Editing Virginia Woolf

Interpreting the Modernist Text

Edited by

James M. Haule

and

J.H. Stape

First published 2002 by
PALGRAVE
Houndmills, Basingstoke, Hampshire RG21 6XS and
175 Fifth Avenue, New York, N.Y. 10010
Companies and representatives throughout the world

PALGRAVE is the new global academic imprint of
St. Martin's Press LLC Scholarly and Reference Division and
Palgrave Publishers Ltd (formerly Macmillan Press Ltd).

ISBN 0–333–77045–5

This book is printed on paper suitable for recycling and made from fully managed and sustained forest sources.

A catalogue record for this book is available from the British Library.

Library of Congress Cataloging-in-Publication Data
Editing Virginia Woolf: interpreting the modernist text / edited by James M. Haule and J. H. Stape
    p. cm.
    Includes bibliographical references and index.
    ISBN 0–333–77045–5
    1. Woolf, Virginia, 1882–1941—Criticism, Textual. 2. Women and literature—England—History—20th century. 3. Modernism (Literature)—England. I. Haule, James M. II. Stape, J. H. (John Henry)

PR6045.O72 Z6267 2001
823'.912—dc21

                                                    2001036187

10   9   8   7   6   5   4   3   2   1
11   10   09   08   07   06   05   04   03   02

Printed and bound in Great Britain by
Antony Rowe Ltd, Chippenham, Wiltshire

For Margaret and for Raymond

Contents

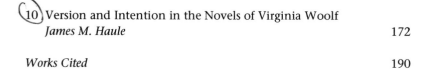

List of Figures

Notes on the Contributors

Anne Olivier Bell is the daughter of A. E. Popham, Keeper of Prints and Drawings at the British Museum, and of Brynhild Olivier, whose father was Sydney Olivier, the Fabian socialist and peer. After studying art history at the Courtauld Institute, she served as a wartime civil servant and, later, on the staff of the Arts Council of Great Britain. She married Quentin Bell in 1952 and worked closely with him in researching and documenting the materials that resulted in his acclaimed biography of Virginia Woolf. Her edition of *The Diary of Virginia Woolf* (5 vols, 1977–84) is itself a widely-acclaimed masterpiece of scholarly intelligence and editorial precision. Sussex University has conferred on her the degree of Doctor of Letters in honor of her scholarship.

Joanne Trautmann Banks is the co-editor of the six-volume *Letters of Virginia Woolf* (1975–80) and the sole editor of Woolf's selected letters, *Congenial Spirits* (1989). She became the first professor of literature and medicine when, in 1972, she was appointed to Penn State's College of Medicine, where she remains an adjunct professor. Sometimes her writing on modern literature and medicine converge as when gerontologists ask what Woolf knew about aging, or literary scholars how clinical case studies demonstrate narrative techniques.

S. P. Rosenbaum is Professor Emeritus of English Literature at the University of Toronto and a Fellow of the Royal Society of Canada. He is a literary historian and the author of *Victorian Bloomsbury* (1987), *Edwardian Bloomsbury* (1994) and *Aspects of Bloomsbury: Studies in Modern English Literary and Intellectual History* (1998). He has edited *A Bloomsbury Group Reader*, Virginia Woolf's *Women & Fiction: the Manuscript Versions of "A Room of One's Own"* and *The Bloomsbury Group: A Collection of Memoirs and Commentary* (revised edition 1995). He is currently writing *Georgian Bloomsbury*, the third volume of the Bloomsbury Group's literary history. He is a member of the editorial committee of the Shakespeare Head Press Edition of Virginia Woolf.

Naomi Black, author of *Social Feminism* (1988) and, with Gail Cuthbert Brandt, of *Feminist Politics on the Farm* (1999), as well as editor of the Shakespeare Head Press edition of Virginia Woolf's *Three Guineas* (2001), is Professor Emerita of Political Science and Women's Studies at York University (Toronto) and Adjunct Professor of Women's Studies at Mount Saint Vincent University (Halifax).

Diane F. Gillespie, Professor of English at Washington State University, is author of *The Sisters' Arts: the Writing and Painting of Virginia Woolf and Vanessa Bell* (1998), co-editor of *Julia Duckworth Stephen: Stories for Children, Essays for Adults* (1987) and *Virginia Woolf and the Arts: Selected Essays from the Sixth Annual Conference on Virginia Woolf* (1997), and editor of *The Multiple Muses of Virginia Woolf* (1993) and *Roger Fry: A Biography* (1996). She is a contributing editor to Bonnie Kime Scott's *The Gender of Modernism: a Critical Anthology* (1990) and has published numerous articles on Woolf, Bloomsbury, and early twentieth-century novelists and playwrights.

Susan Dick did her graduate work at Northwestern University. She is Professor of English at Queen's University, Kingston, Ontario and a member of the Royal Society of Canada, and of the editorial committee of the Shakespeare Head Press Edition of Virginia Woolf. She has edited *To the Lighthouse* for the series, and is currently co-editing *Between the Acts* for it.

Morris Beja teaches at the Ohio State University and has been a visiting professor at universities in Greece and Ireland. He founded the International Virginia Woolf Society and is Executive Secretary and past President of the International James Joyce Foundation. Among his books are *Epiphany in the Modern Novel*, *Film and Literature*, and *James Joyce: A Literary Life*. He has edited a scholarly edition of Virginia Woolf's *Mrs. Dalloway* as well as a number of volumes of essays on Joyce and Woolf, and others on Samuel Beckett and Orson Welles.

Edward Bishop, Professor of English at the University of Alberta is currently studying the publishing history of modernism, and work in progress has appeared in the *Joyce Studies Annual* (1994, 1998), *Proceedings of the 1995 Virginia Woolf Conference* (1996), and *Modernist Writers and the Marketplace* (1996). He has published *A Virginia Woolf Chronology* (1989), *Virginia Woolf* (1991), *The Bloomsbury Group*, *Dictionary of Literary Biography Documents Series* (1992), and *Virginia Woolf's "Jacob's Room": The Holograph Draft* (1998).

J. H. Stape has edited critical editions of Woolf's *Night and Day* (1994) and *Orlando* (1998). He is currently editing critical editions of *Notes on*

Life and Letters (forthcoming 2002) and *Lord Jim*. He contributed two volumes to Macmillan's 'Interviews and Recollections' series – one on Forster (1993) and the other on Woolf (1995), is the author of *An E. M. Forster Chronology* (1993), and the editor of *The Cambridge Companion to Joseph Conrad* (1996). His most recent work includes contributions to The Oxford Reader's Companions to Thomas Hardy and Joseph Conrad (2000). He has taught at universities in Canada, France, and the Far East.

James M. Haule is Professor of English at the University of Texas–Pan American. He is a member of the editorial committee of The Shakespeare Head Press Edition of Virginia Woolf and co-edited *The Waves* (1994) for that series. He is co-editor of the nine-volume microfiche concordance to the novels of Virginia Woolf (1981–88) and the three-volume Garland union concordance (1991). He was General Editor of The Living Author Series that included *John Gardner: True Art, Moral Art* (1986) and *Margaret Atwood: Reflection and Reality* (1987). He has published numerous articles on modern authors, including Virginia Woolf, James Joyce, Edna O'Brien, Angus Wilson, Rosamond Lehmann, and Elizabeth Bowen.

List of Commonly Cited Works

DI–V   *The Diary of Virginia Woolf*, ed. Anne Olivier Bell and Andrew McNeillie (5 vols, Harcourt Brace Jovanovich, 1977–84).

H   The unpublished letters of Virginia Woolf to Winifred Holtby. Winifred Hotlby Collection at the Hull Local Studies Library, Humberside Libraries, Hull, England.

LI–VI   *The Letters of Virginia Woolf*, ed. Nigel Nicolson and Joanne Trautmann (6 vols, Harcourt Brace Jovanovich, 1975–80).

Acknowledgments

We are grateful to the following individuals, publishers, and collections for permission to quote material or reproduce images: The Berg Collection of English and American Literature, The New York Public Library, Astor, Lenox and Tilden Foundations: for permission to use an image (Berg Coll. 89–223) from *Melymbrosia an Early Version of "The Voyage Out"* by Virginia Woolf, New York, 1982, p. 10; Random House for permission to quote from a letter of Virginia Woolf; The Society of Authors as the Literary Representative of the Estate of Virginia Woolf; the late Professor Quentin Bell, to whom we all owe an immeasurable debt, for his permission to quote from the work of Virginia Woolf; Andrew McNeillie and Blackwell Publishers for permission to quote from The Shakespeare Head Press Edition of Virginia Woolf, both text and apparatus; *Twentieth Century Literature* for permission to quote from James M. Haule's article "'Le temps Passe' and the Original Typescript: An Early Version of the 'Time Passes' Section of *To the Lighthouse*" which originally appeared in Vol. 29, No. 3 (Fall 1983); Pace University Press for permission to reproduce a page from *Virginia Woolf's "Jacob's Room"* by Edward Bishop. Mrs. Bell's *Editing Virginia Woolf's Diary* was first published in 1989 in an edition of 200 copies by the Perpetua Press and in 1990 in an edition of 1000 copies by the Bloomsbury Workshop. It is reprinted here with permission.

Introduction: Editing and Interpreting the Texts of Virginia Woolf

J. H. Stape and James M. Haule

Perhaps the only proposition that might be agreed upon in editing literary texts today is that while in practice no definition of it exists, it is nonetheless in a state of ferment driven by commercial pressures, technological change, and debates in literary and cultural studies.[1] The problem of definition is not merely an academic exercise in taxonomy but impinges on the way texts are circulated, marketed, and read, and involves questions of prestige, status, and authority. Indeed, "editing" is now applied to such a wide variety of situations and is so elastically defined that it might be helpful to review briefly the conceptions of it now current.

In common academic parlance, doubtless derived from publishing terminology, an edited text might be (and often is) simply a reprinting of a historical text, whether reset or photo-offset, supplied with an introduction and notes. Cases in point are Salman Rushdie's "edition" of Kipling's *Soldiers Three/In Black and White* (1993) and Edward W. Said's "edition" of *Kim* published by Penguin Books (1987), resettings of the historical editions with minor editorial input. In the specialized field of textual criticism, the term unambiguously refers to the preparation of critical texts, sometimes referred to as "textual editions", involving the gathering of relevant evidence, both pre-print and print, collation and the analysis of variants, and emendation. In the Classics, editors tend to publish the critical text alone, with a separate volume reserved for commentary; in the more impure world of editing modern literary texts, an introduction and notes, aimed, perhaps with some self-contradiction, at both a specialist and a general audience, are now an invariable feature of a critical edition. This practice has helped to muddle the meaning of the term "editing" in general use. It now applies even to a compilation that has had little scholarly input, as, for example, a digital

1

edition of extant pre-print or printed sources. (Mark Hussey's CD-ROM/ on-line archive of Woolf manuscripts is an example.) In the end, editions and editors are, for better or worse, whatever and whoever wishes to lay claim to the title.

Given the elastic nature of the term, such a labored preamble is, we think, wise to contextualize the aims and ambitions of a volume of essays about "editing" Virginia Woolf, a writer whose work has been and very much remains at the forefront of the present-day culture wars that have, not surprisingly, spilled over into editing. "Woolf" is, in some sense, a product of the revision of the canon, serious academic attention to her writing parallelling and expanding with the rise of feminist studies in the 1960s, particularly in the United States. To edit her work is thus necessarily to be involved in the various political and ideological polemics now determining discourse within many fields, textual studies and literary and feminist criticism, in particular.

With the exception of Leonard Woolf's early effort at preparing *Between the Acts* (1941) for publication and editing *A Writer's Diary* (1953), the history of editing Woolf is almost concurrent with her rediscovery in the late 1960s and during the 1970s. The edition of her letters (1975–80) by Nigel Nicolson and Joanne Trautmann (Banks) followed quickly on the heels of Quentin Bell's landmark 1972 biography and further stimulated the then growing interest in her life and work. As Trautmann Banks' essay in this volume suggests, the editorial practice of her co-editor and herself was self-consciously culturally and ideologically charged. Nicolson's family connections and intimate knowledge of English social class blended with and, at times, collided with her academic training and, particularly in the annotations, her feminist allegiances. No take on a life ever aims at neutrality, and variously articulated or assumed theories inform any edition of letters that is not simply a diplomatic transcription of handwriting. Even then, merely undertaking the task of collecting, deciphering, and circulating private correspondence is value laden. From its outset, editing Woolf has been an activist engagement not only in historical recovery but also in re-evaluating a literary reputation that had fallen into relative eclipse after the Second World War.

The editing of Woolf's diaries (1977–84) by Olivier Bell and Andrew MacNeillie represented the second phase of editorial work on the documents of Woolf's life history. The selection of a member close to Woolf's family as the primary editor assured that areas of her life that were not public knowledge made their way into the annotations, although, on the other hand, protective attitudes may also have played their part. As Claire Lamont has observed of editing literary texts, an observation no less pertinent to editing letters and diaries: "Annotators should realize that they are operating in a war zone" (51). In the case of Woolf the "war zone" has widened, with competing constructions of her life, based on the same group of primary materials, proliferating as interest in her and her work has grown.

The publication and reception of the *Letters* and *Diaries* played crucial roles in the various constructions of "Woolf" now current, as scholars, teachers, and students drew on the wealth of information that had become available for both critical and editorial projects. A shift in focus from editing the documents of the life to the works themselves was inevitable, but this only became feasible in 1991, when copyright in Woolf's work lapsed in England on the fiftieth anniversary of her death. Publishers cannily hived off different market segments: the paperback and classroom market, the largest one, was claimed by two established players on the scene, and the library and scholarly one went to a press with a reputation in the humanities. In the United States, the copyright situation remained unchanged, and no re-editing of Woolf's texts or re-publication by competing publishers was possible. By and large, then, the texts readily available in the American market are reprints of the historical texts, first published in the 1920s and 1930s, and lacking the historical information, scholarship, and histories of composition variously available in the English texts, leaving aside the Hogarth Press's so-called "Definitive Collected Edition". In the mid-1990s, an American university student posted a question on an unmoderated Woolf discussion group website enquiring about the original for Orlando. Such information, as well as various interpretations and contextualizations of it, was readily available in the English paperback editions of the text, but, in effect, excluded from the American market.

The factors stimulating the partition of the English market were largely commercial. They were unabashedly so in the case of Hogarth's "Definitive Collected Edition", released the year before Woolf came out of copyright in England as a last-gasp effort on the part of the publisher to make money before the floodgates opened. With two exceptions – Elizabeth Heine's critical edition of *The Voyage Out* and G. Wright Patton's of *Mrs. Dalloway* – this collection reprinted the canon, printers' errors and all, that had been previously available in considerably cheaper forms. Prefaces signed by family members, briefly recapitulating a given work's history of composition or glancing at a salient biographical or compositional fact, served as a further selling point. The texts were not accompanied by explanatory annotations. Priced well beyond the means of the average university student, and, aside from the two critical editions oddly appearing in an otherwise popular collection, this edition, which is neither "definitive" nor "collected", is, in scholarly circles, destined to sink without a trace.

In direct competition for the paperback and classroom market were the Oxford's World's Classics series. Under the direction of Frank Kermode and prefaced by a short biography by him, Woolf's texts were provided with the series' now standard paratext, comprising an introduction, note on the text, and explanatory notes. Penguin Books simultaneously aggressively entered the fray with a "feminist edition" in its Twentieth-Century Classics series. (It was not actually labelled as such but clearly so in practice and characterized as such in its general editor's statements about it.)[2] It featured essentially the same paratext as Oxford's series. Apart from some cosmetic alterations of obvious misprints, the texts of both these editions, like those of Hogarth's "Definitive Collected Edition" again served up, in contemporary typefaces, the historical texts already in worldwide circulation.[3] In the case of the Oxford World's Classics series, Woolf's texts were systematically house-styled to conform with its contemporary preferences. The two paperback series were not editorial projects but critical ones borrowing a certain legitimacy and authority by being attached to the primary texts.

Concurrently, Blackwell of Oxford took up the challenge of producing a critical edition of Woolf's fiction, an endeavor marked by a scholarly conference on editing Woolf held in March 1991 at the University of Toronto. An Editorial Board, comprised of veteran Woolf scholars (Joanne Trautmann Banks, Susan Dick, James M. Haule, Andrew MacNeillie, and S. P. Rosenbaum), was struck to oversee, advise on, and assist the work of the edition's individual volume editors. The edition aimed at a thorough recension of the historical texts and their editing in the Greg–Bowers–Tanselle tradition. A list of variants and a list of emendations were to be supplied and a paratext consisting of introduction and explanatory notes provided for the general reader and student. With the exception of Olivier Bell, the contributors to the present volume are all associated with that edition, as volume editors or as members of its editorial board or both.

A full-scale assessment of these projects, as necessary and useful as it might be for Woolf studies, lies outside the scope of this introductory chapter. It would, given our own participation in The Shakespeare Head Press Edition, also be impolitic, opening us to the charge that the players had reviewed the play and were naturally well pleased with their own work. Nonetheless, some comment on them is required to assist the reader, and while neutrality is impossible, we have aimed at fairness. The editions of Woolf's fiction have been variously received, and given that most students of Woolf and most literary critics are not textual scholars, the introductions and notes have, not surprisingly, received the lion's share of attention.[4] Reviewers were content that serious textual work had been done but not especially interested in it or, for that matter, in the main, qualified to judge it or the editorial theories informing it.

While, on the one hand, the annotations of the Penguin series deliberately appropriate the texts to which they are appended (and in some views are now a constituent element of them),[5] the sole scholarly edition lacks an apparatus as complete, for instance, as the critical texts published by Cambridge University Press in its editions of the works of D. H. Lawrence and of Joseph Conrad, modernist authors with longer histories of academic attention. Such elements as word division are noted in the apparatus of both editions and, in the case of Lawrence, punctuation variants in the published texts receive notice. Any print edition of Woolf is obviously unable to deal with the challenges offered by the technological revolution now under way, since, unlike a hypertext version, a conventional book necessarily privileges certain data, not, as some conspiracy theorists would have it, to suppress evidence by relegating it to appendices but as one of the practical limitations of print technology. In short, no last word has been uttered (nor wisely, attempted), and the editing of Woolf, currently entering its final stages for this generation of scholar–critics, remains to be undertaken again, just as translations need to be refurbished every generation. The curatorial work – the discovery of sources and "hard facts" that might otherwise disappear with time – will surely inform future projects, and, this, curiously, seems more urgent in the annotations of the scholarly rather than the paperback editions, the aim of certainty and accuracy in the recension of the text in somewise informing the admittedly interpretive apparatus.

In this necessarily broad and inevitably partial survey of the editing of Woolf, it may also be useful to indicate general trends and ongoing debates, which in the main run parallel with the editorial treatment of other English or American modernists.[6] A signal difference from them, however, is that editorial theory *per se* largely goes unmentioned by the participants in the debate over how Woolf's work should be preserved and publicly circulated.

The marketplace has powerfully determined the parameters of current discussion. Commercial pressures have, for instance, made The Shakespeare Head Press Edition an endeavor with dual aims, not necessarily contradictory but potentially confusing, whereby an empiricist effort (the recovery of data and the establishment of a reliable text through the analysis of variants) is conflated with a straightforwardly interpretive one in the provision of a paratext. The attempted neutrality of that paratext flows from the edition's central empiric thrust, with its aim at the recovery of fact (conceived as deciphering authorial inscription and establishing the history of composition and publication). Not surprisingly, this approach has vexed certain critics, who, setting out with different premisses, expect the edition's critical input to promote an agenda, whether emerging from Woolf's own engagements or not.[7] A clearly commercial necessity, and in some sense unfocusing the clear aims of textual editing, the paratext is nonetheless now indispensable, and for lack of more precise vocabulary in the field has appropriated the term "editing". Since the 1950s and 1960s when scarcely any information, aside perhaps from a short foreword by a "name" critic, was attached to a text for classroom use or the wider paperback readership, paratext has inexorably expanded and is now firmly entrenched in academic publishing. Prefatory matter, notes, and, almost invariably, a note on the text, however well or ill informed, are provided as a matter of course.[8] No critical edition could survive without these, however irrelevant the first two might be to the nitty-gritty work of establishing the history of composition and publication and the recovery of a text in light of the editorial theory adopted.

In the smaller specialist circle of textual criticism, the watchword is also "more". Fuelled by new hermeneutic theories and advances in digital technology as many versions of a text that time and finances allow can be input and collated. In Joyce and Woolf studies, for example, the availability of facsimile or transcribed manuscript drafts permits any reader, however distant from the actual surviving documents, to reconstruct the growth of the text within the limits permitted by the extant materials. In textual studies of Conrad, by contrast, little pre-print material has been published. Indeed, the abundance of such material available for certain modernist authors not only threatens the confines of the traditional printed page but could simply overwhelm a reader, as Robinson's only part tongue-in-cheek question "Is There a Text in These Variants?" suggests. Despite the Oliver-like call for "more", the pre-print versions of Woolf's work now accessible to interested scholars – an area in which Woolf is particularly well served among modernist authors – disappointingly few genetic studies have, in fact, appeared, and critical essays rarely draw on the evidence of the meticulously transcribed pre-print documents and the archives of the Berg Collection and Sussex University Library now available in digital form.

Neither has the greater accessibility of more reliable texts made much impact. It is still common practice for writers of academic articles to use whatever "edition" lies ready to hand, little bothering about its provenance or its fundamental reliability for pursuing a line of argument. Reviewing one of The Shakespeare Head Press editions for a distinguished scholarly journal, a critic, disappointed but also reassured that no textual cruxes had been uncovered – not the main aim of critical editing, after all – lamely concluded that: the "readership for [this edition of] *Orlando* will be limited to those for whom a 'definitive' text is essential" (Baldwin 93). Leaving aside the question of "definitiveness", that the edition's copy-text restored Woolf's own punctuation, and thus rhythms, to her prose is seemingly "non-essential"; the province of the specialist alone. This take on the aims and value of textual criticism, far from being unique, unfortunately indicates how much an uphill battle a proper understanding of editing still is.

While on the one hand preparing a reliable edition of Woolf's canon can be met with casual indifference or a lack of comprehension even in the scholarly community particularly concerned with her work, on the other, to edit her work is clearly to enter into, if not merely a dialogue of the deaf, a "war zone", to borrow Lamont's apt characterization. Given the differing premises in operation, both self-conscious and implicit, no common ground is currently available. An example of the drawing of boundaries is the wholesale erasure of the Shakespeare Head Press Edition by the editors and writers – aside from the two contributions by members of the editorial board of The Shakespeare Head Press Edition – of *The Cambridge Companion to Virginia Woolf*. The volume's editors, associated with the aims and practices of the Penguin edition, neither cite the Shakespeare Head Press Edition nor draw on the abundant historical and archival scholarship present in its introductions and annotations.[9] While the latest and most up-to-date critical theories inform some of the interpretations offered to the reader, the texts on which these are based inadequately represent and even misrepresent the author's work. As it were, old wine and bad wine is merely being served in new bottles.

The past two decades of textual scholarship, particularly McGann's emphasis on a social theory of textuality, have dealt a death-blow to the hoary chimera of establishing "definitive" texts. In this respect the Hogarth Press's unfortunate claim to definitiveness is not only obviously disingenuous but also dated, appealing to a naive audience. The Shakespeare Head Press Edition, while it makes no similar claim, attempts for the first time in the history of Woolf studies to establish a reliable reading text, informed by historical and archival research, textual collation, and the recension of the text. The "editors" of the paperback editions, properly speaking, engaged in little editorial work at all, although their critical projects witness an important scholarly trend in the triumph of subjectivity,[10] summed up nicely by Robinson's statement: "As editors, we transcribe, mediate, interpret...the text is us" (112). In a broad philosophical sense, the paperback texts of Virginia Woolf, particularly those in the Penguin series, are ancillary to the critical projects pursued. Their premiss, implicit if not self-aware, derived from contemporary theory, is that since the author no longer controls meaning, the text is merely a "pre-text" or "pretext", the occasion for the free play of critical ideas it stimulates. Such a project is, not unexpectedly, essentially indifferent to how the text to which it attaches itself has been constituted, questions of copy-text, reliability, and authority all being irrelevant (or possibly even hostile) to the issues at hand. This is partly so because this orientation operates on an assumption that "facts" have no objective existence, being merely social constructions based on, and varyingly reflecting, political engagements. Hence, authorial intention (however naively or subtly construed, and however essentially elusive), documentary evidence, and the history of a text's life through time are of interest only insofar as they can marshalled to promote a critical agenda.

Given these assumptions, it is not especially surprising that "editing" Woolf is generally seen as an opportunity to practice a particular critical theory or to pursue the aims of a socio-political program. This said, programs or ideologies are inherent in any intellectual activity, and the texts of the Shakespeare Head Press Edition are also involved in various covert persuasions, including the propositions that facts can be established, that evidence is not merely or solely a matter of interpretation, and that the work of the author takes precedence over an ideally self-effacing editor–critic.

While some of the general parameters of the debates over editing Woolf have been set, there is still generally too little awareness of the theoretical issues involved. Texts are, of course, edited in and for their time, and although the simplest question – "Is the comma there?" – might, outside philosophical circles, garner consensus and appeal to a metaphorically conceived timelessness, the fact that it is there becomes a matter for interpretation.

The present volume aims at no cutting-edge contribution to the field of editorial theory, more modestly focusing on the work of practicing editors. It is, in any event, possibly too early a stage in editing Woolf to attempt a wider aim. It covers a wide range of Woolf's activity, encompassing almost all the genres she worked in: diary, letter, essay, short story, biography, and novel. It also serves, in a sense, as a supplement to the work undertaken for the Shakespeare Head Press Edition, where limitations on length, and, as outlined above, a tradition of empirical scholarship at times hedged in an editor, who might have wished a broader scope for an individual opinion.

Anne Olivier Bell's and Joanne Trautmann Banks' essays preserve the history of their engagement in editorial projects aimed at preserving and publicly presenting the documentary record of Woolf's life. Both convey a sense of working "in the trenches" to recover the life history of a writer at a moment of a more general critical reassessment of literary modernism in England and in the wake of social transformations then occurring in England and North America in the 1960s and 1970s. The essays by Edward Bishop and S. P. Rosenbaum on the manuscripts of *Jacob's Room* and *Women and Fiction* likewise focus on the transcription and circulation of documents at various stages of development and not intended for publication, addressing questions pertinent to the interpretation and use of manuscript forms. Susan Dick's essay on editing Woolf's short fiction similarly addresses the presentation of texts in flux, particularly where the surviving evidence occasionally lacks clear and unimpeachable authority. Naomi Black's essay on *Three Guineas* and Diane F. Gillespie's on *Roger Fry* describe their work on Woolf's non-fiction, squarely confronting contentious issues of annotation, self-censorship, and the shaping and packaging of a work for a given audience. The contributions by Morris Beja, J. H. Stape, and James M. Haule address selected problems in the critical editing of the central fictional canon, *Mrs. Dalloway*, *Orlando*, *To the Lighthouse*, and *The Waves*, reflecting on the selection and emendation of copy-text and engaging questions of authority. This final grouping also demonstrates how the historical texts are variously corrupt, with the sources for their deficiencies located in their histories of transmission.

While the editors share a certain common ground in attitude and, broadly, in the theories informing their editorial practice, the collection, naturally enough, demonstrates a heterogeneity of opinion. In a quite real sense, moreover, editing Woolf has just begun, the first generation scholarly edition necessarily giving way at some future date before theoretical positions yet to evolve and before new technologies. Whatever evolution editorial theory sees, it does, however, seem clear that the discovery of new materials occasioned by the empirical task of scholarly editing will have a longer life than any single reading of a text, whatever its contemporary appeal and significance. Such work, important as it is for the moment, inevitably dates, appearing shop worn with time.

Notes

1. On changing technology and its current and potential roles in scholarly editing, see the collections edited by Bornstein and Tinkle, Shillingsburg, and Sutherland.
2. For a discussion of the aims of Penguin series, see Briggs.
3. In bibliography, an edition technically constitutes a resetting of type; in this respect the Hogarth Press, World's Classics, and Penguin Book editions, in bibliographical terms, are legitimately described as editions rather than issues (an impression from previously set type) or reprints (via the photo-offset process).
4. See *The Virginia Woolf Miscellany* and *The Virginia Woolf Annual* for reviews by Woolf specialists. Journals devoted to textual scholarship have not devoted much attention to the various editions.
5. Robinson, for example, offers so catholic a definition of text – an extreme example of reader-response theory – that all responses are incorporated into it: "The folio, the quarto, all the printed and staged versions, Tom Stoppard's fifteen-minute and one-minute versions, and my ten-second version: all of them are *Hamlet*" (106).
6. For a survey of a number of issues being debated in contemporary editorial theory and practice, see Shillingsburg 1997. For an overview of the editorial problems of various periods and genres, see Greetham 1995. Both books provide useful directions for further reading in the field.
7. Marcus calls for annotations to include the critical history of the discovery of information. In her view, the Shakespeare Head Press Edition provides "nice clean book[s], without any references to the embattled critics who have fought over the meanings of the novels.... The critics do the (dirty) work precisely because they want to make converts to their ideologies" (5). Both the metaphors and the definition of critical work are singularly revealing.
8. A staggeringly amateurish example of the latter is offered by Mengham, who, in his Abinger Edition of *The Machine Stops and Other Stories*, in addition to informing the reader that he adopts Forster's 1947 text (in fact, 1948, and in any case an invalid choice in light of modern textual theory) as his copy-text, notes, without a word to suggest why, his silent and selective retention of punctuation from "relevant" earlier volumes.
9. No clearer instance of this volume's *parti pris* character can be offered than Laura Marcus' re-writing of the history of Woolf scholarship to suit her ideological and emotive aims. After suggesting that male-dominated New Criticism neglected or suppressed Woolf during its heyday, she refers to Nigel Nicolson as "the" editor of Woolf's letters – effacing the contribution made by Jo Banks – and further claims that Olivier Bell, who edited the diaries with the help of Andrew MacNeillie (likewise erased) "takes on masculine privilege by association" as the wife of Quentin Bell (234).
10. See Berlin for a wide-ranging discussion of the philosophical bases of certain contemporary theories of artistic production, and on the paradigmatic shifts regarding subjectivity, empiricism, and authority, notions crucial to informing editorial practice.

1
Editing Virginia Woolf's Diary

Anne Olivier Bell

Virginia Woolf, when she died in 1941, left a series of diaries or journals, thirty volumes in all, written between 1915 and her death, besides a number of earlier notebooks of a journalizing character. Leonard Woolf, the judge of her writing whom she most respected, had no doubt in his own mind that Virginia Woolf was a great artist as well as a very remarkable literary critic, and, reading through these diaries after her death, had equally no doubt that they illuminated her intentions, objects, and methods as a writer and, though too personal to be published in full at that time, certainly merited publication in part. Accordingly, in 1954 he published a selection he called *A Writer's Diary*, a single volume containing those extracts from her diaries which referred to her own writing. He did so with some hesitation and misgiving, knowing that such a selection would inevitably present a distorted and unbalanced picture of his wife, since it concentrates on a limited aspect of her personality and, although it reveals a moving and absorbing self-portrait of a true artist at work, its publication probably did a good deal to create or reinforce that popular journalistic image of Virginia Woolf, the moody, arrogant, and malicious Queen of Bloomsbury.

Probably as a result of this book, Leonard was soon beset by aspiring biographers, seeking his authority to write the Life of his wife. He temporised; he did not think the time was ripe; he had doubts about the suitability of the aspirants. There was however one anomalous production: having been politely discouraged by Leonard, Aileen Pippett was befriended by Vita Sackville-West who let her study all Virginia's letters to her; and largely on the basis of their relationship, Pippett constructed an extraordinarily ill-balanced and ill-informed "biography" called *The Moth and the Star*, depending heavily upon lavish quotation from those letters – which were of course Leonard's copyright.

He refused his permission for their use; but in the end relented to the extent of allowing publication in America only – where the book made a further contribution to the distorted image of Virginia Woolf.

In 1964 Leonard, now eighty-four and wishing to come to some decision on the matter, suggested to my husband Quentin Bell that he should write his aunt Virginia's Life. Quentin refused, on the grounds that it should not be done by a member of the family and, moreover, one who knew as little about English literature as he did. Eighteen months later Leonard asked him again, and this time Quentin agreed.

This was in January 1966. When Quentin told me (I was in hospital at the time) that he had now agreed to Leonard's request, I felt distinctly alarmed at the responsibility he had undertaken, though at the same time excited and interested by the prospect, in which I knew I could be of help to him, whether or not he thought so. Perhaps I should say here why I thought myself qualified to help him. After my abortive dreams of a career on the stage, I went to the Courtauld Institute, then in its infancy and the only department of Art History in England; they were pleased to accept me as a student (although I had no Latin) since the fact that my father was an eminent authority on Old Master Drawings in the British Museum conferred a reflected respectability which at that time the Institute was concerned to cultivate – being suspected by the University of London of doubtful academic standards and of being little more than a finishing school for debutantes and aspiring art-dealers. When I had finished my course there, I was lucky enough to be employed in the Institute's Conway Library (half-time, £1 per week), pasting reproductions of architecture and artefacts on to brown paper mounts, inscribing their particulars in neat black script, and filing them in scarlet boxes. Then I progressed to a job as secretary/research assistant to a very distinguished refugee Rubens scholar, Dr Ludwig Burchard, who taught me a great deal about probity in scholarship. He, like so many other benefactors of our cultural life, was interned in the Isle of Man in the summer of 1940, and I was called up for National Service. I became a Civil Servant (temporary) in the Ministry of Information, working first in the Photographs, then in the Publications Division (where I was Laurie Lee's dogsbody); and then, at the end of the war, went to govern devastated Germany as a Civilian Officer (equivalent Major) in the Monuments, Fine Arts, and Archives Branch of the Control Commission. I came home to a research job in a publishers who planned to issue lavishly illustrated and very cheap monographs on painters – towards which end I examined all the 17 000 Turner drawings in the British Museum; but these ambitious and laudable plans came to naught and I went to work in the Art

Department of the Arts Council, where all my previous experience came into play and where, doing anything and everything – there were only three of us then to do it – from hanging exhibitions in the Tate Gallery to escorting the masterpieces from the Alte Pinakothek exhibited at the National Gallery back to Munich (four days and nights in various goods trains across the still war-damaged railway system of Europe, with armed police to guard our treasure). But the task that increasingly fell to my lot was the production of exhibition catalogues: writing, translating, editing, checking, designing, proof-reading, and so forth. The common element in all the various activities of my career was the commitment to an ideal of perfection in whatever I was doing. I was always employed to do things properly, to get things right; and the question of the expense of so doing was never my responsibility – thank goodness. I understand nothing about money.

Well, I met and in 1952 married Quentin Bell, reluctantly left the Arts Council, went to live in Newcastle-upon-Tyne and then Leeds, and had three children; and here we are again at 1966 when Quentin was embarking on the preliminary research for his biography of Virginia Woolf.

Leonard Woolf naturally offered all the help he could; and the first help Quentin asked for was Virginia's diary. It appeared that Leonard had had the thirty manuscript volumes transcribed and typed out; he kept the top copy in a cabinet at home at Monks House (the originals were in the Westminster Bank in Lewes), but he sent us the carbons, and these turned out to be in tatters. Leonard, a practical and economical man, in selecting his excerpts for *A Writer's Diary*, had done so with scissors: he simply cut the bits he wanted out of the carbon copy and sent them to the printer. He put the remnants back into manila foolscap envelopes and these he sent to Quentin, explaining, reasonably enough, that together with the published copy he now had the complete text.

It wasn't quite so simple: the remnants were often shorn of their date and impossible to place; though each year was in a separate envelope, the contents were in a muddle and some bits were clearly missing. Largely because it gave me an excuse to read Virginia's diary, which I longed to do, I decided to reconstitute our copy, typing out the published excerpts and pasting them together with the remnants, referring to Leonard's master copy at Monks House when wholly nonplussed. When I had done this – or perhaps while I was doing it, for it was hardly the work of a moment – I conceived the idea of making a sort of scaffolding of facts which Quentin could depend upon in planning his biography. I took a 6 × 4 inch index card for each month of Virginia's life, I had them printed with lines back and front to accommodate all the days in a month, and entered on them when she had written her diary (she did not do so every day), indicating briefly what she had written – where she was or had been, who she had seen, and so on. I was so pleased with these cards that I got *tête-montée* and had more printed on different colours, using (when the relevant documents became available) green for letters from Virginia, yellow for letters to Virginia, and pink for letters between other people referring to her. Later on, when we were living in Sussex and after his death, I copied pretty well all the laconic daily entries in Leonard's pocket diaries on to such cards too. It seemed perhaps a fatuous labour at the time, but it proved absolutely invaluable.

After we moved from Leeds to Sussex in 1967 we saw a great deal more of Leonard. At Monks House he would show us bundles and boxes of papers and letters, or copies he had made of papers and letters which he had sold – those from Lytton Strachey or T. S. Eliot for instance. At one time he had considered publishing Virginia's letters, and had assembled a considerable number before deciding not to pursue the idea; some of these were originals which their recipients had given him; some were copies of originals he had returned to their owners. Bit by bit we brought all this material to our house, and from time to time Leonard would turn up and turn out of his pockets something he had come across that he thought might interest us – fifteen letters to Virginia from Katherine Mansfield for example. From Quentin's old home at nearby Charleston we brought Virginia's letters to her sister Vanessa and to her brother-in-law Clive Bell, to marry with theirs to her which we had from Monks House. I set to work to sort out and tidy up all this material. I put the letters into folders in alphabetical order of correspondents, whether *to* or *from*; so naive a system that I am rather surprised to find it perpetuated in the University of Sussex Library where most of these letters now are. Then in order to strengthen my scaffold – my chronological card system – I had to try and date all these letters when they were undated (and in early days both Virginia and Vanessa were great ones for putting *Tuesday* and no more). And here is where the case for working with original documents is very strong: apart from the information supplied by the actual ink and paper, some of the letters I was dealing with were in envelopes, postmarked; but most were not. And this led me to my great discovery. In the long-past heroic days of the GPO, when the price of a stamp was a penny or a penny-halfpenny and there were four posts a day, post-office workers used to thump the postmark on by hand; and if they were sufficiently enthusiastic, the blind echo of their thump could be impressed upon the folded sheet within the envelope. So, if one refolds a letter and examines it under strong and raking light, sometimes, eureka! the blind postmark is revealed – as it might be WELLS SOM/4AU 08. I rather fear that in the superior conditions in which manuscripts are now preserved in institutions such evidence, and the possibilities for its detection, will have been ironed out. Of course there are other clues and straws in the wind, references to public events or private arrangements, which help one in dating undated letters, or at least in narrowing down the possibilities, and if you have that sort of mind, it can be a great if rather obsessional pleasure solving such riddles. Anyway, I did all this tidying and dating and entered the results on my cards, which Quentin, when he was writing, would spread out before him with his own notes and drafts to keep his chronology in order.

While working through Virginia's diary, I also made another, alphabetical, card index of all the people she named, finding out what I could about them, noting the date they were mentioned and giving a tiny precis of what she wrote. The greater number of people mentioned in the earlier years I had never heard of. For a time I could ask Leonard: Who was Totty? Who was Snow? But for most of them I had to use my own resources, and the resources provided by books – volumes of *Who Was Who*, old Debretts or Kellys or Whitakers; and innumerable biographies – this giving me a splendid excuse to indulge one of my weaknesses – second-hand book shopping. In the end I accumulated four long boxes of my index cards, two chronological, two biographical. All this painstaking scaffolding I constructed to keep Quentin straight; and it often led to painful confrontations: "You can't say that there; she didn't *meet* Violet Dickinson until 1902"; or "No, it was in *June* not August 1916 that Bernard Shaw (as he later claimed) fell in love with Virginia at the Sidney Webbs". Quentin, who naturally had a far greater imaginative grasp of Virginia's life and character than I had, was often tempted to strike me dead. But somehow our marriage survived, the biography was written, and was perhaps none the worse for being factually accurate. (I might add that I also provided the punctuation, the references, the chronology, the bibliography, and all the proof-corrections; Quentin did the index.)

The biography was written, and was published in 1972. Quentin was able to read the earlier chapters aloud to Leonard before he died in 1969. Some fifteen years before this, he had succumbed to the persuasion of two American dealers in literary manuscripts (no one in England had shown the slightest interest), and agreed to sell them Virginia Woolf's diaries, provided they paid him then and there, that they ensured that the manuscripts went to a major public archive, and that he, Leonard, retained possession during his lifetime. The poor ladies used to come back year after year hoping to claim their purchase and reimburse themselves for their considerable capital outlay – I think it was $20 000 – but Leonard remained obstinately alive and alert until his eighty-ninth year. Only after his death and some legal argy-bargy over his will were the diaries taken from the bank in Lewes and surrendered to America and their final resting-place, the New York Public Library.

Leonard left the copyrights in Virginia Woolf's writings to her sister Vanessa's surviving children, Quentin Bell and Angelica Garnett; her remaining papers went to his residuary legatee and through her came to rest for the most part in the University of Sussex Library, although some joined the diary and other manuscripts already in the New York Public Library. Leonard himself had published several volumes of those of Virginia's shorter pieces that he thought merited posthumous publication or re-publication, as well as his selection of excerpts *A Writer's Diary*. But the problem of what was to be done about Virginia Woolf's letters and diaries he left to her heirs.

It is no sinecure being a literary heir. Of course there are welcome pecuniary benefits in the form of royalties – taxed at 85 per cent until a so-called radical administration saw fit to temper the wind to the suffering rich. Quentin, who undertook the chief burden on behalf of himself and his sister, was already reaping the advantages and disadvantages of the success of his biography, and soon found that interest in Virginia Woolf was reaching quite phenomenal proportions, and that he was continually applied to, by post and in person, for information, interviews, testimonials, advice, permissions, lectures; sometimes there were television crews – and they don't come in less than half-a-dozen souls – and directors spread over our house for days at a time. Indeed the house became a sort of honey-pot with all these Woolf-addicts buzzing around; I had to provide some of the honey in the form of food and drink. Earnest seekers after the truth armed with tape recorders came from Tokyo, Belgrade, or Barcelona; others we came to refer to as "beard-touchers" – those for whom it was obligatory to be able to state "I consulted with Professor Bell" when submitting their doctoral dissertation on "Mythic Patterns in *Flush*" or whatever it might be. Reluctant if well-intentioned recipients of so much attention, and providers of so much hospitality and help, we have sometimes found it hurtful to read articles or reviews by those we have entertained and informed and given up our time to, to the effect that we operated a sort of Bloomsbury closed shop; a protection racket maintained for the purposes of self-aggrandisment and financial gain.

Meanwhile, in New York, the aficionados descended upon the Berg Collection which now housed Virginia's diaries and many of her letters and manuscripts, and soon there came a hail of requests for permission to quote passages from them to enhance or illuminate or justify theses, biographies, works of literary criticism, learned or less-learned articles. ...It was clear that some policy on how to handle such requests must be reached before the diaries and letters were gutted of all quotable bits, or actually fell to pieces from wear and tear. With Leonard's partners in The Hogarth Press, the decision was reached to withhold all permission to quote from unpublished writings, and to prepare to publish both the letters and diaries in some form or other. The question was, what form should publication take?

First, to consider the letters: in 1956 Leonard Woolf and James Strachey published the correspondence between Virginia Woolf and Lytton Strachey – and a great mistake it was; it shows them both at their most affected. Vita Sackville-West always maintained (as oddly enough did nearly all Virginia's correspondents) that Virginia's letters to her were the best she ever wrote, and urged Leonard to allow them to be published on their own; but again he procrastinated. I think that it was after his, and Vita's, deaths that her son Nigel Nicolson raised the matter again; and it became apparent that to publish Virginia's letters to X, or Virginia's letters to Y, separately, would be a thoroughly unsatisfactory proceeding. What would become of the half-dozen letters, of extreme interest, that she wrote to A before her marriage? or the three to B, explaining what she was trying to do in writing *Mrs. Dalloway*? To publish a broad selection of Virginia Woolf's letters would entail collecting as many as possible from which to make the selection; and then on what criterion should it be made? Which to include? What to reject? It was agreed that the case for publishing all the letters that could be traced was justified; and Nigel Nicolson, a very experienced and distinguished biographer, editor, and publisher, who had known Virginia since his childhood, was asked to undertake this task. And this he and his co-opted co-editor Joanne Trautmann achieved, with tremendous energy and skill, in six volumes published by The Hogarth Press between 1975 and 1980.

So to the Diaries: from the thirty manuscript diaries Virginia Woolf wrote between 1915 and her death, Leonard had extracted and published in *A Writer's Diary* considerably less than one-fifth. Those who had read any or all of the remaining four-fifths were unanimous in their view that here was one of the great diaries of the English language which must unquestionably be published sooner or later. Time the Great Reaper had in the nature of things gathered up many of the *dramatis personae* whose sensibilities Leonard had been concerned to shelter twenty years before; others, it had to be accepted, might not live much longer. Should the question of publication be shelved until everyone mentioned was dead and gone? Should another tactful, but more generous selection be made? But on what principle? and so forth. The upshot is manifest: an unabridged publication of the complete series of diaries was decided upon; and it was decided that I should be the editor.

Although this choice no doubt seemed, and seems, to many people a typical example of Bloomsbury nepotism, there were objectively respectable reasons for making it. I was already familiar with the material; I was familiar with many of the characters, with the country, the houses, and to some extent the political and social history of the period covered by the diaries; I knew the tone of voice, the style of humour, the social situation of the Stephens, the Woolfs, and the Bells. I already had a very considerable research apparatus. There is another aspect to the charge of nepotism: the economic one, where the verdict may be the reverse of what is assumed. It is true that half of Virginia Woolf's royalties (taxed) benefit her nephew, my husband; but with these royalties her nephew maintained me, her editor, and her editor's assistant. So that the editor of her diaries (who could not have survived on her own royalties which averaged less than the wages of a hospital cleaner) did not need to seek for funds or foundations to subsidise her work, was not granted sabbatical leave on a University salary at public expense, was not answerable to a paymaster; and was thus free to pursue the aim of excellence without subjection to external pressures. (I could never quite work out how to square my dependence upon Virginia's posthumous earnings with her, and my own, attitude to the dignity and rights of women.)

But such freedom from financial monitors brings problems of its own; that is, I had to decide for myself how to proceed, what to do, and how to do it. No grand Editorial Committee to advise me. It was indeed an intimidating prospect. I began by getting photocopies from the Berg Collection of the 2317 pages of the original diaries (they tried to persuade me to have microfilm but I resisted, and got full-scale sheets – else I would be blind by now). Then I had to check Leonard's transcription – my old patchwork copy – against the autograph pages. Virginia's writing can be very clear and elegant; it can also be extremely difficult to read; and quite often even Leonard (or his transcriber) read it wrong. But undoubtedly it was a great help having his transcription, though by the time I had corrected it against the autograph it looked such an illegible mess that I had to have it all typed out again. Then I had to count the words (not even a pocket calculator in those days) and work out how best to divide the whole into how many volumes. I imagine one of the blessings of a grand Editorial Committee, or of being one of a team of editors, would be that there is bound to be someone on it competent to do this sort of thing. At all events it seemed natural to me to start each volume at the beginning of a year, and to end it at the end of another. But Virginia's years proved rather resistant to a tidy division into equal volumes; and as a matter of fact my first division was altered as I went along, a year being shunted forward from the end of one volume to the beginning of the next, largely due to the publishers' impatience. Inevitably there was a bit of a pile-up in the last volume.

The detail of my operations are hardly of compelling interest; enough to say that the insidious 6×4 inch index card gained new ground. All the passages in the Diary which seemed to me – or later, to us, for I soon realised that I, an active householder, housewife, parent, cook, gardener, hostess, had taken on too much to accomplish single-handed, and imported the invaluable Andrew McNeillie from Oxford to help me – all those passages, I say, which needed elucidation were lettered in the text and copied on to index cards filed in chronological order in boxes; and on to those cards would be entered whatever we could find out about the point in question. Of course the finding out is the fun, or can be; and was an education for me, if a somewhat superficial one, pursuing Virginia's flight over so many territories – personal, political, literary, social, topographical, genealogical, geographical, gastronomical, horticultural, musical, dramatical, historical and poetical. Fortunately we had a very extensive library in our home to begin with, including the *Dictionary of National Biography* edited by Virginia's father, the *Encyclopaedia Britannica* (two editions), most of the standard works of English and French literature, collected letters, poetry, essays, history and art history, and the works of those you might call the Bloomsbury writers; and this was progressively augmented by my bookshopping activities. So a great deal of research could be done at home, which saved time and money spent in going out but did carry its own pitfalls, offering as it did such opportunities for time-wasting or lingering self-indulgence. For instance, Virginia writes: "I happened to read Wordsworth; the poem which ends 'What man has made of man'".[1] I do not know Wordsworth well enough to recognise that poem, and the only way I could find it was to go through a volume of his collected poetry looking only at the last lines. When I had found "What man has made of man" it would have been a silly act of renunciation to close the book without reading the poem from the first line to the last, and possibly others too. Or Virginia in Scotland, noting: "How Scott must have come this way – near

Jedburgh. Burke Sir Walter." Virginia's father Leslie Stephen had a passion for Walter Scott, whom he used to read aloud to his children, a passion inherited by Virginia. I knew next to nothing about Scott, but there are twenty-five double-column pages devoted to him in the *Dictionary of National Biography*, written by Leslie Stephen, so I was able to learn a good deal about him, and to say what "Burke Sir Walter" signified to Virginia when she crossed the Scottish border in 1938.

Some problems consumed an amount of time out of all proportion to their real importance. But there is a challenge in this pursuit of enlightenment which one is reluctant, or too proud, to evade. In June 1920 Virginia records that she dined with Walter Lamb and Mrs Madan at Hounslow. "In this old manor house (cream coloured & black) Miss Arnold used to lie drunk." And there is a good deal more about Mrs Madan and her house. I knew who Walter Lamb was, and identified Mrs Madan. But a Manor House at Hounslow? And a Miss Arnold *drunk*? I started on the Manor House at Hounslow; that is, I started in the Topographical Section in the back cellars of the London Library (the bliss of the London Library is that one can fumble about undisturbed among the stacks), hoping that I might find mention of a manor house in (what soon became apparent) was even in 1920 a very nondescript, unattractive, and un-manorial district. A comparatively recent book on Middlesex however struck me as being exceptionally thorough and well-informed, and I wrote to the author, one Michael Robbins, c/o his publisher, to ask if he could possibly throw any light on my problem. It turned out that he was the Managing Director of London Transport, and was indeed well-informed *and* well-disposed. But he very much doubted the existence of an old manor house (cream coloured and black) in the Hounslow district in 1920, and suggested that Virginia might have been mistaken in the place; he kindly said he would pursue some enquiries. Almost at this moment, an excellently well-documented book called *Ethel Sands and her Circle* by Wendy Baron appeared – Virginia Woolf figured in that circle – and it was full of interesting and relevant information for me. But for the present purpose the most pertinent information was that Mrs Madan, with whom Virginia had dined in that old manor house so long ago, was still alive. I wrote to Wendy Baron, who sent me Mrs Madan's address. I wrote to Mrs Madan and was eventually answered from Scotland by her daughter Lady Campbell of Croy, who said that unfortunately her mother was old and frail and her memory was clouded. She thought her parents had certainly started their married life in a pretty old house, she thought at Twickenham. Stalemate. But a week or so later she wrote again, enclosing a letter from her aunt, her father's sister, who remembered staying in the house in question, which was called The Old Manor House and was at Whitton, in Middlesex. (Whitton is in fact between Hounslow and Richmond, where Virginia was living at that time.)

So to Miss Arnold. I thought that of their nature, all Arnolds were sober and high-minded, none more so than Mrs Humphry Ward, the most prominent member of the family to Virginia's eye, and the one with whom her own family were acquainted. I looked out the lives of Mrs Humphry Ward (there were two), and yes, she did have an unmarried sister, Ethel Arnold, over whom not so much a veil is drawn as about whom nothing whatever is revealed. I wrote to the author of the more recent book on Mrs Humphry Ward, Enid Huws-Jones, who replied that she had been told that Ethel, poor thing, became an alcoholic, but that the authority on all Arnolds was now Dr Arnold's great-great-grand-daughter Mrs Mary Moorman (equally an authority on Wordsworth), the wife of a bishop who might not, she thought, appreciate any suggestion of inebriety in a member of the Arnold family. I wrote to Mrs Moorman with suitable tact. She thought that this "Miss Arnold" probably was Ethel, Mrs Humphry Ward's youngest sister – "an odd bird, who did have a house somewhere in that part of the world... I thought it was at Richmond." Almost by the same post I heard again from Lady Campbell of Croy, who said that in an interval of lucidity her mother did appear to think that it was Ethel Arnold who had lived in the Old Manor House before she did, and had recalled that at the end of her life Ethel had lived in Chelsea in the house of Logan Pearsall Smith, and he it was who had maliciously spread it about that she drank. And finally I had another letter from Mr Michael Robbins, my Middlesex authority, who confirmed from the Isleworth Rate Book for 1919 that the Occupier of the Old Manor House at Whitton was at that time Miss E. M. Arnold. (The house no longer exists; it has given way to a housing estate.)

On page 46 of Volume II of *The Diary of Virginia Woolf* these researches are encapsulated in a six-line footnote.

That was rather an extreme case of persistence, happily rewarded. But from that long tale one or two *morals* (as in Belloc) may be drawn. One, that it is nearly always necessary to find out about ten times as much about your problem as you will eventually use in elucidating it. Two, that the element of luck, of serendipity, in research is very arbitrary but often immensely valuable. The question is, how best to court it? I rather suppose that my amateurish approach paid dividends in this field. I suspect that dependence upon the marvels of modern technology in some areas of research, though no doubt saving time and thus money – does reduce the opportunity the fumbler enjoys of happening upon something he would never have happened upon if he could only get at the printed page through the medium of a co-ordinated publication data catalogue or micro-reader. I suppose I did waste hours, and certainly got very dirty, lugging out the great bound volumes of *The Times* in the London Library, and turning over their decaying pages to establish which string quartets it was that Virginia heard at the Wigmore Hall in, say, February 1922; but, in turning over the pages one's eye might be caught by a headline: "Mr Bevan apprehended in Vienna" . . . Bevan? Mr Bevan? and the whole scandalous and fascinating story of the mysterious Mr Bevan, a financier and the then owner of Littlecote, whom Virginia's friend Violet Dickinson had mentioned in her random gossipy talk, is unfolded day by day. Of course there are invaluable indexes to *The Times* and its supplements and to the obituaries since 1950 (perhaps they go back further now). But in searching for information on somebody I thought might qualify for a posthumous mention or tribute in *The Times* before 1950, there was nothing for it but to go steadily through the index, four volumes to a year, seeking and hoping to find their name. And even this monotonous exercise sometimes yielded a bonus to the straying eye. But the great and inestimable advantage of having actual contact with books is the freedom to pick and dip: to take them off the shelf, sample the index, scan the introduction, the illustrations, the information, in order to establish just one small fact perhaps, rather than having to select a book from a catalogue (now alarmingly computerised) and send for that, only to find it may divulge nothing to the point – a tedious and repetitious business. What, I wanted to know, were "the tremendous words" over the door of St Patrick's Cathedral in Dublin which so moved Virginia? There is a whole stackful of books on Dean Swift in the London Library, and I had a very happy and instructive time finding out, and finding out a good many other relevant things about the Dean and his memorials too, which no one single book would have given me.

I found the most difficult part of my work, after deciding what in Virginia Woolf's Diary required explanation, and gathering the material, was the actual writing of the annotations. I pinned up before my desk a notice with the words: accuracy/relevance/concision/interest; and these were my objectives. There must be tens of thousands of details on all manner of things in the footnotes to the five volumes, and every one of them should be right and true. I do not claim to have been 100 per cent successful, though I've not been very far short. The justification for burdening Virginia's swift and lovely flight of words with such a heavy load of annotation is that different readers need different things elucidated (and if they don't, they don't have to read the footnotes), and that a large number of her readers are on the other side of the Atlantic, and young, or perhaps not yet born – for this edition remains in copyright for fifty years – and are thus not perhaps familiar with matters we islanders, or we pensioners, might take for granted: the result of the 1929 General Election, for example; or that Rabbit's Ears are vegetable, not animal.

As I indicated before, Leonard's publication of *A Writer's Diary* set off a revival of interest in Virginia Woolf, who had rather sunk to the bottom in public esteem after her death, and aroused a curiosity about her life and personality which was fed by his own five autobiographical volumes, and by no means satisfied by Quentin Bell's biography. *A Writer's Diary* gave, as Leonard was aware, a very oblique portrait; in the story of his own life, we see much more of her; and Quentin's work, one would have thought, portrayed her full-length and in the round. However these home-produced books launched a veritable avalanche of studies, both of Virginia's work and of her life, many of the latter purporting to demonstrate that both Leonard and Quentin had completely misrepresented her, and by concealing or cooking the evidence to which only they had access, had been able to present their preferred image – and one in which Leonard himself figured as hero. These studies were sometimes largely based upon interpretations of Virginia Woolf's fiction – a questionable approach to biography it seems to me – and usually reveal more about the writer's prejudices and obsessions than they do about Virginia. Thus we have had Freudian, Christian, Celtic, mystical, existential, Marxist, Feminist – and you can say that again – analyses and accounts of her life and work. Perhaps the most grotesque manifestations of this line of approach have been those which discern that it was the fundamental antagonism, sometimes fueled by Virginia's alleged anti-Semitism, between her and Leonard which drove her, not only to periods of despair, but to suicide; indeed, it has been suggested that he practically pushed her into the river.

There is more documentary information concerning Virginia Woolf's life and work available to scholars than there is perhaps on any other considerable English writer, and now practically all of it is published (what is not is accessible to students either in Sussex or New York), one might hope that the pursuit of ingenious theories and wild speculations about this remarkable woman's motives and feelings might cease, or at least take account of the evidence. But of course evidence can be selected to bolster theories, and with the help of the excellent indexes to her *Letters* and *Diaries* provided by Nigel Nicolson and me, it is all too easy to find words from Virginia Woolf's own pen to support pretty well anything you like; after all, she never stopped writing for half a century.

But let us not think of Virginia Woolf's writings as an arsenal of ammunition for literary in-fighting, but rather as a direct source of pleasure and enrichment for readers. After some twenty years working with her diaries I still find them wonderfully enjoyable – brilliant, funny, informative, moving, a record of her life and observations set down with unsurpassed felicity of language by a woman of extraordinary intelligence, courage, humour and imagination: in short, a genius. But, even if one does not subscribe to the belief in her creative genius and find her novels unreadable, her diaries do constitute a document of enormous literary, social, and historical interest and cannot (I think) fail to seize the interest of any reader. My part in making these diaries accessible to the reading public is an ancillary one which I hope I have not appeared either to overrate or to trivialise. But it does certainly boost my ego when Dr Rylands praises my editing as sane, sensitive, scholarly and companionable; and when I read in the *Washington Post* that Leon Edel thinks my footnotes more satisfying than any he has ever known, or written himself. There's Glory for you – for me, I mean.

Note

1. The following account was written in the first instance at the behest of Professor S. P. Rosenbaum of the University of Toronto, who in 1979 bullied me into addressing a seminar of real editors – an occasion of extreme dread, for, although there is a histrionic strain in the Olivier family (which indeed at one time I hoped to exploit myself), I have never overcome my stage-fright at the prospect of speaking my own words before an audience and had always managed to avoid doing so. However, apostrophizing myself in the words of the immortal diarist – "Be spirited!"; "Be in earnest to improve!"; "Be fine old Scots Laird!" (an exhortation often, if inaptly, employed in our family) – I managed to survive the ordeal, and even to repeat it; and on the last occasion it was put into my rather swollen head that my paper merited publication, although it is patently intended for listeners rather than readers.

2
The Editor as Ethicist

Joanne Trautmann Banks

In an earlier essay entitled "The Editor as Detective", I explained the *how's* of our editing process – that is, how Nigel Nicolson and I collected, dated, transcribed, and annotated over 4000 letters written by Virginia Woolf. In this companion piece, I want to discuss the *why's* of that editing process, as well as their causes and consequences. Why, for instance, did Woolf's manuscript letters survive? Why did we have the right to publish them? Why, having agreed to publish a complete edition, did we omit certain lines and letters? The answers to these questions arise partly from existing principles – some explicit, some assumed, some unexamined until now – but also, inextricably, from the experiences, perceptions, and values of the people involved with the project.

For me, this agile internal dialogue between principles and personality is the core of ethics, as I understand that basic human endeavor. Since Aristotle, ethics has been considered a matter of bringing certain agreed-upon principles of right behavior to bear on specific cases and competing choices. Ethics is a process, an action, something one *does*. To bring this concept back to editing Woolf: if we agree that our ethical goal is the utilitarian one articulated by Jeremy Bentham (the greatest good for the greatest number), then publishing essentially private, but socially valuable, letters is the right course to take. But how can we believe that principles by themselves are enough to guide ethical decisions when they are always personal and therefore always messy? If telling the truth is the aim of an editor or a biographer (the ethical distinction between the two roles is not very great), what should he or she do if a friend insists upon a lie? This was, in fact, Woolf's circumstance when she wrote the biography of Roger Fry. An old friend and daughter of John Addington Symonds wavered about Fry's saying that Symonds was "the most pornographic person" he had ever met (Fowler). Fry said it; why couldn't Woolf print it since the man in question was dead and there-fore could not be libeled? She also had to decide whether or not to hide Fry's technically adulterous love affair with her own sister, Vanessa Bell (*LVI*: 285). Moreover, the Fry sisters, who had authorized the biography in the first place, had to be placated (Gillespie: xxix–xxxi). I am saying that ethics is not only principles applied to (or modified by) specific cases, it is also a part of the life story of the people involved with a decision. An ethical choice derives from the present-day settings, plots, and characters, as much as it is does from the values that a civilization has inherited from its past. In short, ethics is narrative in nature (Newton).

Because ethical decisions are embedded in narrative form, there is a certain element of chance in them. I do not mean to cut ethical deci-sions adrift from lasting principles, leaving us with the "situation ethics" that simultaneously enthraled and appaled an earlier generation (Fletcher). Not at all. I am using "chance" in the same sense as the influential literary philosopher Martha Nussbaum uses "luck". Briefly, her reading of clas-sical literature has led her to assert that some Greeks turned their backs on the Platonic ideal of a self-sufficient, rational being who makes prin-cipled ethical decisions. Nussbaum's Greeks saw people as active ethical agents, but also as acted upon by powers in the external world beyond their control. They thus lived with "limited risk"(10) in making their ethical choices. This conception of the ethically contingent self has been reduced in the popular American graffito to "S— happens." In Nuss-baum's universe, "Good happens" as well, and both play a part in ethical situations.

Here, then, is a narrative about why the Woolf *Letters* exist in their present form. It is a story of people and principles, of chance and choice, at every turn. From the beginning, our edition depended heavily upon chance. "So does every other human project", Nussbaum might validly object. "And every contemporary theory of textual editing", an editor might add, "denies the existence of the ideal text and tends toward an adventitious one". True, but it is nonetheless stunning, I think, to realize how very much the six-volume *Letters* – predicted by its editors, its publishers, and, thankfully, a majority of its reviewers to be definitive for at least fifty years – hangs on happenstance.

The project's ultimate shape – its narrative frame, as it were – began with the choice of its editors, which, in turn, hinged on the concurrence of several events, both large and small. Without doubt, the first of these was the 1972 publication of Quentin Bell's life of his aunt. A success, both critically and popularly, the biography appeared just as the culture was ready to grant major-writer status to Virginia Woolf. I think it is fair to say that she had been considered a fine but minor novelist since her death in 1941. Now, a sufficient number of years having passed, she was ripe for rediscovery. The world into which she was resurrected was a galvanized feminist one. Women and politically sensitive men were looking for an English-writing, female author to place beside James Joyce and D. H. Lawrence. Virginia Woolf was suddenly an obvious choice. So she was called back – like De Gaulle waiting outside Paris – to serve as leader and rallying point. About the same time, Nigel Nicolson was preparing the joint biography of his parents, Harold Nicolson and Vita Sackville-West. *Portrait of a Marriage* (1973) immediately caught the interest of the literary, historical, and the nascent gay activist cultures on both sides of the Atlantic. The medical community treated it as a classic on homosexuality, even while significant numbers of potential and actual readers were shocked by the son's revelations, particularly about his mother, whose lesbianism dominated the volume.

The German abstraction *Zeitgeist* begins to convey the cultural state into which the *Letters* were born. For me, I see now, the milieu was more concrete. It was simultaneously mirror and web (two favorite Woolf images), which implied both clarity of perception and a degree of entrapment. Woolf herself used an English translation of *Zeitgeist* in *Orlando*, where it becomes the spirit of the age. People in her version of cultural history may bargain for a greater degree of freedom, but finally there is no comfortable escape.

None of this activity went unnoticed by a shrewd director of The Hogarth Press, Norah Smallwood. Mrs Smallwood had an exquisite nose for the way the cultural breezes were stirring. In consultation with Quentin Bell, she approached Nigel Nicolson about editing a single volume of the correspondence between his mother and Woolf, certain to be of great interest to the newly reorganized reading public. Nicolson was prepared not only as a writer, a son, and an acquaintance of Virginia Woolf, but also as an editor, having served in that function for his father's *Diaries and Letters* (1966–68). Nonetheless, he decided that he needed scholarly assistance for what everyone agreed would have to be a very careful volume. But who in 1972 was a serious student of both Woolf and Sackville-West?

By chance, I was. I had spent the academic year of 1971–72 at Sussex University, where I met Quentin Bell, who was Professor of Art History there and just completing his biography. On learning that I was writing about *Orlando*'s biographical associations, he gave me an introduction to his friend Nigel Nicolson, who generously met with a rather anxious assistant professor for a taped conversation before lunch at Sissinghurst

Castle, Kent. Since Nigel was then overflowing with his plans for *Portrait*, we had scarcely sat down when he said: "Did you know that both my father and mother were homosexuals, and that my mother and Virginia Woolf were lovers?"[1] I did not. The tape recorded 40-seconds of my silence. In the end, Nigel must have thought, the conversation had gone well enough. A later meeting had too, so when he needed a co-editor, he remembered the *Orlando* scholar. That I was an American was useful because, he already knew, Woolf's letters to his mother had been sold to the Berg Collection at the New York Public Library. That I was a woman and a moderate feminist was valuable because of the political climate. By the time the invitation had been accepted, however, the initial proposal had already been scrapped. Nigel's very next letter informed me that Hogarth now wanted to publish a definitive edition of Woolf's letters. I was 30 years old, free of encumbrances, and replied simply, "Let's do it". Apart from broadly judged competence, we had been selected because of relationships. Is this just? Is it ethical? Did it serve Virginia Woolf and her public in the best possible manner? Perhaps not, but in my experience editors are seldom selected any other way, and, after their selection, cannot imagine a different outcome.

At any rate, Nigel Nicolson and I, together with the bargains we had made with the spirit of the age, joined forces to construct Virginia Woolf the letter writer. Our working relationship was the best professional experience I have had in my life. We did not, finally, disagree about any major decision. Of course, there were distinctions between our backgrounds and, therefore, our points of view. Nigel and I differed in work experience (he had been a publisher, parliamentarian, and self-employed writer; I, an academic), nationality (British; American), gender (male; female), age (57; 30 when work began), and, let me say it straight out, class (Nigel's grandparents were Lord Sackville and Lord Carnock; mine, a lawyer and a miner). From these dissimilarities arose some mild dissension. For instance, I felt frustrated when Nigel wanted to begin the annotation for a woman with the identity of her husband because "he was more important than she was". Never mind that Nigel was historically accurate; I still wrinkled my nose. Even when a woman's marriage was the only information we could obtain on her I grumbled and continued to look for something distinctive about her. Nigel would say, "Well, she was born a Darwin, and she married a painter". I would reply, "but she wrote a memoir". I did not realize fully that I was chafing at past constrictions and the "historians of great men", as they came to be known, rather than at our editorial policy. But I still regret the unfair tone of some of the annotations.

I did win the occasional point. We had determined that our annotations would not condescend to her English or North American audiences. In meeting this obligation, Nigel spoke as ambassador for his entire country, and I for mine. "You cannot possibly explain the Adirondacks", I objected as we dealt with the very first letter, wherein six-year-old Virginia was asking James Russell Lowell if he had been staying there. "My people will be insulted". Nigel agreed: "It would be like telling an English audience what the Cotswolds are". That the first letter had American references was a fluke, and thereafter I had frequently to ask for clarification of English references on behalf of the folks back home. "But *every* Englishman knows *that*", Nigel would usually insist, leaving me for an instant with a vision of Americans as sea-to-sea ignoramuses.[2]

There were certain points of honor between us. One time we came across the term "pump shipping" in connection with T. S. Eliot's embarrassment about mentioning money. Virginia wrote: "It's on a par with not pump shipping before your wife." (*LII*: 572) "What's that?" I asked. "We'll certainly have to annotate it". "'Pumping ship means urinating", Nigel replied patiently. "Every Englishman knows that". "I challenge you", I said. "Let's test your generalization". So the typists, the cook, and my infant's nanny were asked. Nigel's children were asked, as was every guest at Nigel's next dinner party: "By the way, my dear, does 'pumping ship' mean anything to you?" Only one man knew, a physician, as it happens. I say "as it happens", because Nigel determined that it was not the doctor's profession that led to this particular genito-urinary information, but his age and his school. "Only Old Etonians over 50 know about 'pumping ship'", Nigel announced. We annotated it.

One of Norah Smallwood's roles was to remind us of costs and profits: simply put, the first was rising, and the second was falling during the years that we labored on the letters. Could we not then omit more of those short, often undatable notes that had nothing to contribute to either enjoyment or literary history? As a former publisher – he is the Nicolson of Weidenfeld and Nicolson – Nigel was sympathetic to The Hogarth Press' situation. I, on the other hand, tended to see the firm as a charming English version of the generous North American granting agencies. Of course, I knew that Hogarth was not a university press, where budgeting was at that time less important than academe's responsibilities for bringing new knowledge to the public. But I expected the Press to fund our work and stay out of our way. With age, I am no longer so naive (and neither are university presses). I still believe, however, that one of my roles was to represent the scholarly community who wanted the so-called "complete" letters of Woolf to be just that. I can recall colleagues wincing when I told them about the notes we had omitted: as the Henry James of *The Aspern Papers* knew, there is nothing so seductive to the scholarly mind as the unpublished document. I think that Nigel and I changed each other's opinions a little, and that, together, we moved Norah and the Press a few inches. Nigel had great respect for my scholarly colleagues, even when he deplored their otherworldliness. For my part, I came to think of the short, undatable, unaddressed notes as the "Come-to-teas", and rather callously joined in consigning them back to the archives from which they had lately arisen.[3]

Sometimes Nigel would remember wistfully that, when he had edited his father's selected papers, he could omit a letter that was difficult to annotate or simply boring. Indeed, what bored Nigel often did not bore me, and vice versa. He came alive when Woolf touched on the European history in which he had participated, while, to my shame, I plodded through it. On the other hand, he frequently moaned, "Not another servant letter" during the editing of Volume II when Woolf seemed to be writing nearly daily to her sister Vanessa about the difficulty of getting her a maid or a nurse for the new baby or whatever she might need to run her complicated household. "Couldn't we just omit this one?" Nigel might plead, knowing full well that we could not. Nor did I want to. I was fascinated by how a woman to whom professional or artistic work was a life sustainer managed her house and children. Women in my world were still dealing with the same issue.[4] Nigel also grew tired of what he considered the endless stories of Woolf's own servants, Nellie Boxall and Lottie Hope, but, as a feminist and an American, I was as intrigued as Virginia was with the "lives of the obscure",[5] and so followed the fortunes of the two young women with more interest. I wondered too about the effect on Woolf's work and therefore on English letters if Nelly quit, as she so often threatened, whereas I got the sense that Nigel was relieved when Nelly was at last dismissed.

Looking back, I see clearly that we were not the only people closely involved with editorial choices. No one ever writes expansively about the people named in the acknowledgments because research is considered impersonal, and researchers like to believe that they alone control their decisions. Woolf parodied this peculiarly scholarly version of name-dropping in *Orlando*, but sometimes, for her and for us, the people named have significant influence. Skipping over the research assistants and typists, who had influence but no power, I have to say that Quentin and Olivier Bell had a prominent effect on our work at a policy level. I am not speaking of their immense practical help, which I have described in "The Editor as Detective", but of their conceptions of biography, the research process, and of Virginia herself. Olivier had not yet begun her own magnificent editing work on the *Diary*, so we were the first to hack our ways through that particular jungle.[6] Otherwise, the Bells were influential not merely because of their special family position, but also because of the information they, especially Olivier, had accumulated during their preparation for the biography. It is not so much the information itself that I want to stress here, but the way they wielded it. In this respect, they were opposites, at least on the surface. (Like all happily married couples, they had incorporated numerous bits and pieces of the other.) I have worked with scientists all my professional life. As her essay in this book demonstrates, Olivier Bell stands with the best, most careful, of them in her respect for what the scientists are pleased to call "hard knowledge". The relationship between Olivier and the verified facts of Woolf's life was a kind of romance that I beheld with wonder and not a little envy. This was especially true in the early days before I had established my own special relationship with our mutual subject. My point is, if Nigel and I were ever tempted to write interpretive annotations, the image of Olivier rose up in our minds to deter us.

We did not, however, write the same sorts of footnotes. We had decided that ours would be written telegraphically. Even after we saw Olivier's full and fascinating annotations ("they rather put us to shame," said Nigel once), we chose to remain as invisible as we could because we did not wish to distract readers from the letters themselves. This editorial stance is very nearly prescribed among scholars and, when carried off well, is the trait most frequently praised by reviewers of edited letters and diaries. I wonder if there were not also some less obvious, more personal, reasons for our decision. Literary critics when young, as I was then, tend to see themselves as serving the authors who are their subjects. Their own ideas about life are suppressed, their first-personhood, denied. Granted, feminist critics have since modified these conventions, but the approach remains the largely unexamined norm even among senior critics. As for Nigel, he was the son of famous parents, whose reputations he still serves, long after their deaths. He is modest about his own distinguished accomplishments. Olivier is too, but she had accumulated so much data in preparation for the biography, data that did not always find its way into the book, that she must have been eager to use it all. She pledged her allegiance to accuracy rather than to the academy's approval, and I believe that, for her, accuracy is achieved through completeness. Whatever her motivations, the resulting annotations are a text in themselves, which could be studied as such. Over the years, they have inspired me to rethink the relationship between author and editor. I still choose comparative anonymity for the editor, but I am no longer so certain that it guarantees either editorial objectivity or authorial precedence.

Quentin's influence on our general approach to editing was subtler and harder to express, but I am convinced that it was just as real and should be made known. Every reader of Quentin Bell's work will have inferred that the man behind them was, in a word, hilarious. From each one of our frequent meetings with Quentin, we came away not only with more information, but with the relaxed state that comes from having been amused for two hours straight through. Add to Quentin's wit, Woolf's own, which I think became clear to the public only after the appearance of her *Letters*, plus the co-editors' preferences for days peppered with amusement, and you have a milieu that is bound to affect the work. But how? An essay entitled "The Effect of Humor on the Editing of Texts" might not extend beyond the title. Moreover, it would inevitably alarm textual scholars: could it mean that editors should not take their work seriously? In our case, I firmly believe that we were the pickiest of nit-pickers, that we used combs so fine-toothed they could have groomed a bald man. Yet there is such a thing as editors' taking themselves and their tasks so seriously that they push the data too far, twisting them to make them fit, or even pushing past fact into fancy. Examples would make my argument clearer, but using the instances that spring to mind would be ungracious.

The daily presence of humor also allowed us to forgive ourselves for failures and, therefore, to go on with the confidence that is essential for achieving satisfactory results in editing. Because the volumes were tightly scheduled, we had to turn immediately to the next one, which in each case we had only a year to prepare. If, after diligent search, we could not find the information we sought, we still had to make the publisher's deadline. If we discovered after a volume had gone to press that we had made an outright error, we could not afford to dwell on it. How, for instance, did we manage to turn the Argentinean Victoria Ocampo into an Irishwoman (a Ms O'Campo) on every single heading of Woolf's letters to her in Volume V? Then there was the evening I arrived for a dinner party at a house in Georgetown to find Nigel flustered and waiting for me near the door: "I've just been introduced to [name omitted]," he said, indicating a wisp of a human being in the next room. "Didn't we say in the last volume that he was dead?" Fortunately for us, though not of course for the man, it was his wife whom we had, accurately, declared dead.

The basic element of chance in any edition of correspondence is which letters happen to survive to be published in something like their original form. This cultural residue is the result of editing by that anti-scholarly committee, Time, Carelessness, and Decay. In Woolf's case, an astonishing number and proportion of letters survived. Not much time had elapsed between her death in 1941 and our edition, for one thing; and the managers of her literary estate were unusually interested in preserving and promoting Woolf's reputation. For another, her correspondents were largely chosen from among that segment of society which valued letters and, therefore, kept them. However avant garde they tended to be, their intellectual beginnings were in the 19th century, that Age of Biography, of multi-volume *Lives and Letters*. Woolf herself professed this interest often, urging her correspondents to publish their own and their ancestors' memoirs and letters, even when they were not in the first rank of fame (for example, *LVI*: 73 re. Bertrand Russell's parents; *LV*: 15 re. Ethel Smyth's memoirs; *LII*: 512 re. Violet Dickinson's great aunt).

In her earliest letters, Woolf wrote to family and, then a little later, to aristocratic ladies, such as Violet Dickinson, who were family friends. They too kept her letters, but in smaller proportion to the number she must have written since there is every reason to assume that she loved letter writing from a very young age – we have letters written when she was about five years old – and there are far larger gaps in our first than in our subsequent volumes. Violet Dickinson is the exception: she kept nearly every one of the approximately 400 letters that she received from her young friend Virginia Stephen and, years after their correspondence had waned, had most of them typed as a gift for her. Violet had her reasons for hording Virginia's letters, one of which was probably the romantic nature of their friendship. Virginia outgrew it, but the never-married, never-partnered, Violet did not. Violet's expressed reason was her belief in Virginia's genius and her still-unrealized plan to become a novelist. Whatever the cause, without Violet and her cache of letters, there would be no clear epistolary picture of Woolf in her early twenties. That we do have one may be a mixed blessing. Joyce Carol Oates, for one, implies that the letters are embarrassing. The Oates character called Vincent Scoville, whose dissertation had been on "the minor works of Virginia Woolf" (what can Ms Oates possibly mean?), describes the letters of Virginia Stephen as "Sprightly breathless phrases . . . dashes, exclamation marks . . . underscorings of banalities" (132). "Underscorings of banalities" – what a decidedly bad review for our Volume I. For my part, I am left with the impression that Woolf took longer to mature, emotionally and even linguistically, than might have been expected from someone of her brilliance. Yet who among us would look sophisticated if our early love letters were read by the public?

On the other side of the chance construction of Woolf as letter writer lie the letters she must have written to Katherine Mansfield, who was both influence and rival in Woolf's life (Banks, "Woolf and Mansfield"). Only two have thus far been found, the second having come to light in time for my edition of selected correspondence, *Congenial Spirits*. This fact is rather odd since John Middleton Murray was obsessed with every detail of his late wife's public presentation, and he surely thought that being a friend of writers like D. H. Lawrence and Virginia Woolf was an important part of Mansfield's image. But Katherine Mansfield was tubercular and poor in her pathetically short life. Therefore, she moved around a great deal, which makes keeping letters difficult. Woolf's English correspondents, in contrast, tended to have the same address for years. To me, that ability to turn a house into a habitat was one of their finest traits. If someone found the missing Mansfield letters, they might add to our enjoyment of Woolf's skills, or shed some light on Mansfield, or possibly on their mutual influence, but I doubt if they would change our picture of her as an encouraging-if-critical literary friend.

There is, however, a group of absent letters that might add significant shading to Woolf's portrait. No one has ever uncovered even a few of the many letters that Woolf must have written to her brother Adrian. As a result, his biography is disappointingly thin (MacGibbon 1997). We have letters to her half-brother, George Duckworth, whom she professed to despise. Why are there no letters to her brother, whom she only disliked? Is it *because* she disliked and condescended to him and his family that he neglected to put the letters in a safe place?

Several other reserves of letters were lost at the beginning of our project, but turned up in time to be published, if only in the "too late" appendix to Volume VI. Often the new cache lit up other facets of Woolf's character, talent, or desire. For instance, her letters to the admittedly careless Duncan Grant were found by his alert, agile granddaughter, Henrietta Garnett, under a bed in a family house in France. They demonstrated Woolf's deep affection for her *de facto* brother-in-law.

Of course, a number of letters came to light only after our project was finished. Known to us as the "too-too lates", they have been published – by me and others – in several sites. Letters to Woolf's nephew, Julian Bell, were discovered by Quentin and Olivier and showed how Virginia hurt Julian by her frank criticism as well as how she grieved because of it (Banks, "Some New Woolf Letters"). In a box removed from Charleston in the mid-1980s, Olivier found Woolf's earliest letters to her mother, in which Virginia's narrative impulse is already apparent at age four or five: "Mrs Prinsep says that she will only go in a slow train cos she says all the fast trains have accidents and she told us about an old man of 70 who got his legs caute in the weels of the train and the train began to go on and the old gentleman was draged along till the train caute fire and he called out for somebody to cut off his legs but nobody came he was burnt up." (Banks, *Congenial Spirits*, 3) The imaginative view of gender that would show up again in *Orlando* and elsewhere is already in evidence too: "I am a little boy and Adrian is a girl" (*Congenial Spirits*, 2). Only a few years ago, a researcher discovered what Nigel Nicolson and I had not – that his mother's ancient desk in the Tower at Sissinghurst Castle concealed a secret drawer, from which the researcher pulled four letters to Vita Sackville-West that caused Woolf to appear a good deal randier than had previously been thought (Banks, "Four Hidden Letters").[7]

One of the reasons we know so much about the life of Virginia Woolf, as well as several other English modernist writers, is because of "the ladies" (as they were known to Norah Smallwood), Miss Hamill and Miss Barker of Chicago. They were manuscript dealers, who read English obituaries to see which writers had lately died. They then arrived on the doorsteps of the freshly aggrieved, offering to buy the literary remains for sums so small that they afterwards made a good deal of money selling them to both private and public collections. This was good business, but was it ethical? If the means were suspicious, the ends were certainly good as far as Woolf scholars are concerned. After all, the foundation of the major Woolf manuscript collection at the Berg was achieved through "the ladies". It never occurred to me until much later to concern myself with the way in which the ladies had taken advantage of certain people. Why had Nigel and I to pay for the ladies' shadiness? (I admit that the logical extension of this argument is a little harder to dismiss: why must we pay for damage done by others to, say, European Jews during the Second World War or to American blacks before the Civil War?)

It is sobering to contemplate that had Hamill and Barker been successful in their first plan – to sell the Woolf manuscripts to an eccentric collector called Frances Hooper – there would have been little or no Woolf editing, and not as much biography and criticism, until the late 1980s after Miss Hooper's death. Her interest in Bloomsbury waned, whereupon she stashed what material she had in her attic, to which no one was admitted – least of all, anyone who worked with Nigel Nicolson, "that dreadful man," Miss Hooper said to me by phone, "who wrote that terrible book [*Portrait of a Marriage*] about his own mother." When Miss Hooper died, the Woolf manuscripts (including all her letters to Lytton Strachey, plus one of the two extant letters to Mansfield) went to her alma mater, Smith College. I felt nothing but elation at this news: I am afraid that the search for manuscripts sometimes blurs the edges of an editor's sympathies.

Another type of ethical assumption operated as we transferred the letters, word by word, letter by letter, to what would become their standard version, cited by scholars for a very long time. We behaved as though the letters that we edited were the letters that Woolf wrote. Yet that was not precisely true. Each of us spent a good deal of time with the originals, but those pieces of blue (for the most part) stationery covered with blue or purple ink were too precious to be handled more often than absolutely necessary.[8] The major public collections – the Berg, Texas, Sussex, King's, and others – duplicated the originals for us, thereby corrupting them to a certain extent: for instance, was that mark at the beginning of an illegible word an apostrophe, a slip of the pen, or an artifact, that is, a by-product of the copying process? There may have been artifacts that we did not recognize as such because we had no trouble, or thought we had not, in deciphering the words in question. But there were instances that brought home to us that we were not working with the actual letters. In a letter to her husband Leonard in November 1912, just three months after their wedding, Virginia wrote: "Shall you get any [*illegible*] from Craig?" The sentence in question is shown in figure 2.1.

We knew that Craig was Dr Maurice Craig, a neurologist who had treated Woolf for mental illness. Nigel did the first reading of the letter because its original was housed on his side of the Atlantic, at Sussex University. (There were "his" letters at Sussex and King's, Cambridge, and "mine" at the Berg and Texas.) He read the mark as an apostrophe and the word as "'assions", a code word for condoms. I thought the reading ingenious, remembering the private, appallingly coy language that Virginia (like the wife in "Lapin and Lapinova") often employed with those she loved. But that was always animal language. With Leonard, for instance, she saw herself as a baboon, and once invited him to inspect her colorful rump (*L*II: 35). But if the bride in this particular marriage reminded her husband to bring home some birth control devices, she was quite a good deal more heterosexually aggressive than is conventionally thought, the baboon rump notwithstanding. And what about her comment to Violet Dickinson just two months earlier that they wanted to have children (*L*II: 23). The only other possibility for the odd word was "onions", in which case the extra mark on the copy was an artifact of some sort, but treating a neurologist as a greengrocer was

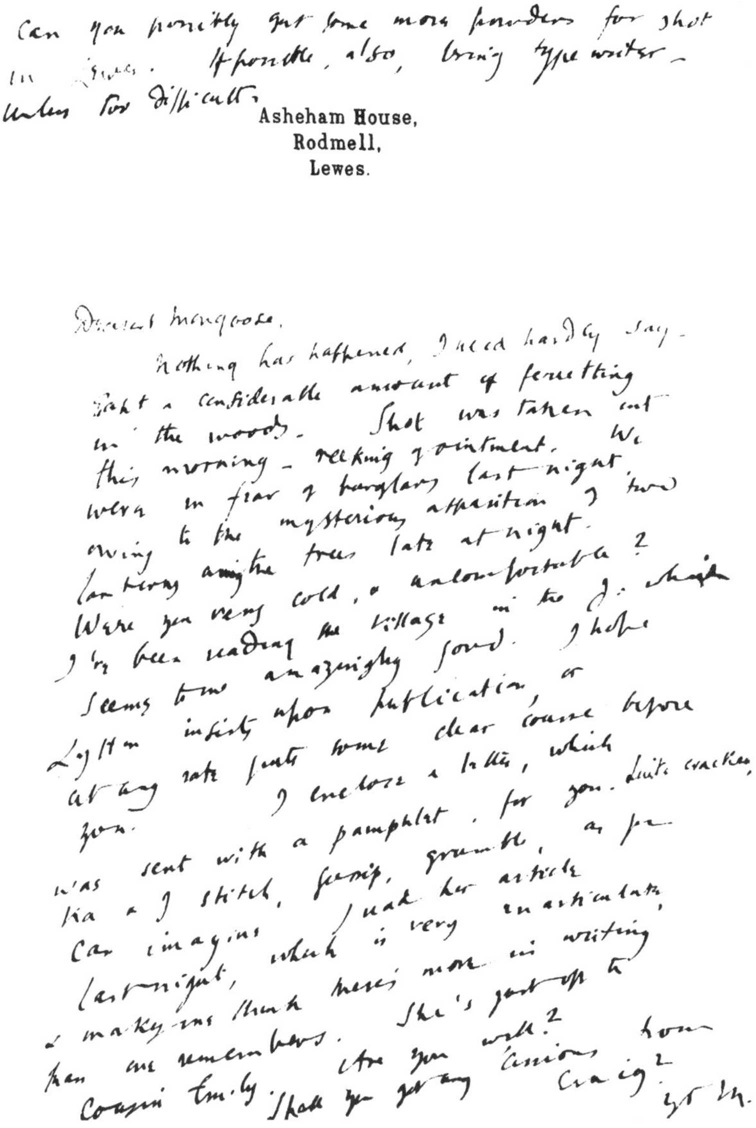

Figure 2.1 An example of Virginia Woolf's handwriting from *The Letters of Virginia Woolf*, vol. II, 12 (letter 652)

preposterous. Checking the original of this letter solved one problem: on the manuscript, there was in fact an ink mark ahead of the word; the copying process had not introduced it. Therefore, in our edition Woolf is forever asking her husband to hurry home with the contraceptives. So far as I know, only Stephen Trombley has commented on our reading. He says that the contraception reading is "unlikely" without saying why (185).

Neither of us was completely comfortable with it either, so in his *Memoirs* (1997), Nigel put the problem before the public again. One of his readers suggested that the troublesome word was "anions", the electrically charged parts of an ionic solution that, when dissociated as in electrolysis, go to the negative anode. ("Cations" are their positively charged counterparts.) Colin Davies, a self-professed "gentleman scientist", went on to recall that electricity was used in various ways by physicians in the 19th century. He had himself been treated as late as 1967 by Galvanism, an 18th-century method in which paralyzed muscles were stimulated by connecting them to a battery. Nigel was not persuaded. He pointed to the apostrophe and to the absence of this technical word in any other Woolf writing. As for me, after looking into the history of electricity in medicine,[9] I believe that "anions" is a slightly more likely reading than "'assions". In my reading, the mark at the beginning of the word is either a slip of the pen, which we occasionally see in Woolf manuscripts, or an inverted comma without its partner, which we see more often, or the result of her confusion about a technical term. To cite its fuller context, Virginia asks Leonard: "Are you well? Shall you get any 'anions from Craig?" Histories of electro-therapy reveal that a method called, among other terms, "electrophoresis" or "iontophoresis" was used by the late 19th century and through the Second World War to drive medications into the body. The process was used for what would seem to clinicians today to be an impossibly broad list of illnesses and symptoms, but they included the sort of muscular problems, namely tremors, from which Leonard Woolf had suffered since his service in Ceylon.[10] Thus is knowledge built, bit by sometimes serendipitous bit, during the editorial process.

In another consideration of manuscript matters, biographer Panthea Reid looked at the originals of Woolf's three suicide notes to suggest a variation of our dating of them (Reid, *Art and Affection*, 471–7; Banks, "Reid's Redating"; Reid, "On My Redating"). She agrees with Nicolson and Trautmann that the letters were written on three different days, whereas Leonard Woolf and Bell had concluded that they were all from the same day, Woolf's last. Reid also agrees that Woolf's note to her sister Vanessa Bell was written five days prior to the suicide in response to a letter from Vanessa that we found at Sussex and cited as part of our suggested time table. Thereafter, Reid challenges our dating of the other two letters based on comparisons of Woolf's stationery, ink, and handwriting as well as on a comparison of language and levels of mounting intensity. So far, Reid's evidence is conventional, even if her argument is, in my opinion, contrived. Her next gambit is the one that most intrigues me. Reid continues her narrative on the basis of creases in the manuscript letters (which she illustrates with elaborate diagrams), ripped and unripped envelopes, levels of soiling, Vanessa's name on the "outside" of one of the letters, and a dusty, dirty drawer. I won't go into our rebuttal of Reid, which is available elsewhere and is built on our intimate knowledge of Leonard's as well as Virginia's habits. I simply want to underscore how readings of manuscripts corrupted by such things as folds, dirt, and subsequent handling may affect the author's identity as it passes down to later generations. In Reid's version of Woolf's last days, she declares her intention to kill herself between 23 and 25 March, doing the deed without writing again on the 28th; in ours,she first decides a full 10 days ahead and writes again to her husband before leaving the house for the last time. What does the difference suggest? I suppose that Woolf's suicide is a more considered decision in our telling (ten days' meditation as opposed to three). Our Woolf thinks pointedly about her husband at the end; Reid's recycles a letter written several days earlier. Probably most important, the Woolf that our editing creates is someone who wrote at least one letter on the last day that she lived. But which tale is true cannot be known with certainty. As in the justice system of the United States, we must be satisfied with the preponderance of evidence.

Reid went back to the originals, as we did from time to time. I had to return to them for a number of questions about the selected letters too. It's easy to imagine, however, that in the near future very few people will be allowed to see, let alone to touch, original, especially handwritten, manuscript material, so vulnerable are these increasingly quaint means of communication. We will then have to rely on the eyesight of curators, I suppose, or on artifact-laden microfilms or -fiches, or on the newer forms, fax and e-mail, plus future inventions. As communication technologies continue to move toward more trustworthy reproduction, how long will it be before scholars stop worrying about the tiny but sometimes meaningful artifacts that these processes may still introduce?

There was one philosophical problem, normally central to textual editing, that we did not have. Nor did Olivier Bell. In editing Woolf's letters and diaries, there is, of course, no question of choosing a copy-text because there are no true variants. We found only one draft letter (to Ben Nicolson, *L*VI: 419–21), which differs so markedly and interestingly from the final version (421–2) that naturally we printed both. The letters to the young Nicolson are, in any case, more like her published "Letter to a Young Poet", and we know how often Woolf revised when she intended to publish. I have long had the sense that she wrote drafts of her early letters to Clive Bell and maybe to Lytton Strachey, if only because they are so stilted. Leonard Woolf speaks of finding this quality in his wife's letters to Strachey, saying that the two were "always on their best behavior" when writing to each other (vii). And here is Woolf herself on the subject, in 1926: "ten years ago I did write drafts, when I was in my letter writing days, but now, never" (*L*III: 247). If she is telling the truth, she apparently destroyed the drafts. Some of the letters to Gerald Brenan also sound like revisions to me, but I have only a sense and no evidence. It is not surprising that every one of these correspondents is a young, male intellectual, a species of whom she was a little wary. Yet most of the time, writing letters was a complete delight for Woolf as well as for her fortunate correspondents. "A mere tossing of omelettes", is the way she described her letters' effortlessness; "if they break and squash, can't be helped" (*L*III: 80).

Because there was only the one draft, it never occurred to us to spend much time defining what a Woolf letter was. I have not seen this issue discussed anywhere else, but I suppose that the usual assumption by those who edit complete correspondence – it was ours – is that the text of the letter is the uncut missive as received by the correspondent. We made a further assumption at the beginning of our work: we were editing the letters that Woolf sent privately; we would exclude the letters that she sent to papers and periodicals because, in essence, the public letters were more like an essay, and an already published form, besides. When I edited the selected letters, I changed my mind about this decision – not, frankly, because I rethought the question of genres, or because I thought that the issue involved an ethical responsibility to scholars, but because the public letters were so very good that I coveted them for my readers.

Thus I made an aesthetic, rather than an ethical, judgment. Or did I? Long considered mutually exclusive categories in Western culture, aesthetics is finally, in my opinion, a subset of ethics because art for art's sake is an unattainable, if worthy, ideal. The very choice to pursue an art proudly isolated from cultural, and therefore impermanent, elements is a decision made in conflict with that part of society that looks to art to improve life. The conflict itself is ethical. When editors make decisions intended to achieve aesthetic ends, ethics is the basic mode in such questions as, will this form be accessible, and therefore valuable, to more or fewer readers than that alternative form? And, would an alternative form move readers toward a better (in some sense) view of life's patterns? And, should I choose a form that pleases me, even though others are paying for my work?

Let me illustrate my contention with a discussion of the form of the Woolf *Letters*. The organization seemed obvious, but there was a different possibility considered. Once we knew about how many letters we had, we divided them into six volumes that would be comfortable to hold, comfortable to read, and comfortable for the publishers to price. They were to be chronological, each book ending with a completed year. What resulted is an edition that scholars can consult easily. They can follow along with the biographies and the *Diary*, if they like. They can dip into a subject through the indexes, which Nigel structured in such admirable detail, or pursue a particular time period. The chronology, plus the publication plan of one volume per year, required us to put at least an approximate date on the many incompletely dated and undated letters before we started, so that we would not come across a Volume II letter while we were editing Volume IV.

For a brief time, we considered a less obvious organization – that is, into themes. There might be volumes on her own writing, on writing or painting by other people, on friendship and love, on travel and place, on social or political ideas, and on family and psychological matters. This plan would have meant that we did not have to date letters at the start, only categorize them. But what a difficult and ultimately illogical course we would then have followed, for all human categories overlap. Furthermore, we would have ended by cannibalizing Woolf's letters to find a paragraph on literary method, and, farther along in the same letter, a few lines on feminism. And what would we then have done about a subject like homosexuality, which she usually treated as love but sometimes as an element of someone's psychological makeup? I think that Norah Smallwood would have vetoed the idea anyway because the final volumes would have varied so much in length that they would have been hard to sell, and harder still to sell as a set. I thought at the time that the idea appealed to the part of Nigel who understood that the common reader might like to purchase, say, "Virginia Woolf on Love", but I have lately realized that he also sees his own life thematically, as the chapters of his *Memoirs* – "The Bloomsbury", "The Soldier", "The Publisher", and so on – indicate. Of course all of us are free to import what categories we please into our own lives. Had we imposed them on Woolf's life, however, ethical dilemmas arise, as all biographers know. In that inspired phrase by Susan Dick, the *Letters* are already "book[s] she never wrote". Thematically organized *Letters* would have been books she never even imagined.

For what is finally important about the organization we chose is that it is representative of our goal to remain comparatively invisible as editors. The chronological form of the *Letters* imposes on them only the pattern that human beings generally have agreed to follow. I mean that, by convention, we arrange our affairs chronologically in a linear fashion; thus, such an arrangement for epistolary texts does not draw attention to itself. A quantum physicist might reply that linearity is every bit as contrived a pattern as a thematic one that ignores time, but the physicist's perspective is not, not yet, at any rate, the one we employ on a daily basis. I do not think, by the way, that a thematic volume would have appeared free from the constrictions of time; I only mentioned timelessness to make the contrast between plans more vivid. Within the volume on, for instance, friendship and love, Nigel and I would have imposed a further pattern, either time (that is, first Woolf loved Violet Dickinson, then she flirted with Clive Bell, but afterwards she continued to love Violet) or person (all the letters to Violet, followed by all the letters to Vita Sackville-West, and so on).

From the beginning, Nigel wanted to create a general reader's text, so many of the decisions he urged were intended to achieve this objective. For instance, he wanted to divide the letters into sections, which were tacitly understood to mean the number of letters that an imagined reader could comfortably process. But there were no rules about where the divisions should come other than they should appear to be natural. It seems to me that a well-schooled sense of narrative rhythm often determined the matter, but there were some more objective markers, such as travel or change of house from London to the country. The reader was also intended to benefit from the short narrative that began each section. The narratives summarized the events in the subsequent letters and, if necessary or merely lively, filled in gaps with information from the *Diary* and elsewhere (Vita Sackville-West's private diaries about their sexual activities, for example). The linking passages were also mildly interpretive, not by virtue of what they said, for they were fairly straightforward summaries of what the next letters revealed, but because they inevitably stressed certain events rather than others. After all, we could not foreshadow every outer and inner event in a section, so the values of the editors were inevitably involved. Did we thereby make Woolf's life tidier than it actually was? Of course. Every biographical statement does so.

I have no idea whether or not our imagined readers appreciate three other decisions made on their behalf. We substituted the word "and" for Woolf's regular use of the ampersand because we thought that a page peppered with "&s" would make readers dizzy with distraction. They can easily decide for themselves because, when Olivier Bell came to edit the *Diary*, she took the purer course and retained the ampersands. We also made new paragraphs, typographically, where Woolf had not but clearly intended them. We hit the indent key whenever she left wide gaps on the same line and afterwards began a new subject. We entitled each volume, but the titles were not designed for a reader's pleasure so much as to get his or her attention. They were requested by Norah Smallwood, as I recall, who thought the books would sell better if they sported a beckoning theme. (Later, when I did the selected letters, the salespeople at The Hogarth Press rejected my first title, and marketeers chose *Congenial Spirits*). Nigel and I took each year's title from a letter in the volume being prepared. We generally agreed on them, but I disputed his suggestions of "A Mere Tossing of Omelettes" (from *LIII*: 80) as too gastric, and "More Mustard to My Meat" (*LIII*: 113) as even more gastric, as well as too suggestive for the juvenile part of the American mind. On the other hand, I championed the last volume's "Leave the Letters Till We're Dead" against his objections that the title would be too long for the dust cover spine. On the North American side of the Atlantic, our editor at Harcourt, John Ferrone, decided that the more straightforward title – *The Letters of Virginia Woolf*, volumes one through six – would be better suited to the audience he served, whom he saw as needing no sales inducement beyond Virginia Woolf's name and reputation.

I come now to the most delicate editorial decisions that we made, each of them ethical in the most specific sense of the word. Just as they are in society at large, some of these moral matters were decided by reference to the law – in our case, the law of libel. Lydia Lopokova, the ballerina who was married to John Maynard Keynes, was still alive in 1977 when we came across Woolf's summary of Lopokova's sexual experiences in thirteen vivid words. Lady Keynes had the affection and protection of her distinguished brother-in-law, Geoffrey Keynes, so it would not do, legally, to publish Woolf's potentially libelous language. Thus the passage appears with "thirteen words omitted" (*LIII*: 52). Following the death of Lopokova, the words were restored in *Congenial Spirits*, where no one, including this editor, commented on "however many Russian Generals and Polish princes or Soho waiters she's lain with" (172). In contrast, there was no ethical issue at all with Gerald Brenan, who wrote Nigel: "I really don't mind what she [Woolf] or anyone else says about me. Nothing should be suppressed". Indeed, in *Personal Record*, Brenan wrote frankly about his own equivalent of the generals, princes, and waiters.

The case of Mary Hutchinson was more complex. We had heard from several sources that the lady, still alive, did not like the Bloomsbury publicity that was already beginning to dominate English journalism and would not co-operate with us as editors. So we read with care Woolf's comments on Hutchinson when they began to appear in Volume II letters. They covered some of the years when Mary Hutchinson and Clive Bell were lovers, though each was, technically, married to someone else. Their relationship was hardly uncommon in Bloomsbury, so in the midst of 600 pages of other excitement, we passed on to the Press a few sections like this one from a letter of 11 April 1920 to Vanessa Bell: "You'll be glad to hear that the amorous Parakeets [Woolf's favorite image for the lovers] are flourishing. They suddenly proposed a visit to Monks House – and came to dinner here instead. Why, when they're together, do they produce such an atmosphere of the Brighton pier? Something brazen and yet sterile; nothing but double asters and lodging house windows and pierrons flourish in it; all my sensibilities have salt dropped on them. I think I feel this more and more, and if you did your duty as a wife, you'd provide another mistress. I think Clive ought to have a change. I've nothing against them separately – indeed I thought Mary humane and even pathetic, like a small kitten".

I cannot now remember what we said about our decision at the time, but I suspect that I urged publication, while Nigel urged caution. I know that, in my thirties, I thought Brenan's jolly frankness about his life admirable. More, it was positively Bloomsbury. Now that I am older, I rather regret how hard I pushed to include each and every instance of Woolf's gossip, no matter about whom, no matter how far-fetched. As an editor, I was like a pig hunting for truffles: it seemed to me that the public we served had a right to know everything we could uncover, particularly when it was articulated so amusingly by that splendid letter writer, Virginia Woolf. Now that I have, I trust, a deeper understanding of the phases of life's stories, and have lived longer with love, death, guilt, and grief, I see that published language has the power to cause considerable suffering. In fact, there is in Volume III another missing name that I could restore here because the person whose bedding behavior Virginia describes has recently died. But I find that, for me, legal permission is no longer congruous with ethical choice.

At any rate, while we were reading through the proofs for Volume II, Nigel "was struck by conscience," as he later admitted to the readers of the *Virginia Woolf Miscellany* (1). He sent the passages on Mary Hutchinson to her son, Jeremy, who, in consultation with his sister (but not their mother), decided that Mary would be deeply wounded by the ridicule of a relationship that had meant a great deal to her. By then it was too late (read: too expensive) to recast the pages, so the volume had to appear with distracting lines of dots taking the place of the offensive language.

In April of the very next year, Mary Hutchinson died, thereby allowing us to ignore the law (the dead cannot be libeled) and rethink our ethics. Nigel wrote again to her son to inquire whether or not Mary received any letters from Virginia, and where those letters might be. We quickly learned that the letters we sought had been deposited with the Humanities Research Center at the University of Texas (from which we had already taken copies of many other Woolf letters). Apparently, we had not known about them because Mary had put an embargo on their publication for 20 years following her death. Now Nigel asked Jeremy Hutchinson, as his mother's executor, to consider waiving the embargo for our edition. He agreed. So there are a number of Woolf–Hutchinson letters in the too-late section at the end of Volume VI.

At the time, nothing in the light-hearted letters caused any concern at all. Having read Virginia on Mary, I assumed that the letters were hypocritical performances. Rereading them later by themselves, however, I realized why they had probably worried Mary Hutchinson. She goes from the conventional address, "My dear Mary" (*LVI*: 508), to "Dearest Weasel" (527). The nickname was inspired by Mary's toothiness, but it was not intended to be hurtful. Close readers of Woolf's letters know that when a woman is addressed by an animal name and/or presented with Virginia under the guise of an animal, Woolf is vaguely, and often more particularly, aroused. The practice goes back to her cousin Emma Vaughan ("Toad") and her sister Vanessa Bell ("Sheepdog", "Dolphin"). It continues during two romantic friendships begun in her twenties: to Violet Dickinson, Virginia signed herself "Wallaby", "Kangaroo", and "Sparroy", (a combination of bird and monkey), and she addressed Madge Vaughan as "Barbary Ape". Vita, with whom of course there was a mutually loving physical affair, was "Sheep dog", (like Vanessa) and "Donkey", or, more generally, "Creature" to Virginia's "Potto" (a small, woolly primate). Even 70-year-old Ethel Smyth, who was openly in love with a bemused Virginia, had her own animal names, albeit affectionately insulting ones – "uncastrated cat", "hedgehog", "befogged and besotted owl".

To this list I tentatively add Mary Hutchinson, the "Weasel", and submit that Virginia's arousal by her is linked to her affair with Vita. In the first place, Virginia uses words about Mary that vaguely echo words used four years earlier to describe Vita. Here is Woolf on Mary: "My vision of you is almost entirely unreal. You come out at night; you drop orchids in the mud, and have them washed in warm water with cotton wool" (*L*VI: 526). And on Vita: "I have a perfectly romantic and no doubt untrue vision of you in my mind – stamping out the hops in a great vat in Kent – stark naked, brown as a satyr, and very beautiful" (*L*III: 198). About Mary, Virginia confessed that she was "very much charmed . . . chiefly because she has such pretty legs" (*L*III: 133). Vita's legs are also alluring: "Then there was Vita, very striking . . . so dashing, on her long white legs with a crimson bow. . . . I like the legs" (*L*III: 380). More convincing to me, Woolf uses overtly flirtatious and sexual language with Mary: "I like Weasels to kiss: but as they kiss to bite: and then to kiss. I like alternations and variety" (527). It was not so much their mutual attraction to Clive, I think, that prompted Virginia to explore these feelings with Mary, but Mary's unchaste night with Vita. Virginia responded with anger, couched in negative and aphrodisiac animal language: "Bad, wicked beast [Vita]! To think of sporting with oysters, lewd lascivious oysters, stationary cold oysters, – to think of it, I say. Your oyster has been in tears on the telephone imploring Clive to come back to her – thats all the faith there is in oysters" (*L*III: 395). In the letter as originally published in Volume III, we had omitted as an act of kindness the words "imploring Clive to come back to her" that identified Hutchinson.

To these ethical issues Nigel brought an additional element: he knew some of the people involved – had known some of them, in fact, for years. He had been at university with Jeremy Hutchinson, for instance. I think that Nigel also had a different, I don't say "better", sense of propriety than I did, perhaps a British sense, aligned with his birth and background, of what simply is not done. It was his practice to send Woolf's potentially hurtful lines to people still alive for their information and vetting, a practice that I have usually followed ever since. If all this seems surprising for the man who wrote a book about his mother's scandalous lesbian affair in *Portrait of a Marriage*, I say that the information instead reveals something of the painful soul-searching that he did before writing a word.

His reflection was made easier by his mother herself. She had left her version of the affair where she knew her literary executor, Nigel, would find it after her death (*Portrait*, vii). Her words seemed to address a public reader. Thus, in a sense, she consented to publication. But did Virginia Woolf consent, in the same sense, to our publishing her letters? That is the basic ethical question that faces most editors of private papers such as letters and diaries. To some people, it is a matter of etiquette – that is, of propriety – rather than ethics. In 1929, the then United States Secretary of State Henry L. Stimpson, proclaiming that "Gentlemen do not read each other's mail", ended the Department's code-interception program. Safely behind our academic cover ("We are in the pursuit of the truth") and non-celebrity ("No one will ever wish to read my letters, thank goodness"), we gentlemen- and lady-scholars relish the reading of other people's mail.

Ethicists are not interested in etiquette but in principles. They have conceived this issue of agreement as "informed consent" in medical research and practice, where subjects and patients must be fully informed about a procedure or treatment before they sign permission papers. Philosophers have for years debated about whether consent is ever completely informed: for example, many seriously ill patients are too stressed to think clearly. Nonetheless, doctors and scientists must make the effort or forfeit an element of humane, civilized behavior. In certain cases, a qualified substitute acts on behalf of an impaired person, trying to observe that person's wishes. Obviously, a deceased person – I return to Woolf – cannot give informed consent to the publication of her letters. Legally, there was no problem in our case. Quentin and Angelica Bell as Woolf's heirs had the right to give consent because they held copy-rights that were still in effect. Nonetheless, Nigel and I were drawn to the ethically humane question: what would Woolf have wished? The most powerful evidence against publication was her last statement to Leonard: "Will you destroy all my papers" (*L*VI: 487). Without wishing to seem harsh, it must be said that the line is practically a convention in a suicide note. In any case, Leonard seems not to have doubted that he should ignore the request. He edited a number of her papers himself, including that remarkable book, *A Writer's Diary*. The evidence that Woolf would have agreed to publication is implicit throughout a life-time spent reading memoirs, lives, and letters: "Letters and memoirs are my delight – how much better than novels!" (*L*VI: 87). She claimed to be furious when her correspondents read her letters aloud to others as entertainment (see for example, *L*III: 368), but she knew that Leonard "should make up a book from" the diaries, "and then burn the body" after she was gone (*D*III: 67). And to Ethel Smyth, who wanted to publish their correspondence while they lived, she wrote the line that gave our last volume its title: "Lets leave the letters till we're both dead. Thats my plan. I dont keep or destroy but collect miscellaneous bundles of odds and ends, and let posterity, if there is one, burn or not. Lets forget all about death and all about Posterity". (*LVI*: 272) This is as close as we can get to Woolf's informed consent to our edition.

I have pursued this question because, in my opinion, it is not asked often enough. The academic community, and indeed the general public, simply assumes that society has the right to know the private and semi-private thoughts of writers who have been awarded laurels and thus, in a sense, belong to all humanity. The assumption goes unexamined when the writer corresponds with a literary friend about a work in progress, but suppose the same writer compares a female novelist's lips to "the private parts of a large cow" (*LII*: 426)? Is it an important part of the culture's understanding of a great writer to know that she is capable of this sort of vulgarity? Would it be censorship to omit the description? To these questions I am inclined to answer "yes" and "yes", but the answers are by no means self-evident.

There is a quintessential story that has been passed from one editor of letters to another until the tale has attained the same status among editors as an urban myth among the public at large. It seems that a certain English writer, usually said to be Philip Larkin, was speaking at a university campus. As part of his host's entertainment of him, he was taken to the library, where the curator of manuscripts proudly showed him the school's latest acquisition – dozens of letters Larkin had written to a long-discarded lover. That the visiting poet might be outraged had never occurred to his hosts. A psychologist might say that editors tell this and similar stories as a gesture of counterphobia – that we immerse ourselves in that which we fear in order to desensitize ourselves to its impact. Maybe so, but I have to confess that, in the end, I felt no more than an ethical *frisson* about editing Woolf's complete letters.

A special obligation is thrust upon the biographer or editor who is a family member or close friend. As we have seen, Woolf, acting as the biographer of her great friend Roger Fry, made concessions to the truth so that she might serve her sister, among others, rather than posterity, and, given the spirit of the age, no one can validly fault her. Moving into our own age, and our own books, I have heard readers complain caustic-ally of the *Letters*, *Diary*, and even the *Essays* that "Bloomsbury is editing Bloomsbury", or that, in the case of the early biographies, "Bloomsbury has anointed its own sons as its historians".[11] The complaints are obvi-ously inaccurate. For one thing, Andrew McNeillie and I are tossed in because of our relationship with, and, granted, a certain dependence on, the Bells and Nigel Nicolson. Nonetheless, I acknowledge the concern, assuming that it cannot be put down to cynicism or envy. How do we assess the impact of a close relationship between author and subject?

Readers get an automatic reward in view of the special knowledge possessed by the writer, but how do they trace the nearly inevitable shading of the subject? (The bias, by the way, is not always complimentary – think of the *Mommy Dearest* genre of revenge biography.) What must Quentin Bell have felt when writing about his father's affairs, his mother's unhappiness, and his aunt Virginia's perfidious flirtation with his father? How did he process his family's standard opinions – every family has them – about his aunt? Since I cannot answer these questions, I will let them stand as examples of a general ethical dilemma that needs more attention and go on to a question to which I can give a more informed opinion – that is, how did Nigel Nicolson handle his editorial responsibilities during the preparation of Volume III, the one that most concerned his mother? I can attest to his maintaining scrupulous control and distance at that time, even when we were consulting his mother's frank diaries and generally reliving her life. Only when we had completed our work on the last day did Nigel allow himself to express his stored grief.

I regard as the ultimate ethical issue an affiliated topic that frequently arises as a ghost story. Biographers will say in casual conversation that they have lived with the specter of their subjects. Editors of diaries and letters will declare that they know their subjects better than they know themselves. I have myself been asked such questions as "what would Virginia Woolf have thought of e-mail?". I have answered without thinking twice: "she would have adored it". My questioner and I were playing for very low stakes, but sometimes a biographer or editor makes a more serious decision that presumes that he or she has temporarily taken on the identity of the subject. D. C. Greetham speaks of an editor's choice sometimes coming down to "intuition", which Greetham believes is a "critical process... based... on *becoming* the author for that moment" in order to make what he does not hesitate to call an "interpretation" of the text. This is an awesome business with extremely high ethical stakes. Greetham continues: "if one must indeed become Langland or Melville (or Shakespeare, Joyce, Woolf, Beethoven, or Michelangelo) in the phenomenology of reconstruction, then clearly textual scholars are making very large claims for themselves, and those claims extend beyond narrow, technical, philological aims" (123). Just so, and editors must compensate for these claims with a great deal of humility. I suppose that a certain amount of identification with one's subject cannot be avoided. Woolf herself used a procreation metaphor, casting Roger Fry in the part of mate when she pondered the biography she had written of him: "What a curious relation is mine with Roger at this moment – I who have given him a kind of shape after his death – Was he like that? I feel very much in his presence at the moment: as if I were intimately connected with him; as if we together had given birth to this vision of him: a child born of us" (*DV*: 305). But many a biographical and even a critical piece has been spoiled by over-identification. Emotion has hurled a writer beyond the facts into an unreasonable interpretation or defense. More than a scholarly failure, such a piece is also, I have been implying all along, a major ethical defeat.

Notes

1. These words are not part of the interview as it was published in the *Virginia Woolf Quarterly* because I was asked to keep confidential the information that would soon be available in *Portrait of a Marriage*. In contrast, by the way, to the usual practice for scholarly pieces, I have here used first names for friends such as Nigel Nicolson, Quentin Bell, and Olivier Bell, and for people such as Virginia Woolf and her correspondents because that was the way they were known to us while we worked on the letters. Using surnames everywhere would make the fundamentally narrative structure of this essay unnatural as well as inaccurate.
2. This paragraph and the next are borrowed from "The Editor as Detective".
3. Lists of the notes omitted from the complete as well as the selected letters have been deposited with the Berg Collection of the New York Public Library and the Sussex University Library. Sussex also holds the "Nicolson Papers", Nigel's letters to and from various people about our edition. I still have in my possession other letters on the subject.
4. When I brought my infant to Sissinghurst, no fewer than six people offered to come as nanny. Four had PhDs in literature, and one was an MD. I hired the sixth precisely because she had never heard of Virginia Woolf.
5. The title of a book that Woolf planned in 1927–28 (see for example, *D*III: 198), but did not complete.
6. As Volume I's scanty annotations demonstrate. I do not count as a worthily edited text the Leonard Woolf and James Strachey edition of the correspondence between Woolf and Lytton Strachey (1956). The selection is capricious, the censorship heavy-handed, the transcriptions faulty, and the annotations both few and haphazard.
7. See Kirkpatrick and Clarke, 413–17, for other late letters. Since the bibliography's appearance in 1997, additional letters have been edited by Stephen Barkway, Stuart N. Clarke, and Hermione Lee. There are plans for future publications by Clarke, Mark Hussey, and Andrei Rogatchevski.
8. Precious for coming literary generations, I mean. But the monetary meaning of "precious" operates too. I have known one manuscript dealer offer a Woolf letter for sale at Canadian $6000, an enormous increase from the £1 apiece paid by Hamill and Barker for her letters to Vita Sackville-West.
9. With the excellent help of Elizabeth Ihrig, curator of manuscripts at The Bakken: A Library and Museum of Electricity in Life, Minneapolis, who led me to two histories of electricity, one by Licht, the other by Rowbottom and Susskind.

10. Jane Marcus says in passing, and with no citation, that Woolf received "electrical stimulation" (4) as part of the treatment in her early rest cures under Dr George Savage. But Trombley, who devotes a chapter to Savage, does not mention electricity. In any case, it is not likely that in this letter Woolf is asking about anions for herself since the treatment could not be transported by a layperson.

11. It is true, of course, that central and peripheral Bloomsbury people, plus their younger friends, have written a great deal of the era's history, whether by memoir (as in Frances Partridge's case), edition (David Garnett's editing of Carrington's letters), or critical work (Richard Shone on the artists). The number of these books may be greater in the case of Bloomsbury, but the close relationships between any artist and some of his or her interpreters is a given in our culture, and, therefore, seldom analysed in ethical terms.

3
The Writing of *A Room of One's Own*

S. P. Rosenbaum

"By a miracle I've found all the pages", Virginia Woolf wrote to Ethel Smyth three years after the publication of *A Room of One's Own* (*LV*: 136).[1] She wanted to donate the manuscript to the nearly bankrupt London and National Society for Women's Service, but the Society asked her to sell it for them in America. Unsuccessful inquiries were undertaken, and in the end Woolf was advised to try and sell the manuscript in England. There the matter seems to have dropped.

While making some inquiries as to the whereabouts of his wife's manuscripts after her death, Leonard Woolf received a request from the Director of the Fitzwilliam Museum in Cambridge, for something of Virginia Woolf's. Leonard Woolf responded appropriately and with great generosity, giving back to Cambridge (but not to Newnham or Girton, not to King's, and certainly not to Trinity's library) the manuscript that had its beginning there.

The Fitzwilliam manuscript bears the title *Women & Fiction* and consists of 134 holograph leaves. It is divided into five chapters plus a conclusion, and bears various dates between 6 March and 2 April 1929. A closer examination reveals, however, that Virginia Woolf did not miraculously find all the pages. The Fitzwilliam manuscript is really two manuscripts. The rhetoric of interruption in *A Room of One's Own* together with the disconnectedness of its composition sometimes make it difficult to recognize breaks in the manuscript's progression. But it is evident that the heading "Chapter 4. Cont." is not simply a continuation of the third chapter that it follows. The manuscript paper is also different.

The third chapter of the Fitzwilliam manuscript is continued, however, in an untitled, undated manuscript of twenty leaves to be found in the Monks House Papers at the University of Sussex. (Also to be found in these papers are a brief variant opening for *A Room of One's Own* and a page of notes for the conclusion of *Women & Fiction*.) The paper of the Monks House manuscript is the same as the Fitzwilliam manuscript, except for the last few pages. But discontinuities remain. The fourth chapter of the Fitzwilliam manuscript does not carry on from the Monks House manuscript. It refers, for example to the imaginary novelist Mary Carmichael, who had been called Chloe in the Monks House manuscript. Parts of the drafts for *A Room of One's Own* are therefore still missing and must be presumed lost. To make matters more complicated, some scenes in the Monks House manuscript have been redrafted again in the following Fitzwilliam leaves. These different drafts, it is clear from the dates in the Fitzwilliam manuscript, were all done within days of each other, for the entire drafting of the book that became *A Room of One's Own* took little over a month. One reason for this remarkable speed, as Virginia Woolf noted in her diary, was that "the thinking had been done & the writing stiffly unsatisfactorily 4 times before" (*DIII*: 218–19, 221–2). She had prepared a paper to be given to undergraduates at Newnham College in May 1928, interrupting the writing of *Orlando*, but illness and the pressure to finish that book led her to postpone until the autumn her visits to both Newnham and Girton (the only other Cambridge college where women could study) which had also asked her to speak. The papers delivered at those colleges in October 1928 are now lost, but Woolf did publish an article on the subject of her papers in the American *Forum* the next year. She called her Forum piece "Women and Fiction". This would also be the working title for *A Room of One's Own* as well as the heading for the paper that the speaker is trying to write in that book. If one counts the talks to Newnham and Girton as separate papers, then this was the fourth time she addressed the subject. (The first was the version prepared the preceding spring.)

The idea of making a book out of her Cambridge lectures does not seem to have occurred to Woolf until the spring of 1929. For three years she had been trying to write a book on the theory of fiction for The Hogarth Press Lectures on Literature series. The success of Forster's *Aspects of the Novel* provided a stimulus for the book because Woolf thought, as she said in her two reviews of Forster's book that he had not paid enough attention to the art of fiction. She had begun "Phases of Fiction", as the book was called, in 1926, but became bored with it and turned to *Orlando* instead. Woolf took up "Phases of Fiction" again and finished drafting it before going to Cambridge in October 1928. She rewrote it in November and December, and still had 10 000 words to do, when another book of fiction intervened.

Woolf says in her note to both *Women & Fiction* and *A Room of One's Own* that they are "based" on the paper or papers read at Cambridge. A comparison of the *Forum* article "Women and Fiction" with *A Room of One's Own* makes the nature of this basis clear. It shows how the experience of coming to Cambridge and reading a paper to a women's college on the topic of women and fiction became the narrative basis for the book that Virginia Woolf would begin to write in March 1929. With the recovery of the manuscript versions of *A Room of One's Own*, it is now possible to follow this modernist transformation through the beginnings, endings, interruptions, repetitions, cancellations, insertions, and marginalia of Woolf's creative process.

Soon after she finished drafting *Women & Fiction*, Woolf wrote a short biography of Mary Wollstonecraft in which she said of works like *A Vindication of the Rights of Woman* what readers have come to feel about *A Room of One's Own*: "they seem now to contain nothing new in them – their originality has become our commonplace". The drafts of *A Room of One's Own* allow us to defamiliarize the text and re-experience the originality of a work so influential that it has become our commonplace. In *Women & Fiction* the narrative structure of *A Room of One's Own* is clearly visible yet almost every sentence of the book was revised in some way during the course of composition. Again and again Woolf rewrites her text as she strives to fuse the diverse forms of lecture and fiction, feminist argument and literary criticism, polemic and prophecy. *Women & Fiction* reflects, like *A Room of One's Own*, the fantasy of *Orlando*, which she had just published, and the mysticism of *The Waves*, which she was about to write. Yet the study of its composition differs from those of Woolf's novels because *A Room of One's Own* is a more discursive work. In its manuscript versions one can watch Woolf creatively developing her arguments through reasoning and association in images and scenes.

The writing of *Women & Fiction*

Early in 1929, the Woolfs visited Vita Sackville-West and her husband Harold Nicolson in Berlin, where he was serving as a diplomat. After their return Virginia Woolf was ill: for three weeks she lay in bed, and for perhaps another three could not write. It was a creative illness. As she wrote later, "I believe these illnesses are in my case – how shall I express it? – partly mystical. Something happens in my mind. It refuses to go on registering impressions. It shuts itself up. It becomes a chrysalis." (*D*III: 287) Woolf had wanted to begin *The Waves*, but the subject of her

Cambridge papers and article forced itself on her again in a new form now, which she described as half talk and half soliloquy. Woolf began making up *Women & Fiction* in her head as she lay in bed. Then in what she called "one of my excited outbursts of composition," the book was drafted in about a month. "I used to make it up at such a rate," she noted when beginning her revisions in April, "that when I got pen & paper I was like a water bottle turned upside down. The writing was as quick as my hand could write; too quick for I am now toiling to revise; but this way gives one freedom & lets one leap from back to back of one's thoughts" (*DIII*: 218–19, 221–2). It was too quick also for any easy deciphering of her manuscript. The scrawl of her handwriting confirms the extraordinary speed with which *Women & Fiction* was written. Woolf's novels were usually written in a bound quarto notebook; the morning's work would be revised when she typed it up in the afternoon. *Women & Fiction*, however, was written on loose-leaf paper and not typed up until the holograph draft had been completed. There are no indications in the manuscript or her diary that she referred to her Cambridge lectures while composing the book that was based on them.

The first date in the manuscript of *Women & Fiction* – "Wed. 6th March 1929" – appears at the start of Chapter II. The opening chapter is undated and undesignated even as a chapter. In the note that describes its basis in a paper read at Newnham and Girton, *Women & Fiction* is not called an essay, nor is there any mention of expanding the paper, as in *A Room of One's Own*. Woolf may not have known yet where her essay–story was going as she began it. The opening words pick up the original title, to which the speaker–narrator keeps returning. Women indicates a dangerous subject, and Fiction lands her in the swamp and maze of literary criticism. The license of fiction is invoked and illustrated with the image of a medieval pedlar, a device Woolf used in one of her earliest stories. Mary Beaton, Seaton, and Carmichael are all mentioned, but none is developed much as persona. There is less emphasis on the fictiveness of the narrative at the start of *Women & Fiction*; college names are undisguised, for example. But the conclusion that will be symbolized in the revised title is present from the beginning. Watching Woolf create the narrative that seeks arguments for women having "money & a room to themselves" is among the most absorbing aspects of *Women & Fiction*.

The episodes of walking on the forbidden grass and being turned away from the library, of the luxurious luncheon party and the bleak fare at Newnham, were all drafted in the first chapter of *Women & Fiction* together with observations on the wealth of men's colleges, on the nature of luncheon parties and poetry before the war, and on the causes of the comparative poverty of women's colleges. The process of drafting involved more than crossings out, insertions, and marginalia. It was an interruptive process. The writing starts, stops, and repeats. A number of pages are unfinished, breaking off sometimes in the middle of a sentence or a series of notes. The next page often starts over again, sometimes in the middle of a sentence. The drafts of *To the Lighthouse* and *The Waves* were to some extent also written this way, but the process seems to have more significance in the writing of what became *A Room of One's Own* because its narrative is so discontinuous. The very writing of the manuscript seems to illustrate the interrupted lives that women lead. Some of the most abrupt changes in the finished book, such as the sudden appearance of soup in the midst of a reverie on some terrible reality, are present from the beginning. The seasonal dislocation in the first chapter, where the speaker prefers to describe the beauty of spring even though it was October, is originally heightened by anachronism. In *A Room of One's Own*, the reference to the great Newnham classicist Jane Ellen Harrison is an anachronistic fantasy, for she had died in April 1928, but in *Women & Fiction* the more descriptive allusion is fancifully extended back almost a generation to include the well-known dons Verrall and Sidgwick.

Some passages in the first chapter, and not always important ones, are reworked a number of times. Five versions appear in the manuscript of the joke about the professor who is said to gallop if someone whistles. Woolf heavily revised the complaint about luncheon parties in novels that describe talk instead of food. Sometimes the first version of a familiar episode or phrase is revealingly different in small details. Freud is mentioned to avoid explaining how a train of thought was started by the sight of a Manx cat. The narrator's anonymous hostess at Newnham is first described as going to Australia to farm ostriches and then identified as a science lecturer named Mary Seton (as the name is now spelled). Finally, after leaving the college at the end of the chapter, the speaker briefly becomes another of Woolf's night walkers, experiencing a sense of isolation after escaping from some thraldom: "The day's skin is neatly rolled off; thrown into a hedge". In *Women & Fiction* it has not yet been described as "crumpled" with accumulated impressions and emotions.

The second chapter, now so designated and also dated, was written in six days. As in *A Room of One's Own*, it consists of a walk through Bloomsbury to the British Museum for a comical attempt to research the causes and consequences of the financial disparity between the sexes. Reflections follow, at lunch and during the walk home, on the angry power of the patriarchy and the advantages of an independent income for a woman. The general resemblance of the British Museum scenes in the manuscript to those of the book is illustrated by the similar satirical list of topics in each. Elsewhere there are various differences in detail, such as Professor X, the author of a great work on the mental, moral, and physical inferiority of women, who is given a German beer-hall setting, but not the title of "von".

More remarkable, however, are the revisions of Chapter II that reveal Woolf thinking about anger. The word first appears, is crossed out, then reinserted. The narrator's doodle of the very angry professor leads to speculation as to the uses of his anger. The narrator's anger is admitted and explained, but for ten pages Woolf tries to answer the question of why men are angry. In *Women & Fiction* these thoughts occur in a French restaurant – twice described before being dropped – whose excellent cooking continues the concern with food in Chapter I. A pencilled note at the bottom of a page gives the conclusion that will be amplified several pages later: "Anger:/ desire to be superior/ importance to have some one inferior". Evidence of patriarchal power in the restaurant is supplied by a newspaper (identified here as the *Evening Standard*), as in *A Room of One's Own*. And a looking-glass theory of male psychology is accompanied by a digression on men as bores, which illustrates the sex's superiority complex. Then Woolf introduces a passage on an amazing tribe of women in Central Asia who have a poet equal, perhaps, to Shakespeare. At first this tribe is read out as a fact from the newspaper, to the irritation of a young man lunching nearby. On the next page it is rewritten as a hypothetical example of male rage and deception, for if such a group were found to exist, men would either destroy the women's works or claim them as their own. These thoughts the narrator offers to her audience, again on the understanding that they are all women, for "there are many things that no woman has 'yet dared to say' to a man". The tribe without this qualification survived into the typescript of *A Room of One's Own* before finally being deleted.

The aunt whose legacy frees the speaker from women's jobs and allows her to think of things in themselves is, like her niece, unnamed in *Women & Fiction*. Nothing can take away the £500 a year as long as the narrator does not gamble in the stock market. This reservation was also deleted in *A Room of One's Own* (which ironically was then published just days before the great crash of October 1929). With that income she is spared the acquisitive torments of men, torments that indicate that in this respect their privileged education was more imperfect than women's. The sky and trees are no longer blocked by – Woolf originally wrote the cryptic phrase "Milton's bogeyman", then changed this to "the large & imposing figure of Professor X". In *A Room of One's Own* she returned to her Miltonic allusion and substituted for Professor X the large, imposing gentleman Milton recommended for her perpetual adoration. She remembered the cancelled bogeyman, however, and brought him back in the revised conclusion to her book. At the end of the chapter a contrast, which remains only implicit in *A Room of One's Own*, is made between domestic rooms where "there was quiet thought and happiness" and the "flying chaos and terror" of the street.

Drafting *Women & Fiction* as fast as her hand could write (and faster in places than can now be read), Woolf took less than ten days between 12 and 22 March to produce the long Chapter III. But just when and where Chapter III ended and Chapter IV began in *Women & Fiction* can now no longer be determined. The third chapter returns to the narrator's unwritten paper on women and fiction and then moves backward and forward between history and fiction. From G. M. Trevelyan's account of the situation of women and the extraordinary heroines of Shakespeare and later writers, a composite being emerges. Recorded history is a little dull for women, however, and the speaker wishes some of her audience would try using the two great searchlights of history and literature to write biographies of average Elizabethan women. Calling them "lives of the obscure" (a title Woolf herself had already used) is still an advisable dodge in October 1928. The passage about the need for biographies of the obscure is then reworked again, and references are repeated to the Pastons and others as nearly the only sources for them.

Without such lives, the speaker is forced into fiction, and the result is a remarkable illustration of Woolf's creativity as she drafts a version of her famous myth of Shakespeare's sister. Born in Warwickshire around 1564, the woman is given the name of Shakespeare's mother, Mary Arden, as an afterthought. The brief life of this additional Mary in *Women & Fiction* contains most of the essentials that will be reworked into Judith Shakespeare's life, except for an episode in which she is beaten by her father for gallivanting about the woods dressed as a man. There is also a cancelled passage asking how the end of her story can be told genteelly. Its evolution in her draft indicates that the fiction of Shakespeare's sister was not part of Woolf's original Cambridge talk. After going on for a page about how other women writers have been hindered from pursuing their art, Woolf breaks off and begins Chapter III again from the beginning. Here and elsewhere, the manuscript of *Women & Fiction* consists of overlapping drafts.

The revised beginning of Chapter III brings it closer to the published book. Some of the details from Trevelyan as well as the life of Mary Arden are skipped over and then put back into *A Room of One's Own*.

The revised story of Shakespeare's sister is left unfinished; it ends not with her death but in a discussion of chastity, the difficulties of women writers, and the possessiveness of men again. Then Woolf comes back to a fundamental concern of both *Women & Fiction* and *A Room of One's Own*, which is the state of mind best suited to the creation of literature. Shakespeare is the standard. The writer is compared to the carrier of a precious jar through a crowd. Examples of indifference and hostility to male writers are cited to suggest how much more discouraging is a woman's situation, and how important it is, as Emily Davies realized when founding Girton College, for women to have rooms of their own. Trying to explain the result of a discouraging environment on artists, Woolf returns to Shakespeare's state of mind, and jots down the single word "incandescent" in the margin opposite a reference to *Antony and Cleopatra*. This play and image will recur in the theory of creativity that is so important in *Women & Fiction* and *A Room of One's Own*. Shakespeare's creative mind consumed all the personal impediments, the grudges and grievances, that remain in the work of Jonson, Donne, or Milton, which may explain why we have less sense of his personality than theirs. For three pages Woolf tries to describe Shakespeare's state of mind in the imagery of metallurgy.

The thought that such a molten state of mind was impossible for any woman of Shakespeare's time begins a new paragraph. In *A Room of One's Own* this is where the fourth chapter begins. But in the manuscript Chapter 3 continues on for another half dozen pages with discussions of pre-nineteenth-century women writers. Winchilsea, Newcastle, Osborne, and Behn are all referred to, but more briefly than they will be in the revised text. The quotations to be used are identified only by first line and page number. These women are the forerunners of Jane Austen, George Eliot, and the Brontës, whose masterpieces are first likened to waves of the sea and then more familiarly described as the result of thinking in common for many years. With the debts that these nineteenth-century novelists owed to their predecessors, the first part of Woolf's Fitzwilliam manuscript stops in the middle of a page – one-third of the way through what will be Chapter 4 in *A Room of One's Own*. The second part of the manuscript picks up the story in the middle of what will be Chapter 5 some 30 pages later in the book.

The gap between the two parts of the Fitzwilliam manuscript is partly filled by 20 leaves of the undated Monks House manuscript. In it Woolf continues, on the same paper as the Fitzwilliam manuscript, some time between 12 and 22 March, the survey of women writers from Aphra Behn into the nineteenth century, as in *A Room of One's Own*. There are significant differences in both organization and detail between this version of the manuscript and *A Room of One's Own*, however. The discussion of *Jane Eyre* does not immediately analyze the awkward break in sequence that is attributed a little later to Charlotte Brontë's indignation. It is interesting to follow Woolf in the Monks House manuscript while she works tentatively towards a moral aesthetic of the novel as a structure of emotional relations depending on the author's integrity for its maintenance. One can begin to see here how her concerns with feminism, creativity, and the future of the novel all come together. Sometimes Woolf's judgements are blunter in *Women & Fiction*; Rochester's description in *Jane Eyre*, for instance, is "the portrait of a man by a woman who is afraid of men", rather than one drawn in the dark and influenced by fear. The much commented upon statement "for we think back through our mothers if we are women" first occurs as a parenthetical remark. Woolf does not yet work into her argument the quotations of men hostile to women's literary aspirations that will appear later in her manuscript and book. Without saying yet that the form of a woman's novel should be adapted somehow to her body, Woolf speculates through her narrator on the kind of poetic novel women may write. In *A Room of One's Own* this marks the beginning of Chapter 5, but in the Monks House manuscript only a line-space separates it from the preceding discussion.

Virginia Woolf begins her section on contemporaries by noting the variety of books now written by women. She then digresses to describe how a visit of Emily Davies and Barbara Leigh Smith to a family of six middle-class girls moping around the table led to the founding of Girton and the writing of such books. Suddenly the speaker blushes for her topic of women and fiction, apparently because such enquiries into only one sex "sterilise and embitter". Then in the remaining ten leaves of the Monks House manuscript Woolf's narrator describes and reflects upon a novel written by a woman, an Oxford graduate with £300 a year, who was born at the beginning of the century. The narrator jumps into the middle of the book to get a sense of its style, which is described as plunging up and down like a boat, using too many words, putting in the wrong things and leaving out the right ones. Still, the novelist was not trying to write a realistic novel, the typical detail of which is satirized. But the test of the book will be the novel's final situation. The work does conclude successfully, but before we reach the end Woolf drafts some of the most interesting pages of *Women & Fiction*. In these passages on the possibilities of contemporary fiction by women she continues the double fictive frame of her book by describing her narrator's reactions to the imaginary novel as she reads it. The novelist's sentence "Chloe liked Olivia ... " changes the current of the narrator's thought. Changes in current – from the first interruption on a college lawn to the last scene outside her window when a young couple come together – are one of the fundamental metaphors by which Woolf organizes her book, as well as one of the sources for the work's humor and irony.

In *A Room of One's Own* the speaker prefaces the suggestive ambiguity of the phrase "Chloe liked Olivia ... " by breaking off to be sure there are no men, no magistrates like the one who judged *The Well of Loneliness* obscene, hiding in cupboards. Originally, however, Woolf's comic interpolation follows the phrase, which is given as "Chloe liked Olivia; they shared a—". The pages of the book stick together at this point, and before she can separate them to read the next word, which is only "laboratory", a fantasy trial, verdict, and book-burning flash through her mind. After some cancellations a more serious current of thought is started, which has to do with the immense literary change that Chloe's and Olivia's relationship signifies. Until Austen wrote, all great women in literature, such as Shakespeare's jealous Cleopatra, were seen primarily in relationship to the other sex. If Chloe likes Olivia and can write – these last crucial words are inserted by Woolf – then Olivia offers readers the extraordinary opportunity of illuminating a cave where no one has been before. Woolf stops in the middle of a sentence and page here, and starts again on different paper with Chloe, who is somewhat confusingly both a character in the novel and its author. (There is no mention of Mary Carmichael.) Chloe has the great opportunity of observing the obscure lives of organisms like Olivia, whose life is "so highly developed for other purposes so *extraordinarily* complex, so sensitive ... ". Woolf will return to these words in the second part of the Fitzwilliam manuscript and extensively redraft the part that follows them in the Monks House pages.

The Monks House version of this section has to do with what Chloe's novel might be about. As a naturalist–novelist (the more interesting contemplative kind is not mentioned), she watches and writes about various rooms and lives of women, such as the ancient lady, seen crossing a street with her daughter, whose life of Monday and Tuesday has passed unrecorded, or the vagrants, whose faces reflect so differently the meeting of a man or a woman. Chloe might even write about shopping rather than golf or shooting, and thus win the approval of the anonymous critic who said recently that "female novelists should only aspire to excellence by courageously acknowledging the limitations of their sex". Woolf took the partial quotation from the August 1928 issue of the new periodical *Life and Letters* that her Bloomsbury friend Desmond MacCarthy had started editing and to which she contributed. Woolf had been disagreeing in print with MacCarthy about the capabilities of women since 1920, when she criticized a review of his on some books about women (*D*II: 339–42). That criticism anticipates the arguments of *A Room of One's Own*. MacCarthy's remark in *Life and Letters* comes at the beginning of his review of a young woman's novel. Its autobiographical relevance appears in a further part of the quotation omitted by Woolf: "If, like the reporter, you believe that female novelists should only aspire to excellence by courageously acknowledging the limitations of their sex (Jane Austen and, in our own time, Mrs. Virginia Woolf have demonstrated how gracefully this gesture can be accomplished)...." After the publication of *A Room of One's Own*, in which Woolf used the same elliptical quotation, MacCarthy wrote in *Life and Letters* that he was horrified to find his unhappy sentence used so acidly when it was inspired by a wholehearted admiration of Woolf's work. He went on to praise her again, but still concluded obtusely that we should applaud the way she recognized her limitations. Later, however, he delighted Woolf with his favourable review of her book in the *Sunday Times*.

Twice Woolf gives the partial quotation in *Women & Fiction*, mocking the reviewer who knew the limitations of women writers but did not specify them. Were they allowed to describe shops, for example? (The reviewer is compared with the bishop who, in an anecdote referred to a number of times, was certain no woman could equal Shakespeare and no cat go to heaven.) The narrator finally comes back to the last scene of Chloe's novel. It represented something about the immensity of the soul, but had little to do with sex. Thus we come back to the start of the speaker's thoughts about women and modern fiction, and at this point, which corresponds to the end of Chapter 5 in *A Room of One's Own*, the Monks House manuscript also ends.

The discrepancies in chapter divisions between *Women & Fiction* and *A Room of One's Own* remain in the second part of the Fitzwilliam manuscript. Virginia Woolf began the chapter, which she headed "Chapter 4. Cont." on 22 March 1929, continuing for ten leaves a chapter whose beginning is not indicated in the surviving manuscripts. Further evidence that part of the draft of *Women & Fiction* is missing appears with the reference several pages later to Mary Carmichael. Where Chloe the novelist turned into Mary is now unknown. How much material has been lost is uncertain; it may be only five to ten pages. The second part of the Fitzwilliam manuscript begins again with the words that had been used to describe the "highly developed", the "infinitely intricate capacities of

Olivia", though they are not the exact words used in the Monks House manuscript. The narrator is vexed that she has slipped into praising her own sex, especially when there is yet no way of measuring its ability. All she can do is note the dependence of great men upon women. The account of this is close to that in *A Room of One's Own*, but it was not part of the original draft in the Monks House manuscript. The rooms of these women are then emphasized, and here one can watch the central symbol of the book emerging. The valuable differences of the sexes are stressed, and in a remark later cut, the speaker says that nothing would please her more than if some explorer discovered yet another sex somewhere. Next, the different rooms and lives of women that Mary Carmichael will have to represent are described, as in the Monks House manuscript. But instead of a discussion of whether she is allowed to describe shopping, a brief description of a shop is given. Returning to Carmichael's untitled novel, the speaker comments on her abilities and discusses the challenge of the last scene at greater length than in the Monks House draft. A racecourse metaphor is repeated and extended to include the men of Cambridge and the authors of books and reviews (MacCarthy's phrase echoes again) who advise and warn from the sidelines. Woolf's narrator places a bet and urges the novelist to ignore the men and think only of the jump itself, which she successfully does. The chapter ends, as in *A Room of One's Own*, with the prediction that in a hundred years Mary Carmichael will be a poet.

It took Virginia Woolf four days to write the continued fourth chapter. On 26 March, five months to the day after giving her paper at Girton, she began Chapter V of *Women & Fiction*. In just one week she drafted both it and the concluding chapter – a total of 34 manuscript pages. The structure of Chapter V, which becomes approximately the first half of Chapter 6 of *A Room of One's Own*, is generally similar to that of the book, though much more disjointed and tentative. The chapter opens with the narrator observing a London street scene. She begins to sketch a theory of androgynous states of mind, and then considers masculine self-consciousness in the work of several unandrogynous modern writers. At the end of the chapter the narrator returns to the description of creative states of mind. The writing of the fifth chapter of *Women & Fiction* was far from being straightforward, however. Much of its interest lies in watching Woolf's attempts to create a scene that will lead her to reflections on the unity of mind required for good writing. The culminating scene of *A Room of One's Own* in which a couple get into a taxi begins in *Women & Fiction* with a girl in patent-leather shoes whom a taxi-driver chooses to pick up instead of a man. Reworking the scene, trying to describe first the sexual current that sweeps all along the street and then the relief experienced at seeing the girl greet a young man, Woolf's narrator tries to explain what she means by unity of mind. Again there are allusions to Tennyson, Rossetti, and Shakespeare.

Three more or less distinct drafts of a plan for the soul can be traced in the writing of this chapter as the narrator tries to write the first sentence of her paper on women and fiction. Only the last version mentions Coleridge and androgyny. In the first version the lack of repression felt by the speaker as she sees a young woman and man together leads to the realization that she can think back through her mothers or her fathers. She can make herself an inheritor of her civilization or an alien in it. Instead of letting her consciousness flow undivided, she can for some special purpose accentuate the dominant sexual half of her brain, as the narrator had been doing in thinking back only through her mothers. A brief fantasy intervenes of some primeval woman who regrets her destiny of having to people the jungle instead of being free to swing through the trees. Towards the end of the first version the sexual imagery of a marriage is used to describe the creative process as one in which the author draws the curtain and sinks into oblivion. While the male and female halves of his brain mate, he may look at stars, pull the petals from a rose, or watch swans. (The pronouns are Woolf's.) The imagery recurs again at the end of the fifth chapter, as it does just before the conclusion in *A Room of One's Own*.

The street scene of a young couple meeting also begins the second draft plan of the soul's male and female powers. The narrator turns to books by living authors, identified as Messrs A, B, C, and D, to try out her theories on men's writing. She begins by noting with some irony that despite all their advantages, men write books that lack the power of suggestion. A self-centred male's novel is mentioned, then the work of Kipling and Galsworthy, before Woolf begins the section again, this time referring to Coleridge and the androgynous mind of Shakespeare. After the suffrage campaign is identified as the cause of modern sexual self-consciousness, the text takes up again the ego–phallic novel of an author identified as Mr A. The reworked account is essentially that of *A Room of One's Own*, including allusions once more to Victorian poetry; the characters of the novel are not named, however, and the speaker's confession of boredom is more defensive. In his review of *A Room of One's Own*, MacCarthy thought the novelist was a gifted contemporary and clearly recognizable under his initial. Woolf, writing to express her pleasure at the review, asked if he meant D. H. Lawrence, and added, "He was not in my upper mind; but no doubt was in the lower" (LIV: 130). Just who, if anyone, might have been in her upper mind she does not say. Lawrence's *Lady Chatterley's Lover* had been privately printed in Italy in 1928, and at the end of the year his old friend S. S. Koteliansky told Woolf, who had probably not read the novel, that it was disgusting (DIII: 217).

After referring to the critic Mr B, whoever he may be, the narrator of *Women & Fiction* moves on to Mr C who turns out to be Churchill. She feels crushed by the furniture of his rhetoric – the size of the sentences, the weight of the metaphors. Victorian preachers were less vociferous. Works by Galsworthy and Kipling are criticized next, and in more detail than in *A Room of One's Own*. Their purely masculine values bore her horribly and thoughts of Mussolini's Italy follow. A list of androgynous and masculine writers, to be discussed in *A Room of One's Own*, is jotted down on the back of a manuscript page at this point. Then Woolf suggests again that the cause of all this literary cock-a-doodling lies in the work of reformers like the founder of Girton. (In *A Room of One's Own* she blames no individuals.) This leads once more to the narrator's blank page headed "Women and Fiction", and for a dozen lines she tries to formulate what will eventually become the first sentence of the paper – that it is fatal for writers to think of their own sex. Once more she tries to imagine the violence as well as the calm, unselfconscious freedom of Shakespeare's state of mind while creating a scene in *Antony and Cleopatra* or writing a line like "Daffodils that come before the swallow dares". The marriage-night metaphor is used again to conclude the chapter.

The last chapter of *Women & Fiction*, entitled simply "Conclusion", corresponds to what follows the dropping of the persona in Chapter 6 of *A Room of One's Own*. The manuscript's conclusion is briefer than that in the book, however. Woolf had jotted down notes for her conclusion in a reading notebook, used them at the start of her chapter, then cancelled them. Anticipated objections to her insistence on money and *A Room of One's Own* (the phrase first appears in the manuscript here) start with the material one rather than the comparative merit of the sexes, as in the book. The same quotation from Quiller-Couch is invoked as a reply to these anticipated criticisms. Woolf began a reference to Florence Nightingale, crossed it out, and then expanded it in the book. Justifying the necessity of women's books leads to the speaker's admittedly selfish complaint about the monotony of her modern reading and the need for books to influence each other.

The important discussion of what Woolf's narrator means by reality and unreality follows from the attempt to justify the existence of good books, and it differs significantly from *A Room of One's Own*. In *Women*

& *Fiction*, the narrator attempts twice to justify its indefinable intuitive basis before giving up and just illustrating what she means. As in *A Room of One's Own*, Woolf connects the experience of reality with the mystical moments that the speaker has experienced at Cambridge and in London. Masterpieces express reality too, and the list in the manuscript includes *Lycidas* and *War and Peace*, which is cancelled. Examples of the effects of unreality are more extended in *Women & Fiction*; they include muffling, swaddling, drugging, numbing, and being knocked senseless or into torpor. There is no escaping unreality. Civilization requires it, but one can fight with pen, brush, piano, or talk. We are close here to Bernard's final efforts in *The Waves*. Nowhere else in Woolf's writing, except perhaps in the late "A Sketch of the Past", does she attempt to describe so explicitly the mystical enmity of unreality that she associated with what she called her madness.

There are no perorations in *Women & Fiction*, no disagreeable quotations from men, no references to liking women and wondering again if a magistrate is in the cupboard. The women of the audience are called upon to get to work – not to write fashionable books, but to conspire, anonymously perhaps, to bring Shakespeare's sister back to life. This they can do if they are free to regard human beings in themselves, to look past Milton's bogey at reality. Such an effort, the speaker maintains, "is worthwhile". These are the last words of both *Women & Fiction* and *A Room of One's Own*.

The revising of *A Room of One's Own*

Virginia Woolf finished *Women & Fiction* in London on 2 April 1929. The next day she went to Monks House to arrange for a new room of her own – two rooms in fact, a bedroom opening into the garden with a sitting or work room above – to be added onto Monks House. Ten days later she complained to her diary that *Women & Fiction* had been written too quickly, and now she was toiling over revisions. But she thought it had conviction and predicted "some sale" for this book of "half talk, half soliloquy" (*DIII*: 221). After a month of revising the manuscript as she typed it up, Woolf announced, again to her diary, that the final version was finished, but she was now uncertain whether it was a brilliant essay or a mass of opinions "boiled down into a kind of jelly, which I have stained red as far as I can" (*DIII*: 222). Leonard was to read it after tea. But still the process of revising continued.

The revisions of *A Room of One's Own* were apparently made while Woolf was trying once again to finish "Phases of Fiction". (In the reading notebook that contains the page of notes for the conclusion of *Women & Fiction* Woolf actually started a page on "Phases of Fiction" under the heading "Women and Fiction" then struck it out.) She was trying to finish the rewriting of "Phases of Fiction" even as it was being serialized in America. In her letters she was calling it her dullest and most hated book. At one point, Woolf jotted down the final title for *A Room of One's Own* and a new opening that emphasized the speaker's train of thought.

Woolf was dismayed when Harcourt Brace suggested in the middle of May that "Phases of Fiction" be published in the autumn of 1929 and *Women & Fiction*, as it was still being called, kept over until the following spring (*DIII*: 227). On 16 May, however, Leonard wrote firmly to Donald Brace in an unpublished letter that his wife preferred to postpone "Phases of Fiction" until the next year and bring out *Women & Fiction* under a different title in the autumn of 1929. This is the first mention of a change in title.

In the event, "Phases of Fiction" was never published as a book. Virginia Woolf felt she had been wrongly pressured by her husband and Rylands into writing it for The Hogarth Press. Despite the title, "Phases of Fiction" is far less historical than *A Room of One's Own*. Forster's aspects had been elements of the novel, but Woolf's phases were kinds of novelists classified as truth-tellers, romantics, character-mongers, comedians, psychologists, satirists, fantastics, and finally poets. Some women writers are discussed – Radcliffe, Austen, Eliot, Emily Brontë – but few of the novelists considered really fit into their categories. Woolf's phases also fail to meet her objections to Forster's aspects, for there is little analysis of the art of fiction in them. Forster had argued in the introduction to his Cambridge lectures that the novel was a mirror unaffected by such things as the women's movement because subject matter had nothing to do with the mirror acquiring a new coating of sensitiveness. He amusingly imagined all the novelists writing their novels together timelessly in the Reading Room of the British Museum. In the book that Woolf developed from her Cambridge lectures, however, women are depicted as writing their novels in parlours or bedsitting rooms. The British Museum is where the speaker goes to find out why women are poor and why men are angry. *A Room of One's Own* is, in its way, a more direct and effective response to *Aspects of the Novel* than "Phases of Fiction" was.

Sometime after Leonard Woolf wrote to put off the publication of "Phases of Fiction" as a book, Virginia Woolf sent Harcourt Brace the typescript entitled *A Room of One's Own*, now in the Monks House Papers

at Sussex. Just how hard she had toiled to revise *Women & Fiction* into
A Room of One's Own can be shown through a brief chapter by chapter
comparison of the typescript with the manuscripts of *Women & Fiction*
and also with the published book. Much of the typescript is identical to
this final version, but there are also numerous, significant holograph
additions and cancellations. Some of the chapter divisions of the typescript are still tentative, and a few pages present overlapping passages.
Even at the typescript stage, *A Room of One's Own* was still in the process
of composition.

The most obvious difference between the manuscript and the typescript
is, of course, the new title's emphasis on the work's principal symbol. In
Chapter 1, still undesignated as such, Woolf incorporates into her typescript the new opening and reworks the speaker's novelistic solution to
the problems of lecturing on women and fiction. The frame story of the
three days (revised to two in the book) that preceded the Cambridge
paper is established, the image of the pedlar is dropped, and some of
the Cambridge names are disguised, including Jane Harrison's, which is
reduced to her initials. Footnotes are added to document the history
of women's colleges. One interesting addition is the passage on how
child-raising makes it impossible for women like Mary Seton's mother
to acquire the kinds of fortunes that men have amassed or inherited.
The revised first chapter ends with a recapitulation of the day's
incidents.

In revising the second chapter of *Women & Fiction*, Woolf introduced
a comparison of research with the aloe that flowers once in a hundred
years, and this harkens back to a similar comparison of the plant with
a don's life in her sketch "A Society". The descriptions of the kind of
men who attend to women and of the student working next to the
narrator have not been muted in her revisions. Footnotes are added
again for sources on men's opinions of women, and some of the literary
allusions are dropped, as is the description of the cooking in the restaurant where the speaker has lunch. Also deleted is the digression on male
bores. But Woolf retained the Asian tribe of women whose achievements
rivalled those of Shakespeare and Einstein. She cut it only when revising
the typescript for the book. In the typescript Mary Beton is given now
as the aunt's name that is also the speaker's. Another addition to the
manuscript involves Desmond MacCarthy again. About a month before
she gave her Cambridge papers, Woolf listened to MacCarthy expressing
his irritation at Rebecca West's saying that men were snobs. She retorted
by criticizing his condescension in *Life and Letters* about the limitations
of women novelists (*DIII*: 195). How the later remark was worked into

Women & Fiction has been discussed; but now in her revisions Woolf took up the earlier comment, included a description of West as an "arrant feminist", and then ascribed it all to "Z, the most humane, the most modest of men". The remark is introduced again at the revised opening of Chapter 4. Woolf also revised the account of male acquisitiveness, adding an observation on how large groups of people are driven by instincts beyond their control. (This, incidentally, was one of the central tenets of Leonard Woolf's political theory.) At the end of the typescript's second chapter Virginia Woolf resolves the chaos and terror of the London machine into a fiery fabric with flashing eyes; in the book it is defined further as a hot-breathed tawny monster.

Chapter 3 of the typescript is quite close to the final version of *A Room of One's Own*. The details of Mary Arden's life are worked into Judith Shakespeare's. A comparison of the artist to a jar-carrier is omitted, the portrait of Oscar Browning developed more astringently, an allusion to Lady Bessborough brought into the text from the back of a page, and a collection of opinions on male superiority called cock-a-doodle-dum is imagined. The beginning of Chapter 4, which is missing from *Women & Fiction*, begins in the middle of a page, rather than at the head of it, as the second chapter had. Woolf's continuing uncertainty about chapter divisions reappears at the end of the next chapter.

The revised discussions of women writers in Chapter 4 are more detailed, especially in the analysis of *Jane Eyre*. Additional references to other writers appear. An allusion to Mary Wollstonecraft is dropped, but the significance of Dorothy Osborne's letters is developed. There is no indication in the typescript of the gap that is to be found in the Fitzwilliam manuscript at the point where nineteenth-century women and fiction begin to be considered. The prevalence of masculine values is emphasized, and then MacCarthy on the limitations of female novelists is brought in and criticized together with another quotation from T. S. Eliot's *New Criterion* in which the reviewer of a Hogarth Press book asserts that a metaphysical obsession is particularly dangerous in a woman. From this Woolf turns to the discussion of men's and women's sentences, giving holograph examples of both in the typescript. The woman's sentence, taken from *Pride and Prejudice*, was deleted from the final version of *A Room of One's Own*. At the end of the chapter Woolf reworked in her own hand the remarks on the future form of women's writing.

That Virginia Woolf had not yet sorted out the organization of the book in her typescript is apparent from the brevity of Chapter 5 and the confusion over the numbering of Chapter 6. The fifth chapter is only five pages long. It begins with the various kinds of books which modern women write (she later included Vernon Lee on aesthetics) then suddenly veers into a fantasy on Florence Nightingale that exists only in the typescript. There is nothing like it in *Women & Fiction*. In her best *Orlando* manner, Woolf imagines a shell from the Crimean War crashing through the drawing-room door of Nightingale's house; out steps the lady with a lamp, which marks the end of women's servitude. Quotations from Nightingale's *Cassandra* follow. Harriet Martineau is mentioned, and then Woolf brings in the anecdote from the life of Emily Davies that she had used in *Women & Fiction* when beginning to discuss modern women's books. There the chapter ends.

Two Chapters 6 are to be found in the typescript of *A Room of One's Own*. In the first Woolf's speaker continues, as in the fifth chapter of the final version, her discussion of living writers by analyzing Mary Carmichael's novel. Now called *Life's Adventure*, the novel also has named characters and a style that fears sentimentality and breaks the sequence like a switchback railway (instead a tossing boat). The satire of realistic fiction in the manuscript is removed, and the reaction to Chloe's liking Olivia changed. Woolf also adds to the discussion of women's friendship in fiction a reference to George Meredith's *Diana of the Crossways*. But no indication is to be found in the typescript of the discontinuity between the end of the Monks House and the beginning of the second part of the Fitzwilliam manuscript. There is, as well, considerable evidence of Woolf's rewriting in the typescript. The speaker now distinguishes between the naturalist and contemplative species of novelist. She criticizes the multiplication of books on Napoleon, Keats, and Milton while the lives of obscure women go unrecorded. Woolf also added a passage about the spot in the back of the head that only the opposite sex can describe. References to Thackeray and Flaubert are reworked and new allusions made to Juvenal and Strindberg.

The second Chapter 6 of the typescript corresponds to the sixth chapter in the book, yet the substantial differences between them indicate the degree to which Woolf would revise her typescript again for the final printed version of *A Room of One's Own*. The crucial scene of the young couple getting into a taxi is more succinctly described in the typescript, and to it Woolf added a remark about the union of men and women making for the greatest happiness. She eliminates the passage on the primeval woman and confined the marriage-night metaphor of creation to the end of the chapter. Her theory about the mind's unity becomes the familiar one of *A Room of One's Own*, except for the retention of the botanical term "gunandros" as a companion for "androgynous". The remainder of the chapter's first part, where the theory of androgyny is tested on some modern men's books, is quite different in detail from both the manuscript and the published book. Mr A, for example is referred to as a descendant of Oscar Browning, and his female characters are described not only as boneless but also as "jelly fish adapted to his lust". Churchill is reduced to his initial; the ridicule of his rhetoric now likens his metaphors to stuffed Wagnerian ravens and his ideas to poor little things rigged up in rouge and brocade – all of which she then drops again from the book. Another passage follows in the typescript describing a banquet at which the narrator wanted to shout the praises of unknown charwomen in response to the Prince of Wales's extolling of fishermen. Woolf revised the more extended criticism of Galsworthy's Forsyte books in the typescript before finally cutting it from her book. She retouched the description of Fascist Italy and worked into the text from the margin the list of androgynous and unandrogynous writers, to which a comment on Shelley's sexlessness was added. Also revised before being cut was a description of the violent state of mind that Shakespeare's composition of *Antony and Cleopatra* must have involved.

A line in the typescript separates these discussions from the conclusions that Woolf now brought in from the last chapter of *Women & Fiction*. Only later in revising the typescript for the book did she accomplish the transition by abandoning her narrative persona. The conclusions of the typescript nevertheless differ significantly from those of the manuscript. Woolf crossed out a beginning that defended the symbolism of money and rooms by citing Quiller-Couch on the material conditions required for the writing of poetry. In her second attempt she moved closer to the book by recapping the episodes of the previous few days. She added a scornful criticism of the comparative merits of the sexes before coming to the Quiller-Couch quotation again, and after it made an allusion to Florence Nightingale. In defending the value of good books, she altered the description of reality, which she refused to define; she gives instead more examples of it but deletes the illustrations of unreality in *Women & Fiction*.

In the typescript Woolf introduces the peroration called for by the conventions of male eloquence, and then evades it by urging her audience simply to think of things in themselves. She does not stop with an emphasis on ends, the means to which are £500 and *A Room of One's Own*, but goes on to remark in the typescript that current writing calls for something very unpleasant when a woman addresses women. Another joking allusion is made to the magistrate of *The Well of Loneliness* trial who may be yet lurking in a cupboard. And then one more ironic quotation, which Woolf had used before in her writing, is given about how women will cease to be necessary when children cease to be wanted. The raising of these topics at the end of *A Room of One's Own* makes its criticism of the patriarchy's sexual standards stronger than that in *Women & Fiction*. Indeed there is little in the manuscripts to suggest that Woolf is softening or censoring her text to make it more acceptable to male readers, as is sometimes claimed about her revisions. At last, after urging young women on to the next stage in their sex's career, Woolf returns once more to fiction for the final invoking of Shakespeare's sister.

During the last two weeks of June 1929, Woolf worked at correcting what must have been the typescript of "that much corrected book, *Women & Fiction*" (DIII: 237). It is odd that she should revert to its original title on the same day, 30 June, that she signed the contract for *A Room of One's Own* with Harcourt Brace (LIV: 71). Two days later Woolf began the first draft of *The Waves*.

The proofs for *A Room of One's Own*, which allowed more opportunity for correction, were corrected in July and August. They do not appear to have survived, but Woolf's correspondence indicates that she had to send Harcourt Brace revised proofs containing additional alterations in the first two chapters or so (LIV: 76). On 19 August, more than four months after finishing her manuscript, she opened her diary to record

> the blessed fact that for good or bad I have just sent the last correc-
> tion to *Women & Fiction* or *A Room of One's Own*. I shall never read it
> again I suppose. Good or bad? Has an uneasy life in it I think: yet feel
> the creature arching its back & galloping on, though as usual much
> is watery & flimsy & pitched in too high a voice. (DIII: 241–2)

The next day she expressed her delight with Vanessa Bell's cover, which showed a view through a curtained arch or window of a room with a clock on the mantle. The clock's hands form a "V", which Woolf thought would cause a stir (LIV: 81). The published dust-jacket of The Hogarth Press first edition also has a blurb describing *A Room of One's Own*. From what is known about the operations of The Hogarth Press, it is reasonable to assume that this description of the book has authorial status. Woolf would continue to comment publicly and privately on the book and its reception, but the summary on the dust-jacket can be given here as, in a sense, the last act of the book's composition. Its opening comment's generic paradox, the description of the author as an outsider, the emphasis on the relation of the sexes, and hopeful fore-cast of a freer future for women are all completely characteristic of Woolf's writing and thought:

This essay, which is largely fictitious, is based upon the visit of an outsider to a university and expresses the thoughts suggested by a comparison between the different standards of luxury at a man's college and at a woman's. This leads to a sketch of women's circumstances in the past, and the effect of those circumstances upon their writing. The conditions that are favourable to imaginative work are discussed, including the right relation of the sexes. Finally an attempt is made to outline the present state of affairs and to forecast what effect comparative freedom and independence will have upon women's artistic work in the future.

Notes

This chapter is a revised version of the preface and introduction to the transcription of Virginia Woolf's *Women & Fiction: The Manuscript Versions of "A Room of One's Own"* (Oxford: Blackwell's Shakespeare Head Press, 1992).

1. The edition of *A Room of One's Own* used here is the first English one published by The Hogarth Press on 21 October 1929. B. J. Kirkpatrick's *A Bibliography of Virginia Woolf*, 4th edition (Oxford, 1997) is the indispensable source for the history of Virginia Woolf's writings. In addition to Woolf's letters and diaries, also essential are the *Letters of Leonard Woolf*, edited by Frederic Spotts (New York: Harcourt Brace Jovanovich, 1989) and Brenda R. Silver's *Virginia Woolf's Reading Notebooks* (Princeton: Princeton University Press, 1983).

4

"Women Must Weep": The Serialization of *Three Guineas*

Naomi Black

When I agreed to edit *Three Guineas* for Blackwell's Shakespeare Head Press edition of Virginia Woolf, I knew that the task would be complicated by the rather complex history of the texts, but I believed that the serialization would be the least of my problems. The book started in January 1931 as a lecture and then developed along with Virginia Woolf's hugely successful 1937 novel *The Years*. Between 1931 and 1937, while concentrating on the novel, Woolf collected materials for what began as a book about women and professions; from time to time, she jotted down notes and fragments of draft. A slightly fictionalized and fully documented version of the factual underpinning of *The Years*, *Three Guineas* itself was finally completed in the winter of 1937 and spring of 1938. Soon after, it was published in slightly different versions, first in Britain and then the United States. In addition, it was serialized in two instalments under the title "Women Must Weep", in the American magazine, *The Atlantic Monthly*, in May and June 1938, overlapping with the appearance of the English and American first editions in June and August respectively.[1]

Kirkpatrick's magisterial bibliography of Virginia Woolf had dismissed the serialization as "a summary" (175). I had read "Women Must Weep" and had even once used it as a shorter version of *Three Guineas* for an undergraduate class. Obviously the book's 124 endnotes and five photographs were missing from the serial version. But my impression was the same as Kirkpatrick's, that *Three Guineas* had simply been reduced to two articles. Since I did not anticipate anything either difficult or important emerging from the version in *The Atlantic Monthly*, I postponed the necessary collation with the book as just one more chore of many. But I was wrong.

In the process of editing *Three Guineas*, I learned a lot, including that I had vastly underestimated what the project involved. For example, it required lengthy correspondence with worthies such as the Norroy and Ulster King of Arms to identify the regalia displayed in *Three Guineas'* photographs; their subjects turned out, in one of Woolf's little jokes, to be well-known dignitaries hidden under generic titles like "A General" or "An Archbishop".[2] Checking the references that Woolf used in *Three Guineas* was something of a nightmare, since she did not always date or identify newspaper clippings when she cut them out of six different daily and weekly newspapers, and she often edited citations with a fine disregard for precise wording. Annotation was a seemingly endless process for an ironic and allusive book that developed over a very long period. But, above all, editing the text made clear to me the craft, as well as the passion, that went into Woolf's presentation of her arguments.

Three Guineas is the fullest statement of Virginia Woolf's feminism, anticipating to a startling degree the concerns of second-wave feminism. "Women Must Weep" has to be taken seriously as one of the versions of the book. And the big question for me was, increasingly, is "Women Must Weep" more or less feminist than *Three Guineas*?

The serialization of *Three Guineas* is not in any simple sense a summary, as is acknowledged in the most recent edition of the Virginia Woolf bibliography, where it is described as "an abridgement with some additional passages" (Kirkpatrick and Clarke, 107). This is still somewhat of an understatement about what happened to *Three Guineas* before it appeared in *The Atlantic Monthly*. To begin with, there is the title. "Women Must Weep", the overall title of the two instalments, is already far more evocative than the rather obscure *Three Guineas*. In addition, Woolf expanded the title for the second instalment, adding four words that make it into a strong feminist statement: "Women Must Weep – or Unite Against War." Here she echoed standard and recognizable feminist rhetoric, familiar in both England and the United States. She also added to the serial a passage making a feminist argument not to be found in any of the other texts related to *Three Guineas* or, indeed, anywhere in her writings. Yet, at the same time, the text of "Women Must Weep" concludes more tentatively than *Three Guineas*, and it seems possible that its final impact might be different than the book's.

Woolf left no records of how or why she made changes in readying the book for magazine publication. Still, it is worth trying to get clear just what happened, and we can certainly speculate about the results. In this study I shall, therefore, look at the composition of "Women Must Weep" and then compare the text with *Three Guineas*, drawing on what I learned while editing the book.

I

The life of *Three Guineas* as a serial can be dated to 1931, shortly after Virginia Woolf delivered on 21 January the speech about professions for women that would become both *The Years* and the closely related polemical *Three Guineas*. We know that she spent several days revising and likely expanding the speech, putting it aside reluctantly at the end of January to continue finishing *The Waves* (DIV: 7). About two weeks later, on 10 February, she wrote to literary agent Nancy Pearn about placing "more than one" article in *Good Housekeeping* magazine. The book she had "to some extent finished" was not appropriate, but "I have some vague idea that I shall turn a speech I made the other night into a sequel to *A Room of One's Own*".[3] So perhaps she already saw what she was then calling "A Knock on the Door" as something that might be suitable for serial as well as book publication (DIV: 7).

In 1933, the only other work of Woolf's to appear in serial form was published in four parts in *The Atlantic Monthly*. This was *Flush*, Woolf's parody biography of Elizabeth Barrett Browning's spaniel. In this case the sequence of serial and book editions was different than for *Three Guineas*, for the last instalment of *Flush* appeared in the October issue of the magazine while the book itself was issued in both Britain and the United States on 5 October (Kirkpatrick and Clarke, 292–3). An unpublished letter in *The Atlantic Monthly*'s archives indicates that on 6 September 1933 Woolf told its editor, who seems to have asked for another serial, that "the next book will be long, and not ready for some time".[4] *The Years* was indeed long, even though she cut it drastically in proof. And it took Woolf four more years to complete it, putting off the final composition of *Three Guineas* until after the publication of the closely related novel in 1937.

We do not have any record of when or why the decision was made to offer *Three Guineas* for American serialization. After at least three refusals, it was once more *The Atlantic Monthly* that accepted, but they wanted only 12 000 words of text (DV: 130).[5] Assuming that the magazine did not want the not-yet-completed endnotes, which eventually added up to 166 pages, that still left more than 60 000 words to be cut to fewer than one fourth. Printed in the same font as the first English edition, it meant reducing 261 pages of text to the equivalent of fewer than 70. Woolf managed this feat neatly: the two instalments took the form of 20 double-column pages with no more than 650 words on each page.[6] The figures imply massive compressions or omissions, and close examination shows that both occurred.

There is no reference at all in Woolf's diaries or letters to preparing the serial text although it must have been a tedious enough task, and she grumbles in her diary about how boring the completion of the book became: "too much drudgery donkey work" (*DV*: 132). On 10 March 1938, she notes that she is "working 5 hours a day to finish off those notes, those proofs", with a six-day deadline if the book is not to be postponed until the autumn (*DV*: 128).[7] Two days later she records the serial's acceptance but does not comment on the need to compress the text.

Perhaps Woolf fitted in work on "Women Must Weep" after the galley proofs of the main text of *Three Guineas* went back to the printer and before she tackled the notes. There is no way of telling. But we do have some evidence about how she composed the serial. What seems to have happened is that she marked up galley proofs to produce the required shorter text. Although no proof version of *Three Guineas* has survived, the Massachusetts Historical Society owns what appear to be two pages of instructions to a typesetter for *The Atlantic Monthly*. The first page makes it clear that Woolf herself made the revisions, including cuts, insertions, and rewriting.[8]

At the top of this page is written, not in Woolf's handwriting, "All sections to be used are indicated by brackets in the margin." Notes by the same person, possibly a copy-editor, indicate page numbers of galley proofs[9] and locations for inclusions and omissions in a way that corresponds to the differences between the book and the serial. Then, for "page 13", a cut-out piece of paper is stuck on. Here we find in Woolf's familiar eccentric typewriting the instructions to change "a Grenfell point of view; a Knebworth point of view; a Wilfred Own [sic] point of view; a Lord Chief Justice's point of view" to "the soldier's and airman's point of view; a Wilfred Owen point of view; the patriot's point of view". The copy-editor labelled the new passage "Insert A". A second passage, labelled "Insert B", is in the same handwriting: "Even the clergy, who make morality their profession, give us divided counsel – in some circumstances it is right to fight; in no circumstances is it right to fight."[10] Here we can guess that Woolf had written a new summary passage on the script she handed over and the copy-editor had transcribed her difficult handwriting for the typesetters. The final substantive item on this page of instructions is another new summary, again typed by Woolf and stuck on, in order to add to a new page 19 the phrase " – no weapons but an illusionary 'indirect' influence, the hard-won vote, and one other".[11]

As can be seen, specific allusions ("Grenfell" and "Knebworth" points of view) are changed to more general ones ("the soldier's and airman's point of view").[12] Sometimes such changes are necessary simply because lengthy specific examples have been removed and there must be a summary as replacement. In this way, "Insert B" about the contradictory guidance received from "the clergy" takes the place of a passage referring explicitly to the Church of England and quoting disagreements between the Anglican Bishops of London and Birmingham (*Three Guineas*: 19). Sometimes, as in the last typed insertion, a short new phrase bridges over a substantial deletion, in this case a discussion of the informal, necessarily limited influence exercised by great ladies and how even such influence was not available to women like Virginia Woolf (*Three Guineas*: 24–9).

At first sight, the copy-editor's instructions suggest that Woolf was making some concessions to her American audience, for the deleted references and examples are very English. But so are almost all of the examples in *Three Guineas*, so that any shrinkage or omission of detail was bound to cut down on the book's Englishness. "Women Must Weep" does use American spellings, as the first American edition of *Three Guineas* does not,[13] but in the serial version there are only two changes and one omission that look like possible adaptations to an American audience: "bunch of spillikins" becomes "box of matches" and "wireless" becomes "radio" while "tattoos" are omitted from the list of military celebrations to be boycotted.[14] In general, it seems clear that no allowances have been made for possible American ignorance. For example, Woolf deletes eight pages about the two women's colleges at Cambridge but leaves in the statement that the preference for a "belettered staff" disadvantages students at Newnham and Girton (*Three Guineas*: 47–55; WMW: 590). One has to wonder if American readers would recognize the names of the colleges, let alone know that in 1938 their graduates were not granted university degrees even when they had completed all the normal requirements.[15]

Adaptation for American publication thus does not seem to be a significant element in the serial's uniqueness. Certainly it does not obviously explain the different title. The uninformative title of *Flush* was retained for America, so presumably Woolf could have kept *Three Guineas* had she wished; its meaning is made clear in the text, and the highly bestselling *The Years* had made her so well known in the United States that even an obscure title surely would have drawn readers. Instead she selected the phrase "women must weep", which sums up the conventional view of female responses to catastrophe and the loss of life.

The serial title most likely comes from Charles Kingsley's poem "The Three Fishers": "men must work and women must weep". That is, there is nothing for women to do but wait and lament while the men go off to sea. They weep because some of the men will not survive; they do the same in response to war and its losses. The women activists who from early days opposed traditional gender roles and claimed for women an entitlement to resist the brutalities of the public sphere rejected such stereotypes of female passivity and domesticity. Furthermore, Kingsley's precise wording was conspicuous in pre-suffrage feminist rhetoric. For example, Josephine Butler, the mighty campaigner against evils associated with prostitution, wrote that she had "rejected the old ideal of division of labour 'that men must work and women must weep'". She was reporting a prayer meeting held in 1883 towards the end of the successful attempts to obtain repeal of the Contagious Diseases Acts.[16] As Butler came into the room, many women were weeping but "a venerable lady from America rose and said: 'Tears are good, prayers are better, but we should get on better if behind every tear there was a vote at the ballot box'". We can assume that Woolf read this account; not only does she cite Butler's memoirs in *Three Guineas*, but she also refers to a footnote that was attached to that same passage about weeping women when it was included in a 1927 pamphlet honouring Butler (Butler, 82–3; *Three Guineas*: 290, 269; Fawcett and Turner, 101).

The title's reference to the Kingsley poem, identified neither by Butler nor in *The Atlantic Monthly*, also links the serialization to feminist activists contemporary with Woolf. Of these, she knew best the leaders of the National Union of Women's Suffrage Societies (NUWSS), the moderate suffrage group headed by Millicent Garrett Fawcett and members of the Strachey family. In a relevant example of feminist discourse, we find Helena Swanwick, then secretary of the NUWSS, explicitly referring to "The Three Fishers" in September 1914 and adding, "As long as men think that women must only weep for the errors of men, they will not trouble much" (Whittick, Appendix 2: 296). Swanwick was the sister of the painter Walter Sickert, about whom Woolf wrote an important essay in 1934; in *Three Guineas* Woolf quotes Swanwick's memoirs to amplify the suffrage history she drew from *The Cause* by Ray Strachey, who was also secretary of the NUWSS (Woolf, 1934; *Three Guineas*: 286).

It is not obvious, however, that the serial's title is more feminist than the book's, even though *Three Guineas* itself, as a title, is increasingly likely to seem baffling, even distasteful, to the feminist reader. The notional sum of a pound plus a shilling is meaningless outside the United Kingdom, where indeed the guinea itself, even as a concept, is almost obsolete. It is class-linked, because the imaginary guinea was typically used for payments to highly paid professionals such as doctors, lawyers, and fashionable tailors, as well as for purchases of fine art and race horses. Guineas were also used, but not by members of the working-class, for charitable donations. The guinea is, therefore, also gendered, since even now, luxury services and goods are purchased far less often by women than by men while men continue to have larger disposable incomes available for supporting charities.

However, in the context of Woolf's own class position – among people who actually used guineas – the reference to charitable donations, guineas or not, can be thought of as feminist because of her unusual choice of two out of three good causes: a women's college and a support group for women professionals. The third recipient of a guinea is less obviously feminist, for it is a peace society headed by a man. Here Woolf reflects reality: such societies are run by women but usually have men in charge. As a result, her insistence that she will not join the organization, although she will support it by a donation, is what asserts women's autonomy. So that the original title of *Three Guineas* can itself be seen as having a set of feminist references, and no evaluative conclusion can safely be drawn from the change.

Whatever the title's implications, in "Women Must Weep" the general argument remains what it is in *Three Guineas*. However, the emphasis on preventing war becomes stronger because so much of the material about the women's movement and individual women is removed, either as part of the missing endnotes or, in more active intervention, with the cuts made to the text. For example, in "Women Must Weep" there is no more than a reference to Elizabeth Barrett Browning's struggles for independence, to the diplomat Gertrude Bell, to Josephine Butler, or to the first heads of the women's colleges at Cambridge. Sophia Jex-Blake's unsuccessful struggle to get her Victorian father's permission to work for pay is retained, but there is nothing about her role as leader of the "battle of Harley Street" that won for women the right to become doctors (*Three Guineas*: 115–16). Missing also are the discussions of Sophocles' Antigone and nearly all of the indictment of the Church and the Civil Service for sexism.

The biggest loss in the serial, however, is the endnotes. Woolf might well have felt that it did not matter if she omitted formal documentation for her argument; after all, the first English edition of the book was due out just after the first instalment of the serialization, and the first American edition was to appear not long after the second. In any case, 43 of the 124 notes are merely citations of sources. As far as the other endnotes go, the adaptation in "Women Must Weep" is very skillful, as we might expect. Only in one case does there seem likely to be a significant problem for the reader, who will look in vain for a definition of the important term "educated man's daughter". But in 1938 the term was apparently easily comprehensible, as can be seen in *The Atlantic Monthly* itself. "The Contributors' Column" that appears before the second instalment, which refers the reader to *Three Guineas* for a fuller statement of the arguments presented, sums up the serialization and the book as urging "'the daughters of educated men' to unite in concerted opposition to man-made war."[17]

Without the endnotes, however, the book, though comprehensible, is incomplete. Removing the endnotes does more than remove documentation; as their absence makes clear, their other main function is not explanatory but expansive. It is striking to what extent the deletion of the endnotes removes memorable parts of the book. It is in the endnotes, not the text, that Woolf jeers at the academic teaching of English as sipping literature through a straw, and it is in the notes that she invokes *Lysistrata*, derides Mr Justice McCardie, cites Walter Bagehot's horrible letter about professional women, expounds her views on chastity and veiling and St Paul, and quotes Walt Whitman, S. T. Coleridge, and Georges Sand on the nature of equality and freedom.

It is evident, too, that in "Women Must Weep" Woolf's feminism seems less complex because of the loss of the additional comments, often lengthy and substantial enough to be considered short essays, that are to be found in the endnotes. For example, in *Three Guineas* Woolf justifies coining the term "educated man's daughter" on the grounds that "our ideology is still...inveterately anthropocentric". Although the clumsy coinage "anthropocentric" never caught on, here is Woolf, in 1938, identifying androcentrism. In the same endnote she rejects the conventional leftist definitions of class, as applied to women: "Obviously, if the term 'bourgeois' fits her brother, it is grossly incorrect to use it of one who differs so profoundly in the two prime characteristics of the bourgeoisie – capital and environment" (*Three Guineas*: 265). This explanation is important for the continuing discussions of Woolf's sensitivity to the material conditions of women's lives and relevant to any attempt to label her a socialist. Absent also from "Women Must Weep" is a long note about Sergeant Amalia Bonilla that Woolf excerpted from a French journalist's reports on the Spanish Civil War (*Three Guineas*: 313). With this excision we lose a clear indication that Woolf is no essentialist about women and war, but instead was well aware that under some circumstances females may become fighters.

Furthermore, the deletion of the endnotes removes a whole dimension of satire. As they stand in *Three Guineas*, the endnotes themselves constitute a feminist undercutting of the masculine scholarship they utilize.

Sometimes they are almost parodies of "malestream" scholarship. For example, Woolf notes slyly that in her account of male indifference to the travails of women at Cambridge, she has described the dons, watching an anti-women riot, as sipping claret instead of the more correct port. "Strict accuracy", she writes, is "here slightly in conflict with rhythm and euphony" (*Three Guineas*: 306).

Without the endnotes, the book thus becomes a far more conventional text in both form and tone. In this respect it is less feminist, and it is also less fun to read. As has often been pointed out, *Three Guineas* is an angry book. It is also often amusing, at least for those who are not its targets, but most of the comedy is to be found in the endnotes. Nor is the omission of the illustrative photographs trivial, for they too provide ironic and comic comments on the male elite and its trappings.

II

Virginia Woolf did not just cut *Three Guineas* to make it into "Women Must Weep", however. She also rewrote, and in three cases the changed wording is worth attention. The first of these rewritings relates to the important word and concept "feminist":

> another celebration seems called for. What could be more fitting than to write more dead words, more corrupt words, upon more sheets of paper and burn them – the words, Tyrant, Dictator, for example? But alas, those words are not yet obsolete. We can still shake out eggs from newspapers; still smell a peculiar and unmistakable odour in the region (1E: 186)

> a celebration seems called for. What could be more fitting, now that we can bury the old word "feminist", than to write more dead words, corrupt words, obsolete words, upon sheets of paper and burn them – the words "tyrant", "dictator", for example? Alas, those words are not yet obsolete. We can still see traces of dictatorship revealed in newspapers, still smell a peculiar and unmistakable odor of masculine tyranny in the region (WMW: 752).

In *Three Guineas*, in passages missing from "Women Must Weep", Woolf discusses the word "feminist" at some length. She insists that nineteenth-century activists such as Josephine Butler were not really, or not just, feminists, for they were working for the rights of all rather than just the rights of women. As "feminism", it is obsolete because feminism means the quest for the rights of women, and "the only right, the right to earn a living" has now been won. As a result "men and women [can work] together for the same cause" (*Three Guineas*: 184–6).

Butler herself wrote, in a similar vein, that her campaigns were "much less of a simple woman's war against man's injustice than it is often supposed to have been". She added, "It was as a citizen of a free country first, and as a woman secondly, that I felt impelled to come forward in defence of the right". As a result, however, she became even the narrowly defined sort of feminist that Woolf decried, for it was necessary "also to work against all those disabilities and injustices which affect the interests of women" (82–3).

In "Women Must Weep" the whole of *Three Guineas'* discussion of nineteenth-century feminism is missing, and the word "feminist" is dealt with only in passing. As can be seen in the passage cited, the word is to be buried instead of burned as it is in *Three Guineas*. We have gained the phrase "masculine tyranny", which is not to be found in *Three Guineas*, but because the discussion of "feminist" has been deleted, it is unclear why the word is to be grouped with "tyrant" or "dictator".[18] As a result, the section on feminism sounds simply like a rejection of that term. In fact, even as it appears in *Three Guineas*, the passage about the obsolescence of feminism persuaded some readers that Woolf was not a feminist in spite of the fact that she strongly supported women's rights and saw a continuing role for women's experience, perspectives, and organizations.

Narrower and wider definitions of feminism are at issue here, and Woolf is disposing of a narrow one. In a diary entry she used the term "feminist" to identify those women who continued in the interwar period to focus their activism on what Josephine Butler had called the "disabilities and injustices which affect the interests of women". Woolf was pleased that such women existed, for "its [sic] the feminists who will drain off this black blood of bitterness which is poisoning us all" (*DII*: 167).[19] Today, in a somewhat similar usage, the word "feminist" is often read as referring only to activists or, more narrowly, those activists who take a confrontational posture in regards to men. But the term has also been rehabilitated to include the larger goals that both Butler and Woolf refer to.

Whatever she thought of the label, Virginia Woolf was a feminist because she was committed to a vision of women as different, as valuable, and as potential transformers of the imperfect present world. She was also a feminist in her reliance on women's activism, whether in the existing groups, colleges, and societies, or in her virtual society, the Outsiders. And her goals, like Josephine Butler's, were wide ones that encompassed all sorts of inequality and, indeed, the very concepts of inequality and hierarchy. But in the absence of the fuller discussion found in *Three Guineas*, in "Women Must Weep" all we have is a brief dismissal of an ambiguous label.

At the same time, in "Women Must Weep" some points were sharpened by rewriting and by the need to state briefly the points the book could make at leisure. "What reason is there to think that a university education makes the educated against war?" Woolf asks crisply (WMW: 589). And one new idea is added. It is to be found in the second half of the serial text:

> First, [members of the Outsiders Society] would bind themselves to earn their own livings. The importance of this as a method of ending war is obvious; sufficient stress has already been laid upon the superior cogency of an opinion based upon economic independence over an opinion based upon no income at all or upon a spiritual right to an income to make further proof unnecessary (E1: 200)

> But there is another way in which the Outsiders can bind themselves to carry out this duty – a more positive, if a still more difficult way. And that is by earning their own livings: by continuing to earn those livings while the war is in progress. History is at hand to assure us that this method has a psychological influence, a strong dissuasive force upon war-makers. In the last war the daughters of workingmen proved it by showing that they could do their brother's work in his absence. They thus roused his jealousy and his anxiety lest his place should have been filled in his absence, and provided him with a strong incentive to end the war (WMW: 753).

Woolf has just explained, in both *Three Guineas* and "Women Must Weep", that Outsiders must avoid encouraging militarism and chauvinism. She then shifts to considering possible economic actions that might help prevent or end wars, beginning with economic autonomy. In "Women Must Weep" a new section of the text now begins.[20] After stating, as in *Three Guineas*, that Outsiders must earn their own livings, she inserts the unique passage beginning "by continuing to earn those livings while war is in progress". If middle-class women go on working during the war, Woolf argues, middle-class men fearing permanent loss of their jobs to women will hasten to make peace as working-class men did for similar reasons during the First World War.

In both book and serial texts Woolf is making the same general point: women need to have an independent source of income if they are to influence war-makers. In both, she had suggested earlier that, unlike middle-class women, working-class women could in principle have an economic impact by withholding their labour from the industries necessary for war (*Three Guineas*: 24; WMW: 588). But the argument about middle-class women found only in "Women Must Weep" is not so much economic as psychological. Woolf may have been influenced by Ray Strachey's account of male reactions to women's First World War movement into industry (in *The Cause*, a source that Woolf used repeatedly for *Three Guineas*). Strachey describes one of the reasons for the initial resistance by male skilled workers to the "dilution" of their trades by women: "it filled them with fears for the future. . . . if [women] were brought in, and especially if, when they were brought in, they did well, where were the men's position be in their 'own' trades after the war?" (342).

However, there is no evidence that men of any class wanted or needed to end the First World War in order to retrieve their jobs from women. British unions were able to ensure that women had no permanent claim on positions in which they replaced men. They also managed to avoid adverse impact on pay or working conditions for unionized jobs that women held on a temporary, wartime basis. As a result, women received the same salaries as men had received, an enormous increase for them and possibly, though improbably, an incentive for working women to favour the continuation of the war. After the war ended, women were, in fact, turfed out of their wartime positions in deference to returning veterans. And, although Woolf seems not to have noticed, this also is documented by Strachey immediately after her discussion of the hostile male reactions to women's wartime work.

Woolf's fantasy about the impact of war work is one of two places where "Women Must Weep" differs significantly from *Three Guineas*. The other is the conclusion:

> Let us leave it to poets to tell us what the dream is; and fix our eyes upon the photograph again: the fact.
>
> Whatever the verdict of others may be upon the man in uniform – and opinions differ – there is your letter to prove that to you the picture is the picture of evil. And though we look upon that picture from different angles our conclusion is the same as yours – it is evil. We are both determined to do what we can to destroy the evil which that picture represents, you by your methods, we by ours. And since we are different, our help must be different. What ours can be we have tried to show – how imperfectly, how superficially there is no need to say. But as a result the answer to your question must be that

we can best help you to prevent war not by repeating your words and following your methods but by finding new words and creating new methods. We can best help you to prevent war not by joining your society but by remaining outside your society but in co-operation with its aim. That aim is the same for us both. It is to assert "the rights of all – all men and women – to the respect in their persons of the great principles of Justice and Equality and Liberty". To elaborate further is unnecessary, for we have every confidence that you interpret those words as we do. And excuses are unnecessary, for we can trust you to make allowances for those deficiencies which we foretold and which this letter has abundantly displayed.

To return then to the form that you have sent and ask us to fill up: for the reasons given we will leave it unsigned. But in order to prove as substantially as possible that our aims are the same as yours, here is the guinea, a free gift, given freely, without any other conditions than you choose to impose upon yourself. It is the third of *Three Guineas*; but the *Three Guineas*, you will observe, though given to three different treasurers are all given to the same cause, for the causes are the same and inseparable.

Now, since you are pressed for time, let me make an end; apologising three times over to the three of you, first for the length of this letter, second for the smallness of the contribution, and thirdly for writing at all. The blame for that however rests upon you, for this letter would never have been written had you not asked for an answer to your own. (E1: 260–1)

This is the picture that has imposed itself upon this letter. It would seem that it is the same picture that has imposed itself upon your own letter – the same picture, but looked at inevitably from a different angle. We are both agreed that the picture is the picture of evil; we are both determined to do what we can, you by your own methods, we by ours, to destroy the evil which that picture represents. And we may both be wrong, not only in the methods by which we attempt to destroy that evil, but in our judgment.

Many men of highest education maintain that the picture is a picture, not of evil, but of good. War, it is argued, brings out the noblest qualities of mankind. The Dictator, it is claimed, is neither a menace nor a monster, but, on the contrary, the consummation of manhood. He is the embodiment of the State; the State is supreme; both men and women must obey its commands, whether they are just or unjust. Obedience is all.

On the other hand, some men also of the highest education also maintain that the picture is the picture of evil. War is inhuman, horrible, unnatural, beastly. The Dictator is a monster. His commands must be disobeyed. The State is not supreme. The State is made of human beings – of free men and women, who must think for themselves.

What judge is there to decide which opinion is right, which is wrong? There is no judge; there is no certainty in heaven above or on earth below. All we can do is to examine that picture as clearly as sex and class allow; to bring to bear upon it such illumination as history, biography, and the daily paper put within our reach; and to examine both reasons and emotions as dispassionately as we can.

That is what we have attempted. The Society of Outsiders – to give it too pompous a name – is the result. The rules – to speak too pedantically – are an attempt to embody the findings of that enquiry. At length, then, we have reached what must serve, temporarily at least, for an answer to your question. Given our sex, our past, our education, our traditions, the best way in which we can help you to prevent war, is to keep these rules. The best way in which we can help you to prevent war, as society is at present and as we are at present, is to remain outside your society. I have every confidence, Sir, that you will read these words aright, and therefore will not elaborate them further.

To return, finally, to the form which you have sent and ask us to fill up, we will leave it, for the reasons given above, unsigned. But in order to prove as substantially as possible that our aims are identical with your own, here is the guinea: a free gift, given freely to help you to assert "the rights of all – all men and women – to the respect in their persons of the great principles of Justice and Equality and Liberty" (WMW: 758–9).

Woolf seems to have had some difficulty with the last part of the book; at the late date of 22 March 1938, well into her revision of proofs, she wrote in her diary that she had "once more tried to recast the last page" (*DV*: 131). But we have no way of telling if the "Women Must Weep" version was written before or after what she left as the book's conclusion in the first editions. All we know is that the endings of *Three Guineas* and "Women Must Weep" are substantially different, and that the serial version is both less assertive and strikingly less feminist.

As can be seen, at the end of "Women Must Weep" the Society of Outsiders, the organization without officers or official identity that will replace for women the existing peace societies, is presented diffidently.

Woolf writes that its name is too pompous, and it is "pedantic" to refer to the group's "rules" as she does in both book and serialization. This though we know that Woolf and her feminist readers were all deeply committed to the concept of outsider activity.

Most notably, in its last pages "Women Must Weep" emphasizes disagreements about the possible value of warriors, war, and authoritarian society. In both *Three Guineas* and "Women Must Weep" the narrator states that she and her peace society correspondent agree that the figure of the virile, militaristic Fascist man in uniform is abhorrent: "it is evil". In both cases, like a good liberal, she then notes that others may disagree. But the emphasis is very different. "Opinions differ" is all she says in *Three Guineas* (260). In "Women Must Weep", she writes instead, "And we may both be wrong, not only in the methods by which we attempt to destroy that evil, but in our judgment". Two substantial paragraphs then repeat the arguments for and against war, obedience, and the supremacy of the state, and a third says, rather desolately, "What judge is there to decide which opinion is right, which wrong? There is no judge; there is no certainty in heaven above or on earth below". These are sentiments Woolf expressed elsewhere in *Three Guineas* in much the same words, but she did not choose them for the conclusion of her argument.

The end of "Women Must Weep" also omits the linkages between domestic and public tyranny. Of the title's three donations, only the guinea to the mixed-sex peace society is mentioned. Woolf has also removed the crucially important statement that the *Three Guineas*, "though given to three different treasurers are all given to the same cause, for the causes are the same and inseparable" (*Three Guineas*: 261). And the quotation that ends "Women Must Weep", although it is once again taken without attribution from Josephine Butler, is the most sex-neutral possible version of social activism.

III

Those critics who faulted *Three Guineas* for linking the status of women with war, who found it too insistent and too class-linked, would surely have felt more comfortable with the conclusion of "Women Must Weep" than with that of *Three Guineas*. And perhaps the title "Women Must Weep" or "Unite against War", which might strike us today as more overtly feminist than *Three Guineas*, was in fact milder and more acceptable because of its reference to conventional sex-role expectations. Women "uniting" against war is an unthreatening enough prospect. "Women Must Weep" also lacks those annoying endnotes and photographs that can leave male readers feeling so uneasy, as if the joke is on them in some way they do not quite understand.

It seems likely, in short, that the irritation provoked by Woolf's feminism and by the dense, whimsical, and semi-academic style in which she expressed it in *Three Guineas*, would not have been as strong in response to "Women Must Weep". But for all the cutting and pasting, the basic argument is still as radical, and certainly as feminist.

Notes

1. The first instalment of the serial was in the May issue of *The Atlantic Monthly Magazine*, 161:5, and the second in the June issue, 161:6. The first English edition of *Three Guineas* was published on 2 June 1938 and the first American edition on 25 August 1938. Citations in this essay are to the first English edition (1E) and to the serial publication (WMW). In addition, Woolf's posthumously published essays included "Professions for Women", an expanded version of the original lecture. For a detailed account of the history and writing of *Three Guineas*, see my introduction to the Shakespeare Head Press edition, 2001.
2. Thus, "A General" was Sir Robert Stephenson Baden-Powell, 1st Lord Baden-Powell of Gilwell, the hero of Mafeking and the founder of the Boy Scouts, wearing the full dress uniform of a colonel in a Hussar Regiment, with the neck decorations of the Order of Merit and a Knight of the Order of the Bath along with the Sash of a Knight Grand Cross of the Order of St Michael and St George. Letter dated 22 October 1997 from Mrs S. K. Hopkins, Head of Department of Uniform, Badges and Medals, National Army Museum, Chelsea.
3. Unpublished letter of 10 February 1931, Berg Collection, New York Public Library.
4. Archives of *The Atlantic Monthly* magazine.
5. The magazine published *Flush*, only 190 pages long, uncut.
6. The title pages and the conclusion were somewhat shorter.
7. The deadline must have had some flexibility, for although Woolf seems to have completed work on the proofs of the main text by 26 March, she was still correcting proofs of notes on 31 March (*DV*: 132). However, what she referred to as "proofs" were being shown to "Miss Hepworth's friends the bookseller" in the third week in March; he found them "exciting" (*DV*: 131).
8. The second page is merely a list of numbers in the same hand as the instructions at the start of the first, relevant page. The two sheets are part of the Harcourt Brace Archives, held by the Massachusetts Historical Society, Boston.
9. The references are evidently not to page proofs, for their pagination corresponds neither to the first English nor the first American edition of *Three Guineas*.
10. The passage is both indented and inserted in quotation marks by the copy-editor.
11. There is no full stop, but the quotation marks are as given.
12. Such material was usually also documented in the endnotes, if not in text omitted from "Women Must Weep". In "Women Must Weep" Woolf cites

material about Francis Grenfell and Antony (Viscount Knebworth) without attribution; in *Three Guineas* she identifies the sources in notes. In *Three Guineas* she attributes to the Lord Chief Justice the remarks that in "Women Must Weep" she calls simply "the patriot's point of view" (586 and 587; by contrast, see Notes 4, 5, and 7 to the first chapter of *Three Guineas*: 265 and 266).

13. Since the first American edition made no concessions at all to its audience, "Women Must Weep" has no particular resemblance to it. The only significant differences between the two first book editions are in the notes, where the first American edition has four added passages. Most of the other slight differences between the first editions occur in sections absent from "Women Must Weep". When "Women Must Weep" includes passages that are not the same in the first book editions, the serial text is the same as the first English edition, with only two exceptions. One of those passages already differs considerably in the two editions; in the other case, the relevant passage was substantially rewritten in "Women Must Weep".

14. In both cases, the two texts are the same in both first editions.

15. By 1938 women did receive equal treatment at other British universities including Oxford, but they were not made eligible for degrees or full membership at Cambridge University until 1948.

16. These acts, applicable in English garrison towns, used fear of sexually transmitted disease as a justification for treating all women as potential prostitutes liable to medical inspection and registration, on pain of jail sentences.

17. Vol. 161: 6 (June 1938), unpaginated insert at start of volume. There are no such sections earlier or later, and a new editor seems to have tried this out once. He adds, "[Mrs Woolf] has a definite and trenchant programme, elaborated in her book, *Three Guineas*, which is to be published by Harcourt, Brace and Company, and from which our essay has been extracted". It is interesting to see how Virginia Woolf is then identified to her American audience: "The daughter of Sir Leslie Stephen and the wife of Leonard Woolf, a London economist and man of letters, Mrs Woolf is the moving spirit of 'the Bloomsbury Group'." Their home, we are told, is a "literary centre" where are to be met a list of individuals that adds to Keynes "his Russian wife Lydia Lopokova" as well as Lytton Strachey, Desmond MacCarthy, E. M. Forster, and Arthur Waley, V. Sackville-West, and Lord Berners. It concludes: "Mrs. Woolf's novels, *The Voyage Out*, *Jacob's Room*, *Mrs. Dalloway*, and *Flush*, and her essays, *The Common Reader* and *A Room of One's Own*, have earned her high rank in contemporary letters".

18. In any case, but especially in its truncated version, the argument about getting rid of obsolete words – not yet possible for dictator or tyrant – is confusing, since once tyranny was gone, it would be terms or concepts such as freedom-fighter that would no longer be needed.

19. The reference was to Lady Rhondda, formerly a militant suffragette, who attempted unsuccessfully to overturn the House of Lords' ban on peeresses in their own right, founded and bankrolled the pro-feminist journal *Time and Tide*, and was active in efforts to increase women's role in politics and the professions. Lady Rhondda liked *Three Guineas* very much.

20. The text is divided into sections headed by roman numerals; this is Section III of the second part.

5

The Texture of the Text: Editing *Roger Fry: A Biography*

Diane F. Gillespie

Editing Virginia Woolf's *Roger Fry: A Biography* in retrospect is considerably different from the actual editing process. I knew from the beginning that Woolf's text presented several challenges beyond the usual ones, like choice of copy-text. The two challenges that now strike me as most interesting and memorable both have to do with "texture". The word suggests a tactile, hands-on creative process that is related to Woolf's own later image of the biographer as craftsman, carpenter, and cabinet-maker (*Collected Essays* IV: 277; LVI: 381; DV: 266). These words, in turn, evoke images of selecting and proportioning, adjusting and fitting, smoothing and shaping sometimes obdurate materials. The often frustrating building project for which Woolf accepted the commission is not unlike the job of constructing an edition of that same text. How does a later editor deal in Introduction and Notes with Woolf's earlier role as editor or, as some would call it, censor of both Fry's words and her own text and with the resulting standard criticisms of the biography for its reticences and suppressions? The answer was to reveal, whenever possible, the control Woolf retained over her materials in ways that served her own ends. The second question is related. What control does an editor assume over Woolf's text, and for what purposes? To what extent, in other words, should one create another editorial layer, re-edit Woolf's text by restoring, if only in notes, material she chose to omit or delete; by identifying her sources and defining the uses that she made of them; and by annotating the often unidentified people, places, and events that she included? Is the role of the editor of *Roger Fry* one of overriding Woolf's original decisions? While the answer to these questions is more difficult to frame in anticipation of the essay to follow, essentially it is "yes". What then is the position of an editor in relation both to the author and to the reader? As this question raises others, the answer must emerge in the course of the argument below.

The craft of selection: editing and/or censorship?

The founding of The Hogarth Press, as Brenda Silver and others note, eliminated from Virginia Woolf's pre-publication process "an external editor/censor" (Silver, 196). *Roger Fry: A Biography* (1940) is an apparent exception. The last work to appear in print before Woolf's death was very much a collaborative effort. A number of people – Fry's family members and friends – provided her with books, newspaper clippings, letters, and memoirs, as well as their own written and verbal accounts of Fry's character and activities. Leonard Woolf read a typescript version. So did Vanessa Bell and at least three members of Roger Fry's family, most notably his sister Margery, the main impetus behind the biography in the first place. Vanessa Bell apparently made some suggestions,[1] but in late March 1940 Margery Fry made "some 100 corrections; all to be entered; some to be contrived" (*LVI*: 389). Two months later, Woolf was "entering 3 different Frys comments into the edges of proofs, and altering my own words to admit theirs" (*LVI*: 399).[2]

To what degree were these first readers responsible for the reticences other readers have noted in Woolf's biography of Fry?[3] The corrections and comments of Fry's family and friends certainly raise questions about the relationships, or lack of them, between editing, perhaps even censorship by others, and Woolf's own writing process. As Silver notes, "one recurring issue is the fine line between self-editing and self-censorship, a distinction that is often difficult if not impossible to make ... " (208). Even without an outside evaluator of her unpublished texts, "Woolf continually struggled with the question of what she could say out loud, and in what tone of voice, without alienating her readers. In this way, the specter of an external critic became one of the multitude of factors that inevitably play a role in the process of revision, including the writer's awareness of her audience" (Silver, 208). In the case of *Roger Fry*, though, in addition to her own self-criticism and the anticipated responses of post-publication readers, Woolf was intensely conscious of actual, pre-publication critics. It would be a mistake, however, to assume that Woolf's relationships with them was antagonistic. As Edward Mendelson says of Auden's plays, "the author made his work in part as a gift to those around him, and those who seek to recover authorial intention find, disconcertingly, that that intention explicitly accommodated and included the intentions of others" (163). Similarly, Woolf provides a portrait of Fry that is, in part, a gift to the immediate audience of Fry's family and friends. That gift, however, is not without conditions, one of which is the equal integrity of her own reconstruction of a complex man.[4]

It has become relatively common in Woolf scholarship, at least since the mid-1970s, to examine a published work in the context of earlier drafts and proofs and to perceive, at least, a "composite work" (Silver, 201, 203). Although the Shakespeare Head Press Edition of Virginia Woolf seeks to present in appendices the variants among the versions published during her lifetime, it does not have a composite text as its goal. At the time of Woolf's death in 1941, three printings of the first edition of *Roger Fry*, without any of her corrections, had appeared in England. The first American edition was a photo-offset reprint of the English edition and thus an issue of it. Aside from one deliberate change, it is identical to the English edition.[5] Unfortunately, the proof copy, or other copies of *Roger Fry* upon which Woolf entered changes in response to the suggestions of others have not survived.[6] The only relatively complete, pre-publication version is an undated, 500-plus page typescript in the Berg Collection of the New York Public Library.[7] It occurred to me that a computer collation of this earlier version of the text with the first English edition, my copy-text, might reveal something about the degree to which outside requests for revision played a role in Woolf's alterations. While the collation informs my Introduction and Notes, for reasons of space and consistency with the other volumes, I was not able to publish even a portion of it as an appendix to my edition. Since the collation was important to my work, I am glad to be able to say more about it here.

While the Berg typescript is difficult to date precisely,[8] and while Woolf made many changes after the holograph revisions on this typescript (some of which were not allowed to stand in the published version), a collation of this draft with the first English edition still enables us to see more clearly the direction taken by some of her subsequent changes.[9] With clear evidence about what she deleted and added as she dealt with representative areas of Fry's life – his childhood years with his family, his sexuality and intimacies with women, and his rivalries with other artists and critics – it is possible to observe Woolf exercising control over the materials she presents rather than abnegating responsibility to outside readers or working entirely at the mercy of her own reticence (conscious or unconscious), as Quentin Bell concludes she did (II: 183). The evidence suggests, too, that the published *Roger Fry* is not an inferior version of some original conception that is more forthright on political and social issues. I am not arguing, therefore, for a text that reveals a story evident in the earlier version but submerged in the final one.[10] While agreeing in general with Ruth Hoberman who re-evaluates *Roger Fry* as a successful feminist attempt to "demasculinize historical writing" by rewriting biography "from a less self-oriented point of view" (197), I am arguing that, within a particular cultural context, Woolf conducted in *Roger Fry* an admirable experiment in re-animating a complex man both for the people who knew him and for his time.

Woolf's own most recent conclusions about biography strongly emphasize the cultural context. In "The Art of Biography", written in 1938 while she was struggling with *Roger Fry*, she concludes that biography is a collaborative genre. While fiction "is created without any restrictions save those that the artist, for reasons that seem good to him, chooses to obey", biography is "made with the help of friends, of facts" (*Collected Essays* IV: 222). These facts, moreover, "can be verified by other people". Limited "by friends, letters, and documents", the biographer still is entitled "to all the facts that are available" (*Collected Essays* IV: 225–6). While the biographer is no longer under pressure to exclude unflattering details, even such details "are subject to changes of opinion; opinions change as the times change. What was thought a sin is now known, by the light of facts won for us by the psychologists, to be perhaps a misfortune; perhaps a curiosity, perhaps neither one nor the other, but a trifling foible of no great importance..." (*Collected Essays* IV: 226). One of the biographer's tasks, Woolf thinks, is to test conventions, to determine which ones are no longer viable, and to reassess the kinds of lives potentially worthy of biographical treatment. All in all, Woolf concludes, the biographer is "a craftsman, not an artist", and a biography is not a work of art, but something "betwixt and between". The biographer's creations may be "invaluable", but they are "not destined for the immortality which the artist now and then achieves for his creations" (*Collected Essays* IV: 227).[11]

If the biographer, as Woolf now implied, can and must write not for posterity but for a historically limited audience, then she is justified in treating indirectly or even eliminating sensitive material altogether. She also is freed from much of the explanation and documentation needed by later readers, should they materialize. At the same time, the success of her efforts is bound more closely to the reactions of that initial, more limited audience. It includes many people who had known or heard of Fry, read his writings or seen his paintings, and could measure her portrait against their own sometimes strong, often emotionally charged opinions about his controversial personality and impact.

In the area of Fry's early family life, where one would expect the Fry family hand to have been the heaviest, Woolf's published version introduces believable complexities without sacrificing the general repressive characteristics of his Victorian family that she clearly sought to emphasize. When Woolf reported, with mixed feelings, on 27 March 1940 that Margery Fry had asked for corrections, she also said that she was "very reasonably spattered" with them and that Margery's "kindness and reasonableness is such that I can't ignore". It is important to note that, in spite of Woolf's irritation ("Yet why is filial love so deucedly persistent? And erratic?"), she did consider Margery Fry kind and her requests reasonable (*LVI*: 389).[12] The precise changes that Margery and then the other Frys requested (*LVI*: 399) are unknown, but the alterations Woolf made in her earlier depiction of the Fry family, between the extant typescript and the published versions, are such that the image of reasonableness remains, even to the inclusion of a few references to important roles Margery herself, as well as another of Fry's sisters, Joan, played at various points in his life.[13]

In Chapter 1, for example, Woolf added an observation about the memoir materials on which she relied heavily for her depiction of Roger Fry's early relationship with his strict Quaker family.[14] Fry wrote these recollections, she adds, for a particular, irreverent audience, the Memoir Club, and they should be seen in that light:[15]

> *TS:* Obviously the man, looking back at his past has added something to the impression received by a child of seven.

> *1E:* Obviously the man, looking back at his past has added something to the impression received by a child of seven, **and, since it was written for friends who took a humorous rather than a reverential view of eminent Victorians, no doubt it owed a little to the temper of the audience.** (1E: 22; *Roger Fry*: 17)

Even though Woolf justifiably admits that Fry may have exaggerated in order to amuse his friends, she does not concede that he did so more than "a little".[16]

One of these memoir pieces, which Woolf quotes, describes Fry's "first passion" which "was for a bushy plant of large red oriental poppies". It also describes his first "disillusionment" when he thought he understood his mother to send him to pick "one of the buds of my *adored* poppy plant" and then was reproached for having done so. In two instances (one in Chapter 1 and one in Chapter 7), Woolf changed two words so that their connotations altered the image of Lady Fry's response:

> *TS:* he picked the poppy and was **severely scolded** by his mother for doing so

> *1E:* he picked the poppy and was **gravely reproved** by his mother for doing so (1E: 16; *Roger Fry*: 13)

TS: A red poppy, **a mother's scolding**, a Quaker upbringing, ("scolding" has been underlined in the TS)

1E: A red poppy, **a mother's reproof**, a Quaker upbringing, . . . (1E: 161; *Roger Fry*: 128).

Woolf mitigates the "severe scolding" with its connotations of harshness and shrewishness without diminishing the young Fry's confusion and disillusionment, which are her main concerns.

In her re-creation of the family atmosphere that led to the disagreement between Sir Edward Fry and his son about his choice of art over science as a profession, Woolf qualified the early statements she made about the place of art in the Fry home. She did not change, however, the overall impression that art – and especially the nonrepresentational kind with which Fry was to become associated – was not, and would not, be valued:

TS: But science was part of the home atmosphere; **art was ignored**

1E: But science was part of the home atmosphere; art was **"kept in its place"; that is the Academy would be dutifully visited; and a landscape, if it faithfully recorded the scene of a summer holiday, would be dutifully bought** (1E: 19; *Roger Fry*:15).

Woolf's revision describes the situation in a way no doubt more fair than her earlier version. Yet her repetition of the word "dutifully" and her description of acceptable landscapes as faithful documentations of sites visited do not alter the basic impression of family members who valued art only to the degree that viewing or purchasing its most traditional, referential products was appropriate to their position in society. No love of art, no aesthetic apprehension was involved.

The severe image of Sir Edward Fry is further qualified in Chapter 1:

TS: **he played no games**; he had no skill with his hands

1E: **bowls and halma were the only games he tolerated; and** he had no skill with his hands (1E: 24; *Roger Fry*: 20).

While again the revision is in the direction of greater accuracy and complexity, Woolf's use of the words "only" and "tolerated" does not diminish significantly Sir Edward's austerity.

When Roger Fry was sent to Sunninghill School, the headmaster promised his Quaker parents that the students were not subjected to physical punishments. Fry's letters home, however, indicated that floggings were part of the routine. An essay Fry later read to the Memoir Club, much of which Woolf quotes, describes the floggings in graphic detail. One added word, however, relieves Fry's parents of complete hypocrisy and complicity:

TS: In spite of these very plain hints that Mr. Sneyd-Kynnersley was not keeping his promise, the parents made no protest

1E: In spite of these very plain hints that Mr Sneyd-Kynnersley was not keeping his promise, his parents made no **effective** protest, ... (1E: 31; *Roger Fry*: 26).

Although Woolf includes details to indicate that Fry's experiences at the school were varied, and although her point in raising the issue of the floggings is to explain Fry's life-long horror of violence, why his Quaker parents left him at a school with practices so against their principles remains a mystery that does not reflect creditably upon them.

Woolf altered her actual quotation from Fry's memoir of the floggings at Sunninghill by deleting a reference to his first experience of his sexuality, his first erection. Here we do have cases both of censorship – of Fry's account – and of self-censorship – of Woolf's own earlier version:

TS: I do not know what complications and repressions lay behind it but their connection with sex was suddenly revealed to me one day when I went back to my room after assisting at an execution [omit?] **by my having an erection. So far as I can remember it was the first I had ever had. It was a great surprise to me. I had not even then the faintest idea of the function of the organ whose behaviour so surprised me for** all ideas of sex had been deeply repressed in me in my unremembered past.

At some point Woolf marked the passage in the typescript for possible omission, and then did omit it (1E: 34; *Roger Fry*: 28), but not without considerable thought. On 6 January 1940, she noted in her diary that she had asked Maynard and Lydia Keynes if they thought she could "mention erection". Maynard Keynes thought not: "I should mind your saying it. Such revelations have to be in key with their time. The time not come yet". Although Woolf had wondered if Keynes was "right, or only public school", she ultimately accepted his advice (*DV*: 256).[17] As her narrator notes in *Orlando*, "the transaction between a writer and the spirit of the age is one of infinite delicacy, and upon a nice arrangement between the two the whole fortune of his works depend" (152). Perhaps this is also another instance of the woman writer feeling impeded, as Woolf notes in "Professions for Women", by "the extreme convention-ality of the other sex" (*Collected Essays* II: 288). Her decision was, in any case, in line with her observation in "The Art of Biography" that bio-graphers must test conventions and determine which have become obsolete (*Collected Essays* IV: 226). Panthea Reid, assuming that Woolf marked the passage for possible omission after talking to the Keynes and then bowed to Margery Fry's wishes in the matter, concludes that Woolf proved herself "as anal as Roger had claimed she was" (421).[18] Other explanations are possible. Woolf's deletion was in line with her satire in *Orlando* of biographers who reduce women (in that case) to their sexuality (for example: 154). However poetic the justice, would it have been fair to treat a man's life in a similarly reductive way? The deletion also has the final effect – at least on some early twenty-first-century readers like myself – of eliminating an all-too-important symbol of masculine power and privilege.[19]

Possibly some of the same dynamics are at work in Woolf's treatment of Fry's intimacies with women, an area of his life where she frequently is charged with undue reserve. A comparison of the typescript with the published version does not reveal, however, that she deleted references to the women in Fry's life. On the contrary, at some time later than the Berg typescript, she added significant, albeit periphrastic, passages. One such addition, in Chapter 4, indicates the importance of the older woman – still, it is true, unnamed – who educated "him in the art of love":[20]

> TS: But for all his susceptibility, he knew the difference between "the many ways of love"

> 1E: **And among these fleeting attachments to young and lovely faces there was a more serious relationship with a lady who was neither young nor beautiful, but old enough to be his mother. She it was who undertook to educate him in the art of love, much as Symonds had educated him in the art of painting. Endowed, he said, "with enough fire to stock all the devils in Hell", she stormed at his stupidity, laughed at his timidity and ended by falling in love with him herself. He profited by the lesson and was profoundly grateful to his teacher. Had she not taught him what was far more import-ant than the art of dissecting the livers of drunken men or of**

discriminating between a genuine Botticelli and a sham? So he thought at least, and to the end of life pupil and mistress remained the best of friends. Thus instructed he lost his Cambridge callowness and learnt to distinguish between "the many ways of love" (1E: 94; *Roger Fry*: 75).

The other addition emphasized the importance of Vanessa Bell – still, it is true, called a friend, not a lover – in his life:

1E: And he felt that confidence, that determination not only as a painter. All his doubts and difficulties, he said, seemed to have left him. He had found himself at last – he could deal with life, he could deal with people. It is easy to find reasons, whether they are the right or the sufficient reasons, for the change. There was the relief from the long strain of his wife's illness – the relief that comes naturally and healthily when a struggle has ended and defeat has been faced. There was the new friendship with Vanessa Bell, who, as a painter belonging to the younger generation, had all the ardour of the young for the new movements and the new pictures and urged him away from the past and on to the future. There was her painting and her studio and the younger generation arguing with him and laughing at him, but accepting him as one of themselves. All this brought about a change that showed itself even in his face, so that a friend meeting him in the street exclaimed, "What's happened to you? You look ten years younger." He repeated that saying, and added that, strange as it was, at last, at the age of forty-four he found himself where most people find themselves twenty years earlier – at the beginning of life, not in the middle, and nowhere within sight of the end (1E: 162; *Roger Fry*: 128–9).

Although Fry and Bell were lovers during 1911 and 1913, they remained good friends for a much longer period – until his death, in fact, in 1934. One could argue that Woolf's reference to friendship, therefore, is more characteristic of the long-term relationship than is the relatively brief affair she implies but does not mention directly. Woolf again emphasizes the longevity of the friendship by adding Vanessa Bell's name at least twice in the last two chapters of the published version as a recipient of the Fry letters from which she quotes.

In the area of Fry's rivalries with his contemporaries, in several instances Woolf deleted names and insulting references to certain hostile people, notably Wyndham Lewis, from the Fry letters quoted in the typescript, another instance of censorship both of Fry's writing and her own earlier version:

> *TS:* **bottom of the question. I suspect that Lewis had never been in the Omega except for what he could get out of it and that even before we came back from Italy he had formed a "cave".** I quite agree[21]

> *1E:* bottom of the question. . . . I quite agree (1E: 193; *Roger Fry*: 154).

Again positing that her biography of Fry would be read primarily by her contemporaries, Woolf's alterations reveal her understandable choice not to carry on his battles – not only with Lewis, but also with other living rivals like William Rothenstein – beyond the grave.[22] Just as Fry refused to defend himself in the case of the Ideal Home Exhibition conflict with Lewis, so Woolf also chose to delete from Chapter 8, presumably in proofs, a letter affirming that the commission had been given unconditionally to Fry.

These few, but representative examples from the collation of the Berg typescript with the first English edition of *Roger Fry: A Biography* indicate that some of Woolf's later alterations were dictated by at least three principles: fairness; justice to the complexity not only of Fry, but also of other people with whom he was involved; and a definition of biography as a collaborative genre necessarily limited by the culture of the time. The collation, in combination with Woolf's letters and diaries and her essay, "The Art of Biography", enable us to look critically at the common evaluations of this text. We see Woolf, not so much as a passive victim of censorship or self-censorship, either by Fry's family or because of her own inhibitions, as an active, thoughtful editor, writer, and biographical theorist, aware of her audience, aware of her options, and capable of making careful choices among them.[23]

The architecture of annotation

Written, at least in part, as a gift to family and friends who could read not only the lines but also between them, *Roger Fry* nevertheless was printed both in England and America for wider mid-twentieth-century audiences. Although Woolf suggests in "The Art of Biography" that she does not envision a life for such a book among readers of subsequent generations (*Collected Essays* IV: 227), such unanticipated readers still exist, and their responses and requirements are different. Indeed, the editorial committee for the Shakespeare Head Press edition of Virginia Woolf (Joanne Trautmann Banks, Susan Dick, James M. Haule, Andrew McNeillie, and S. P. Rosenbaum) rightly indicated from the outset that a major challenge for the editor of *Roger Fry* would be responding to the need for extensive annotation. What, more precisely, did that entail? The committee encouraged the editors to annotate in ways that would not date the volumes unduly: "The brief identifications of literary allusions, historical figures, places, events, ... should be as factual and non-interpretive as possible", read our guidelines; "Annotations should be 'factual' and not 'theoretical' or 'speculative' in emphasis", reiterates the style sheet. Although these directives are clear, they raise questions about the often unexamined assumptions governing both the practice and the reception of annotation. The degree to which notes can be "factual" or objective is only part of a larger issue, their purpose, and larger still, the implied relationship between editor and reader, editor and author.

To some scholarly editors, annotation is taken for granted and thus is not an issue. To others, like many of the contributors to an academic symposium and ultimately an essay collection on annotation edited by Stephen A. Barney, contemporary readers should be wary of the editorial authority with which their need for information is met (for example, Mayali, 185). Editors, so the argument goes, seek less to be helpful to readers than to assert themselves; they display their own learning in notes that pander to the kinds of readers and institutions trained to produce, expect, accept, but rarely use them (McFarland, 158, 161–3). Responses to an earlier culture from which both annotator and contemporary readers feel alienated, annotations at the same time canonize texts for "some critical community" to which the annotator belongs. In so doing, annotators may well create their audiences as well as the authors whose works they edit (Hanna, 178, 181). Annotators, as Barney's collection represents them, then, are anything but "Dictionary Johnson's" "harmless drudges".

These self-conscious interrogations – for who writes essays about annotation but annotators? – deserve thoughtful rebuttal at a time when, as Anthony Grafton points out, many publishers cut footnotes "to a minimum or banish them to the ends of books, where they may escape notice" and when even younger academics dismiss annotation as "little more than one of the rhetorical devices by which the scholars of older generations created a myth of intellectual authority". Grafton defends annotations as both evidence of adequate research and invitations "to argue with authors about their interpretations of the record" (59). Adding "to argue with editors about their selections from the record", I would like to suggest a parallel perspective. Behind the notion that annotating a text is primarily about the editor's ego is the hierarchical model of conflict and competition Woolf challenges in *Three Guineas*. One can substitute for this adversarial model mediation, negotiation, and collaboration among editor, author, text, and reader. One can look at editions in general and annotations in particular, not as authoritative and final, not as threats to the autonomy of the literary text, but as selections from currently available information, as efforts to preserve fragments of human history, and thus as dialogic in their relation to the text and its readers. The problem is less with the format of scholarly editions and more with readers who submit to what they define as "authority" and who do not think critically about what they read.

Different editorial procedures or even publishing formats are not necessary, just a different way for editors and readers to *think about* editing in general and annotating in particular. As the yearly selected papers volumes from the Annual Conferences on Virginia Woolf increasingly demonstrate, talk of the *criticism* of her texts is an on-going dialogue or conversation – as opposed to ignorance or one-upping of what has gone before – is expected and affirmed. Similar talk about the *editions* of Woolf's works is now beginning. A good example is Margaret Connolly's review of three recent editions of *Night and Day*: "Reading the volumes side by side", she says, "one gets a sense of the choices that yet inform a seemingly self-evident, certainly painstaking, and often thankless task" (8). She concludes a series of comparisons of the features of the three editions and of selected annotations with an apt reference to "all of us engaged in the collaborative act of reading Woolf's texts" (9).

In addition to the editor/reader relationship, there is an editor/author issue – whether or not an editor's practice of annotation should somehow reflect the author's own values. In George Bornstein's collection of essays on editing modernist texts, however, only one contributor discusses annotation. Unlike the works of Pound, Eliot, and Joyce, A. Walton Litz points out, William Carlos Williams's poems have not been annotated adequately, largely because the New Critics viewed him as "an anti-intellectual poet of concrete, immediate experience" and because of his "antagonism to international modernism". Yet Litz and his co-editor Christopher MacGowan "were amazed to find how much annotation was needed", not only the usual "information that the other modernists expect their readers to command", but also "allusions to 'high culture'", images from the visual arts, and "local references . . . to the American scene" (52).

The assumption that extensive annotation may be inappropriate emerges again in connection with some modernist women writers. As George H. Thomson, annotator of Dorothy Richardson, recognizes, "some readers will object that by interposing so much precise detail and labored documentation I have, so to speak, pinned down the delicate flight and dammed up the ongoing flow of the *Pilgrimage* text. If I have done so", he adds, "it is in the belief that once the facts and the backgrounds have been absorbed the reader may experience an enhanced freedom and appreciation in moving through Miriam Henderson's world" (xi). Some of the commentary on the recent editions of Woolf's texts voices a similar concern. Aimed at a range of markets from scholarly to popular, these editions proliferated after 1992, in Britain at least, during the temporary expiration of the copyright. The assumption of impropriety seems to be behind Julia Briggs' conclusion that Woolf's "commitment to textual indeterminacy and to plentitude of meaning evident in the characteristic contrasts and dialectic generated by her work should act as an awful warning to those of us who have, with the best of intentions, enchained her flying texts and tied them down to the stone breaking apparatus of notes, commentaries and appendices" (76). Yet in the same essay Briggs supports "a carefully edited text with a helpful intro-duction and notes" and thinks the important question is "what informa-tion the good editor should supply, and how much" (67). Contrasting the editing of Woolf by academics with that by nonacademics, Jeri Johnson writes that how one feels about the difference between Hermione Lee's over 30 pages of notes in the recent Penguin edition of *To the Lighthouse* and Margaret Drabble's little more than three in the Oxford edition "will depend entirely on how one feels about annota-tions". Defending them, Johnson observes that only Woolf's "closest readers" have noticed her "erudition and complex, though subtle habit of allusion" even though her allusions "form a significant, deftly inter-woven fabric of meaning in the works . . . " (5). An editorial apparatus like annotation, then, is important to reader understanding and enjoy-ment. Rather than enchaining and breaking a Woolf text, notes can serve as a constructive addition to it.

Woolf's own writing experiments, or what we think she might have approved also are not necessarily valid bases for judging current editions of her works. It is true that Woolf did not take kindly to academics and their methods, and one cannot rule out some degree of parody, or even desperation, when she uses annotations herself. As Bornstein points out, though, "the 'author' changes over time", and "even a given author at a given moment often displays not a monolithic singularity of purpose or desire, but rather a multiplicity of them embodied in a multiplicity of intentions", many of which "may be at cross-purposes and contradiction with each other" (8). *Three Guineas* is a good example. Given the mix of readers in whom she hopes to stimulate thought, Woolf presents the results of her own extensive research in what seems to be a conventional academic way, by means of 124 endnotes. At the same time, she effectively uses such notes, some of them small essays in themselves, to articulate further, to complicate, and to substantiate her arguments.[24] As John Whittier-Ferguson demonstrates, the notes constitute "an unexpected final chapter" (93), exposing the lacunae in English history, assaulting institutions like the Christian church, and challenging the orderly and often monologic forms of annotation itself (94–7). *Roger Fry: A Biography*, which includes only eight brief notes, suggests a different, nonargumentative purpose, and a different anticipated audience. Woolf's own definitions of "The New Biography", however, require that the "granite" of facts be there, if not in notes, then in the text itself, however carefully facts may be selected and arranged to evoke the "rainbow" of personality (*Essays* IV: 473).

Can one provide further "granite" without doing violence to Woolf's conception of the reading experience? A major advantage of the Shakespeare Head Press Edition is that the annotations do not interrupt the "pleasure in reading", as the editorial committee says in the general Preface. Notes appear together at the end, identified by page number, and readers who are not mystified by a reference probably will not even turn to the back for elucidation. While such a practice may imply that the Notes are not essential, it is also a means by which certain kinds of readers can have the original text and contextualize it too.[25] So many sources does Woolf use, and so deftly detailed is the milieu she creates, that the Notes in this first annotated edition of *Roger Fry*[26] add up to over half the number of pages in the biography itself.[27] In addition to the usual kinds of identifications of people, places, events, and objects, they include references to what remains of Woolf's early research and drafting as well as identifications of her published and unpublished sources and comparisons of her uses of them to the originals. In the case of this densely detailed text and the scholarly parameters of the Shakespeare Head Edition, abundant annotations seem neither excessive nor aggressive. The editorial committee – who asked me, for instance, to group the brief identifications of painters and composers into an appendix – advised only minimal pruning.

Initially, I did not plan to search for Woolf's sources. Rereading the biography, however, along with the references in letters and diaries to the overwhelming amount of material at her disposal, I became increasingly curious about her intellectual and creative processes as she shaped the biography. A search for sources led to published Fry letters, his uncollected articles, other people's published memoirs, and numerous reference works found mainly in the Cambridge University Library. Unpublished materials included letters, manuscripts, and memoirs by Fry and others at King's College and at Trinity College Libraries; Fry family papers that Woolf consulted; and Woolf's notes for the biography at the University of Sussex Library. As I became aware of the plethora of materials available to her, read through her many notes, and compared these materials to the typescript and published versions, I was able to identify with Woolf's struggle to shape a coherent yet multi-faceted portrait. I gained an enormous respect for what she accomplished in a relatively short space. Just as people had saved Fry's unpublished letters and memoirs and provided them to Woolf for use in writing the biography, so heirs, scholars, and librarians have since preserved, and in some cases published, many of these same materials. Using these, and thereby providing many of the details Woolf chose to omit, does not constitute a rebuilding of her text as something that never was nor a bid for respect for the editorial carpentry involved. It became more important to increase the admiration of other contemporary readers for Woolf's ability to select from the huge amount of material at her disposal, for her deft biographical writing, and for a work often considered more an anomaly than one central to her career.[28]

The context provided in the Notes to *Roger Fry* also accounts for the tone and nature of some of Fry's remarks. Woolf's treatment of his relationship with Vanessa Bell, already mentioned, provides good examples. Earlier I indicated the ways in which Woolf, as she revised, became more candid about her sister's role in Fry's life. An instance of seemingly contradictory intentions, however, is the selective use of the Bell/Fry correspondence in ways that reveal his state of mind yet conceal her role in causing it. Woolf quotes the despairing letters Fry wrote after Duncan Grant had taken his place in Vanessa Bell's affections, for instance, in "The War Years" chapter without identifying Bell as their recipient. The context implies – in spite of the word "privately" which, in any case, could be read as a reference to his wife's mental illness – that the primary cause of Fry's gloom was the First World War: "So 1917 came to an end; and he noted how the struggle to keep going was almost intolerable; both publicly and privately. He spoke of the 'sadness and numbness of my life'", of feeling as though he had to learn "to live 'only on outside fringes'" (*Roger Fry*: 167). The quotation, as my note indicates, is from a letter to Vanessa Bell (17 January 1917): "The sadness and numbness of my life are what I share with you most intimately.... It's not a constant and sharp pain any more ... but it is a feeling of having lost the central purpose of my life – of living only on outside fringes" (*Roger Fry*: 347). Because Vanessa Bell was the one who had provided Fry's letters and advised Woolf to be truthful (Marler, 450), she would have recognized these references. Most other original readers would not have. Since her sister was one of the primary people for whom Woolf wrote, however, her recognition was important. This note, and others, reveal to contemporary readers of the biography, therefore, that, for certain crucial early readers, there were few suppressions.[29]

It is satisfying to find many of the pieces of a complex puzzle: a wealth not only of quotations from published and unpublished sources, but also of names, titles, allusions, events, places, even objects most of which Woolf does not identify, or identifies only minimally in the text.[30] Some of these, however, proved untraceable, and my editors advised me to eliminate most of the annotations that read, "unidentified". With so many details involved, accuracy was also a concern, as it certainly was for Woolf. Although at the end of her Preface to *Orlando*, Woolf mocks the man who frequently writes to correct her facts and, in the same tone, encourages his continuing corrections (8, 195), in the case of *Roger Fry*, she wrote more seriously to one of Fry's sisters, "I'm sorry I put you in the wrong house, and where was Roger born?" (*LVI*: 423).[31]

Missing pieces and factual accuracy, however, are not the only problems with large numbers of facts. Which of the many references in the text does one identify for audiences considerably more diverse than Woolf's own, for readers living generations later and, in many cases, from different social classes and cultures? The editorial committee overseeing the Shakespeare Head Press Edition of Woolf's works responded to the proposed annotations for *Roger Fry* with a world-wide audience in mind. Still, the five editors sometimes responded differently, disagreeing about what should or could be annotated. This edition of *Roger Fry*, it is true, is not likely to be picked up by readers who are not of a studious inclination. Yet even many bright and curious graduate students of twentieth-century British literature initially know little or nothing about Fry and his prominent Quaker family, the school system in which he was educated, or the art scene of which he was a controversial part. How does one provide the references some groups need without insulting or patronizing other groups, such as British scholars, art historians, and

European travelers to whom more of these references are familiar? While "halma", which I identify as "a game played on a board with 256 squares", may constitute a superfluous note to some (Spalding, "Editorial" 3), I had never heard of it before. If one cannot avoid offense, one should err, if err it is, on the side of helpfulness.

Finally, what kinds of information does one provide in an individual note? Sometimes that depends upon the thoroughness of the research, and, if it has been thorough, what one selects from a number of available facts.[32] Among the post-1992 editions aimed at, and (in affordable paperback form) accessible to a wider audience, the Penguin editions under Julia Briggs' general editorship are seemingly at the opposite pole from the Shakespeare Head Press Editions. In the context of the approaches to Woolf of previous decades, these are edited unabashedly "for the nineties" by women with explicit, albeit broadly defined feminist assumptions (Briggs, "The Story", xxviii).[33] If those who claim that there are no ideologically neutral annotations, that even the apparently self-effacing and objective annotator is, in some complex way, a cultural construction,[34] are right, however, then the general differences between at least the annotations in these two editions are likely to be less in kind than of degree. The Introductions to the Penguin editions discuss, and the Notes include, much that is not explicitly or stereotypically "feminist", and the tone is not "hostile or aggressive or even aggrieved" (J. Marcus, 17). Similarly, although there is no feminist Penguin edition of *Roger Fry*, some of my notes might have been appropriate for an edition so defined. Whenever possible, I relate people or places to Fry, to Woolf, or to both of them. Woolf mentions Oscar Browning, for instance, among the "Cambridge characters" Fry encountered (*Roger Fry*: 36). Fry's comment in a letter home on Browning and his rooms was appropriate for the note (*Roger Fry*: 269). So was Woolf's ironic reference to him in *A Room of One's Own* where he appears among those men who consider themselves qualified to pronounce upon women's abilities (*Roger Fry*: 269; *Room*: 81). Does the inclusion of Woolf's earlier treatment of Oscar Browning, however, constitute, in some broad sense, a "feminist" interpretation? The note suggests, albeit without comment, some of Woolf's own likely gendered associations when she encountered "O. B." in Fry's letters about the university experiences she had been denied. For that reason, or for some other, a different editor might not have included it.

My note on the conservative Pitt Club to which Fry was elected at Cambridge is an example of a note as "factual" as requested. All Woolf says about the Club is that Fry decided the honor was not "worth the very big subscription". Refraining from any political commentary (perhaps unnecessary for her original audience) beyond the implication that it was a club for the very wealthy, Woolf only says that, in contrast, Fry had "no doubts" about joining The Apostles (*Roger Fry*: 40). My note on the Pitt Club reads:

> Founded during the first half of the nineteenth century, its chapters promoted the political ideals and candidates of the Tory party. The club was named for William Pitt the Younger (1759–1806), statesman, who was educated at Pembroke Hall, Cambridge (M.A., 1776), became Chancellor of the Exchequer (1782), and was made Prime Minister at age twenty five (1783–1801). RF reported his decision not to join the club in a letter to Lady Fry on 16 May 1886 (FP) (*Roger Fry*: 275).

Since this essay is in part about "editing and interpreting" processes and procedures, however, it is amusing to imagine a note that prefaced these facts with the way some of them materialized. Such a note, modifying Woolf in *A Room of One's Own*, might read:

> Because a famous Club has been cursed by a woman is of no significance to the famous Club. Women are barred from the Pitt Club meeting rooms in Cambridge which my husband and I came upon while walking down Jesus Lane one day. My obliging partner climbed the stairs, therefore, and explained in his American accent that his wife needed some information about the Club for an explanatory note. Although a young man questioned him suspiciously about my intentions, he provided this male assistant not only with the necessary facts but also with a glass of wine. I, the female editor, cooled her heels for twenty minutes downstairs. Founded during the first half of the nineteenth century, etc.

While this kind of note would justifiably provoke charges of an aggrieved version of feminist bias, not to mention egotism, the actual note, conforming to the traditional, seemingly objective style, inadvertently reifies the patriarchy and conveys seriousness and respect that is not necessarily merited. Objectivity becomes a matter not only of degree but also of definition.

Editing and censorship, as well as subjectivity and objectivity are poles on a continuum between which, in most practical applications, authors, their editors, and the general editors or editorial committees at presses slide in sometimes unexamined, sometimes contradictory ways.

If *Roger Fry: A Biography* was a collaborative project, a gift to the people who loved its subject and deluged her with information, and a reanimation of a controversial and mercurial man in and for his time, if it was an editing and shaping project requiring all her cabinet-making skills, and if it was, in addition, Woolf's (pro)creation of her own friend, what she calls "a child born of us" (*DV*: 305), then the distinctions among these various roles are virtually impossible for a later editor to sort out completely. Similarly, while the editorial apparatuses of Introduction, Variants, Annotations, and Appendices suggest scholarly control, a knowledgable editor inevitably must reflect, in and by means of these instruments, the blurring of boundaries inherent not only in Woolf's biographical writing but in the contemporary editorial enterprise itself where editors edit and/or censor themselves and themselves are edited and/or censored, however minimally. The question is not whether annotation is appropriate for Woolf's work but whether we, as intellectually curious readers, can produce and learn to read both scholarly and more popular editions of her texts in a dialogic manner, aware not only of their strengths and limitations but also of our own. No edition, however carefully wrought, and no editorial apparatus is "definitive" or "authoritative".[35] Using the resources available at the time of its publication, each edition joins as well as influences the conversation about a text. In the case of *Roger Fry: A Biography*, the Shakespeare Head Press Edition inaugurates the dialogue. It is not the last word on the texture of this text.

Notes

I presented a version of the first part of this essay for the International Virginia Woolf Society panel on "Woolf and Technology" at the MLA Convention, December 1994, San Diego, and quite a different version of the second part for a panel on editing at the Eighth Annual Conference on Virginia Woolf, June 1998, St Louis. I wish to thank the editors of this volume as well as Leslie K. Hankins and Beth Rigel Daugherty for their suggestions.

1. The typescript Vanessa Bell read was "uncorrected" (Marler, 462). In an unpublished letter to Margery Fry, March 19 (1940), Woolf reported that Vanessa had given her some ideas for changes. I am grateful to Joanne Trautmann Banks for letting me see this unpublished letter.
2. At some point during her extended period of work on what became the long last chapter (11), whether in 1939 or during the later revision stages, Woolf asked Helen Anrep, with whom Fry lived during the last years of his life, to read that portion of her manuscript. A letter from Helen described how excited and moved she was by Woolf's recreation of Fry, especially the description of the Queen's Hall lecturing. She also sent some corrections of the French for

Woolf's long quotation from Fry's history of his earlier relationship with the Frenchwoman Josette Coatmellec; and she corrected an anecdote Woolf used about Fry's treatment of an enthusiastic American visitor. Although the letter is dated, in Leonard Woolf's shaky hand, 1938 (Monks House Papers, University of Sussex Library), the diary entries would place it in at least 1939, perhaps even later.

3. See, for instance, Bell II, 183, 214 and Spalding, ix.

4. See Goodheart who says, in relation to D. H. Lawrence's work, "If the making of a book is a collaborative process, authorial intention relinquishes much of its authority to publisher and audience. In a sense, authorial intention is always already determined by a sense of its audience. It may also be determined by a desire to resist its audience, to tell it a story it may not even wish to hear" (238).

5. After the books were printed, four pages of the first American edition were reset in order to alter two sentences Woolf had quoted from Fry which the family of J. Pierpont Morgan considered derogatory. In part because Woolf expressed her reluctance to make the alterations and because they do not exist in all copies of the first American edition (*Roger Fry*: xxxii–xxxiii), I chose the first English edition of *Roger Fry* as my copy-text.

6. Neither is *Roger Fry* a good example of Woolf's practice of introducing variations in her published texts "as she corrected two sets of identical page proofs, one for The Hogarth Press and one for her American publishers" (Silver, 196).

7. While the typescript is in the Berg Collection at the New York Public Library, Philip H. Smith Jr's printout of the collation as well as my selection from it of significant variants eventually will be available in Manuscripts, Archives, and Special Collections, Holland Library, Washington State University, Pullman, Washington, where the Leonard and Virginia Woolf Library and Bloomsbury Collection are housed. Some of the differences between the two texts are mentioned in my Introduction and Notes to my Shakespeare Head Press edition of *Roger Fry*.

8. In the Berg Collection, the typescript is divided into nine parts and put in folders stamped "Ann Watkins, Inc.", the name of a New York agent to whom The Hogarth Press wrote on April 5, 1940 (Berg Collection). According to the letter, the typescript was being sent to be considered for "partial serialization" in the United States. Even if we could be sure that all or some of the pages in the folders are those sent to Ann Watkins – which is unlikely – it is still uncertain when the holograph revisions on them were entered. For one thing, in Chapter 7 of the typescript – where the Borough Polytechnic details appear in the published version – Woolf has left blank lines. This part of the typescript at least must have been produced prior to October 24 (1938) when Woolf wrote to Vanessa Bell to ask if she and Duncan Grant would "write something quick about the Borough Polytechnic" (LVI: 294–5). On November 2 (1938) Woolf wrote to thank Vanessa for having sent the facts (LVI: 298). If Woolf added the information shortly thereafter and recorded completion of her first sketch of Fry on March 11, 1939 (DV: 207–8), it is highly unlikely that in April 1940 – a year later – she would have sent a typescript to Ann Watkins in New York without the addition. At various times there must have been other copies, differently revised, of the typescript. A later version incorporating the holograph revisions on the NYPL typescript, as well as other revisions like the Borough

Polytechnic facts, must have been the one given to Vanessa Bell, various Frys, and Leonard Woolf to read in March 1940.

9. While I saw to the typing into the computer of the texts of the first English edition and the typescript, the actual collation of the two texts was done by Philip H. Smith Jr.

10. It is useful to keep in mind Pizer's four tests of self-censorship: (1) what we know about the origins and creation of the work; (2) what evidence we have of the reasons for making revisions; (3) what we conclude about the respective quality of the earlier as opposed to the revised work; and (4) whether there is reason to consider the first published version, established for fifty years or more, as a "historical artifact" that deserves continued reading even if self-censorship is apparent (150–1).

11. Contrast Woolf's earlier essay, "The New Biography" (1927), in which she emphasizes the artistry of the genre (*Collected Essays* IV: 229–35).

12. In contrast, she considered "unreasonable" the request from J. Pierpont Morgan's family through Donald Brace, her American publisher, that she delete Fry's two references, in passages she had quoted, to Morgan's mistresses.

13. It is possible that Woolf made these changes herself in a typescript subsequent to this one and prior to the one Margery Fry read. In this case, the kinds of changes would indicate an intense awareness of the family audience. More likely, however, the changes point to a family member or members who expressed a desire for a more complex representation of Roger Fry's family.

14. Fry's memoirs are in King's College Library, Cambridge.

15. Here, and in the examples that follow, *TS* refers to the Berg typescript and *1E* to the first English edition, while my editorial remarks are in parenthesis. The differences between the two versions are signaled by boldface type. Woolf's holograph insertions are in square brackets.

16. Another good example of Woolf's use in the Fry biography of memoir material intended for reading to the Memoir Club is Clive Bell's *Roger Fry: Anecdotes, for the use of a future biographer . . .*, which I was not able to include as an appendix to the Shakespeare Head Press Edition but which I have published separately. Another potential appendix I edited and published separately is a sketch by Woolf entitled *Roger Fry: A Series of Impressions*; an effort perhaps closer to what she would have liked to have done in memory of Fry's life had she not found herself responsible for a full-length biography.

17. Rosenbaum briefly discusses Woolf's deletion in the larger context of Bloomsbury education in *Victorian Bloomsbury*, pp. 102–3.

18. As Reid notes, Woolf had found an application of Freud appended to a 1919 letter from Fry to Vanessa Bell: "Virginia's anal and you're erotic." (419)

19. I am indebted for this idea – although the application to *Roger Fry* is my own – to Neverow, "Defying".

20. As Spalding notes (47–8), the woman was Mrs Cecelia Widdrington.

21. Fry's allusion is to David's escape from Saul and his gathering of the discontented men of the region into the cave Adullam (I Samuel 22: 1; see Sutton II: 373 n. 1).

22. The "older artists", including William Rothenstein, who in the typescript "refused to co-operate with" Fry to mount the second Post-Impressionist Exhibition, become in one instance in the published version "the older artists" who "held aloof" (1E: 169; *Roger Fry*: 136). Examples of those who charged

Fry with having been part of "a mutual admiration society" are named in the typescript: "M. Jacques Blanche and Sir William Rothenstein". The names are crossed out, however, and the "some observers" of the published version are added (1E: 293; *Roger Fry*: 241).

23. Daugherty documents the change from "the late 1960s and 1970s" when Woolf scholars tended to define her revising as loss to more recent critics who, "though often taking a 'bi-directional' view, emphasize Woolf's revising as gain, imply a more positive relationship with the reader, and portray Woolf as having more agency". (168–9)

24. Neverow argues persuasively, like Jane Marcus before her, for tracing "*Three Guineas* to its sources" in "Tak[ing] our stand openly . . . " (22).

25. As Cole says, "Obviously everyone has parts where they don't need notes & that's very easy to deal with. At the bottom of a page it's so difficult to ignore notes . . . .placed at the end, you can more easily be selective."

26. The Hogarth Press reissued *Roger Fry* in 1991, the only change from the 1940 edition being a new introduction by Frances Spalding.

27. Shone, for instance, refers to the "extensive notes" which he also says are "fascinating and take into account Woolf's working papers, annotations and preliminary drafts" (51–2). See also Bull who, irritated because Woolf's status has precipitated such a "meticulously annotated" edition of her biography of Fry when "almost all Fry's writings remain unread and (at least in Britain) unavailable" (12), writes an essay on Fry instead a review of the edition. Stansky who counts pages of notes and, while he says it is "a splendid job" and expresses gratitude for much "is invaluable and vastly enriches the text", still thinks I may have done "a bit too much" (6).

28. Daiches early sets the tone of heavily qualified praise when he says that "the book, though written in a style at once simple and sensitive, lacks that final touch of artistry which the reader expects from her work" (151).

29. For a fuller discussion of the "*menage a trois* (Vanessa/Roger/Virginia)" Woolf creates in *Roger Fry* and Woolf's simultaneous appropriation of Fry from Vanessa and the gift of Fry to her, see my "The Biographer and the Self in *Roger Fry*".

30. McFarland notes that "the three greatest biographies in English are usually considered to be Boswell's *Life of Johnson*, Lockhart's *Life of Scott*, and Froude's *Life of Carlyle*", none of which are annotated by their authors. McFarland mentions several biographical essays, among them Leslie Stephen's essay on Coleridge (*Hours in a Library*), that also avoid the annotations that "would tend to disperse their intensity" (156–7). J. G. Lockhart's *Memoirs of Sir Walter Scott* (1882), was a gift to Virginia Stephen from her father in 1897. Woolf's experience of these books would have been different from that of their original audience and, whatever her decisions about annotation may have been, she had an intense awareness of the relation between reader and text. She owned Leslie Stephen's copies of Froude's *James Anthony Thomas Carlyle: A History of His Life in London, 1834–1881* (1884) and Boswell's *The Life of Samuel Johnson* (1876), both with notes and comments by her father, an inveterate writer in the books he owned. Her father's edition of Boswell's *Life* already contained numerous additions by John Wilson Croker and had been revised and enlarged by John Wright. Woolf's copy of *Hours in a Library* also has her father's notes and corrections of his own writing. All of these are in

Manuscripts, Archives and Special Collections at Washington State University, Pullman.

31. I too welcome corrections, solicited or unsolicited. Shone has found one failure in my "indefatigable sleuthing after dates and identities" (52); Spalding alerts readers to two more (3). Clarke has sent me "a very small list of corrections" (letter, February 23, 1996).

32. Briggs cites the example of the reference in *Between the Acts* to the rape of a woman lured by members of the guard at Whitehall to a barrack room to see a horse with a green tail. One annotator (Frank Kermode) identifies White-hall while another (Gillian Beer) was able to cite Stuart Clarke's article on the actual incident, much in the previous year's newspapers, and, in so doing, place Woolf's allusion in the context of women's issues of the time (including not only rape, but also a subequent abortion) ("Editing Woolf", 72).

33. In addition to her positive response to the early Shakespeare Head Press editions in general, Marcus thinks that the Penguin editions, in spite of their "nineties" approach, are "built to last" (18). A comparative analysis of the other post-1992 British editions of Woolf's works is beyond the scope of this essay. Attempts have been made by others, however, notably Briggs ("Editing Woolf", "The Story"), Marcus, and Johnson.

34. "No annotation is neutral", Derrida, for example, says "annotation, directly or indirectly, can express judgments, give advice, or provide an order for reading . . . ; they can constitute a sort of ethics or politics of interpretation". (196)

35. Ironically, the recent editions of Woolf's works called "definitive" by Random-Century (now owners of The Hogarth Press) are for the most part reprintings with new jackets and introductions.

6

A Book She Never Made: Editing
The Complete Shorter Fiction of
Virginia Woolf

Susan Dick

Leonard Woolf began his work as the editor of Virginia Woolf's posthumous publications with *Between the Acts*. This appeared in July 1941, just four months after his wife's death. *Between the Acts* was followed by *The Death of the Moth and Other Essays*, and then by *A Haunted House and Other Short Stories*. In the Foreword to this collection, he explained that in 1940 Virginia Woolf had decided to publish a collection of short stories. This would have included most of the works in *Monday or Tuesday*, the only book of short fiction she had published, some stories that had appeared in magazines, and some unpublished ones. He was now, he said, fulfilling her intentions. *A Haunted House* contained six of the eight pieces from *Monday or Tuesday* (he knew she wanted to omit "A Society" and was quite certain she also meant to exclude "Blue & Green"), seven stories that had been published in periodicals, and five previously unpublished stories.[1]

For nearly thirty years most readers assumed that Virginia Woolf's short fiction was limited to these eighteen stories. Then in 1973, Stella McNichol published *Mrs. Dalloway's Party: A Short Story Sequence*. This contained seven stories: "Mrs. Dalloway in Bond Street" (a short story published in *The Dial* in 1923 but not included in *A Haunted House*), four stories from *A Haunted House*, and *Two Stories* that had not been published before. *Mrs. Dalloway's Party*, which had an introduction but provided no bibliographical information about the texts of the stories, appeared during a decade that marked a turning-point in Woolf scholarship. In 1972, Quentin Bell published his two-volume biography of Woolf, in which he made use of a great deal of unpublished manuscript material. Soon other scholars could consult this material in the Berg Collection of the New York Public Library and the Monks House Papers at the University of Sussex, the two repositories of the majority of Woolf's manuscripts. Carefully edited volumes of her letters and her diary began to appear, along with editions of the holograph drafts of *The Waves*, a portion of *The Years*, and *Moments of Being*, Woolf's autobiographical writings. Interest in Woolf's life and work was growing and the editorial standards applied to her writings were becoming increasingly rigoros.

Questions that had been raised about the texts of the stories in *Mrs. Dalloway's Party* led to my going in 1983 to the Berg Collection to compare McNichol's texts with the manuscripts (Hulcoop; McNichol). I found there not only holograph and typescript drafts of many of the stories in *A Haunted House* and *Mrs. Dalloway's Party*, but also drafts of eight unpublished stories. At Sussex I found among the Monks House Papers additional drafts of stories in the Berg as well as drafts of yet more unpublished stories. There were in all 28 complete unpublished stories by Woolf.[2] The earliest of these, "Phyllis and Rosamond," was written in 1906; the latest, "The Watering Place", in 1941, about three weeks before her death.

A pattern in the posthumous publication of Woolf's writings was by 1983 well established. Editions of selections of her essays, letters, and diary had been or were in the process of being replaced by complete editions of those writings. Also, draft versions of her novels continued to be published. The Hogarth Press readily agreed to publish a complete edition of Woolf's short fiction, one that would include both the previously unpublished stories and sketches and those already published.

What, in this context, did "complete" mean? Like her long fiction, Woolf's short fiction is experimental and thus challenges the conventions of the genre. I took as my standards the works Woolf had herself published as short fiction: the eight pieces in *Monday or Tuesday*, and the ten others she had published separately between 1918 and 1939. The range among these 18 works is great. There are reveries ("The Mark on the Wall", "An Unwritten Novel"), prose poems ("Blue & Green", "Monday or Tuesday"), impressionist pieces inspired by a place or event ("A Haunted House", "The String Quartet"), narratives shaped by the rhythm of repetition ("Kew Gardens", "In the Orchard"), narratives that focus on characters over a brief segment of time ("Mrs. Dalloway in Bond Street", "The New Dress"), or a long one ("The Duchess and the Jeweller"), and narratives that place characters within a well-delineated plot with a beginning, middle, and end ("Solid Objects", "Lappin and Lapinova"). The unpublished stories also fall into these broad and overlapping categories.

All the works included share two characteristics: they are short and they are primarily fiction. The second characteristic may seem as obvious as the first, but it can at times be difficult to decide whether a work by Woolf is, for example, a fanciful biography (that is, more fact than fiction), or a work of fiction cast as a biography and making use of biographical facts. Booksellers faced this question when *Orlando* was published. I excluded "Old Mrs. Grey", for example, which Leonard Woolf published in *The Death of the Moth*, because a passage in Woolf's diary led me to assume that it was a portrait of an actual person. Similarly, I excluded the unpublished "The Cook", which according to Quentin Bell and the evidence of Woolf's diary and memoirs, was a portrait of the Stephen family cook, Sophie Farrell. While most of Woolf's stories contain details drawn from her life, I considered as fictional those in which the scenes, characters, and events were not primarily biographical or autobiographical.

It was also necessary to make a distinction between personal essays, such as "To Spain", "Gas", or "The Moment: Summer's Night", and other short pieces, such as "Three Pictures" and "The Fascination of the Pool", which closely resemble them. I again used the dominant presence in them of fictional scenes, characters, or events as the deciding factor.

Since I intended to establish the text of each story, it was important at an early stage to ensure that I had located not only all of Woolf's existing short fiction, but also all the drafts of the 46 works in my preliminary table of contents. Although the majority of Woolf's manuscripts are in the New York and Sussex collections, some were sold or given to other libraries and some were still at that time in the possession of Quentin Bell. My enquiries turned up no new separate works, but some additional pages of the untitled series of "Portraits" were found by Anne Olivier Bell among their papers. Eventually I had before me a stack of over four hundred photocopies of Woolf's holograph and typescript drafts, received from five libraries and one private collection in England and the United States.

In neither *A Haunted House* nor *Mrs. Dalloway's Party* were the stories arranged in chronological order. Leonard Woolf placed the six stories from *Monday or Tuesday* first, followed by the seven that had been published in periodicals (which he did not arrange in order of publication), followed by the five previously unpublished works, also not arranged chronologically. I decided to place Woolf's short fiction in chronological order, for I felt that this arrangement would contribute most to our understanding of both Woolf's development as a writer and the important role her short fiction played in that development. Works she had published would be placed by their date of publication unless I could determine that they had been written at an earlier date. Unpublished works would be placed according to the date of the latest draft. Thus the unpublished works would not be separated from the more polished published ones.

Many factors came into play as I worked on this arrangement. Seven of the unpublished stories were dated by Woolf. These, along with those she had published, served as benchmarks for dating the others. In addition, the holograph drafts of other works – such as *Jacob's Room* and *Mrs. Dalloway* – notes she made in various manuscript books, and especially the eleven volumes of Woolf's detailed diary and letters, all helped me to evolve a kind of biography of the short fiction. The earliest story in the edition, for example, now known as "Phyllis and Rosamond", has a date in place of a title at the top of its first page: "Wed. June 20–23rd 1906". The same date occurs in the third paragraph. The undated story "The Mysterious Case of Miss V." closely resembles "Phyllis and Rosamond": both are written in black ink on large sheets of white paper in Virginia Stephen's small, spiky handwriting. Also, in both stories, which are studies of the lives of women in contemporary London, the narrator speaks at the beginning from the perspective of a social historian. The same perspective and tone are found in many of Woolf's 1906 journal entries and in the long undated, untitled story known as "The Journal of Mistress Joan Martyn", which Woolf's letters and biography also indicate was written in the summer of 1906.

Several times during her career Woolf wrote stories in clusters, as she appears to have done in 1906. One of the most complex and interwoven of these is the group of short works she wrote between 1916 and the publication of *Monday or Tuesday* in 1921. In the summer of 1916, while recovering from her severe mental breakdown of 1915, Woolf began her second novel, *Night and Day*. She later told Ethel Smyth that she wrote this long realist work, which she likened to copying "from plaster casts, partly to tranquillise, partly to learn anatomy" (*LIV*: 231). Some of the "little pieces" published in *Monday or Tuesday*, she added, "were written by way of diversion; they were the treats I allowed myself when I had done my exercise in the conventional style". One of these was "The Mark on the Wall", which she told Smyth she wrote "all in a flash, as if flying, after being kept stone breaking for months". In July 1917, "The Mark on the Wall" became, along with Leonard Woolf's story, "Three Jews", the first publication of The Hogarth Press, *Two Stories*. In thanking David Garnett for praising "The Mark on the Wall", Woolf wrote, "In a way its easier to do a short thing, all in one flight than a novel. Novels are frightfully clumsy and overpowering of course; still if one could only get hold of them it would be superb. I daresay one ought to invent a completely new form." (*LII*: 167)

While she continued to write *Night and Day*, which she would submit to George Duckworth in April 1919, she was clearly enthusiastic about the potential of the "short things" she was also writing and about the freedom The Hogarth Press gave her to publish these without the intervention of editors or publishers (*LII*: 167). She was also happy to be collaborating with Vanessa Bell, who illustrated "Kew Gardens" (probably begun by Woolf in August 1917), which The Hogarth Press published in May 1919. References to several of the stories of this period in letters to Vanessa Bell helped to establish their chronological sequence. In one written on July 26, 1918, for example, Woolf returned Vanessa Bell's illustration for "Kew Gardens" and wrote, "I hope you will do as many more as you can both for that story, and for the one about the party" (*LII*: 262). This piece of evidence enabled me to place the writing of the unpublished, undated story, "The Evening Party", in the summer of 1918. The story also seemed to belong to this period because the two typescript drafts resembled others that could be dated. Further, like most of the other short fiction Woolf was writing in 1918, "The Evening Party" reflects her desire to break the "plaster casts" she was copying in *Night and Day* and find a new form for fiction. The opening paragraphs are written in the poetic style which she took to extremes in "Monday or Tuesday" and "Blue & Green" and would perfect in her novels. These paragraphs especially bring *The Waves* to mind as this sentence which closes the second one illustrates: "The room is full of vivid yet unsubstantial figures; they stand upright before shelves striped with innumerable little volumes; their heads and shoulders blot the corners of square golden picture frames; and the bulk of their bodies, smooth like stone statues, is massed against something grey, tumultuous, shining too as if with water beyond the uncurtained windows" (*CSF*: 96–7). The rest of the narrative is an intense, sometimes cryptic conversation among unidentified people at a party.

The other undated, unpublished story of this period is "Sympathy". In it the narrator recreates her immediate response to a newspaper announcement of the unexpected death of a friend. The date of his death is April 29, which the narrator says was a Tuesday. This date, along with the similarities among the typescripts of "Sympathy", "The Evening Party", and "Kew Gardens", led me to believe that the story was written in the spring of 1919, when April 29 fell on a Tuesday. Also, the narrative of "Sympathy" closely resembles that of both "The Mark on the Wall" and another work of this period, "An Unwritten Novel". All three are shaped by tracing the immediate reflections of a narrator who is responding to an object, person, or event that has suddenly come into her life.

There was additional evidence to consider in dating "The Evening Party" and "Sympathy", and discussion of that brings me to *Jacob's Room*, Woolf's first experimental novel. Many links exist between the short fiction of this period and *Jacob's Room*, which Woolf began to write in April 1920. The idea for it came to her in January of that year: " . . . conceive mark on the wall, K[ew]. G[ardens]. & unwritten novel taking hands & dancing in unity", she wrote on January 26, as she described the "idea of a new form for a new novel" she had just envisaged (*DII*: 13–14). She was probably writing "An Unwritten Novel", which was published in the *London Mercury* in July 1920, at this time. She continued to write short fiction after she began to work on *Jacob's Room*. In January 1921, she interrupted the first draft of the novel to write a portion of "The String Quartet" (published in *Monday or Tuesday*) and several short sketches. One of these was called "A Death in the Newspaper", which was a reworked, extremely condensed version of "Sympathy". Woolf revised three of the short sketches in the *Jacob's Room* manuscript, including "A Death in the Newspaper", and grouped them in an unpublished work she called "Cracked Fiddles". The fourth short work in "Cracked Fiddles", "The Evening Party" (which she placed first), is the evocative two-paragraph opening of the longer version of the story. The first two pages of the second typescript draft of the longer version are missing and must have been removed by Woolf when she assembled "Cracked Fiddles". A comparison of the two typescript drafts of "Sympathy" with the holograph and two typescript drafts of "A Death in the Newspaper" in "Cracked Fiddles" shows a pattern of revision which indicates clearly that here, too, the longer work was written before the shorter version.

In arranging the eleven stories in the "1917–1921" section, I relied on both internal and external evidence. The four stories published before *Monday or Tuesday* and the two unpublished stories that seemed to have been written before it, preceded the five stories that had appeared only in that collection. These five were arranged according to their order in *Monday or Tuesday*. I placed "Cracked Fiddles" in an appendix since much of it derived from *Two Stories* in the main body of the collection. This was the most extensive group of stories in *The Complete Shorter Fiction*, and the trickiest to arrange.

By contrast, the group of stories set at *Mrs. Dalloway's Party* was written over a short period of time and the order of their composition was relatively easy to determine. These eight stories evolved from a plan Woolf had sketched out as she was completing *Jacob's Room* in 1922. She thought her next book would be made up of short separate chapters, each of which would be complete. The first of these, "Mrs. Dalloway in Bond Street", soon "branched into a book", however (*DII*: 207), and the second chapter, "The Prime Minister", was left unfinished (*CSF*: 316ff). As she was completing *Mrs. Dalloway* in the spring of 1925, she began to think again of writing a series of stories. These would be set at Mrs. Dalloway's Party and would function as a "corridor" leading to another book (this became *To the Lighthouse*, which she began to write in August). The "Notes for Stories" in her notebook include two lists of titles; a third list appears in another notebook that contains drafts of the stories. The order of the drafts matches the order of the titles on Woolf's lists. Thus in arranging these stories chronologically, only one of which, "The New Dress", she had published, I followed the order of the titles on her lists. The *Two Stories* that intervene in the collection between "Mrs. Dalloway in Bond Street" and the earliest of the other Dalloway stories, "The New Dress", are children's stories. The first draft of "Nurse Lugton's Curtain" appears in the holograph of *Mrs. Dalloway* and was probably written in the autumn of 1924. I could not date "The Widow and the Parrot: A True Story" so precisely, but since it had appeared in *The Charleston Bulletin*, a comic family magazine produced by the Bell children in the 1920s (Lee, 48), I placed it with the other children's story.

Two other lists proved useful for dating a later story, "Scenes from the Life of a British Naval Officer". In a bound exercise book, dated June 1931, entitled "Additions to Waves, &c. Fragments of possible stories. Corrections & Additions to Second Common Reader", Woolf wrote: "Caricatures. 1. The Shooting Party. 2. Scenes from English life. The pheasants. Scenes: Life on a Battleship". These notes are followed by the holograph draft of the opening pages of "The Shooting Party", dated January 19. In another notebook, following some notes dated February 1932, and headed, "Revising Second Common Reader", Woolf wrote, "Caricatures Country House Life, The Royal Navy, The Great Jeweller". The earliest of the two typescript drafts of "The Shooting Party", dated January 19, 1932, has on its separate title page, "CARICATURES: Country House Life". Although the typescript drafts of "The Duchess and the Jeweller" and "Scenes from the Life of a British Naval Officer" are undated, it seems likely that they were also written early in 1932. The three stories do not appear together in the collection, however. The unpublished "Scenes" was placed according to its probable date of composition, early 1932, and the other two stories according to when, as we know from her diary and letters, Woolf revised them in 1937 for publication in *Harper's Bazaar*.

Establishing the texts of the stories in the collection was the other major challenge of the edition. My sources varied a good deal. Only the published texts exist for eight of the 18 stories published by Woolf. One of these, "The Mark on the Wall", appeared three times (1917, 1919, 1921) and another, "An Unwritten Novel", twice (1920, 1921). She revised both stories when she reprinted them, and the revised versions were the ones I used. The most extensive variants were given in the notes. Her revisions in both stories took the form of deletions. For example, in the 1917 version of "The Mark on the Wall" the narrator says of the previous owners of the house: "She wore a flannel dog collar round her throat, and he drew posters for an oatmeal company, and they wanted to leave this house...." In the 1919 version "dog" is removed; in 1921, the entire passage disappears and "they wanted to leave this house..." becomes the beginning of a new sentence (*CSF*: 83). The most interesting and extensive deletions from "The Mark on the Wall" are two paragraphs Woolf removed when she reprinted it in *Monday or Tuesday* in which the narrator complains of her housekeeper, who has the "profile of a police-man" and whose social pretensions she finds menacing (*CSF*: 297). Perhaps Woolf later felt that this servant resembled too closely the eccentric Maud who cleaned for them in 1915 and whose "secret obsession", Woolf suspected, was "that she is a lady" (*DI*: 31).

Typescript and in some cases holograph drafts of the other ten stories published by Woolf exist. These provided useful information about the evolution of the stories, but generally did not affect the texts, since I assumed the published versions were the latest ones. In one instance I was, however, tempted to modify my method. An entire paragraph occurs in the typescript of "Kew Gardens" that is not in the story as Woolf published it, twice in 1919, a third time in *Monday or Tuesday*, and a fourth time in 1927. Although it is probable that Woolf overlooked the omitted paragraph, since there is no indication on the typescript, which contains holograph revisions, that she intended to cancel it, I could not assume that it was omitted by mistake, partly because she had several opportunities to restore it. So it too was placed in the notes.

The decisions that had to be made about the unpublished works were frequently much more complex. In most cases Woolf had not prepared these for publication. As Leonard Woolf wrote in his Foreword to *A Haunted House*, when the idea for a story came to her, it was "her custom ... to sketch it out in a very rough form and then to put it away in a drawer". Later, she might take it out and revise it for publication. Only four of the 28 unpublished works, "Memoirs of a Novelist", "The Searchlight", "Gipsy, the Mongrel", and "The Legacy", had reached that final stage. For eight of the unpublished stories there is only one type-script; for four there is only a single holograph draft. But for 15 there exist multiple drafts. (There was only a published text for "Three Pictures", which Leonard Woolf had included in *The Death of the Moth*.)

Woolf's first drafts are like the underpainting upon which a finished picture takes shape. The incremental process of revision began on the first drafts themselves, which are filled with cancellations, sentence fragments, and interlinear and marginal revisions. She clearly knew that the first draft was just the beginning of the writing process. Transcribing and editing these drafts was fascinating work. When there were multiple typescripts of a story, I could order them by studying the revisions, for a change that appeared in holograph in one draft would often appear typed in the next. Some typescript drafts are made up of pages from several drafts. Especially in her later years, Woolf seems to have needed to type a complete new copy of a story at each stage of revision. The files of the late story "The Legacy", for example, contain a holograph, two complete typescripts, and fragments from at least six typescript drafts, totaling 48 pages of material, only 11 of which are the final version of the story. It is no wonder Woolf was annoyed when *Harper's Bazaar*, which had requested the story, failed to publish it (*LVI*: 463, 469).

When establishing the text of a story, I incorporated into my tran-scription all the revisions Woolf had made in the version I had decided was the latest. I was deeply aware as I did this that I was making what appeared to be a finished text out of one that was actually a work in progress. I was also aware that the choices I made as I deciphered Woolf's revisions were not necessarily those Woolf, or another editor, would make. Her revisions are often sketchy and difficult to read, the sort of notes most writers make to themselves in anticipation of further revi-sions. In a critical edition, all variants would be recorded, but there was not room for such full documentation in this collection, whose intended audience was common readers as well as scholars. When words or punc-tuation needed to be added for the sake of clarity, they were placed within brackets; words I was unsure of were enclosed within brackets and followed by a question mark. The addition of conventional punctu-ation (full stops, opening or closing quotation marks, and so on), which Woolf often overlooked as she wrote or typed, and the correction of obvious typing errors were done without comment. Some unconventional punctuation was left alone, however. Woolf often uses colons and semicolons where another writer might choose either a comma or a full stop. These affect the rhythm of her prose and were not changed. Also, occasionally words within a series are not separated by commas, as in this phrase from "Happiness:" ". . . on one's high swift safe sledge" (*CSF*: 179). The rhythm of the sentence would be altered if commas were added. Selected variant passages were placed in the notes, along with the bibliographical history of each text. I hoped that these details would remind readers that a text that looked on the page as though it had been finished had in fact been left by Woolf unrevised. The locations of all the manuscript drafts were given in a bibliographical summary at the end of the book.

I can illustrate some of these issues with "A Summing Up", the last of the Dalloway stories. The final three pages of a holograph draft and a five-page typescript with holograph revisions exist. Leonard Woolf included this story in *A Haunted House*, and some of the writing on the typescript is his. He explains in his editorial note to *The Death of the Moth* that he regularly went over his wife's manuscripts before they were published, making small verbal corrections and adding punctuation. In this story, for example, he is probably the source of many of the commas added in holograph to the typescript. (His handwriting can usually be distinguished from hers, but not small marks, such as commas.) He also habitually wrote over revisions Woolf had made which he probably felt the printer would find hard to decipher. In one passage in "A Summing Up", he also made a correction of his own. Virginia Woolf had typed: "But then Bertram putting his arm through hers in his familiar way for they had known her all her life remarked that they were not doing their duty and must go in". Besides adding commas after "Bertram", "way", and "life", Leonard Woolf crossed out "they" and wrote "he" above it, making the phrase read "for he had known her all her life". I felt that Leonard Woolf had a special role as editor of his wife's works and I included this correction without comment.

Both Leonard Woolf and Stella McNichol assumed that "A Summing Up" ended with the paragraph that comes at the bottom of page 5, the last page of the typescript. The final page of the holograph fragment, however, contains a one-sentence paragraph that brings the story to a significantly different close. In it, Sasha Latham, who in the previous paragraph has been imagining her soul as a bird soaring away, is brought back by her companion's trivial words to the mundane world of the party: "It now appeared that during the conversation to which Sasha had scarcely listened, Bertram had come to the conclusion that he liked Mr Wallace, but disliked his wife – who was 'very clever, no doubt'"

(*CSF*: 211). This sentence nicely rounds the story out and repeats the rhythm of escape and return that shapes all the stories in the group. Since it seemed possible that a sixth page of the typescript had gone missing, I decided to include the ending from the holograph draft and to explain its source in the notes.

The most fragmented of the unpublished works is "Portraits", which is made up of eight short sketches. On February 19, 1937, Woolf wrote in her diary that she and Vanessa Bell were discussing a collaborative book of illustrated incidents. On February 21, she recorded that she had "done" eight incidents; three days later she mentioned writing "Faces & Voices" (*DV*: 58–61). After that, no further reference is made to the project. Eight sketches, preserved in two collections, appear to be these "incidents". They were typed on a mixture of blue paper and white paper; some were stapled together; and they all resemble another sketch, quite confidently placed in this time frame, called "Uncle Vanya". There are two drafts of two of the portraits (the earlier blue, the later white) and only single drafts of the others (four blue, two white). One is called "Portrait 3", and I used it as the basis for ordering the others and for the title of the work as a whole. I arranged the eight portraits in a way that makes a progression in setting from France to England, and a change in tone from the crisp and lively diction of the first sketches to the more somber individualized voices heard in the later ones. While she worked on these portraits, Woolf was awaiting the publication of *The Years*, and as in 1917, she seems to have felt the need to write freely and extravagantly after being tied to another long and burdensome realist novel.

A word needs to be said about the notes in the edition. Besides giving the relevant biographical and bibliographical information about each story, along with occasional variant passages, the notes contain annotations. These identify historical figures and events, writers, artists, and so on, with which I thought readers might be unfamiliar. They also give the sources of quotations and allusions and explain details readers might find obscure. The latter often remind us that, although Woolf died during the Second World War, she lived the first 18 years of her life in the nineteenth century. One example of the historical context that she knew first-hand, but which most modern readers will need explained, occurs in "Portrait 6". The speaker, who says he wishes he had been born in the 1880s, refers to London "bus drivers wearing the Rothschild pheasants slung on their whips" (*CSF*: 245). This puzzling image is clarified once one knows, as Woolf remembered from her childhood, that during the Christmas season the Rothschilds gave pheasants to the bus drivers who drove past their houses in Piccadilly. They acknowledged the gifts by decorating their whips and bell cords, not with pheasants, as the speaker thinks, but with ribbons of blue and amber, the Rothschild racing colors (*Moments of Being*: 121).

The major omissions from the annotations are notes that point out passages in the stories that are echoed in Woolf's longer fiction and essays. In "The Evening Party", for instance, the speaker recalls a moment during childhood when "as one stepped across the puddle or reached the window on the landing, some imperceptible shock froze the universe to a solid ball of crystal which one held for a moment – I have some mystical belief that all time past and future too, the tears and powdered ashes of generations clotted to a ball; then we were absolute and entire; nothing then was excluded; that was certainty – happiness" (*CSF*: 98). The passage compellingly foreshadows two of Rhoda's visions in *The Waves* (41, 145), as well as Woolf's description in "A Sketch of the Past" of one of the "Moments of Being" she experienced as a child (*Moments of Being*: 78). Another, less resonant, example is the narrator's realization near the end of "The Lady in the Looking-Glass: A Reflection", that Isabella's letters "were all bills" (*CSF*: 225). The same is said of Isa in *Between the Acts*, who "had only bills" (252). There simply was not enough room in the edition to note all such echoes. The pleasure of finding them is left to the reader.

Leonard Woolf said in his Foreword to *A Haunted House* that he felt "some hesitation" in publishing stories Virginia Woolf had not finally revised. I certainly shared this feeling. Woolf would undoubtedly have revised all the unpublished stories, many extensively, before she published them. Indeed, there is no way of knowing how many of these unpublished stories she would have wanted to publish at all. Leonard Woolf's hesitation made him conservative in his choice of stories to include in *A Haunted House*, but it did not stop him from publishing the collection. With the earlier publication of *Between the Acts*, he had established a precedent that he and later editors would follow. He had also begun to nurture an enthusiastic audience of common readers and scholars who continue to welcome the publication of previously unpublished fiction, essays, diaries, and letters of Virginia Woolf, not only for their high quality, but also for what they tell us about a remarkable writer. The previously unpublished works in *The Complete Shorter Fiction* highlight especially the playful side of Woolf and the great range of her experiments with narrative and language. She tries out techniques in these stories that are not used in any of her other writings, as we see vividly, for example, in the comic poem, "Ode Written Partly in Prose on Seeing the Name of Cutbush Above a Butcher's Shop in Pentonville". Thus even the incomplete stories and sketches, which were added to the second edition, enhance our appreciation of Virginia Woolf's unprecedented achievement.

Notes

1. In his Foreword to the first edition of *A Haunted House*, Leonard Woolf said he thought "Moments of Being: 'Slater's Pins Have No Points'" had been published, but since he could find no record of it, he was printing it from the typescript. It had appeared in *Forum* in January 1928, and although he states this in later editions, he continued to reprint the typescript version, which differs from the *Forum* version at several points (see *The Complete Shorter Fiction of Virginia Woolf* [hereafter *CSF*] 9–10, 215–20).
2. In 1987 S. P. Rosenbaum found "A Dialogue Upon Mount Pentelicus" to be complete. It was included in the 1989 enlarged edition of *CSF*. Thus there were 27 previously unpublished stories in the 1985 edition and 28 in the 1989 edition, to which ten incomplete stories and sketches were also added.

7
Text and Counter-Text: Trying to Recover *Mrs. Dalloway*

Morris Beja

> What was she trying to recover?...
> Ever so many books there were; but none that seemed exactly
> right....
>
> *Mrs. Dalloway* (Shakespeare Head Press, 9–10)

Traditionally a textual editor, even while recognizing the wisdom of being aware that no book, no edition, will ever be "exactly right", nevertheless presumably strives to make it so and attempts to recover – or uncover or discover – the book itself, the literary work as it may best be presented to the reader.

In these reflections on the preparation of a scholarly edition of *Mrs. Dalloway*, let me start with a personal note. Over the years during which I worked on that edition, a bit to my own surprise I never felt that I was becoming a Melvillian "sub-sub librarian", some "mere painstaking burrower and grub-worm of a poor devil of a Sub-Sub" (*Moby-Dick*: ix). Perhaps I deceived myself. In any case, I did often wonder how much the fascination I ended up developing with textual editing itself would have come about, or in contrast faded rather quickly, had I not been increasingly convinced that I was working on and with one of the truly major works of fiction in the English language. Immersing myself in the details of Woolf's novel only enhanced my awe of her achievement. But I was also encouraged by my growing and intensified realization that there was a genuine *need* for a good edition.

Of course, nowadays one possibility would have been to produce not an old-fashioned book as such, but a digital or hypertext version (or multiple hypertext versions) of *Mrs. Dalloway*. I hope that someday such a hypertext, in a CD-Rom format, or on line, or in some yet-to-be-developed technology, will indeed come about. The value of such a

project – which could include both first editions, the surviving sets of
proofs, and perhaps facsimiles or transcripts of the extant manuscripts
as well – would be immense. But the result would not be the "book", at
least not in the traditional sense of that term. A hypertext may be an
aid in reading the book; or beyond that it may be an alternative to the
book itself (and for some indeed a preferable alternative). In the end,
however, it is not the book, and retrograde that I am, that would seem
to me a major disadvantage: only one disadvantage but in itself a cardinal
and even insurmountable one.

Still, a major benefit of such an electronically generated project is that
it would provide scholars and critics with all that would be needed to
enable them, as it were, to come up with their own "editions", by in effect
providing what a number of Woolf scholars have called in a frequent
trope a "palimpsest" of the entire work in all its available or discernible
versions.[1] Some textual scholars regard that process as not only extremely
valuable but as, in fact, the only appropriate goal of an editor. I disagree,
although let me reiterate my realization that such a goal is extremely
appropriate for a project aimed primarily or solely at literary and textual
scholars. I hope, and in my hubris believe, that the Shakespeare Head
Press edition of *Mrs. Dalloway* addresses their needs (and their curiosity,
too), but those needs and that curiosity were not foremost or absolutely
primary in my mind in preparing the actual text, as distinct from the
apparatus and scholarly defenses that also appear in the same volume.
For, at the risk of offending some of my closest friends, I would argue
that the literary scholar is not the single most important reader of
Virginia Woolf, the one whose needs we must keep uppermost in mind.
That reader is, to coin a phrase, the common reader, the person who
does not want to put a book together, but to read one.

Every novel tells a story, but it also has its own story – the story of its
creation and publication. The particular need for a new and scholarly
edition of *Mrs. Dalloway* came about from its publishing history. What
became the novel had begun by the spring of 1922 with a short story,
"Mrs. Dalloway in Bond Street", centering on Clarissa Dalloway, who had
appeared as a secondary character in Woolf's first novel, *The Voyage Out*.
The short story – the first line of which was "Mrs Dalloway said she
would buy the gloves herself" – was published in *The Dial* in July 1922
(*Complete Shorter Fiction*: 152). By then Woolf was already thinking of
expanding the material into a book that she at first contemplated calling
At Home: or The Party. She seems to have envisioned a work of related
stories rather than a "novel" as such: "a short book consisting of six or
seven chapters, each complete separately", though "all must converge

upon the party at the end."[2] Soon, by October 1922, she wrote in her diary that "Mrs Dalloway has branched into a book; & I adumbrate here a study of insanity & suicide: the world seen by the sane & the insane side by side – something like that. Septimus Smith? – is that a good name?" (*DII*: 207). In one of the stories she was writing around her central idea, "The Prime Minister", she planned to have Septimus commit suicide only after having killed the Prime Minister (*Complete Shorter Fiction*: 322).

We have several short stories Woolf wrote centering on Clarissa Dalloway's party and also have parts of the manuscript for *Mrs. Dalloway* itself, in the Berg Collection of the New York Public Library and in the British Library. (The latter manuscripts take up where those in the Berg Collection end, after Peter Walsh's visit to Clarissa's home in the morning.) An extremely useful and fascinating edition of the British Library manuscripts, and the relevant material in the Berg Collection, has been published as *The Hours*. When *Mrs. Dalloway* was published, for the first time in Woolf's career her novel appeared simultaneously in England and the United States, in 1925 (as did, incidentally, *The Common Reader*). Woolf had finished a typescript of *Mrs. Dalloway* late in 1924, and Leonard Woolf had read it by January 1925, when it was sent to the printers. (That typescript is now lost.) Woolf received three sets of proofs very shortly after that, one to be used for The Hogarth Press edition in England, one for the Harcourt Brace edition in the United States, and one for herself. (What happened to the latter copy is interesting and will come into my discussion shortly.)

Two of the sets of marked proofs are extant and available. Because publication of *Mrs. Dalloway* was simultaneous on both sides of the Atlantic, Harcourt for the first time was unable to set its edition from an already published English text. Consequently, Woolf had to correct two sets of proof, presumably at or around the same time, although it has been cogently argued that she worked on the Harcourt set first.[3] Those proofs are now in the Lilly Library, Indiana University. The Hogarth proofs have not survived, presumably having been destroyed during the Second World War. (But I find myself particularly if perversely fascinated with the possibility that they and other sets of proofs were in fact used by the Woolfs as toilet paper [Bell, II, 123].) Woolf did, in any case, also make some limited corrections in her own set of proofs. In a major departure from her usual practice, since usually only Leonard Woolf was permitted to read her books before their publication, she then sent that marked copy to a friend, Jacques-Pierre Raverat, who was dying in the south of France. Woolf had genuine affection for Raverat and his wife,

Gwendolen Mary Darwin (Charles Darwin's granddaughter). Although she had not seen Raverat for several years, she decided to send him an advance copy of her new novel in the form of the extra set of proofs, inscribed "Jacques/with love/Virginia/6th Feb. 1925". Shortly before his death on March 7, 1925, his wife read the book to him, and he responded in a way that gave Woolf "one of the happiest days of my life" (*D*III: 7).

It might be expected that Woolf would not have bothered to correct the proofs she sent to Raverat, but starting on page 91 she did begin to insert limited and sporadic corrections after all. That set has also survived and is in the University Research Library at the University of California, Los Angeles. Both it and the Harcourt set of proofs are corrected by Woolf in her favored purple ink, with a typescript (interestingly different in each case) inserted with revisions for the section on Septimus Warren Smith's death. (The Harcourt proofs also have pencil annotations by the Harcourt editor, for the printer.) It was in the Harcourt set that Woolf made notably extensive corrections – and, it should be stressed, revisions as well. Clearly, too, these corrections and revisions were not identical to those she must have made in the Hogarth proofs. Unfortunately, no doubt, Woolf was a great novelist rather than a meticulous textual editor and was more driven by her creative urges than by the desire for bibliographic consistency or the pressing needs of future scholars. As a result of those clearly lamentable deficiencies, the differences between the two first editions are interesting and substantive. Claire Tomalin's note on the text of the novel in the Oxford World's Classics series declaring that there are "no significant differences" between the two texts is patently incorrect (xxxiii).

One possibility, which struck both me and the general editors of the Shakespeare Head Press edition as untenable, would have been to opt for a "hybrid" edition; one that would select whichever variant or version of a particular passage that I happened to favor, resulting in a compilation that would in some odd way be something that I would have come up with as an editor, rather than an edition as close to Woolf's creation as we can get. So instead I had to choose a copy-text, the version of the novel that would be the base text, from which any variations would have to appear in the form of emendations to be duly listed, explained, and, when necessary, defended. The two obvious candidates were the English and American first editions.

There was for example a strong rationale for favoring the English first edition, since Hogarth was Woolf's own firm, and she could have had access to the proofs for it at a later stage and could have made changes subsequent to those she made for the Harcourt edition. And it could be argued that even where the Hogarth edition does not include corrections to be found in the American proofs, that omission could reflect in at least some instances a change of mind on Woolf's part. Glenn Patton Wright's 1990 edition of *Mrs. Dalloway* for Hogarth, however, which calls itself "the definitive" edition, reveals some of the problems of selecting the Hogarth first edition as the copy-text, as Wright does. Most of those problems are purely textual, although some are also, admittedly subjectively, aesthetic. For example, near the end of the novel Clarissa reflects about Septimus, in the first American edition, that "He made her feel the beauty; made her feel the fun".[4] That sentence – of which, for example, Sandra Gilbert and Susan Gubar make much in their study *No Man's Land* (284) – appears in neither the first English nor Wright's "definitive" edition based on it. The loss is surely significant. But I shall return to the issue of how much we should permit such considerations to dictate or even affect editorial decisions.

In contrast, there are also persuasive arguments for favoring Harcourt's first American edition. Perhaps even the mere fact that we have the proofs for it argues in its favor, however differently we might have felt had both sets of proofs survived. Moreover, there are *numerous* instances in which the Hogarth edition does not include corrections that appear on the American proofs. (Faced with the new necessity to work on two sets of proofs, Woolf was careless in transferring alterations from one set to another. Therefore, confident assertions about her uniformity of intentions are difficult.) As E. F. Shields argues, it is difficult to believe that both sets provided basically similar corrections or "revises" and that, in so many instances, Woolf went on to change her mind and restore the original version for the Hogarth edition with a "stet" (174). Another way to express that reservation is to observe that in the case of the American first edition we at least *know* when Harcourt deviated from Woolf's wishes, as indicated in her corrections on the proofs; whereas in the case of the Hogarth first edition we can only guess about whether the deviations have any – in that euphonious phrase – authorial authority.

Woolf did cooperate with future scholars in one important way: once she published her novels, she tended to leave them alone. So we do not have the problem of competing editions of *Mrs. Dalloway* within her lifetime that we do, for example, with Herman Melville (as in the case of *Typee*), or Stephen Crane (as with *Maggie, A Girl of the Streets*), or William Faulkner (as with *The Sound and the Fury*) – or with special frequency in the oeuvre of poets such as William Wordsworth, Walt Whitman, William Butler Yeats, Marianne Moore, or W. H. Auden.

All those considerations led me to choose as the copy-text neither first edition, but rather the extant marked proofs from which the American first edition was prepared. (Comparable conditions led Susan Dick to make a similar decision for the Shakespeare Head Press edition of *To the Lighthouse*.) That choice preserves Woolf's punctuation and spelling, although in fact the Harcourt edition did preserve those as well, and also provides her own revisions and corrections. In contrast, the Oxford World's Classics edition alters both Woolf's spelling and punctuation, in order to conform to the publisher's house style or the editor's sense of what the "Note on the Text" terms "current standard usage" (xxxiii) – an approach that would produce fascinating results if applied to authors as various as Henry Fielding, Jane Austen, Charles Dickens, William Faulkner, or . . . well, other writers too. Glenn Patton Wright made more sophisticated changes in his edition, but they too are ones that, I would argue, are ultimately unjustified and unjustifiable.

Consider, for example, the question of the color of the dress Elizabeth Dalloway wears at the party at the end of the novel. In all editions published during Woolf's lifetime, the dress is referred to as "pink" in a couple of instances up to the party itself, when it becomes "red". Wright's edition changes the word "red" to "pink", remarking that "Woolf simply overlooked the error in factual details" and citing as supportive corroboration the fact that a similar "correction" was made in a British edition published in 1947, six years after Woolf's death (179–80, 214). Similarly, Wright changes one reference to Peter's age as 52 to 53, to conform with previous references (180), just as he changes a reference to Lucrezia Warren Smith's "sisters", in the plural, to "sister", because elsewhere in the novel Lucrezia has been called the "younger" daughter, not the "youngest".[5] Yet Wright claims that his textual edition of *Mrs. Dalloway* is "conservative" (181). I wonder.

I assume, in any case, that an editor's goal ought not to be to "improve" the novel, but rather to provide an improved text of it. When a dress is red in one passage and pink in another, is it an editor's role to worry about that discrepancy so much that one takes it upon oneself to do away with it, rather than point to it in an appropriate and unobtrusive note? After all, we cannot be sure that there may not be a point in the apparent inconsistency. I saw my role as falling short of re-writing *Mrs. Dalloway*, all the more so as I thought that there might be at least the possibility that I might not come up with a better novel than Virginia Woolf managed to write.

So while an editor must inevitably make aesthetic decisions insofar as they cannot be entirely separated from purely "textual" ones, she or he must be wary and even suspicious about making them. Earlier, I mentioned my sense of the loss in other editions of the sentence, "He made her feel the beauty; made her feel the fun". Another passage from the same section of the novel demonstrates similar issues. Clarissa ponders about Septimus that "She felt glad that he had done it; thrown it away" (Beja, 138). Woolf had deleted on the proofs an added phrase that still appears at the end of the sentence in the Hogarth edition, which reads "thrown it away while they went on living".[6] The additional words seem to me to amount to overkill, yet surely an editor would be out of bounds omitting them on that basis, for we then enter a realm in which textual editors confuse the need to make corrections or emendations with what would entail their own revisions. Obviously there is no point in immortalizing in our reading texts clear typographical or other textual errors; otherwise, why produce a new edition in the first place? Nor, however, should an editor who is preparing a reading text in effect renounce responsibility for any decisions.

As I have observed, multiple ("palimpsestic", if you will) texts can be extraordinarily valuable to those who wish to study and examine a great novel, and doing so is, I firmly believe, an estimable task. So, after all, is reading a great novel. Textual scholars must of course resist false "definitive" labels for their texts, but neither should we be so ill advised that we end up exclusively with results that provide not so much a novel, say, as an intricate series of complicated alternative texts. Those texts would be of great interest, certainly, but not necessarily to readers, as such, so much as chiefly or solely to scholars (and too often, if the truth be told, only to textual scholars at that). The work of textual scholars is of inestimable importance for many reasons, including the central role that an understanding of how texts are arrived at must play in any critical interpretation of a work of literature; but nothing justifies textual scholarship more than the final product it produces, the reading text.

My own approach can perhaps best be clarified and, if needed, defended, by contrasting it with that of an editor of another modernist text whose approaches and assumptions are intelligently and consciously held, but that lead to results I regard as wrong-headed: Danis Rose, who has produced a "Reader's Edition" of James Joyce's *Ulysses*.[7] (I wonder for whom the other editions have been intended.) Rose regards the belief that "the extirpation of mere printers' errors, important as it is, is the sole or even the primary function of a textual editor" as a "widespread fallacy" which ought to "have passed away" (xi). That sounds sensible enough, although one must also realize where Rose heads when he goes beyond the errors made by "printers". Who else makes errors?

Well, authors do. Fine, they do, in fact. (But what sorts of errors?) Anyway, what authority do we have to correct authors' errors? Rose's response is, in effect, to urge us to question the authority of the author and to recognize that "traditional" textual scholarship is myopic in believing that any literary "work is entirely the work of the author alone" (xv). In this claim Rose is influenced by the work of Jerome McGann,[8] but he also recognizes that he goes beyond him in asserting that the "logical conclusion" of his own approach is one that sees an editor taking on major responsibilities and authority that include producing "an edition that is *of its own time*" (xv; emphasis added). So we are back to the claim of the Oxford World's Classics edition that it is appropriate to provide us not with Virginia Woolf's "usage" but with "current standard usage". According to Rose, the conviction that the goal is an edition "of its own time" allows an editor to "follow sound practice. (I say sound practice rather than best practice because sound practice changes over time and also varies depending on the author and the kind of book that one is editing.)" (xvi)

For the "kind of book" that *Ulysses* is, the results of Rose's approach are disastrous. For example, Rose feels entitled to revise and correct the mathematical and scientific assertions that form a major basis of the Ithaca chapter. Most notoriously, he has felt free to present Molly Bloom's final monologue with the punctuation that Joyce so emphatically and effectively left out. So much for mere "authorial intention". Even Rose recognizes the questionable nature of that particular decision, so he provides as well the "more experimental format of the first edition" (xxv), that is, a version without his own added punctuation, although only in an appendix. Rose may, of course, be seen as correct in making his revisions if one grants his assumptions and follows them to their "logical conclusion". One wonders where they would take us in the works of Virginia Woolf. In *The Waves*, certainly another odd "kind of book", the word "said" that introduces each monologue is not on the face of it "logical". The characters do not "say" anything. So why not have us read, "'I see a ring,' thought Bernard..."? ("Pondered Bernard"? "Mused Bernard"? Or "Bernard did not really say, as such"?)

But while editors can get carried away, they must do their job – must make decisions and present us with a reading text. And in doing so they must be answerable to other scholars. They should demonstrate the rationale for their decisions and, in a clearly discernible manner, the results of those decisions, for example in lists of variants. My goal in supplying for *Mrs. Dalloway* a complete list of variants for the two first editions and the proofs, including the two sets of marked proofs, was not simply to show the differences between the English and American first editions. Still, let me stress that those differences are substantive and interesting. Consider one passage, centering on Sir William Bradshaw, that does not make syntactical sense in the Hogarth edition: "If they failed, he had to support him police and the good of society...." As corrected by Woolf in the proofs for the Harcourt edition, it reads, "If they failed him, he had to support police and the good of society.... "[9] Later, sitting on the window sill and about to commit suicide, Septimus thinks, "Life was good. The sun hot. Only human beings – what did *they* want?"[10] In the uncorrected proofs, the last phrase reads "what did *they* want of one?": Woolf crossed out the words "of one". In the first English edition, the sentence reads simply, "Only human beings?" (Hogarth, 1925, 225), lessening the impact and force of the threat personal Septimus feels from all humanity.

An interesting example of a variation in a single word is the appearance in the first American edition of "vagulous" (as Clarissa sees "that vagulous phosphorescence, old Mrs. Hilbery)".[11] In the first English edition, under the apparent assumption that there is no such word as "vagulous", the word was changed (almost certainly not by Woolf) to "vagous". The latter word also appears in the Hogarth "definitive" edition, which cites "vagulous" as a "misspelling" (Wright, ed., 155, 212). It seems, actually, to be a neologism: Woolf uses "vagulous" elsewhere (for example, *D*I: 291), and the second edition of the *Oxford English Dictionary* (1989) defines it as "wayward, vague, wavering" and cites it as appearing "only in the writings of Virginia Woolf" (see Beja, "Notes", 158).

Especially enlightening is the record we attain, through the variants, of the differences between the proofs and the published versions; these enable us to become "genetic" critics and scholars, to see Woolf working on and revising her prose and clarifying it – or, sometimes, making it more enigmatic. Brenda Silver has compared the resulting interpretive process to the "tunneling process" that Woolf felt she had discovered while writing *Mrs. Dalloway*, and that enabled her to reconstruct "the past by instalments" (*D*II: 272; see Silver, 194). Previous lists of the variants for *Mrs. Dalloway* had been highly selective, employing the now largely abandoned if not discredited distinction between "substantive" and "accidental" variants. I wanted to present a complete list, and the results show, I believe, that many so-called "accidentals" are far from minor. Still, that is not to deny that some variants and revisions are more intriguing than others, as when Woolf makes a passage less explicit. I have already mentioned the instance in which she deleted the reference (preserved in the Hogarth Press edition) to Clarissa's sense that Septimus had "thrown it away while they went on living".[12] Among many other examples is one much earlier, when Lucrezia puts her wedding ring in her purse and Septimus thinks that he should now be free, "since his wife had thrown away her wedding ring; since she had left him"; in the unmarked proofs, the second clause reads, "since she hated him, and had joined his persecutors. . . ."[13] Other passages, in contrast, expand upon the original version and intensify it, as in the one I have pointed to in which Woolf inserted, "He made her feel the beauty; made her feel the fun" (138). On the previous page, the passage in the Hogarth edition which reads, "Odd, incredible; she had never been so happy", was changed to, "It was due to Richard; she had never been so happy".[14]

Inevitably, I sometimes had to deviate from the version in the copy-text, and present my rationale for such decisions in the list of emendations. For example, in the first American edition, during his consultation with Bradshaw, Septimus wonders, "Would they let him off then, his torturers?" (Harcourt, 1925, 148). The first English edition reads, "Would they let him off then, Holmes Bradshaw?" (Hogarth, 1925, 149). The corrected version in the Raverat proofs is, "Would they let him off then, Holmes & Bradshaw?" The Shakespeare Head Press edition, altering the ampersand to "and" as Woolf obviously assumed would be done, thus reads: "Would they let him off then, Holmes and Bradshaw?"[15]

I have attempted through such decisions to present the most reliable and readable text possible, the one closest to what we can determine the author (not the editor) would have wished us to have. No word raises more red flags within textual scholarship than "intention".[16] But I feel strongly that while we may not be able (and, in theory, may not wish or may not need) to know how an author might have intended us to *interpret* what she wrote, we have an obligation – in theory and in praxis – to attempt to determine what she actually intended to *write*.

Yet while I can and do explain and defend my own decisions in striving to provide what Woolf actually wrote and intended to write, I have no illusions about having provided a "definitive" text, as The Hogarth Press edition of 1990 is rashly called. There are too many judgment calls in the entire process of editing for one to feel entirely free in using that dated term. I wonder if one could in full confidence come up with a "definitive" version of a short story, say "Bartleby" (or should it be "Bartleby the Scrivener"?), or a short poem, say "I heard a Fly buzz – when I died", or even perhaps "I Wandered Lonely as a Cloud", (or should it be "I wandered lonely as a cloud", or for that matter "Daffodils"?), much less of a full-length novel.

I also made other, non-textual, decisions, such as one to include as an appendix Virginia Woolf's own Introduction to *Mrs. Dalloway* for the 1928 Modern Library edition (I have never understood why other editions have not done so) and, as well, a map of "The London of *Mrs. Dalloway*".[17] I had special fun working on the annotations, particularly in finding the sources of allusions that had never been published before, like the one to the "house with the China cockatoo" (9), or the reference to the "absurd statue" in Regent's Park (43). Or in showing what the words "the black" refer to, when Peter notices "all the exalted statues, Nelson, Gordon, Havelock, the black" (40): the reference is to the image of a crew member looking upon the dying Nelson in a corner of the relief by J. E. Carew on the pedestal of the Nelson column in Trafalgar Square, facing Whitehall. (A major incidental benefit of working on the annotations was the chance to get to know London more intimately.)

I was also able to correct previous attempts to "date" the novel, by showing that references to Ascot indicate that the events take place on June 20, 1923. We know the day is a Wednesday in June 1923, and during that year Ascot took place from Tuesday the 19th to Friday the 22nd; that date is further supported by references to sporting and other news that can be found in newspapers for June 20.

Such scholarly detective work was both challenging and pleasurable, as I had expected it to be. I had expected immersion in textual scholarship to produce gratifying results, but, in all honesty, I was less prepared for its seductiveness as well, but that work proved to be no less absorbing and engrossing. I hope I may be forgiven for being reminded of Peter Walsh's feelings at the end of the novel, as he wonders what fills him with such extraordinary excitement. In my case it has been *Mrs. Dalloway*. For there it is.

Notes

1. On the advantages of such a "palimpsest" in providing multiple texts, see for example Silver, who stresses, however, that in her essay she is not concerned "with the editorial questions surrounding the choice of copy-text for a critical edition of a novel and the place of the extant holographs, typescripts, galleys, and page proofs – the various versions – in this process" (195–6).
2. Holograph working notes in a notebook of manuscripts for *Jacob's Room*, in the Berg Collection, New York Public Library. See Woolf, *The Hours*, 411.
3. See Shields, 157–75, and Wright, 241–61, and the latter's edition of the novel. Also see *The Hours*, xiv–xv (Wussow, ed.).
4. Beja, ed., 138. See, also, the list of "Textual Variants", 195.

5. Wright, ed., 207. The notes to the Shakespeare Head Press edition point out that both in this and another passage, later in the novel, all editions published during Woolf's lifetime referred to "sisters" (Beja, 150).
6. *Mrs. Dalloway* (Hogarth, 1925, 280), and Wright, 165. See the Shakespeare Head Press edition, "Textual Variants" (Beja, 195).
7. I cite Rose's edition for my own present purposes, but I am grateful that the many and knotty questions aroused by the competing editions of *Ulysses*, and by the theoretical bases of those editions, are beyond the scope of this essay.
8. See especially *A Critique of Modern Textual Criticism*.
9. Shakespeare Head Press edition (Beja, 77). The uncorrected proofs read "If they failed, he had to support police . . . "; see "Textual Variants" (179).
10. Beja, 111; Harcourt, 1925, 226; see Beja, "Textual Variants", 187.
11. Beja, 130; see Beja, "Textual Variants", 192.
12. See the "Textual Variants" in Beja, 138.
13. Beja, 52; see "Textual Variants", 172.
14. Beja, 137; see "Textual Variants", 195.
15. Beja, 74; see "Emendations", 161–2, and "Textual Variants", 178–9.
16. For an important discussion of the concept of "intention" as it relates to textual studies, see Tanselle, "The Editorial Problem of Final Authorial Intention", which begins: "Scholarly editors may disagree about many things, but they are in general agreement that their goal is to discover exactly what an author wrote and to determine what form of his work he wished the public to have. There may be some difference of opinion about the best way of achieving that goal; but if the edition is to be a work of scholarship – a historical recon-struction – the goal itself must involve the author's 'intention'" (167).
17. One of life's little triumphs: after I had published a much earlier version of that map, in 1977, a Londoner had written to correct my – and Woolf's – placement of the statue of General Gordon in Trafalgar Square, since it can be found in the Victoria Embankment Gardens. I was for a brief time disconcerted by my "error" and very surprised at Woolf's. But it turned out that the statue was, in fact, moved to the Embankment in 1953.

8
The Alfa and the *Avant-texte*: Transcribing Virginia Woolf's Manuscripts

Edward Bishop

> Forms effect meanings
> – D. M. McKenzie

The black Alfa Romeo snarled out of the parking garage and headed toward the East River, weaving through the 5 o'clock surge of yellow cabs. At Second Avenue the driver snapped the gearshift down into second gear, whipped the car left across two airport buses and headed uptown through Harlem.

"The Duty of the Editor is to Edit," she declared, taking up my question about manuscript transcriptions.

"Yes but . . ." I said, nervously watching the tach spin toward the red line.

"You have to make decisions," she said, slicing across three lanes of traffic to hit Harlem River Drive, "cut extraneous material." She cut off two gentlemen in a coupe de ville – the passenger gave us the finger and the driver seemed to be mouthing something about his mother.

"Readers want a clean text," she said. "They don't want to have to read through all those squiggles, or figure out flying brackets, square brackets – shit!" the Italian air horns blared at some poor station wagon that had dared to slow for the exit ramp, "or any of those symbols."

She swung round the wagon, geared down, and flung the Alfa into the tightening curve. My stomach was tightening too – we hit third gear, 60 mph, and the deck of the George Washington Bridge all at the same moment.

"But a manuscript is . . ." I started.

"Exactly. The original manuscripts are accessible. So why reproduce them?"

We were heading west now, into the spitting rain, across to New Jersey. I held fast to the grab handle, and tried to hang on to my position.

> *I tried again. "The manuscripts are 'accessible' if you live in New Jersey or Manhattan but what about scholars further afield?"*
>
> *The Pirellis were singing in the rain and the not-so-muted roar of the big Alfa six made conversation difficult.*
>
> *"Look," said Louise, raising her voice (for it was Louise DeSalvo, editor of* Melymbrosia), *"I consulted the MLA committee on editing and they said 'clean text'".*
>
> *We were going 80 now and she seemed to have a grudge against some semi-trailer who wanted into our lane. We were wheel to wheel like in the Ben Hur chariot race – except that the semi's wheels were bigger than our whole car.*
>
> *"Ok ok," I conceded. MLA, semis, what the hell. I didn't expect to reach Jersey alive anyway.*

But I did, and now I want to re-open that argument, having produced a holograph edition of the *Jacob's Room* manuscript, and am no longer trapped in a speeding Alfa.[1] I begin with an anecdote because, as the vignettes in Woolf's own essays remind us, whether it is a beadle barring the way to an archive or a young man sedulously extracting nuggets of ore in the British Library Reading Room, personal dynamics impinge upon scholarship. My own encounter raises issues of ownership and power, access and appropriation, mastery and privilege, issues that materially affect the texts we reproduce yet that are always disavowed. For instance, DeSalvo's argument about the manuscripts being accessible was based not only on proximity (a New Jersey-centric conception of the world in which you needed only to hop across the river to consult the originals), but also upon a presumption of access to the privileged space of the Berg Collection, a room guarded and aloof from the rabble of the main reading room. Too often we treat manuscript work as if it were value-neutral: you discover the document, you reproduce it accurately, and you keep the scholar out of the text. But the scholar is in the text whether she or he wants to be or not, and we are wrong to pretend that this is not so. In this essay I will examine the three principal transcription models – the "clean text" of *Melymbrosia*; the edited and annotated text of *Pointz Hall*; and the facsimile transcription of *The Waves*, which I used for *Jacob's Room* – not to provide readings of particular passages in the texts, but to explore the mediations of the form, to consider the implications of format and annotation styles. My argument is that we must "read" the page: for page design, ostensibly innocent, has designs on us.

To contextualize this discussion briefly, in little more than the quarter-century since Graham produced his edition of *The Waves* there has been a revolution in the status of drafts, as genetic criticism and French editorial theory have influenced Anglo-American critical practices. In the introduction to "DRAFTS", the 1996 special issue of *Yale French Studies*, the editors declared, "Today we tend to be fond of works that have managed to retain something of the aura of their potentialities. . . . The classical notion of the monumental and stable work is now being contested by a growing interest in that part of the work that is move-ment, action, creative gesture, solidified ephemera" (1, 4). What this means is that where "in the past, editors aimed to establish a text in what they hoped would be a definite edition [now] genetic critics have put the text back into motion" (2). This shift in attitude has given rise to the term *avant-texte*.[2] Where "draft" carries associations of "rough draft", something to move beyond, to cast off, *avant-texte* (like *avant-garde*) implies something forward looking, if incomplete and fragmentary, something with intrinsic value (De Biasi, 26; Robinson-Valéry, 59).[3] Further, as Christine Froula says in one of her indispensable articles on modernism and genetic criticism, "Genetic texts not only document the evolution of literary works through the stages of their compositional history but . . . emphasize their interdependence with historical condi-tions" ("Portraits", 513).

Woolf herself was one of those intrigued by the idea of texts in motion. In *A Room of One's Own* she notes how it shocked Charles Lamb to think "Lycidas" could have been different. In a footnote to his 1820 essay "Oxford on Vacation" Lamb raged against the instability of the *avant-texte*: "There is something to me repugnant, at any time, in writ-ten hand", he said,

> The text never seems determinate. Print settles it. I had thought of the Lycidas as of a full-grown beauty – as springing up with all its parts absolute – till, in evil hour, I was shown the original written copy of it. . . . How it staggered me to see the fine things in their ore! interlined, corrected! as if their words were mortal, alterable, displaceable at pleas-ure! as if they might have been otherwise, and just as good! as if inspi-rations were made up of parts, and those fluctuating, successive, indifferent! I will never go into the work-shop of any great artist again.[4]

Woolf (or her persona), on the other hand, has already decided as she walks across the quadrangle, to "amuse myself with wondering what could have been bettered, where Milton had thought twice" (8).

As recent critics have noted, in the modern period a delight in possib-ilities replaced Lamb's terror of textual instability, not only in writing but in other art forms as well. Francis Marmande argues that the valorization of perpetual becoming is best exemplified in that quintessential modernist form, jazz: "The best improvisations have never been 'takes,' they are played elsewhere, tomorrow, on a night when nobody was there, among musicians, on a smoky dreamlike night in a world that leaves no trace and there's no second take" (156). In modernist sculpture, Judith Robinson-Valéry cites Rodin as one who, by including unworked or half-worked stone in pieces such as *Les Bourgeois de Calais*, *Danaïde*, and *La Pensée*, suggested "the necessary part played by the 'rough' in making the 'polished' possible – no longer as a *negation* or *correction* of the 'rough' but rather as its completion" (64). Thus the draft and the final work mutually define one another, and are in fact ultimately inseparable. Vincent Kaufmann, in "Valéry's Garbage Can", contends that genetic theory "is *an effect* of modernism: it systematizes the modernist promotion of the 'work' of writing" (70), and he cites Valéry as one for whom the published book is always circumstantial, and often the result of a commercial order. Lacan calls publication *poubellication*: the creation of garbage, and for Valéry "the published work is an accident", it represents a discontinuity in its own genesis (80).

Similarly, though Woolf declares in "Mr. Bennett and Mrs. Brown" that as she is forced to "make a dizzy and dangerous leap" from one line of *The Waste Land* to the next, she cries out "for the old decorums", she is already taking us beyond those decorums. As Froula points out, when Woolf's narrator in *Women and Fiction* compares her first chapter to a "bucket of splinters" we immediately think of *Jacob's Room* ("Portraits", 520, 525). Indeed, Froula argues, drafts and fragments "become modernity's quintessential forms . . . the major epistemological shift of the modern period [is] the dissolving of the object as such into action, process, a history in which ghostly traces of what is not there can resonate almost as palpably as what is" ("Villanelle", 113, 117).[5] In tracing that action, that process, that history we must rely on transcriptions, for the original manuscripts are even less accessible than they were in the mid-1980s. Yet though these transcriptions can provoke heated debates about the accuracy of the linguistic text, the iconic aspects of the transcription are often ignored.

In viewing the page of the *Jacob's Room* manuscript (see Figure 8.1), the reader can see how Woolf has worked it, with interlineations, four sections of marginalia down the left, big sweeping loops encircling material to be moved, horizontal strikeouts through portions of lines, and, in the centre of the page – though these are harder to see – lazy vertical squiggles deleting four lines of text. What strikes the reader first

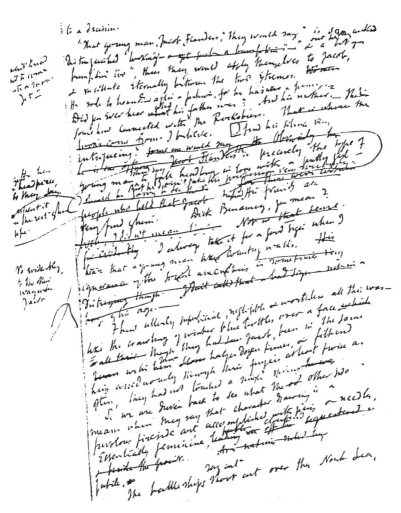

Figure 8.1   Jacob's Room manuscript, Notebook 2, p. 215

is not any particular passage but the page itself, the activity and energy displayed there. In short, we read the page as well as the text.

In the DeSalvo *Melymbrosia* we read the text (see Figure 8.2). As Louise said to me in the Alfa, "It looks like a book. Graduate students like it because they can read it". This is true: the variants are tucked away at the back (on page 273) allowing us to consult them if we want them, but encouraging us to read the text unimpeded. But as George Bornstein points out in discussing the protocols of reading variorum editions, "the paradoxical effect . . . is to enshrine whatever version the edition uses as its base text . . . and cause the reader to skip over the very apparatus that would allow reconstruction of alternate versions" ("Modernist Poetry", 164). Elsewhere he quotes Jo Ann Boydston's blunt description in her presidential address to the Society for Textual Scholarship of such apparatus: the "dreary lists that no one uses at the back of critical editions" ("Yeats", 246).

The title-page defines the audience for this text: it is a Scholar's Edition, published by the New York Public Library. Further, the copyright page has the MLA seal of approval: "Center for Scholarly editions/AN APPROVED TEXT/Modern Language Association of America".[6] This emblem has a history. Peter Shillingsburg notes that "the roots of modern textual criticism lie in classical and biblical scholarship which generally speaking assumes an ur-text", usually conceived to have been single and completed, and this idea of an archetype or ideal text was carried over into modern textual criticism ("Inquiry", 55). The governing assumption was that the author's intentions were paramount, and that the editor's job was to serve the author. The one concession to serving the reader in American scholarly editing was the "clear reading text, uninterrupted by footnotes or note indicators". More than anything else, Shillingsburg argues, "this principle reflects . . . [a] belief in the established definitive text, the recovery of Pure Virgin Text" ("Inquiry", 56), and he draws attention to the implications of format: "English editions have tended to use notes at the foot of the text page, indicating, tacitly, a greater modesty about the 'established' text and drawing attention more forcibly to at least some of the alternative forms of the text" ("Inquiry", 76, n. 8).[7] This, then is the trade-off: clear text militates against an awareness of alternatives.

Unlike DeSalvo's edition, Mitchell Leaska's transcription of the *Pointz Hall* typescript (see Figure 8.3) gives a great deal of intertextual information on the page: the first bracketed insertion tells us that this is page 38 of the Early Typescript, draft 1, scene 5, and that it corresponds to the Hogarth Press edition, pages 22–34, and the Harcourt Brace Jovanovich edition when examined. Consequently he issued facts more frequently than ideas; and was never in a muddle about his feelings. While he sipped his tea, and cut his toast into long bars, he was cracking many a doubtful idea up in his workshop. How far should one let oneself be influenced by her beauty in judging Helen's niceness? Some kinds of beauty probably set up an emotional fiction which it is the right to submit to. Yes that was undoubtedly present, to some extent, in this case. Blandly he passed her the jam. She was talking nonsense, but not worse nonsense than people usually do talk at breakfast. It is never right to yield because a woman is a woman. Therefore, he stuck to his "I do not know." Then he rambled. About marriage, for instance. It is advisable in certain circumstances; for when childbirth is over, there remains companionship, which has obvious advantages over solitude. There must be many small things one can say to a woman when one is undressing; but after a certain age the formation of habits is an insuperable bar. Are habits bad? He reviewed his habits. He committed not only poetry but prose to heart a good deal; he was fond of dividing numbers; [5, 28: E2/5] he read Petronius in May, and so on. But the human affections are the best things we have. His circumstances had not been altogether favourable. Condemned to toil for twelve years in a railway station in Bombay, he had seen few women that commanded his respect. He had applied his mind to the service. He had perfected a system. There was nothing to regret in his life, except fundamental defects, and no wise man regrets them. There is always the present. He looked round the table, and smiled.

"What's that old thing smiling for?" Rachel mused. "I suppose he's chewed something forty seven times."

"Chewing" summed up much – too much; indeed the poor man was nothing but a summary of middle age to her. One person stood for age, another for business, another for society. It was a convenient short cut. More often than not they gained in the process, becoming featureless but dignified. The figures of elderly women, and beautiful young women in particular, gained a beauty like that of people on the stage, which they would not have had, if Rachel had dispensed with symbols. The cruelty of the process was now shown; she met Mr Pepper's smile with an intelligent stare, and possibly clouded his conviction that their understanding was deep and lasting, though not a thing one talked about. So kindly was the morning, showing blue through the windows, that she pitied him – a man who had no future, a man who knew all about himself.

"Are your legs bad to day, Mr Pepper?" she asked, with the smooth and charming voice of youth, which conveys balm if not sympathy.

10 / Chapter Three

Figure 8.2   Melymbrosia, p. 10

56

"To nail the placard," she said, standing beside his chair.

The words were like the first peal of a [peal]<chime> of bells; while the first peals, you hear the second; while the second peals, you hear the third; and so on,

[*Page 38, ETS, Draft 1, Scene 5, HP: 22-34, HBJ: 16-26*]

the first being half the second. Isa knew that she would say next: ". . . for the entertainment."

And he would [say] <groan,> "Tonight? Damn it!"

"If it's fine," she would say, "they'll act in the garden."

"And if it's wet," he would reply, "in the Barn."

"And which will it be?" she would continue. "Wet or fine?"

And then — as they were doing now — they would both look out of the window.

Every summer for seven summers now, she had heard the same talk; about the hammer; the nails; the entertainment; the weather. Every year they said the same things; every year it was either wet or fine.

Every year the same chime followed the same chime; it seemed impossible that any thing should change the chimes; or change the picture; of children fifty years ago, fishing in the stream that ran through the meadow. But she changed; it changed — the thing that was behind <the wall>: today <"it" was> "the girl screamed; and hit him about the face; they dragged her to the bedroom in the barrack and held her down. . . ."

"The forecast," Oliver said, taking up the paper, "the forecast is: Variable winds; fair,

[*Page 39, ETS, Draft 1, Scene 5, HP: 22-34, HBJ: 16-26*]

average temperature; rain at times."

That was the report given by the Meteorological Office where they noted down the buzz and flicker of the very sensitive instruments that recorded pressure, velocity, density, humidity and other phenomena provided incessantly by the sky. The sky continued its mysterious, its incalculable, its incessant [operations] <manoeuvres.> It was green in the garden one moment; grey the next. It was as if an <expanded> eye beamed approval, then withdrew in melancholy reproach. It was as if some one felt illimitable joy; <an immense rapture!> then sympathy, sorrow, <compassion,> so great that it covered its face and forebore to look on human suffering. The movements of the clouds, however, were

Figure 8.3   Pointz Hall, p. 56

pages 16–26. I mention this first because that is what my eye is drawn to first on the page. John Graham in his transcription of *The Waves* puts an asterisk in the margin and uses a footnote to mark the corresponding published texts – Leaska's reference slices across the page. Having noted the page correspondences with other texts, I start reading, and learn in the second line that Woolf first wrote "peal" and then "chime". At least that is what I think she did, so I reconsult the list of abbreviations, and am reminded that angle brackets indicate a word inserted, either above or below the line, or in the margin. But reading in a linear mode I read "peal" first, and I find the first term takes precedence for me, whether it is in angle or square brackets; and I wonder if it is in the margin or not. I am also made uneasy by the note that "Editor's insertions are not indi-cated. A missing *a* or *the* or some such comparable minor oversight has simply been filled in": the language sounds to me paternalistic – Woolf's "oversight" has "simply been filled in" (22).

Further, this edition includes a section called "Notes and References" that is in fact extensive commentary. Note in the middle of the page the line about fishing, leading into the rape of the young girl:

> Every year the same chime followed the same chime; it seemed impossible that any thing should change the chimes; or change the picture; of children fifty years ago, fishing in the stream that ran through the meadow. But she changed; it changed – the thing that was behind the wall: today "it" was "the girl screamed; and hit him about the face; they dragged her to the bedroom in the barrack and held her down".

Leaska glosses this as follows:

> Lucy and Bart "fishing in the stream", so carefully placed beside the girl's rape in the barrack room, assumes added possibilities of inter-pretation as Lucy's memory of that childhood experience begins to multiply in steadily changing contexts. Moreover, Lucy's fascination with taking the fish off the hook and the blood-filled gills (ETS 37) has a much subtler meaning because of the way V.W. uses "hook" in this passage. Chaucer's Prioress wore a pendant containing the words "Amor vincit omnia" (cf. Virgil's "Omnia vincit Amor": "Love con-quers all" *Eclogues*, X, 69). It is not hard to see how "Amor" (love) could easily be confused with "Amus" (hook); and how "vincere" (to conquer) somehow got associated with "vincire" (to bind). So that the hook, in the scene with Lucy and Bartholomew, resonates with

sexual implications. The "hook" is used explicitly in *Jacob's Room* where Jacob's childish love for Mrs. Sandra Wentworth Williams is described as "this hook dragging in his side" (HP: 146; HBJ: 147). (203)

This is a close and subtle reading. Yet the effect, for this reader at least, is to draw attention away from Virginia Woolf's "flight of the mind" and to direct it toward the flight of Mitchell Leaska's mind. The usual ascendancy of text over commentary becomes reversed. As Tribble says, we "necessarily use citation form as a demonstration of mastery" (163), but there are degrees of assertiveness.[8] The style of annotation reflects the *mise en page* of the transcription itself. The Leaska text reminds us every few lines that there is an editor here, shaping the text, and it raises questions about power and authority, about who owns the text. But its function is clear: it encourages what McGann calls "radial reading" – the text is like the hub of a wheel and the spokes lead out to other versions and to other texts.[9] *Pointz Hall* is a work we *consult*, with other texts close at hand.

In his facsimile edition of *The Waves*, John Graham reproduces the holograph draft page-for-page and line-for-line, with interlineations, marginalia, and squiggles. This format produces not only a linear reading (as with the DeSalvo text) or a radial reading (as with the Leaska text) but an iconic reading.[10] The passage here, reproduced as in the transcription, is one of the most famous from *The Waves*, not only a characterizing device for Bernard, but a self-referential commentary on the text itself, and on Woolf's struggle with language:

I have never found the phrase. I
need a little language such as
lovers use. I need some simpler
language, when the storm comes over
the marshes & passes over me
where I lie in the ditch, minute,
unseen. Nothing neat. Nothing
that comes down on the page
on all fours. None of those
resonances & lovely
echoes, that break their
chimes in our blood & beat in
our brains: I have done with
language.

If we read it aloud we find that the text, formatted like an imagist poem, *becomes* a "little language".

This particular page is clean, but in her notebooks Woolf constantly uses her margins. The use of angle brackets to indicate insertions has profound implications for the text. The material in brackets may have been above the line, may have been in the margin, so now it is in spatial limbo, it has no material site. It makes it impossible for us to reconstruct the page in the mind's eye, and thus privileges a purely linguistic theory of text, one that not only ignores but banishes the iconic dimension. In *Margins and Marginality* Evelyn Tribble speaks eloquently of how, with marginalia, the page becomes a "territory of contestation" (55). Because the margin is in a fluid relationship to the text proper, margins allow us to see the competing claims of internal authority and plural, external authorities in the margins of the text. Tribble is speaking of the Bible and its marginal gloss by commentators, but she notes how Derrida in *The Margins of Philosophy* uses the margins to disturb illusion of univocality of the text, and she cites Spivak who remarks in an interview that she is beginning to think of margins as, "the place for the argument, the place for the critical moment, the place of interests for assertions rather than a shifting of the center" (103). The dynamic between margin and text is pointed up forcibly if we ask how the *Rime of the Ancient Mariner* would read if all the glosses were in footnotes. Imagine the "moon gloss" at the foot of the page, or at the end of the poem, or enclosed in angle brackets and placed after the stanza.

The *Jacob's Room* transcription, like those of John Graham and Susan Dick of *To the Lighthouse*, is a facsimile transcription (see Figure 8.4). What may strike us first are the words, "doesn't know how to come into a room yet" – yet in a bracketed transcription the phrase would come in a set of angle brackets after "and yet such a bumpkin". If in editing the draft you erase the distinction between interlinear additions and marginalia, you destroy the dynamic of the page, the multivocal quality of the manuscript, the tensions between text and emendation. Marginalia are not, in the colloquial sense of the term, marginalized, but foregrounded; whereas interlineations are buried. Yet with brackets both are turned into a species of strikeout: both parentheticalized, embedded in the line and second-classed. But the marginal is something Woolf is coming back to, augmenting, giving a second look, not something she is eliminating or emending on the fly in the middle of the line. If we are going to read the drafts *as drafts* we have to be alert to the choreography of the page. And these readings are crucial to our readings of the text as a whole. To quote Louis Hay, manuscripts "give a new power to literary critics...."

240   *Jacob's Room*   [2.215]

to a decision.

"That young man, Jacob Flanders," they would say, "is so very awkward

doesn't know how to come into a room yet" —

distinguished looking - & yet such a bumpkin" - "& a bit of a
but he
'bumpkin too", thus they would apply themselves to Jacob,
& vacillate eternally between the two extremes. Women

He rode to hounds –; after a fashion, for he hasn't a a penny.
who
Did you ever hear what his father was? And his mother? - She's
somehow connected with the Rocksbiers. That is where the
looks come from. I believe. [I find his silence very
intrigueing. some one would say He Obviously he

He has good a head piece, so they say & repent it for the rest of his life

he is one of those Jacob Flanders is precisely the type of
He
they say
young man / to fall headlong in love with a pretty girl -
But he doesn't take his profession very seriously:
I should be sorry to see that. — for there were certain
people who held that Jacob Anyhow His friends are
very fond of him.   Dick Bonamy, you mean?
Well, I didn't mean that   Not in that sense.

No evidently, its the other way with Jacob

for evidently I always take it for a good sign when I
hear that a young man likes country walks. His
ignorance of the social amenities is sometimes/very
distressing though. I don't call that a bad sign - not in a
boy of his age.

How utterly superficial, negligible & worthless all this was -
like the crawling of winter blue bottles over a face, which
For all their though they had seen Jacob, been in the same
Jacob
room with him [severa?] half a dozen times, & filtered
him assiduously through their fingers at least twice as
often, they had not touched a single spring. he was

So we are driven back to see what the od other side
means when they say that character drawing is a
frivolous fireside art, accomplished with pins and needles
feeble   cloistered
essentially feminine, leading all off the sequestered &
& beside the point. Are nations ruled by
futile, a
ray out
The battleships shoot out over the North Sea,

Figure 8.4   Jacob's Room, p. 240

The ways in which the text is laid out on the page, with marginal notations, additions, cross-references, deletions, alterations, in different handwriting styles, and with drawings and symbols, texture the discourse, increase the significations and multiply the possible readings" ("Text", 69).[11] What is at issue here is a sense of textual life and activity that conventional printed documents deny.

I felt strongly enough about the interlineations and marginalia to invest my own research money in paying a designer to mock-up each page. She adjusted each page individually, changing the spacing so the interlineations would fit the text block, changing the type size so that the lines would fit as Woolf wrote them, without wraparounds. I then added the scribbles using a fountain pen with an italic nib. These marks serve two functions: (1) they display the movements of Woolf's creation, but (2) they function in the transcription as a rupture of the holographic into the typographic, a textual scar that draws attention to the metamorphosis going on in this published text. They shatter the smooth surface of the typographic text, where they merely disrupt the original holograph, but they serve here as a reminder of the actual labour of Woolf's writing. And for Woolf it was a struggle: some of the strikeouts look like the lazy motion of a paddle in water, and suggest a reflective decision to delete; others are sharp slashes that recall the shower scene in *Psycho*.

Marta Werner writes passionately about graphic markings. In her introduction to *Emily Dickinson's Open Folios* she declares, "Against an editorial and a critical tradition that has 'normalized text' and focused primarily on its signs, I have introduced facsimiles to 'abnormalize readers' and to emphasize the iconicity of the manuscript pages themselves" (50). Werner reproduces even the backs of pages with the merest squiggle on them, putting in dashes and underlinings by hand because, "the regularizing effect of type utterly eras[es] their instantaneousness and force" (50). Indeed, Woolf scholars have observed how the printed ampersand transforms the character of her drafts: what is a quick flick in the manuscript becomes something as elaborate as a treble clef in the published version – "&".

As Brenda Silver notes, Susan Stanford Friedman associates Woolf's drafts with repression and suppression,[12] and she herself argues that Woolf "illustrates the process of condensing, displacing, or erasing an anger that is culturally forbidden from the 'final', public, published versions" (208). Whether we agree with Friedman or not, the markings on the text provide evidence of different kinds of cancellation.[13] Louis Hay points out that "from the first jottings in a notebook to the final manuscript, we are following a process of socialization of the writing, leading from the most brusquely individual notations to interference by cultural codes and the regulated contours of the text" ("History", 207). If we are to be sensitive to this "process of socialization of the writing", the material embodiments of the texts must, while they cannot duplicate the original, at least allow room for an imaginative engagement with the earlier stages of the work.

We are bound by technology, but we can incorporate signs of resistance within the published text. Helen Wussow's *The Hours* and S. P. Rosenbaum's *Women in Fiction* bracket the interlineations and replace squiggles and slashes with conventional strikeouts, but they do give us marginalia. In producing camera-ready copy these editors have been bound (as I was) by the strictures of the 7½" text block; thus economics determine the shape of the page, and the draft looks much denser than in Woolf's notebooks. Not only are the material conditions of production written on the text, but in some cases the publishing history is as well. Stuart Nelson Clarke's self-published edition of the holograph draft of *Orlando* began life in the early 1980s as a project intended for publication by University of Toronto Press (as in fact did *Jacob's Room*), but the press lost interest in the series and in 1993 Clarke published it himself. Clarke's loss is our gain. One of the attractive features of his edition is that for the draft itself he uses a typeface that mimics his early typed transcription of the draft, while for the front matter and notes he uses a modern typeface with proportional spacing. Thus the pages of Woolf's text, paler in spindly type and laid out double space on generously-sized sheets, are set apart visually from the commentary. We almost feel we are dealing with one of Woolf's corrected typescripts. Clarke's edition invites us not just to consult a particular passage but to read the work, and to read it as an *avant-texte*.

As Jean Bellemin-Noel says, "The difference between *The Text* (finished, in other words: published) and the pre-text is that the former offers itself as an entity spellbound in its destiny, whereas the latter holds and reveals its own history" (quoted in Hay, "Text", 71). "History" is doubly important here because in fact the manuscript transcription, the *avant-texte*, has become an *après-texte*: we come back to the draft not in a circle but in a spiral, reading it (in most cases) *after* reading the published text, and indeed after *studying* the published text. We can never read DeSalvo's text as Clive Bell read early chapters of *Melymbrosia*, long before *The Voyage Out* was published. DeSalvo's title page calls attention to this fact by calling it "a Scholar's text". In transcribing the *avant-texte* we have not "recovered" it: out of the manuscript we have created a completely new work. And reading in this circular or spiral way we move beyond the notion of a text as a finite entity. We are all sophisticated enough to avow the fluidity of the text, to agree with Roland Barthes that it is a methodological field, but in practice it is hard to break free of the notion that texts are closed, fissures are faults, and unity the goal, to be imposed if not discovered. I would argue it is this kind of reading that the clear text of *Melymbrosia*, or in a different way, the edited text of *Pointz Hall* invites. To oversimplify, with DeSalvo we read as scholars, appraising an already-edited work; with Leaska we read more as students, commentary keeping us on a tight rein; with Graham and Dick we read as genetic critics, tracing the process, and consciously or not, Graham and Dick promote a poststructuralist notion of text.[14]

Draft transcriptions should be messy; they should convey the mood of creation. Reading the end of *The Waves* in Graham's edition, watching the pages get shorter, the lines get shorter, strikeouts and marginalia all left behind as Woolf's pen moves swiftly across the page is, for me, a thrilling experience. A thrill inseparable from the contrast between the sure slender lines, and the anguished, clotted pages that precede them.[15] Drafts should also convey the contingency of the process. At the end of *Jacob's Room* we have the ending Woolf wrote and then partially deleted:

> "What is one to do with these, Mr. Bonamy?"
> She held out a pair of Jacob's old shoes.
> ~~They both laughed.~~
> ~~The room waved beh~~ind her tears. (275)

We also have the ending of the manuscript itself. The last passage of *Jacob's Room* in Berg Notebook 3 is the image of the thorn tree at midnight, and Mrs. Flanders going to bed:

> But at midnight when ~~it is perfectly still~~ & no one
>   the thorn tree is perfectly still,
> speaks or gallops, & from nothing stirs, & the
> clock strikes twelve [& the rectory lamp is
> extinguished & the Mrs. Flanders lies down:]
> then it would be foolish ~~espe~~ to vex the moor with
> questions, ~~or to say anything now that It makes no~~
>   Let
> ~~reply~~. The church clock strikes twelve. (293)

A page that takes us to the subtext of the mother's love. Having read these endings we will always read with at least two other possibilities in mind when we re-read the published ending. We still seem to be groping for an adequate metaphor for what goes on here. Louis Hay says, "Perhaps we should consider the text as a *necessary possibility*, as one manifestation of a process which is always virtually present in the background, a kind of third dimension of the written work"(75). Brenda Silver invokes Hans Zeller's image of the textual history of a work as a three-dimensional cylinder (205). Pierre-Marc De Biasi goes one further and insists we need a conception of textuality that "fills out the text with a dimension that had been sorely lacking: the fourth dimension, that of time, where the text of the work reclaims possession of its history"(57). And we need different reading practices. Over ten years ago Susan Stanford Friedman insisted on "the necessity of reading 'both ways' instead of regarding the 'final' texts as the endpoint"(146). More recently Hans Walter Gabler has argued for "circularity", and Michael Groden envisions "the reader oscillating between ... the deep background" and the text (185, 196). What underlies all of these images is a dynamic conception of text. McGann puts it dramatically: "Every text has variants of itself screaming to get out"(10). One thinks immediately of the possibilities of hyper-text: a photo-reproduction of the actual holograph; a facsimile transcription like Graham's to facilitate working with the manuscript; a clear text like DeSalvo's to appreciate the linguistic text of the draft; a full set of annotations linking the draft to published versions, such as Leaska provides; and the published versions of the novel, with reproductions of the dust-jackets, blurbs, and other paratextual features.[16]

However, the basic issue remains. The most important effect of the *avant-texte*, says Genette, is that it "confronts what the text is with what it was, with what it could have been, with what it almost became" (402). In reading Virginia Woolf's manuscripts and typescripts we want to preserve that sense of becoming. Editorial interpretation or clarity of representation should be subordinated to the dance, the struggle, of the page. Marta Werner poses the essential question in her epigraph from Cixous' *Readings*: "Writing is already something finished.... What does it mean to work on texts that are 'near to the wild heart'?" If we are to engage with Woolf's pre-publication texts we need transcriptions that preserve their wildness.

Notes

1. This essay began as a paper delivered at the Virginia Woolf Conference in St Louis, Missouri, in June 1998, where Mark Hussey provided invaluable assistance with the visuals. I would like to thank Jo-Ann Wallace for her suggestions, Jim Haule for his constructive comments on the expanded version, and John Stape for his sharp editorial eye.

   To clarify the often-confused terms *holograph*, *manuscript*, and *autograph*, *holograph* derives from the Greek *holos* and *graphos* and for "wholly written". It is an adjective, not a noun, and it means written entirely in the hand of the author. *Manuscript* of course applies to documents written by hand, but unlike *holograph* it need not be the author's hand. *Autograph* is applied to writings in the author's hand, but the term usually refers to letters, inscriptions, notes, and so on. *Holograph*, on the other hand, is reserved for literary manuscripts. So in editing Woolf we might encounter her *manuscript* notes on other authors for her essays, her *autograph* letters, and her *holograph* drafts. See Carter, 121.

2. Louis Hay credits Jean Bellemin-Noël with creating the term *avant-texte* in 1974 ("Text", 71). Pierre-Marc De Biasi has prepared an exhaustive typology of the *avant-texte*, distinguishing among six different stages and the different kinds of work associated with each (see his chart, 34–35), but I use the term here as most critics do, to indicate the whole range of pre-publication documents.

3. In French it is worse: *brouillon* (rough draft) as an adjective also means careless and untidy, and the term is associated with *brouillard, brouille, brouiller*, and *brouillé*: mist, muddle, quarrel, and scrambled, as in scrambled eggs.

4. *Collected Works of Charles and Mary Lamb*, 2: 311; cited in Rosenbaum, 204. See Froula, "Portraits", 513.

5. See Bornstein's "Once and Future Texts": "Most modernist poems exist in multiple forms, more like a process than a product, with each form carrying its own authorization and validity" (164). See also Rabaté on modernism and the production of the "Ideal Genetic Reader".

6. Moreover, the Preface thanks the MLA's Committee on Scholarly Editions, especially W. Speed Hill and G. Thomas Tanselle, for providing advice. These are names to conjure with in editorial theory; their presence in the preface is akin to having a deconstructive work endorsed by Jacques Derrida or a postcolonial study by Homi Bhabha.

7. Although the CEAA emphasized that the emblem of approval read "An Approved Text" rather than "*The* Approved Text", and the MLA modified this emblem to read "An Approved *Edition*" rather than "An Approved *Text*" (thus emphasizing that the editing was definitive, though the text itself not necessarily so) this was merely, says Shillingsburg, an acknowledgment that "editors attempting to produce a text that best represented the author's intentions were confronted from time to time with inconclusive evidence" (57). The concept of recovering Pure Virgin Text still held sway. See also his "Text as Matter, Concept, and Action".

8. See pp. 16–22 of Anthony Grafton's brilliant history of the footnote for an account of how scholars skewer each other and attempt to master texts through notes.

9. "The elementary sign of a radial reading is probably illustrated by a person who rises from reading a book in order to look up the meaning of a word in a dictionary or to check some historical or geographical reference" (116).

10. See Bornstein and Tinkle's introduction to *The Iconic Page* for a discussion of the "semantics of the page" (1).

11. As McGann (1991) points out, "to read Blake, or any newspaper, is to be reminded of the crucial importance of spatial relations; physical space calls out different modes of reading" (113). We need only think of the difference between the *New York Times* and *USA Today*, or the London *Times* and the *Daily Mail* to feel the force of this. Groden re-animates the dead metaphor "the body of text" to observe of Joyce's notebooks, "the *avant-texte* documents have the appearance of a textual body with appendages jutting out in many different directions" (189).

12. "Read intertextually, 'drafts' are potentially the 'textual unconscious' of the 'final' text. . . . In political terms, the repression of what is forbidden in the change from 'draft' to 'final' text may reflect the role of ideology as an internalized censor" ("Return" 145). Our relationship to pre-publication materials is tricky. Further, where the published text is presented to the reader, drafts, on the other hand, are overheard writing. We are not face to face with the author, we are looking over her shoulder from the side (half-acknowledged) or behind (uninvited and unknown). Or is this true? Genette points out when a writer wants the manuscripts to disappear she or he knows enough to attend to it in person: "The pre-texts retained by posterity are all, therefore, pre-texts passed on by their authors". The message is "'Here is what the author was willing to let us know about the way he wrote his book'" (396). A good point: how many years did Woolf hang on to, and move the 1000-page typescript of *Melymbrosia*?

13. In his catalogue to an exhibition of notebooks in St Louis, Kevin Ray sees struggle in the very etymology of the term: "Just as the notebook is a place of memory and memorialization . . . so too it is a place of conflict and of struggle. Latin notebooks, *pugillares*, 'little writing tablets', are empty spaces, objects and loci . . . interpolated into a place between words derived from *pugio* (boxer or pugilist) and those derived from *pugio* (dagger or poinard), which gives way to *pugna* (fight, battle, combat), *pugnacitas* (desire of fighting), and, as if to link page to pen, *pugneus* (pertaining to the fist)". He goes on to point out a central irony of the notebook: it is "a physical place wherein the fluid is fixed in its fluidity. . . . Even the writer discovers a difference . . . once it is located on the page, a place of revising, of re-reading" (2).

14. But see Brenda Silver, who argues that Graham echoes Tanselle's notions of "authorial intent" and the primacy of the organic work of art in his "Editing a Manuscript: Virginia Woolf's *The Waves*".

15. Read the final two pages, 742–3, and then go back and work through, say, the start-and-stop composition of page 684. Or compare the tentative final page of the *Lighthouse* holograph (366).

16. No one likes reading extended texts on a screen, though as Alan Burdick suggests in a recent article, electronic "ink" (blue and white particles in microscopic ink capsules move around and make new letters in response to a radio signal) may give us the properties of electronic text in a book with actual pages. More problematic, however, are the protocols of reading

engendered by hypertext in any form. In "The Places of Books in the Age of Electronic Reproduction", Geoffrey Nunberg points out that up to now electronic texts have been mainly resource documents like encyclopedias, which are relatively nonlinear; meantime, he argues, "it's likely that the printed book will remain the preferred medium for sustained, serious reading of the kinds of texts associated with literary culture" (19). I confess that for me the blue links are like the doors in Bluebeard's castle, impossible to resist. They induce an extreme of radial reading: I can never hold back for more than three blue words before I click and catapult myself into a new text.

9

The Changing Shape(s) of *Orlando* and the Myth of Authorial Control

J. H. Stape

> ...Lamb wrote how it shocked him to think it possible that any word in Lycidas could have been different from what it is. To think of Milton changing the words in that poem seemed to him a sort of sacrilege.
>
> *A Room of One's Own*, Ch. 1

Such were the thoughts prompting Virginia Woolf's famous abortive attempt to visit the Wren Library at Trinity College, Cambridge. She was herself no less "shocked" to find that "ladies" were not admitted except by special pass. That words might not fall immediately into place and might be changed by the writer is not an especially "sacrilegious" proposition in her case; over the past two decades, scholarship has demonstrated how relentlessly she revised her prose throughout its composition and into the final stages of proofreading. The textual challenges raised by these multiple layers of revision have evoked serious scholarly interest; and although not excessively complex compared to some modernist writers, Joyce or Conrad, say, Woolf's textual situations have garnered increasingly sophisticated comment.

While the sometimes indeterminate and fluctuating shapes of the title-character of *Orlando, A Biography* might playfully be linked to the novel's own various and shifting forms, establishing a critical text on such a basis would seriously misrepresent the thrust of Woolf's painstaking and conscientious writing and revision of her work. The novel's extant pre-printing states amply testify to evolving conceptions, the reshaping of materials, and stylistic perfectionism. Stuart Nelson Clarke's transcription of the holograph manuscript, of which Madeline Moore had earlier presented extracts, and Alison M. Scott's edition of the surviving marked proofs reveal the writer at work in the moment of creation and offer insight into Woolf's compositional methods.

The sheer abundance of these pre-printing materials should not, however, obscure the diverse and compelling evidence that Woolf was working towards a "final" text, although that goal in the end proved beyond her grasp. Nor does it permit the conclusion that the surviving forms are equally valid versions of *the* novel, however revealing they might be about the compositional strains and creative tensions of the work-in-progress. The extant manuscript is in essence a rough draft that by dint of considerable determined effort became a different and considerably more sophisticated text; and the surviving marked proofs offer records of stylistic choices and decisions on rhythmic effects as part of a highly complex process of writing, revision, and rewriting that extended from early October 1927, when Woolf began the novel, to at least July 1928, and possibly even as late as August, when she finished correcting the proofs. That Woolf attempted to see her writing into print in a form that best represented her ideal of it might at one time in the study of literary composition have been self-evident. The siren call for "a *variorum* edition as the standard text for the common reader, the academic, and the critical reader" (Scott, 289), accompanied by the assertion that no "fixed" text can be established, is, from one perspective, more a response to a political agenda seeking to democratize art and the artist rather than a theory of critical editing or a practical approach to its manifold challenges. It begs to be countered by setting out, as fully as the extant surviving evidence permits, the physical and mechanical processes by which the novel took shape and then saw its way into print in England and America. Of no less importance is a careful analysis and evaluation of the textual consequences of these processes.

To this end, the present essay briefly outlines the history of the novel's writing and printing as a prelude to arguing the case for a critical text of *Orlando* based on Woolf's extant revised proofs, emended to incorporate the changes that she made in the now lost Hogarth Press proofs and final revise proofs (proofs returned to the author after initial proof correction for checking the accuracy of the printer's alterations), the readings of which are present in the first English edition. This essay also seeks to give nuance to the widely held view that Woolf's situation as the publisher of her own work allowed her complete control over the final forms in which it appeared and that The Hogarth Press was somehow, and mysteriously, unique or special when it came to the production and printing of its books.[1] Woolf's control over her work once it left her own hands is relative rather than absolute and is more related to the subjects of her fiction and methods of treatment than to the production processes that gave it a public life.

These unexamined assumptions are amply contradicted by the evidence in the first English and American editions of *Orlando*, proofread by Woolf herself, and containing not only printing errors but also interventions by compositors and, for lack of a precise term in the field, "editors" (a word used hereafter to indicate any person other than the author who "improved" or "corrected" the text including, for instance, the compositor unable to resist the urge to tidy what appeared faulty or eccentric or was simply unfamiliar).[2] *Orlando* was, in this sense, subjected to editing. This did not occur in the large-scale way that Edward Garnett played literary midwife to D. H. Lawrence or Maxwell Perkins to Thomas Wolfe, but in the more limited sense that numerous fastidious changes were made to Woolf's wording, punctuation, spelling, and word-division. Some of these alterations are indifferent in the sense that they do not impinge upon meaning; but others, cumulatively, affect both the texture and rhythms of Woolf's prose and thus encroach upon sense. While the "secret sharers" responsible for these intrusions necessarily remain anonymous, following their traces is possible with the evidence available and even in the absence of the marked up setting-copy typescript and final revise proofs. Whether this collaboration is to be assessed as a negative input, the stance mainly taken by the Greg–Bowers tradition of textual editing, or celebrated positively in light of more recently proposed theories of the socialized text, advanced particularly by Jerome J. McGann, is a separate issue too large to consider here.[3]

First shape: the manuscript and typescripts

Woolf began writing *Orlando* on the morning of October 8, 1927,[4] and over the next fortnight, drafted much of the first chapter (*DIII*: 161).[5] On the 15th, then planning "a little book, with pictures and a map or two" (*LIII*: 430), she began the Great Frost episode and on the 29th the second chapter (*Draft*: 48). The sexual transformation and gypsy sections followed on November 20 (*Draft*: 106). On the 29th, she started writing Chapter III, continuing the Archduchess Harriet episode on December 5 (*Draft*: 121, 132). On the 20th, noting in her diary that the book's ambitions had grown, she sketched out plans for further plot developments (*DIII*: 167). She then took some time off for the year-end holidays, blocking out the Dr Johnson scene and the section in which the nineteenth century begins on January 4, 1928 (*Draft*: 179). Nearly a month elapsed before she began Chapter V on February 1 (*Draft*: 183). Despite a bout of ill health, she reached the second Nick Greene section (*Draft*: 247) by the beginning of March and was excitedly moving towards a conclusion. This was tentatively achieved on March 17, the date inscribed on the manuscript's last page. Writing and rewriting likely spilled over into the next few days, and she finished typing the last section on the 22nd (*D*III: 177). With the novel drafted, she foresaw a further "three months of close work" (*D*III: 176), and promptly turned to it, producing a second typescript, a draft typescript having been created concurrently with writing. The setting-copy typescript, which Woolf prepared during April and May 1928, formed another stage in the novel's composition as she made major deletions, reshaped sentences and paragraphs, polished her style, and settled punctuation, the last often absent or slapdash in manuscript because of the flow of composition.

Second shape: the proofs

On June 1, Leonard Woolf posted the first 179 pages of this typescript to The Hogarth Press's printers, R. & R. Clark, Ltd, of Edinburgh (Leonard Woolf). A few days later, he sent the remaining pages, and the Preface and Index followed some time after. The printers set the text rapidly, and Woolf immediately turned to the task of proofreading. Two of the several sets of proofs that were pulled survive. That at Smith College is a mixed set, comprising both "First" and "Third" proofs, the signatures of which are date stamped or dated by hand from 9 June to 22 July 1928. Two corrected versions survive for one of the signatures of Chapter VI. An unmarked set of proofs, once the property of Christopher Morely, is housed at the Harry Ransom Humanities Research Center at the University of Texas at Austin.

As in the case of *Mrs. Dalloway*, *To the Lighthouse*, and *The Waves*, Woolf corrected and revised *Orlando* on more than one set of proofs (Beja, xxv–xxvi; Dick, xxxi–xxxii; Haule, xxxii), transferring alterations with varying accuracy. She revised fairly extensively, particularly towards the conclusion, where her cuts include deleting a brief appearance in the Marshall & Snelgrove scene by "that tiresome *Mrs. Dalloway*" (Pr 268).[6] The extant corrected proofs were forwarded to her American publisher, Harcourt Brace and Company of New York, for use both by them and by Crosby Gaige, who had contracted to issue a special limited edition.[7] The set of proofs corrected for The Hogarth Press edition was almost certainly destroyed by the printers after use, as was customary.

The extant corrected proofs appear to be the more heavily revised of the two sets that Woolf corrected, since the text of the first English edition not only lacks additions Woolf had made but also contains matter she had deleted. For instance, the sentence "The sounds too seemed closed

& concentrated", added by Woolf in proof (Pr 50), appears in the Harcourt Brace and Gaige texts (1A 55.8) but not in The Hogarth Press edition (1E 52.21). Similarly, although Woolf altered "the effect of three honeyed words" (Pr 178) to the more vivid "the poison of three honeyed words" (1A 197.12), The Hogarth Press edition has the phrase as originally typeset (1E 179.12), one of several lapses in transferring a change that Woolf made in one set of proofs to the other. A case for a reversion to her original formulations in the lost English proofs in this and similar instances could, of course, be made; but it would demand sustaining the proposition that she possessed a singularly tin ear in matters of style and would have to discount the probability that she made mistakes in juggling between two sets of proofs. Most critics would agree that these lines of argument are not tenable. The suggestion that Woolf might have been creating separate texts for her English and American readerships is easily countered: she knew virtually nothing about the United States, lacked first-hand experience of it, and showed relatively little interest in its literature, culture, or social organization. In any case, why concessions would be made for such an audience when the novel itself is so preoccupied with things English would in itself be highly curious. In short, weighing probabilities recommends a commonsense and tried-and-true approach to the question: the premiss must be adopted that greater stylistic control is achieved after initial, tentative fumblings, and that the innately error-prone mechanical processes of revision need to be taken into account.

Collation of the surviving proofs with the novel's first English and first American editions reveals not only a pattern of error in transferring changes but also the fact that Woolf made alterations in wording and punctuation in a later set of Hogarth Press proofs, the final revise proofs, now lost.[8] Such changes appear in the first English edition but not in the first American one. Thus, for example, where the proofs and Harcourt Brace and Gaige texts share the phrase "he soon transferred" (Pr 205; 1A 228.14), The Hogarth Press edition, echoing phrasing that appears earlier in the paragraph, reads "the country gentleman soon transferred" (1E 206.12). Likewise, where the proofs and first American edition share "'Sir Nicholas!' she replied" (Pr 248; 1A 276.18), the English first edition reads "'Sir Nicholas!' she exclaimed" (1E 249.8), which justifies the exclamation point and renders dramatic, and perhaps even slightly histrionic, the surprise of a chance meeting after hundreds of years. Missing from both the proofs and the American edition is the sentence "She looked into the darkness" (1E 294.9). On balance, these changes were made in revise proofs, but whether made there or whether they are instances of Woolf's failure to transfer matter from the concurrently revised Hogarth Press proofs does not alter the practical editorial task. The impossibility of determining the exact sequence certainly complicates it; but it neither makes it an exercise in futility nor does it lend validity to a presumption of indeterminacy as an authorial ideal. In the editing of classical texts such problems commonly arise, the highly tangled histories of transmission and the absence of documentary evidence making choices based upon reasonable probability an essential component of their textual criticism.[9]

A more complex instance of alteration in proof reveals multiple revisions of a simple phrase: where the corrected proofs and the Harcourt Brace and Gaige texts share "as she passed through the lodge gates into the park" (Pr 281; 1A 314), a formulation Woolf hit upon in proof, The Hogarth Press edition reads "(she had passed through the lodge gates and was entering the park)" (1E 282.15). This conflates the version originally set up – "(she had just passed through the lodge gates)" – with the altered one. The phrase, which simply narrates Orlando's return home, is relatively insignificant as description, and however much it powerfully suggests a characteristic search for verbal exactitude, is of scant stylistic interest. The reader could nonetheless be presented with all three versions, the brief of a variorum edition; to do so, however, would not only outrightly contradict Woolf's manifest attempt to improve her phrasing, but would even more obviously risk losing the reader's attention in a plethora of detail, some of it trivial. The editor adhering to the Greg-Bowers theory of textual editing would presumably agonize little over dismissing the version originally set up, rejected by Woolf herself during proofreading, and would confront a choice between the other readings. This choice would necessarily rely upon an appreciation of Woolf's general tendency during revising to expand phrasing and aim at greater precision. In this case, then, The Hogarth Press reading is the stronger claimant for inclusion in a critical text, with the relegation of the American edition's variant to the accompanying apparatus.

This is self-evidently an interpretive matter, as is the preference for resolving a conflicting claim of priority itself. To reproduce all the historical versions would likewise, however, constitute an interpretive act. Assuming that a readable printed text could preserve all the variants (a digital version could do so less problematically) from the manuscript (including its excisions) through the first editions, the purpose of producing such a text for "the common reader" as opposed to the scholar and critic interested in stylistics, textual criticism, and publishing history is not self-evident. By incorporating deletions, which, it seems proper to assume, were considered and deliberate, such a text would, moreover, fly in the face of expressed authorial preference, up to now the invariable, if sometimes elusive, aim of the professional textual critic. In any case, while a critical edition based upon Greg-Bowers principles privileges one variant over several others, far from engaging in suppression – the conspiracy theorist's brief against critical editions – its obligatory listing of emendations and variants discloses the evidence underpinning and supporting its decisions while its textual essay analyzes them.

Final shape: the first English and first American editions

Both the first English and first American editions of *Orlando* are mixed texts. The Hogarth Press text contains variants that are later than those in the Harcourt Brace/Gaige text as well as readings that are, because of Woolf's imperfect transfer of revisions in proof, earlier than those in the extant proofs and first American edition. The Harcourt Brace/Gaige text, on the other hand, lacks later readings present in The Hogarth Press edition. By itself, then, each text only partly embodies what Woolf apparently wished to achieve by her laborious revision of the novel's proofs; and because of the procedures involved in their creation, each text varyingly bears traces of an editorial hand at work.

This hand is on the whole considerably more present in The Hogarth Press edition than in the American one. Some of its tidying is unexceptionable, and, indeed, necessary to bring the text into conformity with the standard expectations of the language and to avoid anomalous formatting in print. It would seem self-evident that no reader would be usefully served by the preservation of infelicitous eccentricities spawned at the moment of inscription, such as misspellings, dropped out punctuation, or the like, whatever their impeccable authorial credentials. Woolf herself doubtless did not expect to see these preserved in print; had they been, they would have been distracting and perhaps even irritating.

Despite the various efforts to tidy the text for print, the first editions contain numerous inconsistencies in spelling, punctuation, and capitalization inherited from the proofs. Thus, such forms as, for instance, "order of the Garter" (1E 26.3; 1A 25.7) and "Order of the Bath" (1E 116.20; 1A 126.11), "alms houses" (1E 30.28; 1A 30.16) and "almshouses" (1E 270.29; 1A 301.7), "mountain top" (1E 114.22; 1A 124.6) and "mountain-top" (1E 131.30; 1A 143.17) and "age-long" (1E 132.24; 1A 144.18) and "agelong" (1E 160.4)[10] occur. These forms may reflect Woolf's own variable practice in pre-printing documents, and by common consent should, although they have little if any interpretive consequence, remain unreconciled in a critical edition. In books produced by commercial publishers such inconsistency, whatever else it demonstrates, evidences a pattern of inattentive copy-editing.

The Harcourt Brace text meets a higher standard of printing than the book published by The Hogarth Press. It contains fewer printer's errors and more consistently places punctuation within inverted commas. Its proofreading and house-styling were more careful and, in a word, simply more professional. There are, however, occasional lapses. For instance, in the proofs Woolf's inadvertent deletion of "a" in cutting "a natural" from the phrase "a natural sympathy of blood" (Pr 27) resulted in the article's dropping out (1A 28.20). (The English edition reads "the sympathy of blood" 1E 29.8.) Compositors Americanized Woolf's spelling in a handful of instances; but these are casual compositorial slips rather than a systematic attempt to impose American orthography. The text was, however, subjected to some editorial change, and Woolf's grammar was corrected on one occasion. An attentive copy-editor or compositor intervened to adjust the careless phrase "air of one doing what they do every day of their lives" (Pr 16; 1E 18.3) to "air of doing what he does every day of his life" (1A 16.10).

An attempt was also made to tidy punctuation and regularize spelling in the first English edition. Commas in series occur more systematically than in the corrected proofs or the first American edition, and Woolf's compounds were hyphenated by a compositor (or "editor"). For instance, The Hogarth Press edition reads "small-pox" (1E 32.14) for the "small pox" of the corrected proofs (30), "blood-red" (1E 48.26) for their "blood red" (46), "candle-end" (1E 50.12) for "candle end" (48), and "elk-hound" for their usual although not unvarying "elk hound". Although such alterations rarely affect meaning, they may do so; their presence, in any event, reveals a non-authorial hand at work. The correction of a straightforward grammatical error also reveals the involvement of a hand other than Woolf's own: the proofs and first American edition have "the whole fortune of his works depend" (Pr 239; 1A 266.10) where the English edition reads "the whole fortune of his works depends" (1E 240.1).

Contrary to the assertion that the "proofs and the Hogarth Press edition consistently place terminal punctuation outside closing quotation marks" (Scott, 285), the corrected proofs and the first English edition use inverted commas with a high degree of inconsistency. Double and single inverted commas both occur, and punctuation is placed inside and outside them, occasionally on the same page and even in the same sentence.[11]

Collation of the proofs against the first English edition reveals, moreover, that an attempt was made to regularize punctuation inside closing inverted commas at a stage later than that represented by the extant proofs. While this regularization is an indifferent matter, it encourages two conclusions. Woolf, who was wholly inattentive to this in the surviving marked proofs, was inherently unlikely to have been responsible for it, and, as a corollary, far from being absent, an "editorial presence imposing consistency upon the text" (Scott, 287) is manifestly, if somewhat incompetently, present. This also tends to suggest that the books of The Hogarth Press were accorded the same status as those of other publishers in a highly competitive and mainly conservative trade: house-styling occurred, and once received back, revise proofs were not read by the printers to ensure their correctness, this being the responsibility of the author and publisher. Additionally, if one takes into account the erratic styling and the straightforward, uncorrected printer's errors (somewhat numerous for a day when literals tended to be fewer than, for example, than in the 1950s and 1960s and before the so-called computer age) The Hogarth Press edition of *Orlando* witnesses a less than complete mastery of the basic procedures of seeing a work into print.

While the search for perfection may, indeed, be witnessed on the aesthetic level in Woolf's Flaubertian quest for *le mot juste*, The Hogarth Press, on the other hand, and despite the evident efforts of Woolf herself (as well as others), produced a volume that, while certainly not grossly defective, is not an exemplary instance of book-making. It might be countered that, as publishers, the Woolfs were "not as interested in fine looks as in content" (Lee, 371); but, leaving aside decorative elements such as dust-jackets, fine type, and quality papers – the traditional preserve of small publishers – and even assuming so hard and fast a distinction between vehicle and contents, the contents are, as the above discussion indicates, affected by and intimately dependent upon a control over physical processes. Slipshod proofreading obviously has aesthetic and interpretive consequences. The clearest case of this in *Orlando* is the misprinting of "weary" for "wary" in the following sentence of the hitherto received texts: "Polite, they always were to strangers, but a little weary; with her, they were entirely open and at their ease" (Pr 283; 1E 284.28; 1A 316.21).

From authorial control to editorial intervention

Authorial control over a work submitted for printing is invariably relative, and compositorial expertise and house style varyingly affect both writer and reader. The case of *Orlando* is no exception, and, as the evidence cited above should make clear, intervention occurred as the book moved through production. That this influences interpretive possibilities should be self-evident; it may nonetheless be instructive to concentrate on a few examples where authorial intentions, in as much as the surviving documents can suggest these, were not followed, and where "minutiae" have an impact on creating meaning.

The occasional alteration of Woolf's punctuation for the sake of rule-book correctness normally has more serious aesthetic consequences than modifying spelling or word division since it can impinge on the rhythms of a sentence or paragraph. An editorial hand in The Hogarth Press edition is at work in the following description of Nick Greene's physiognomy, evidently meant as a clue to his character:

(1) The head with its rounded forehead and beaked nose was fine; but the chin receded. The eyes were brilliant but the lips hung loose and slobbered. (Pr 78: original typesetting)

(2) The head with its rounded forehead and beaked nose was fine; but the chin receded. The eyes were brilliant but the lips slobbered. (Pr 78: revised; 1A 85.9)[12]

(3) The head with its rounded forehead and beaked nose was fine, but the chin receded. The eyes were brilliant, but the lips hung loose and slobbered. (1E 80.3)

The problem here is twofold since Woolf's revision in proofs, removing what might be seen as a suggestion of mental deficiency, did not make its way into the English edition. The reader of that edition thus not only encounters a slightly different character but also confronts two instances of editorial or compositorial change: in the first sentence, the heavier semi-colon was replaced by a lighter comma, and in the second sentence a comma was added presumably for the sake of parallelism. The changes subtly affect rhythm, and thus influence characterization, in however minor a way. That Woolf herself made these alterations of punctuation in another set of proofs now lost is inherently improbable. The Smith College proofs demonstrate that she rarely modified punctuation, mostly supplying it where it was conventionally required but missing, either dropped out by a compositor or absent from the setting-copy typescript she herself prepared. On the whole, her keen interest in verbal revision was not matched by her casual indifference to so-called "accidentals"; and she sometimes simply left their settling to compositors, with the result, however, that their determinations also, as they do here, become part of "her" text.

As a consequence of Woolf's general tendency to concentrate on verbal revision and her occasional failure to follow through such revision by altering punctuation, control occasionally slipped from her to the individuals who saw her work into print. The following example of revision demonstrates another such case:

(1) like a shell round a boy's figure—or was it a girl's?—young, slender, seductive—a girl, by God! furred, pearled, in Russian trousers; but faithless, faithless! (Pr 271: original typesetting)

(2) like a shell round figure—was it a boys or was it a girl's?—furred, pearled, in Russian trousers; young, slender, seductive—a girl, by God! but faithless, faithless! (Pr 271: revised)[13]

(3) like a shell round a figure—was it a boy's or was it a girl's—furred, pearled, in Russian trousers—young, slender, seductive—a girl, by God! but faithless, faithless! (1A 303.2)

(4) like a shell round a figure—was it a boy's or was it a girl's?—young, slender, seductive—a girl, by God! furred, pearled, in Russian trousers; but faithless, faithless! (Pr3 272; 1E 272.17)

In the first proofs Woolf transposed the phrase "young, slender, seductive" by circling it, indicating a point for its insertion, and writing the abbreviation "tr" (transpose) in the margin. The American compositor modified her revision at four points: he reasonably restored the mistakenly deleted "a" supplied the apostrophe in "boys" that had dropped out in Woolf's rewriting of the phrase in the margin; missed out setting the question mark; and replaced the semi-colon with an em-dash. The last of these changes not only failed to resolve the syntactical problem Woolf had created but also modified the sentence's rhythm, and, arguably, its sense. The set of third proofs and The Hogarth Edition ignore the insertion.[14] Woolf's retention of the semi-colon in her transposition is seemingly inadvertent. Such punctuation has no sanction in general practice, and the presence of other anomalies suggests hasty inscription and the greater probability that she simply failed to complete her revision by altering its punctuation. The construction she presumably intended, which appears in no historic text, is as follows: "like a shell round a figure—was it a boy's or was it a girl's?—furred, pearled, in Russian trousers, young, slender, seductive—a girl, by God! but faithless, faithless!"

The rhythms imitate the accumulating impact of Orlando's visual impressions and the increasing breathlessness replicates the verbal striptease that moves from clothing to physical form and to the final excited conclusion that a girl is indeed at issue. It seems all the more necessary, given Woolf's reputation as a stylist, to note that such "small" things do indeed count.

The following similar case, with Woolf having made a transposition that carried over the punctuation of the original typesetting, reveals the necessity of emending her prose in order for it to appear as she evidently intended it:

(1) Lying in bed of a morning listening to the pigeons on fine linen; silver dishes; wine; maids; footmen. (Pr 278: original typesetting; 1E 279.22)

(2) Lying in bed of a morning on fine linen; listening to the pigeons silver dishes; wine; maids; footmen. (Pr 278: revised)

(3) Lying in bed of a morning on fine linen; listening to the pigeons; silver dishes; wine; maids; footmen. (1A 311.2)

The original carelessly formulated sentence has the pigeons rather than Orlando reposing "on fine linen". In attempting to repair this, Woolf transposed the phrase "on fine linen" but took over the semi-colon. The Harcourt Brace compositor sensibly supplied terminal punctuation after "pigeons" without explicit direction, and executed Woolf's alteration. This, however, had the effect of breaking Orlando's single continuous act into two separate ones, and the adjustment runs contrary to her apparent intention. Making the reasonable assumption that Woolf retained her semi-colon inadvertently, the crux could be solved and the author better served by accepting the reading of the American text but replacing the semi-colon after "linen" by a comma. Again, The Hogarth Press edition prints an earlier, rejected form and cannot provide an emendation.

So small a slip as the faulty setting of capitalization can also encourage interpretive castles in Spain. The solemn and official declaration of Orlando's sex in the proofs and the first American edition is "Female", a styling that could possibly encourage a feminist critic using the Harcourt Brace text to hypothesize that this somehow privileges or elevates femaleness, either for Orlando or for Woolf herself. As the editor of The Hogarth Press edition recognized, however, the proofs contain a typesetting error, the compositor having mistaken the word as the beginning of a new sentence following upon the closed round bracket:

(1) "My sex", she read out with some solemnity, "is pronounced indisputably, and beyond the shadow of a doubt (what I was telling you a moment ago, Shel?), Female." (Pr 228)

(2) "My sex," she read out with some solemnity, "is pronounced indisputably, and beyond the shadow of a doubt (what I was telling you a moment ago, Shel?) Female." (1A 255.6)

(3) "My sex", she read out with some solemnity, "is pronounced indisputably, and beyond the shadow of a doubt (what I was telling you a moment ago, Shel?), female." (1E 229.27)

The American compositor's three alterations – the placement of punctuation within closing inverted commas, the deletion of the comma after the closing round bracket, and the removal of the faulty opening inverted comma before "Female"–failed to address the syntactical problem. While The Hogarth Press edition retains the proofs' inconsistent punctuation, it corrects the more egregious setting errors including the faulty capitalization.

Responses to these and similar textual situations can certainly diverge. The mere reprinting of Woolf's historical texts, the choice of Penguin Books, of Oxford's World's Classics, and of the so-called "Definitive Edition" released by The Hogarth Press, with or without some cosmetic tidying of obvious printer's errors, perpetuates texts that are varyingly and seriously deficient. By definition, a variorum edition simply records the evidence, leaving to a reader, ideally a preternaturally observant one with infinity at his or her disposal, the sorting out of errors. A conservative critical edition would likely opt for a historic form, emending it only where hard and fast evidence exists in the documents that chanced to survive. An analytical critical edition would take the evidence where it exists, but where it does not, go a further step to make emendation on the grounds of reasonable probability, taking into account the writer's usual if not unvarying practices and the general publishing conditions of the day.

The instances of textual instability cited above, small in themselves, are nonetheless revealing. Taken cumulatively, they demonstrate how diverse factors, some outside Woolf's control, shaped her prose, and they suggest the inherent unlikelihood of playful indeterminacy as a conscious authorial aim. That mechanical processes have consequences for a text's accuracy and, by default, affect an interpretive project's validity is axiomatic. The problem, then, is the age-old one of presenting an accurate and readable text. As crucial as the accumulation of evidence contained

in the novel's shapes, from draft to printed state, may be to certain interpretive projects, the sheer weight of this evidence would overwhelm
most readers. A critical edition offers a highly reasonable and practical
solution to the problem of the novel's varied forms. That it should be
based on the surviving document closest to Woolf's punctuation in her
lost typescript and undergoing least house-styling and interference is
a requirement that, in the case of *Orlando*, is only met by the extant
proofs. That the chosen copy-text demands emendation to incorporate
later verbal changes and to correct errors is a tried-and-true principle of
critical editing, and it proves its value once again when applied to the
textual situations encountered in this novel.

Notes

1. See Laura Marcus for an overview of Woolf's involvement in the Press.
2. Shields reaches similar conclusions about the revision and typesetting of
   Mrs. Dalloway. In speaking of various alterations made by Harcourt "on its own
   authority"(167), however, she avoids using the word "editor".
3. See Tanselle for a wide-ranging discussion and assessment of the general
   theoretical writings on this topic during the 1990s.
4. *Orlando: The Holograph Draft*, p. 3, hereafter abbreviated as *Draft*. Clarke's
   apparatus has its own pagination.
5. The chapter divisions in the manuscript and book text differ. For the sake of
   convenience, the chapter numbers cited here are those of the published text.
6. The abbreviation Pr is used for quotations from the revised proofs.
7. Printed from identical plates, the Gaige text constitutes an issue of the first
   American edition and differs in no instances cited here from 1A.
8. For a list of substantive variants between the first English and first American
   editions, see Stape.
9. For an overview of scholarly editing in various literary periods and of various
   genres, see Greetham.
10. The American edition rationalizes, providing a hyphen here (A1 160.21).
11. In Chapter II, for example, commas occur within closing inverted commas
    13 times, outside closing inverted commas 14 times, full stops within on
    seven occasions and outside once. An instance of punctuation within and
    outside inverted commas in the same sentence is as follows: "'Nothing
    remains of all these Princes", Orlando would say . . . "except one digit,"' (Pr 65;
    E1 67.25). The American edition rationalizes.
12. Deletion of the phrase "hung loose and" involved considerable hesitancy:
    Woolf cut it, then reinstated it with "stet", and then finally crossed out "stet",
    adding delete signs in both margins.
13. This is a diplomatic transcription: Woolf's failure to place "a" before "figure"
    was, as the American compositor noticed, presumably inadvertent.
14. This is either another case of a revision in one set of proofs not being carried
    over into the other or the result of a mix-up during typesetting.

10
Version and Intention in the Novels of Virginia Woolf

James M. Haule

In her 1974 article on the American edition of *Mrs. Dalloway*, E. F. Shields concludes that the "very substantial" differences between the first American and first English editions of the novel leave us with "two versions – both of which can legitimately claim to be authoritative first editions" (175). Much of her argument depends on the evidence of the corrected page proofs that the Woolfs sent to Donald Brace in 1924. Leonard Woolf wanted to publish simultaneously in both countries to avoid copyright problems, and he had other business motives in mind as well, including the desire to see *The Common Reader* appear before *Mrs. Dalloway*. However, Brace never did receive the "finally" corrected proofs that the Woolfs promised. Furthermore, after proofs were sent to America, Virginia Woolf made additional changes to the English proofs that were not transmitted to Brace.

More significant, perhaps, is the issue of the publisher's attempt to be "faithful" to the wishes of the author, certainly a key issue in determination of an edition's authority. Shields offers convincing proof that, despite Harcourt's best efforts, this was not possible for *Mrs. Dalloway*. The culprit in many instances was Woolf herself. Her American publisher "diligently followed all directions" that Woolf provided in her own hand whenever possible. When Harcourt did not follow the author's directions, it was because they were "confusing, or because – if taken literally – the directions would lead to problems with grammar and punctuation" (162). Shields correctly concludes that while some few differences between the two editions of the novel were the result of Harcourt's alterations, "the vast majority originated with Virginia Woolf herself" (175). To explain this, Shields points to diary entries that show Woolf's dislike of proofreading, her lack of a "factual" mind, and her carelessness: "a detail given on one page of the novel might be contradicted ten pages later"

(175). To confuse matters further, the Hogarth "Uniform Edition" is not "faithful" even to the first English edition, introducing numerous new variants of its own.

While the Uniform Edition and, more recently, Hogarth's "Definitive Collected Edition" are certainly "edited editions" with little claim to textual authority, we are still left with two versions of *Mrs. Dalloway*, both of which are first editions. The issue of the legitimacy of versions of a text is often difficult to determine, but in the case of modern editions, specifically those of Virginia Woolf, the problem is not simply the result of the editorial policies or the inattention of typesetters, although both play a part in the creation and transmission of textual variants. More important is the author's role in providing different versions of her own texts, often for reasons that annoy those scholars who still assume that a final, "clean" version of the text can be discovered and transmitted. Virginia and Leonard Woolf often made this task virtually impossible due to inattention or to financial considerations. This was certainly true for *The Waves*. Woolf also prepared different versions of all or part of a work on more than one occasion. When she did so with the "Time Passes" section of *To the Lighthouse*, she initially described it as a chapter of a novel-in-progress but later claimed it was a "story". Clearly, scholars should be cautious about accepting the author's description of her text. As we shall see, the person least credible in such cases is often the artist herself.

On 17 February 1931, Leonard Woolf wrote to Donald Brace that he would send him "a copy of the typescript [of *The Waves*] as early as possible" (*LW*). This was the beginning of a familiar procedure, since the Woolfs often sent a typescript to Harcourt Brace well in advance of corrected page proofs of the first English edition from which the first American edition was set. Among other things, this enabled Brace to offer Woolf a contract for work still in progress. By April 15, 1931, *The Waves* was under contract to Harcourt Brace and was well enough along for Leonard Woolf to assure Brace that "we will of course send you proofs at the earliest possible moment" (*LW*). Leonard Woolf considered August a reasonable goal. Woolf herself was not at all sure that she could meet that deadline. In June she wrote to Sibyl Colefax that "my next year's income depends on sending a book to America in August. It ain't half done" (*LIV*: 351). By August 7 Woolf was nearly finished. She was at Monks House to record in her diary that she was writing *Flush* in the morning to ease the strain of working on *The Waves* (*DIV*: 37). A later diary entry suggests that she did not actually begin correcting the proofs until three days later (*DIV*: 38). That entry also reveals that Woolf's attention was engaged by more than proof correcting. She was writing *Flush*, fighting headaches, and taking time for excursions to London. In the same entry, Woolf also indicates her satisfaction with the first chapter of *The Waves*:

> I have now 10.45, read the first chapter of *The Waves*, & made no changes, save 2 words & 3 commas. Yes, anyhow this is exact & to the point. I like it. And see that for once my proofs will be dispatched with a few pencil strokes. Now my brood mounts: I think I am taking my fences. . . . I am forging through the sea, in spite of headache in spite of bitterness – I may also get a box [?]. I will now write a little at *Flush* (DIV: 38).

This information is important not only because it marks the beginning of a proof correction process that would take ten days (ending on the 17th), but also because it mentions only five changes.[1]

On August 15, Woolf records in her diary that she is "rather a flutter – proof reading. I can only read a few pages at a time. So it was when I wrote it, & Heaven knows what virtue it all has . . . " (DIV: 38). On the next day, Sunday August 16, Woolf is near the end of her correction of the proofs and writes in her diary that

> I should really apologise to this book for using it as I am doing to write off my aimlessness; that is I am doing my proofs – the last chapter this morning – & find that I must stop after half an hour, & let my mind spread, after these moments of concentration. I cannot write my life of *Flush*, because the rhythm is wrong. I think *The Waves* is anyhow tense & packed; since it screws my brain up like this (DIV: 40).

It is clear that Woolf worked slowly but steadily at the proofs for a week, taking a day off for a trip to London. At the same time, she has been writing *Flush*, which she finds too different from the "rhythm" of *The Waves* to make composition possible. The entry of August 16 also mentions that she and Leonard had a particularly enjoyable day on the 15th, setting some poems in type and walking on the marshes (DIV: 40). On the 16th, Woolf also wrote to Ethel Smyth about her work on the proofs, commenting about "that wearysome book [*The Waves*]: I shall finish tomorrow; but must then go through all the corrections again, copy into a second proof, and finally get a revision of one chapter gone wrong" (LIV: 369).

This letter reveals two things. First, Woolf, for some reason, has departed from what appeared to be her usual practice: correcting two sets of proofs at once – one for the English and one for her American publisher, as she did, for example, with *To the Lighthouse*.[2] She is working here with only one set of proofs and must then copy those corrections into another set for the second publisher. Second, she indicates that she must revise a "chapter gone wrong". All of this sounds like an enormous amount of work. The sequence of the work (copying corrections into a second proof then revising a "chapter gone wrong") is also interesting, since it would seem sensible to continue working on one set of proofs until all changes were made before copying into a second set. This would appear all the more natural, since the word "revision" implies an intention to make substantive changes.

However drastic the changes sounded in her letter of the 16th, the next day Woolf records in her diary that she has "done my proofs; & they shall go tomorrow – never, never to be looked at again by me, I imagine" (*DIV*: 41). Her diary entry for August 19 confirms both the completion of the work and the fact that she is done with them forever: "My proofs did go: went yesterday; & I shall not see them again" (*DIV*: 41). Therefore, in the space of ten days, Woolf has corrected one set of proofs, quickly copied the changes into another, and set right a "chapter gone wrong". During that time, she has also taken a day off for a visit to London, rested, set up poetry in type, and written a portion of *Flush*. Her alterations to the novel at the proof correction stage and the changes she made to the "chapter gone wrong" could not have been extensive in so short a time. In the introduction to his transcription of the two holograph drafts of *The Waves*, J. W. Graham concludes that "the revision of Typescript 4 could not have entailed lengthy revision of many sections; and scarcely any extensive revisions could have occurred during the correction of the proofs" (*TWH*: 38).

A computer comparison reveals that the Hogarth edition differs from the uncorrected proofs 634 times, many of these punctuation and other non-substantive changes, some of which are most certainly compositorial. The American edition retains 330 of these differences and records only 19 instances of a reading that is different from both the Hogarth edition and the uncorrected proofs. In other words, in almost all of the instances where the two first editions differ, the American has the uncorrected proof reading. It is, therefore, safe to say that the first English edition is the more revised text, and for this reason it was chosen as the copy-text for the Shakespeare Head Press edition of the novel.

More is revealed here, however, than the evidence necessary to establish a copy-text. We also learn something about Woolf's process of revision and the extent to which her claims about the condition of the text may be believed. If we look again at her description of her changes to the first chapter, we see that she claims to have "made no changes, save 2 words & 3 commas". When the uncorrected proofs are compared against the first English edition, they reveal not five but 35 differences. In the Hogarth edition, there are 20 changes in punctuation and 15 changes in wording, additions, or deletions. In the first American edition, 13 of these alterations of wording appear. Thus only two words are different between the two editions, the very number that Woolf reports.

Even without the aid of corrected proofs, some hints about the revision process can also be found in Leonard Woolf's editorial statement in the introduction to the posthumous collection of essays entitled *The Death of the Moth* and in his unpublished correspondence with Donald Brace regarding the publication of *The Waves*. Leonard Woolf's preface to *The Death of the Moth* notes that he "punctuated them [the essays] and corrected obvious verbal mistakes" since he "always revised the MSS of her books and articles in this way before they were published". There can hardly have been time for him to do this with the proofs of *The Waves* between the time that Woolf completed her review of them and their being sent off to the printer; if he worked on them at all, Leonard Woolf must have done so before Woolf herself saw the proofs. This means that after she made the changes to the proof that she desired, Woolf was herself responsible for copying all the changes into a second set when she finished her work on 17 August.

We also know that Leonard Woolf was unusually eager to get *The Waves* into print. Since the details of publication of *The Waves* were entirely in his hands, his unpublished correspondence with Donald Brace is especially revealing. On August 26, 1931, Brace wrote to him that the "corrected proofs of *The Waves* ready for the press have just come in this afternoon. I am looking forward to reading them this evening, and then we shall go ahead immediately with the printing. We shall aim at early October publication, leaving the exact date to be determined later" (*LW*). On September 16 he cabled Leonard Woolf to ask if he should "wait for any corrections before printing the Book". Leonard Woolf's anxiety about possible elections in England prompted his haste to get the novel into print as soon as possible. His letter to Brace of the 16th reveals why:

> We are in great difficulty here owing to the uncertain political outlook. It looks today as if there will be an election about the middle of November. In that case we must either postpone publication until the spring or rush the book out. With considerable hesitation we have decided on the latter course. I do hope that you will not object or

think that we are treating you badly. It is the last thing I should like to do, but I think you will realize the difficulties here. If one knew definitely that there was to be an election before Christmas, it might be worth while postponing altogether; but with the present uncertainty, we might postpone until next season only to find that nothing happened this side of Christmas and that our publication was again involved in the election. (*LW*)

That same day Leonard Woolf cabled Brace to "Print immediately".

As it turned out, however, Brace could not print immediately, since Leonard Woolf had not sent the copy of Vanessa Bell's dust-jacket Brace needed by separate post, including it instead with copies of the English edition that did not arrive in New York until October 2, 1931. Consequently, while the English edition was published on October 8, 1931, the American was not issued until October 22.[3] Thus the later publication date of the American edition does not indicate any additional care in its revision. It should be noted, too, that Brace's question about possible corrections was not simply a matter of form. Woolf herself had sent corrections to Brace for *Jacob's Room* and *To the Lighthouse* and *Orlando* after Brace had received proofs.[4] In addition, the unpublished letters between Woolf and Winifred Holtby of mid-September 1931 indicate that Woolf did not have a complete set of proofs available to her in the weeks between correcting the first proofs and the publication of *The Waves* by The Hogarth Press. Her part in the process was finished once her marked proofs were sent to the printer. Woolf tells Holtby that since she "had no complete proofs here" (H: September 14, 1931), she would ask The Hogarth Press to send her an advance copy. Her diary entry of September 22 records her pleasure at Holtby's response:

And Miss Holtby says "It is a poem, more completely than any of your other books, of course. It is most rarely subtle. It has seen more deeply into the human heart, perhaps, than even *To the Lighthouse* . . ." & though I copy the sentence, because it is in the chart of my temperature, Lord, as I say, that temperature which was deathly low this time last week, & then fever high, doesn't rise: is normal. I suppose I'm safe; I think people can only repeat. And I've forgotten so much. What I want is to be told that this is solid & means something. What it means I myself shant know till I write another book. And I'm the hare, a long way ahead of the hounds my critics. (*DIV*: 45)

Her answer to Holtby's letter is naturally restrained, but it reveals her relief and her concern for the last chapter of the novel:

> I was about to write, very late in the day, to thank you for what you said about *The Waves*. I was very much encouraged and cheered up. I had got to feel that the book was a complete failure, and conveyed nothing – less than any of my books. I daresay this will be the verdict of the public; but anyhow it is a great pleasure to me to think that it meant something to one reader. I wonder if you liked the last chapter – so much depends on last sections and they have a way of plunging down to ruin. (H: September 29, 1931)

The existence of the uncorrected proofs suggests what went "wrong" with the last chapter and why Woolf worried about "ruin" – a word that exaggerates the actual condition of the text. An inspection of the uncorrected proofs reveals that pages 301 and 302 are missing; the proofs and the text of the first English edition also end on different pages. There is a thirteen-line difference between them. That is, thirteen lines were cut from the proofs on the two missing pages. The proof page 303 (line one) is the first English edition page 302 (mid-line 19). The other differences can be accounted for by many small alterations in punctuation and spacing. The sort of "revision" this suggests could have been accomplished easily in the very restricted time period documented above. This may be what Woolf meant by her insistence that she had to "get a revision of a chapter gone wrong." She had to "get", meaning it now appears, that she had to "understand" or "get at" a major error in the proofs, perhaps something as simple as repeated lines set by the typesetter.

Months after Woolf completed her work on the proofs of *The Waves*, she remained defensive about the style of the novel, worried that it would render it unreadable, or perhaps worse, "unreal". This was precisely the criticism that Hugh Walpole leveled against it.[5] Woolf responded to him in a letter of 8 November 1931. She took issue with the criticism of what is real in the novel, not too subtly suggesting that perhaps her own prior review of his *Judith Paris* might have had some bearing on his opinion:

> Well – I'm very much interested about unreality and *The Waves* – we must discuss it. I mean why do you think *The Waves* unreal, and why was that the very word I was using of *Judith Paris* – "These people aren't real to me" – though I do think, and you wont believe it, it has all kinds of qualities I admire and envy. But unreality does take the

colour out of a book of course; at the same time, I don't see that it's a final judgment on either of us. You're real to some – I to others. Who's to decide what reality is? (*LIV*: 402)

The two authors found the time to discuss "reality" some months later when Walpole visited Tavistock Square. It was then that Woolf presented him with the uncorrected proofs of *The Waves*, writing on them:

Hugh Walpole
not from
Virginia Woolf

Below this gift inscription, Walpole wrote the following:

These proofs were the very earliest of this book. Virginia signed them for me very reluctantly because she said that all the best bits were destroyed by the bad ones many of which were afterwards eliminated. Feb: 26. Tea in Tavistock Square discussing Reality.
Hugh Walpole
Feb: 26. 1932   *Virginia as always work in progress?*

Since Woolf made relatively few corrections to the proofs before publication, whatever else might be true about them, they were certainly hers. Scholars interested in producing a historical reconstruction of the writing and revision of the novel, as Tanselle suggests must be the goal of an edition for it "to be the work of scholarship", would be hard pressed to discover the "author's intention" in such a case (28). Almost as difficult would be an attempt in this case to follow Tanselle's later judgement that a fair copy "holograph is generally the proper choice for copy-text over the first printed text" (195), since, as we have seen, Woolf's corrections at even later stages (typescripts and press proofs) can be so confusing or careless that an editor would be compelled to reject them. This could tempt an editor to produce an edition that depends on an editor's acceptance or rejection of elements of the holograph, typescript, and the first editions based on nothing more than felicitous phrasing. The result would be an edition that Woolf never wrote and certainly never intended to publish.

The case of the middle section of *To the Lighthouse* raises other difficulties with regard to versions and an author's "intentions". "Time Passes", the middle section of the novel, was completed in draft on or about May 25, 1926 (*D*III: 88). The entire novel was not presented to Leonard Woolf for his judgement until mid-January 1927 (*D*III: 123). Woolf spent part of the intervening months revising and correcting this troublesome middle section. For years, the only document known to exist was the early holograph preserved in the Berg Collection of the New York Public Library. A version of the text was published in January 1927: the Charles Mauron translation that appeared in the Winter 1926 issue of *Commerce*. That text was assumed to be little more than a translation of the holograph. Close inspection reveals, however, that it is more than that. Virginia Woolf clearly revised the holograph before presenting it for translation. She was to revise it at least once again for publication in its final forms.

In the preparing the French translation for republication in *Twentieth Century Literature* in 1984, the typescript that Woolf sent to Charles Mauron came to light. Typed by Virginia Woolf herself and containing last-minute alterations in her hand, this document is undoubtedly a version of the text that stands between the early holograph and the published editions. Discovered, too, were two unpublished letters from Virginia Woolf to Charles Mauron that shed some light on the nature of this version of the text and Woolf's opinion of it.

The first of these, dated October 19, 1926, in ink, is the initial letter of inquiry:

> 52 Tavistock Square, London, W.C.1.
> Telephone: Museum 2621
>
> Dear M. Mauron,
> The Princesse di Bassiano has asked me to suggest a translator for a chapter from a book of mine which is being published in *Commerce* in January. Mr. Forster has advised me to ask you if you would do it, as he so much admires your translation of *The Passage to India*. I have told the Princesse that if you are willing, I should prefer her to ask you, and I hope very much that you will agree, if she writes to you. It is about 7,000 words long.
> May I say how much the essays of yours that we are publishing at the Hogarth Press have interested me? I want to read them again, but at the first reading they seemed to me full of int[e]resting and important things.
> Yours sincerely,
>
> Virginia Woolf[6]

This letter acknowledges that the text to be translated is a portion of a novel-in-progress and makes no reference at all to the trouble its

composition continued to cause her. Roger Fry, who encouraged publication, saw the translation before its publication. He dispatched the
proofs and then wrote to Marie Mauron, the translator's wife, on
December 21, 1926, with some observations of his own on its merits:

> I have sent off the proofs of Virginia Woolf in haste and without
> a word so as not to miss another post. I hope it will be all right. Good
> Lord, how difficult she is to translate, but I think Charles has managed
> to keep the atmosphere marvellously. To tell the truth I do not think
> this piece is quite of her best vintage. I have noticed one peculiarity.
> She is so splendid as soon as a character is involved – for example the
> old concierge [sic] is superb – but when she tries to give her impression
> of inanimate objects, she exaggerates, she underlines, she poeticizes
> just a little bit. Several times I felt it was better in the translation,
> because in translation everything is slightly reduced, less accentuated
> and in general better. (598)[7]

Woolf herself acknowledged difficulty with this section while working on the first draft. On May 15, 1926, she wrote to Edward Sackville-
West to break an engagement because she was "overcome by the feeling
that I can't – the truth is I am all over the place trying to do a difficult
thing in my novel [the Time Passes section]" (*LIII*: 272–3). With the
publication of "Le Temps passe", she wrote to Sackville-West again to
say that she was "glad, but surprised, that you like 'Time Passes'. I thought
that between The Princesse Bassiano [the publisher of *Commerce*] and the
translator it had got into a hopeless mess" and claimed that she "was
too ashamed to read it." (*LIII*: 315–16) Her diary entry for February 12,
1927 indicates that she was aware of Fry's criticism:

> I may note that the first symptoms of *Lighthouse* are unfavorable.
> Roger, it is clear did not like "Time Passes". *Harpers* and the *Forum* have
> refused serial rights; Brace writes, I think, a good deal less enthusiast-
> ically than of *Mrs D*. But these opinions refer to rough copy, unrevised.
> (*DIII*: 127)

Even after publication of *To the Lighthouse* (May 5, 1927), Woolf was
particularly sensitive to references to the middle section of the novel.
Her letter of May 15, 1927 to Lady Ottoline Morrell notes that she was

> so glad you like parts of the *Lighthouse* – I accept it all gratefully and
> humbly. I daresay its [sic] flattery, but I like it so much that I swallow

it all the same. I'm specially pleased that you like "Time Passes" – It gave me more trouble than all the rest of the book put together, and I was afraid it hadn't succeeded. (*LIII*: 377–8)

In an unpublished letter of March 27 to her translator, Virginia Woolf acknowledges these fears, yet she does not admit to having seen "Le Temps passe", which she now calls a "story":

27th March 1927
52 Tavistock Square W.C.1

Dear M. Mauron,
I have long had it on my conscience that I never wrote and thanked you for your translation of my story in *Commerce*. The truth is that I had to alter a chapter of a novel for the Princesse, and I so much disliked it when I had done it that I was very reluctant to read it again. Also I was sorry that you had been at so much pains with a piece of work which did not seem to me worth your trouble. I am told now however [sic] that it is not as bad as I had feared; and for this I am sure I have to thank you. Please forgive me for taking so long about it. Yours sincerely, Virginia Woolf[8]

The *Diary* and the *Letters* present ample evidence not just of Woolf's trouble and misgivings, but of her repeated attempts to revise. The Mauron translation, as we now know, was done from a draft considerably different from either published version (English or American) and departs substantially from the holograph as well. Constant, often troubled, revision was not unusual for Virginia Woolf; publication of a draft of a section of an unfinished novel was. If in fact Woolf was so troubled by this section, indeed felt the need to revise it substantially before Leonard was allowed a first crucial reading, why did she decide to publish a version of it in an "unfinished" state? Virginia Woolf was a consummate artist, unable to rest until she was utterly convinced that her work was in its most perfect state. Evidence of this abounds. Louise DeSalvo offers a dramatic account of her painstaking revisions of *The Voyage Out* before and even after initial publication, and Grace Radin recounts the similarly agonizing revisions of *The Years*. Why then did Woolf choose to publish part of an unfinished novel and why this particular version?

While psychological speculation on these matters is tempting, the existence of the holograph in the Berg Collection, the typescript, and the published editions present us with material for a more substantial judgement. In her edition of the *Diary*, Anne Olivier Bell attempts a preliminary conclusion. She sees the differences between the translation and the variants in the English and American editions to be the result of Woolf's reaction to the reported criticism of Roger Fry. In a note to the *Diary* entry February 12, 1927, she concludes that

> several proof copies had been pulled (by R. and R. Clark, Edinburgh) and that three at least had been sent to America. There are discrepancies between the text of the English and of the American edition (printed for Harcourt Brace by Quinn & Boden Company, N.J.), notably in the section "Time Passes". It thus seems likely particularly in view of Roger Fry's reported opinion, that VW made emendations on her proof which were effected by Clark's but not transmitted to America; and thus that the English edition embodies her final revision. (*DIII*: 127–8)

While there is some evidence, as we shall see, that Woolf did indeed react to Fry's opinions, the typescript does not supply convincing evidence of the pre-eminence of either edition. Certainly the substantial differences between the typescript and the published versions indicate that a great many changes appear in both. Regrettably, all proofs have been lost. This makes the typescript all the more valuable. It stands between the holograph and the published versions, allowing us the opportunity to glimpse the changes in approach to theme and character that Woolf felt compelled to make. The nature of these changes is immediately apparent when the typescript is compared to the other extant texts. It is in this way that we can begin to see what Virginia Woolf found so "difficult" and why publication of an early version seems to have played a part in resolving some of the problems she confronted.

Readers of the typescript will notice the conspicuous absence of an element central to the published versions of the novel: the presence, both direct and indirect, of the characters so carefully developed in "The Window" and in "The Lighthouse". The typescript starts with what was to become Part II of "Time Passes". It begins with darkness ("It grew darker"), not with the gradual extinction of light echoed in the brief fragments of conversation given to Mr. Bankes, Andrew, Prue, and Lily. Part I in the final versions leaves a flickering light; Mr. Carmichael is awake with his Virgil. The typescript begins with no mention of specific character and no hint of light. It dwells instead on "ghostly confidantes" that accompany the visions and cries of the unidentified dreamers. The question that the sleepers ask the water and sky ("is the day all") is answered by the wind in the third paragraph. This paragraph contains a poignant identification of water with night, and the wind with a helplessness that leads to a confrontation with nothingness ("Why ... if in truth we only ... weave this garment for nothingness?"). Absent too are the many parenthetical comments on the fate of Mrs. Ramsay, Prue, Andrew, Mr. Carmichael, and on the arrival of Lily Briscoe (and in the Hogarth edition, of Mr. Carmichael "by the same train") at the conclusion of the section.

The addition of characters from "The Window", the suppression of ghostly presences for real ones, and the direct comment on the destruction wreaked by time and circumstance on family as well as on possessions, speak to Fry's objections. It should be noted here, however, that Virginia Woolf had begun this editing process before Fry could have seen the document that was to become "Le Temps Passe". For example, paragraph three in the typescript, remarkable for its despair at the hopelessness of human endeavor, is considerably longer in the holograph. The paragraph that precedes it is also heavily edited. The crucial point here is not the specific changes so much as the clear intent to foreshorten, to reduce the level of abstraction and despair. Certainly part of the reason could well have been Woolf's desire to edit her early version to accommodate, in length and in tone, the requirements of journal publication. This easily could have had some bearing on changes such as these.

A more comprehensive explanation, and one that is encouraged by other changes to be noted in a moment, is that as Virginia Woolf wrestled with form and format, she realized that much of what she had done in her first version did not fit the novel she was writing. Both the holograph and the typescript are very personal statements. To use Fry's term, she "poeticizes" again and again in an effort to reach a statement about human achievement more universal than Mr. Ramsay's fears of intellectual oblivion and Lily Briscoe's struggle with significant form. The holograph was clearly too intense and too abstract. Its focus was so sharp as to separate it almost entirely from the novel she had begun so differently. Before it was severely altered to become an integral part of *To the Lighthouse*, however, she chose to edit it slightly for *Commerce*. Thus it seems likely that Woolf saw periodical publication as a way to present a version of the entire section in a form that conveyed her original intention: a separate but important statement of belief and unbelief. It was not the "corridor" between the two large sections of the novel that she sketched in her notebooks.[9] It had become something more. By publishing this section with the help of Roger Fry and by publishing it in translation, she not only saw it into print, but also accomplished something else. She put it in the hands of a critic she admired and, owing to her severe misgivings about this version, reduced her risk of unfavorable impact from what she claimed was a "hopeless mess" by publishing it in a language other than English.[10]

Although Woolf's intentions cannot be demonstrated conclusively from the textual evidence, certainly the speed of her composition and the carefulness of her repeated revisions make a sweeping reliance on Fry's opinion in regard even to a part of her composition unlikely. There is some textual evidence to support this. Fry's one point of praise centered on the character of Mrs. McNab. In holograph, the description of the "old *concierge* [sic]" that Fry finds "superb" is nearly identical to the corresponding passage in "Le Temps Passe" typescript. There is some additional description in the holograph that is not repeated in the typescript, but it is in almost all respects the same text.

The Mrs. McNab of the typescript is, as can be seen particularly in Part IV, ten years older than in the published editions, and is allowed a measure of forgiveness ("her forgiveness of it all") for the injustices played upon her ("who had been trampled into the mud for generations, had been a mat for King and Kaiser"). Paragraph two of Part IV, following the holograph very closely, is almost entirely eliminated in the published versions. Woolf has reduced the stature of this "superb" character considerably between the typescript and the published editions. Mrs. McNab's "message to a world" is originally "more confused but more profound" than those "solitary watchers" who "pace the beach at midnight" and receive "revelations of an extraordinary kind". The problem is not one of vision but of voice and understanding. The "broken syllables" share a unity with all nature, with bleat and bud. They exceed the significance of the wise and would be revered so if only they were noticed ("could one have read it").

Most of this is absent in the published texts. The Mrs. McNab they present is little more than a pitiable charwoman who "continued to drink and gossip as before" (Hogarth: 204/HB: 198). Woolf saves this line intact and transforms a couple of others that come before it in the holograph and the typescript, cutting the rest entirely. The wisdom, the possible forgiveness, even the extent of McNab's victimization are withdrawn. This is hardly the kind of alteration that we could expect of someone following Fry's criticism; it is, in fact, precisely the reverse.

What this text demonstrates in an especially compelling way is not Woolf's consideration of the advice (however indirect) of a friend, but of her assumption of authorial control. A McNab, presented with a detail that allows for wisdom, compassion, and universal dignity, is a more interesting character, but one that deflects rather than advances the force of the section: the passage of time and its impact on the significance of things. Woolf eliminates a crucial part of her "superb" characterization in the process of creating something more: a direct, headlong plunge through ten years of disintegration. She creates her corridor at last by narrowing the stream of her words and increasing their force. She connects physical events with character in a way vaguely reminiscent of the "Aeolus" section of *Ulysses*, broadcasting in headline-like asides the tragic and the inconsequential events of familiar characters.

Numerous other passages in the typescript represent edited portions of the holograph that did not survive into the published editions. The majority of these changes reduce the emphasis on the unnamed, ghostly presences so eloquent a part of Woolf's original version of this section. Her reliance on the abstract representation of human disintegration and despair and her pointed explanations of the significance of insignificant labor are reduced in favor of a more controlled, more imagistic approach.

Clearly, an author owns her text and is allowed to present a radically different version of it outside the published editions. Ultimately, "Le Temps Passe" may indeed be the "story" that Woolf claimed it was. Certainly it is not a significant piece of evidence for a scholar who wishes to establish a history of the text of *To the Lighthouse*. There are, however, other instances where Virginia and Leonard Woolf made decisions about the texts that indicate the way they viewed them. Elizabeth Steele's edition of *Flush*, for example, documents an instance where financial considerations influenced the text. In this case, The Hogarth Press printed an initial 11 763 copies of the novel before noticing five errors in dates. These were corrected, and another 12 680 copies of the novel were printed with different illustrations. This second issue was bound as the "Large Paper Edition" and released on October 5, 1933. The Book Society distributed 6300 copies of this edition to its members. Rather than discard the first issue with its errors and different illustrations, Leonard Woolf chose instead to cut it down and bind it as the Uniform Edition, tipping in an errata slip on page seven. It also appears likely that some of the copies of the first issue were presented later as the second, confusing matters even more and making the establishment of chronology virtually impossible. Naomi Black, in her edition of *Three Guineas*, also notes that when Woolf serialized the text as "Women Must Weep" in *The Atlantic Monthly* in 1938, she reduced it to a quarter of its original size and removed all endnotes and other documentation of sources. This version is obviously very different from either the American or English editions of the book, a result that may concern scholars a good deal more than it did the author. With this kind of reverence for the text, it is not terribly surprising to learn that visitors "to both Tavistock Square and Monks House in Sussex were sometimes disconcerted to find galley proofs serving as toilet paper" (Rosenbaum, 1998: 115).

These examples make several things clear. First, there is not one version of a text but several. More than one edition is authoritative, and other versions of the text, while not always an issue in the establishment of a copy-text, certainly reveal that Woolf had several things in mind. Of least importance in many cases was the production of a clean, error-free text that would represent her final "intentions". Furthermore, much of what Woolf wrote about her work and its revision is highly inaccurate when set against the actual evidence. The effort to revise could be dramatically exaggerated, as could her participation in the production of the published editions. Woolf was even content to present a version of a work with as much as three quarters of the original text eliminated. In at least one case, her husband did not discard thousands of copies of a first issue that contained textual errors, deciding instead to cut its pages to fit new covers. Thus a scholar would be hard pressed to be faithful to this author's "intentions", and Woolf herself is one of the obstacles to the production of a final, authoritative edition. Without her co-operation, such an edition is surely impossible.[11]

Editors of modernist texts must now realize that the goal is not to reconstruct "intention" in an effort to produce the single version of the text the author had in mind. Modernist texts often exist in several versions and intentions, if ever known, are often dark or misleading. The goal of the editor is not to resurrect a single, pristine text that represents an author's putative final vision but to present a "version" of the text as free as possible from the harm done it by its history of transmission. To do this, an editor must weigh carefully the evidence of the published texts and the pre-print documents as well as the other relevant historical evidence. As the editor negotiates among possibilities, he or she must make choices clearly and openly, determining not to reconstruct the author's mind but to transmit the best possible version of the text.[12] For this important work, not even the author can be trusted implicitly.

Notes

1. It would be useful, of course, to check Woolf's reports of her revisions against the corrected proofs of the novel, but none is known to exist. However, there is a nearly complete set of uncorrected proofs to the first English edition available

in the William Allan Neilson Library of Smith College, Northampton, Massachusetts. In preparing the text of the Shakespeare Head Press edition of *The Waves*, these proofs were input into a computer along with both first editions. A computer comparison was then run, which allowed us to identify all differences between the two first editions and between the editions and the uncorrected proofs. See *The Waves*, eds James M. Haule and Philip H. Smith, Jr. (Oxford: Blackwell Publishers, 1993). I have borrowed at length from the introduction to that edition (now out of print); the edition introduction presents a much fuller account of Woolf's composition of the novel. I am grateful to Andrew McNeillie and Blackwell for permission to present that information here.
2. See the Shakespeare Head Press edition of *To the Lighthouse*, ed. Susan Dick (Oxford: Blackwell Publishers, 1992). See especially Dick's discussion of the corrected and uncorrected proofs (xxx–xxxiv).
3. For details about subsequent editions with bibliographic descriptions and print run details, see B. J. Kirkpatrick and Clarke.
4. Unpublished letters to Donald Brace (Harcourt Brace Jovanovich Archives), August 3 and October 4, 1922, March 1, 1927, and July 22, 1928.
5. Woolf had used the word "unreal" to describe Walpole's characters as early as 1918. See Virginia Woolf, "The Green Mirror", in *The Essays of Virginia Woof*, ed. Andrew McNeillie, II, 215.
6. The letters of Virginia Woolf and Princess Bassiano were supplied by Mme Alice Mauron from her archives at St Remy-de-Provence. They were published for the first time in "'Le Temps Passe' and the Original Typescript: An Early Version of the 'Time Passes' Section of *To the Lighthouse*", *Twentieth Century Literature* (Fall 1983), 29, 3 and are reproduced here with permission. The words "of yours" were added in ink to paragraph two and the last word "things" was typed in after striking over the word "ideas". The "essays" that Woolf so admired were published as *Nature of Beauty in Art and Literature* by The Hogarth Press (Hogarth Essays, Second Series) and were advertised as "an original contribution to aesthetics" in the Spring 1927 publications list. I am deeply indebted to Mme Mauron for her kindness and generosity and to the late Professor Quentin Bell, whose great patience and unfailing aid are acknowledged here as they have been by so many before me.
7. The reason for Fry's urgency is revealed in the correspondence of Princess Bassiano to Charles Mauron concerning his translation of "Time Passes". Extracts thanks to Mme Alice Mauron:

Princess Bassiano to Charles Mauron, de Versailles
11 November 1926
"Voici le texte de Mrs Woolf que je trouve admirable–très difficile à traduire mais s'il y a quelqu'un qui peut le réussir c'est certainement vous-même. Puis-je vous demander si je peux l'avoir pour le 15 décembre".

Princess Bassiano to Charles Mauron, de Beauvallon
16 December 1926
"Voulez-vous me dire le titre en français du texte de Mrs Woolf et aussi à peu prés combien de pages ça prendra dans Commerce? Ça sera composé dans les gros romains. ... Quand pensez-vous le finir? Je vous prie de l'envoyer directement à Monsieur Heret, Imprimerie Levé, 71 rue de Rennes Paris".

Princess Bassiano to Charles Mauron, de Beauvallon
20 December 1926
"C'est si pressé que le texte de Mrs Woolf soit envoyé immédiatement à
l'imprimeur. Je vous prie si M. Fry ne vous l'a pas encore renvoyé de lui
telegraphiéa [sic] à ce sujet lui disant que s' [sic] est trés urgent. Il faut que
nous paraissions fin janvier...celui de Mrs Woolf est le seul qui manque. J'ai
si hâte de voir votre traduction".

Following the publication of *Commerce* at the end of January 1927, Princess
Bassiano wrote to Charles Mauron an undated letter, saying in part:

"Quelle merveille de traduction. Je trouve que vous avez vraiment fait
l'impossible. Je suis certaine que Mrs Woolf doit être enchantée. C'est certainement une chance d'être traduit de cette façon et qui n'est malheu-
reusement pas l'expérience de beaucoup d'écrivains".

Quentin Bell noted that "...Virginia herself thought it [the Mauron transla-
tion] gave her sense better than she could herself" (from a letter to James
Haule June 13, 1983).

8. Mme Mauron notes: "Lettre tapée à la machine, sur papier bleu-violet. La
   date en haut et la signature sous manuscrites (encre violette). Deux Lettres
   ajoutée à la plume: Also I was sorry et howvever [sic]."
9. Virginia Woolf's notebook in the Henry W. and Albert A. Berg Collection of
   English and American Literature in the New York Public Library (Astor,
   Lenox, and Tilden Foundations) marked "Notes for Writing. Holograph
   Notebook, unsigned, dated March 1922–1925", 11.
10. See also Jane Marcus, "A Rose for Him to Rifle", in *Virginia Woolf and the
    Language of Patriarchy*. Marcus concludes, in part, that Woolf published in
    Commerce as a "gesture", an "attempt to gain the attention of French women
    writers and readers, to place her novel about her mother in sisterhood with
    Colette's *Sido* and *My Mother's House*, and to place herself as a writer in
    relation to the powerful community of women artists in Paris in the twenties
    where...women created Sappho's island community" (5).
11. Antiquarian booksellers may also contribute to the problems scholars face
    when attempting a textual history. See Haule, 1996.
12. This is the goal of the Shakespeare Head Press Edition of Virginia Woolf.
    Annotations, variants, and emendations are included at the end of each
    volume, and the introductions include a textual history.

Works Cited

Baldwin, Dean. Review of *Orlando, A Biography*, ed. J. H. Stape. *English Literature in Transition* 43.1 (2000): 89–93.

Banks, Joanne Trautmann, Susan Dick, James M. Haule, Andrew McNeillie and S. P. Rosenbaum, eds. The Shakespeare Head Press Edition of the Works of Virginia Woolf. Oxford: Blackwell, 1992–.

——. *Congenial Spirits: the Selected Letters of Virginia Woolf*. San Diego: Harcourt, 1989.

——. "The Editor as Detective". *The Charleston Magazine* (Spring/Summer 1996): 5–13. Rpt. as "Confessions of a Footnote Fetishist" in *Virginia Woolf and Her Influences: Selected Papers from the Seventh Annual Conference on Virginia Woolf*. Ed. Laura Davis and Jeanette McVicker. New York: Pace University Press, 1998.

——. "Four Hidden Letters". *Virginia Woolf Miscellany* 43 (Summer 1994): 1–3.

——. "Reid's Redating". *Virginia Woolf Miscellany* 50 (Fall 1997): 7–8.

——. "Some New Woolf Letters". *Modern Fiction Studies* 30 (1984): 175–202.

——. "A Talk with Nigel Nicolson". *Virginia Woolf Quarterly* I (Fall 1972): 38–44.

——. "Virginia Woolf and Katherine Mansfield". *The English Short Story, 1880–1945*. Ed. Joseph M. Flora. Boston: Hall, 1985. 57–82.

Barkway, Stephen. "Letters from Virginia" [to Robert Nichols and Margery Olivier]. *Virginia Woolf Bulletin* 3 (January 2000): 4–8.

Barney, Stephen A., ed. *Annotation and Its Texts*. New York: Oxford University Press, 1991.

Beja, Morris. "Introduction". Virginia Woolf, *Mrs. Dalloway*. Ed. Morris Beja. Oxford: Blackwell/Shakespeare Head Press Edition of Virginia Woolf, 1996. xi–xxxi.

Bell, Quentin. *Virginia Woolf: A Biography*. San Diego: Harcourt, 1972.

——. *Virginia Woolf: A Biography*. 2 vols. London: Hogarth, 1973.

Berlin, Sir Isaiah. "The Romantic Revolution: A Crisis in the History of Modern Thought". In *The Sense of Reality: Studies in Ideas and their History*. London: Chatto & Windus, 1996. 168–93.

Bornstein, George. "How to Read a Page: Modernism and Material Textuality". *Studies in the Literary Imagination* 32.1 (1999): 29–58.

——. "Introduction: Why Editing Matters". In *Representing Modernist Texts: Editing as Interpretation*. Ed. George Bornstein. Ann Arbor: University of Michigan Press, 1991. 1–16.

——. "The Once and Future Texts of Modernist Poetry". In *The Future of Modernism*. Ed. Hugh Witemeyer. Ann Arbor: University of Michigan Press, 1997. 161–79.

——. "Yeats and Textual Reincarnation: 'When You Are Old' and 'September 1913'". In *The Iconic Page in Manuscript, Print, and Digital Culture*. Ed. George Bornstein and Theresa Tinkle. Ann Arbor: University of Michigan Press, 1998. 223–48.

——. and Theresa Tinkle, eds. *The Iconic Page in Manuscript, Print, and Digital Culture*. Ann Arbor: University of Michigan, 1998.

Brenan, Gerald. Letter to Nigel Nicolson. 7 July 1976. Nicolson Papers. Sussex University Library.

——. *Personal Record 1920–1972*. New York: Knopf, 1975.

Briggs, Julia. "Editing Woolf for the Nineties". *South Carolina Review* 29.1 (1996), 67–77.

——. "The Story So Far…An Introduction to the Introductions". *Virginia Woolf: Introductions to the Major Works*. Ed. Julia Briggs. London: Virago, 1994. vii–xxxiii.

——. gen. ed. *The Novels of Virginia Woolf*. Twentieth-Century Classics. Harmondsworth: Penguin Books, 1992-.

Bull, Malcolm. "Cezanne and the housemaid: From anarchism to formalism: Roger Fry's View of Post-Impressionism". *Times Literary Supplement* (April 5, 1996): 12–14.

Burdick, Alan. "The Only Book You'll Ever Need to Read". *The New York Times Magazine* (June 11, 2000): 78.

Butler, Josephine. *Personal Reminiscences of a Great Crusade*. London: Horace Marshall & Son, 1896.

Carter, John. *ABC for Book Collectors*, 7th edn. Rev. Nicolas Barker. New Castle, Delaware: Oak Knoll Press, 1995.

Clarke, Stuart N. "Letters from Virginia" [to E. McKnight Kauffer and Victoria Ocampo]. *Virginia Woolf Bulletin* 1 (January 1999): 12–16.

——. Letter to Diane Gillespie February 23, 1996.

——. "Letters to the Spiras". *Virginia Woolf Bulletin*, 2 (July 1999): 4–12.

——. [To Crosby Gaige]. *Virginia Woolf Bulletin*, 4 (July 2000): 4.

Cole, Annabel. Letter to the Diane Gillespie (September 2, 1996).

Connolly, Margaret. "Review: Critical Editions of Night and Day". *Virginia Woolf Miscellany* 51 (Spring 1998), 8–9.

Contat, Michel, Denis Hollier, and Jacques Neefs. "Editors' Preface". *Yale French Studies* 89 (1996): 1–5.

Daiches, David. *Virginia Woolf*. 1942. New York: New Directions, 1963.

Daugherty, Beth Rigel. "Readin', Writin', and Revisin': Virginia Woolf's 'How Should One Read a Book?'". In *Virginia Woolf and the Essay*. Eds Beth Carole Rosenberg and Jeanne Dubino. New York: St. Martin's Press, 1997. 159–75.

De Biasi, Pierre-Marc. "What is a Literary Draft? Toward a Functional Typology of Genetic Documentation". *Yale French Studies* 89 (1996): 26–58.

DeSalvo, Louise A. *Virginia Woolf's First Voyage: A Novel in the Making*. Totowa: Rowman and Littlefield, 1980.

——. *Virginia Woolf's Melymbrosia: An Earlier Version of The Voyage Out*. New York: New York Public Library and Redex Books, 1981.

Derrida, Jacques. "This is Not an Oral Footnote". In *Annotation and Its Texts*. Ed. Barney, 192–205.

Dick, Susan. "Introduction". Virginia Woolf, *To the Lighthouse*. Ed. Susan Dick. Oxford: Blackwell/Shakespeare Head Press Edition of Virginia Woolf, 1992. xi–xxxvii.

Fawcett, Millicent, and E. M. Turner. *The Life and Work of Josephine Butler*. London: Association for Moral & Social Hygiene, 1927.

Ferrer, Daniel. "Clementis's Cap: Retroaction and Persistence in the Genetic Process". *Yale French Studies* 89 (1996): 223–35.

Ferrer, Daniel and Michael Groden. "Post-Genetic Joyce". *Romanic Review* 86.3 (1995): 501–12.

Finneran, Richard J., ed. *The Literary Text in the Digital Age*. Ann Arbor: University of Michigan Press, 1996.

Fletcher, Joseph. *Situation Ethics: The New Morality*. Philadelphia: Westminster, 1966.

Fowler, Rowena, ed. "Virginia Woolf and Katherine Furse: An Unpublished Correspondence". *Tulsa Studies in Women's Literature* 9 (1990): 201–30.

Friedman, Susan Stanford. "The Return of the Repressed in Women's Narrative". *Journal of Narrative Technique* 19.1 (1989): 141–56.

Froula, Christine. "Modernism, Genetic Texts and Literary Authority in Virginia Woolf's Portraits of the Artist as the Audience". *Romanic Review* 86.3 (1995): 513–26.

——. "Modernity, Drafts, Genetic Criticism: On the Virtual Lives of James Joyce's Villanelle". *Yale French Studies* 89 (1996): 113–29.

Fry, Roger. *The Letters of Roger Fry*. Ed. Denys Sutton. London: Chatto & Windus, 1982.

Garnett, David, ed. *Carrington: Selected Letters and Extracts from Her Diaries*. New York: Ballantine, 1974.

Genette, Gerard. *Paratexts: Thresholds of Interpretation*. Cambridge: Cambridge University Press, 1997.

Gilbert, Sandra and Susan Gubar. *No Man's Land: The Place of the Woman Writer in the Twentieth Century*. New Haven: Yale University Press, 1988.

Gillespie, Diane F. "The Biographer and the Self in Roger Fry". In *Virginia Woolf: Texts and Contexts: Selected Papers from the Fifth Annual Conference on Virginia Woolf*. Eds Beth Rigel Daugherty and Eileen Barrett. New York: Pace University Press, 1996. 198–203.

——. ed. *Roger Fry*. By Virginia Woolf. Oxford: Blackwell/Shakespeare Head Press Edition of Virginia Woolf, 1995.

——. ed. *Roger Fry: Anecdotes for the use of a future biographer, illustrating certain peculiarities of the late Roger Fry by Clive Bell*. Bloomsbury Heritage Series. London: Cecil Woolf, 1997.

——. ed. *Roger Fry: A Series of Impressions by Virginia Woolf*. Bloomsbury Heritage Series. London: Cecil Woolf, 1994.

Goodheart, Eugene. "Censorship and Self-Censorship in the Fiction of D. H. Lawrence". In *Representing Modernist Texts: Editing as Interpretation*. Ed. Bornstein, 223–40.

Grafton, Anthony. "Birth of the Footnote". *Lingua Franca*. November 1997. 59–66.

——. *The Footnote: A Curious History*. Cambridge, MA: Harvard University Press, 1998.

Graham, J. W., ed. *Virginia Woolf, The Waves: The Two Holograph Drafts*. Toronto: University of Toronto Press, 1976.

Graham, John. "Editing a Manuscript: Virginia Woolf's *The Waves*". In *Editing Twentieth Century Texts*. Ed. Francess G. Halpenny. Toronto and Buffalo: University of Toronto Press, 1972. 77–92.

Greetham, David C., ed. *Scholarly Editing: A Guide to Research*. New York: Modern Language Association, 1995.

——. "Textual Scholarship". In *Introduction to Scholarship in Modern Languages and Literature*. Ed. Joseph Gibaldi. New York: MLA, 1992. 103–29.

Groden, Michael. "Wandering in the *Avant-texte*: Joyce's 'Cyclops' Copybook Revisited". In *The Future of Modernism*. Ed. Hugh Witemeyer. Ann Arbor: University of Michigan Press, 1997. 181–99.

Hanna, Ralph, III. "Annotation as Social Practice". In *Annotation and Its Texts*. Ed. Barney, 178–84.

Haule, James M. "Introduction". Virginia Woolf, *The Waves*. Eds James M. Haule and Philip H. Smith, Jr. Oxford: Blackwell/ Shakespeare Head Press, 1993. x–xxxix.

——. "'Le Temps Passe' and the Original Typescript: An Early Version of the 'Time Passes' Section of *To the Lighthouse*". *Twentieth Century Literature* 29 (Fall 1983): 267–311.

——. "Virginia Woolf's Revision of *The Voyage Out*: Some New Evidence". *Twentieth Century Literature* 42 (Fall 1996): 309–21.

Hay, Louis. "Does 'Text' Exist?" *Studies in Bibliography* 41 (1988): 64–76.

——. "History or Genesis". *Yale French Studies* 89 (1996): 191–207.

Hoberman, Ruth. *Modernizing Lives: Experiments in English Biography, 1918–1939*. Carbondale: Illinois University Press, 1987.

Hoffmann, Charles G. "Fact and Fantasy in *Orlando*: Virginia Woolf's Manuscript Revisions". *Texas Studies in Language and Literature* 10.3 (1968): 435–44.

Hogarth Press., The. *The Definitive Collected Edition of Virginia Woolf*. London: The Hogarth Press, 1990.

Hulcoop, John. "McNichol's *Mrs Dalloway*: Second Thoughts". *Virginia Woolf Miscellany* (No. 3, Spring 1975), 3–7.

Hussey, Mark. [To Mr. Aubrey]. *Virginia Woolf Miscellany* (Spring 2000).

——. ed. *Virginia Woolf: Works*. Major Authors on CD-ROM. Woodbridge, CT: Primary Source Media, 1997.

James, Henry. "The Aspern Papers". *Henry James: Selected Fiction*. Ed. Leon Edel. New York: E. P. Dutton, 1953. 292–370.

Jenny, Laurent. "Genetic Criticism and its Myths". *Yale French Studies* 89 (1996): 9–25.

Johnson, Jeri. "Woolf woman, icon and idol: The canonization of a sceptical Modernist". *Times Literary Supplement* (February 21, 1992), 5–6.

Joyce, James. *Ulysses*. Ed. Danis Rose. Dublin: Picador, 1997.

Kermode, Frank, gen. ed. *The Novels of Virgina Woolf*. Oxford World's Classics. Oxford: Oxford University Press, 1992.

Kirkpatrick, B. J. and Stuart N. Clarke, eds. *A Bibliography of Virginia Woolf*. 4th edn Soho Bibliographies: 9. Oxford: Clarendon Press, 1997.

Lamont, Claire. "Annotating Texts: Literary Theory and Electronic Hypertext". In *Annotation and Its Texts*. Ed. Barney, 46–66.

Lee, Hermione. "Covered with Honey: Five Unpublished Letters by Virginia Woolf". *Times Literary Supplement* 5057 (March 3, 2000): 14.

——. *Virginia Woolf*. London: Chatto & Windus, 1996.

Licht, Sidney, ed. *Therapeutic Electricity and Ultraviolet Radiation*. New Haven, CT: Elizabeth Licht, 1959.

Litz, A. Walton and Christopher MacGowan. "Editing William Carlos Williams". In *Representing Modernist Texts: Editing as Interpretation*. Ed. Bornstein, 49–66.

MacGibbon, Jean. *There's the Lighthouse: a Biography of Adrian Stephen*. London: James and James Science Publishers limited, 1997.

Marmande, Francis. "The Laws of Improvisation, or the Nuptial Destruction of Jazz". *Yale French Studies* 89 (1996): 155–9.

Marler, Regina, ed. *Selected Letters of Vanessa Bell*. New York: Pantheon, 1993.

Marcus, Jane. "An Embarassment of Riches: Review-Excerpts, Blackwell's Shake-speare Head [Press] Editions of Virginia Woolf". *Virginia Woolf Miscellany* 47 (Spring 1996): 4–5.

——. "An Embarrassment of Riches". *Women's Review of Books.* 9, 6 (March 1994): 17–19.

Marcus, Laura. "On Dr. George Savage". *Virginia Woolf Miscellany.* 17 (Fall 1981): 3–4.

——. "Virginia Woolf and the Hogarth Press". In *Modernist Writers in the Market-place.* Eds Ian Willison, Warwick Gould and Warren Chernaik. New York: St. Martin's Press, 1996. 124–50.

——. "Woolf's Feminism and Feminism's Woolf". In *The Cambridge Companion to Virginia Woolf.* Eds Roe and Sellers, 209–44.

Mayali, Laurent. "For a Political Economy of Annotation". In *Annotation and Its Texts.* Ed. Barney, 185–91.

McFarland, Thomas. "Who Was Benjamin Whichcote? or, The Myth of Annota-tion". In *Annotation and Its Texts.* Ed. Barney, 152–77.

McGann, Jerome. *A Critique of Modern Textual Criticism.* Chicago: University of Chicago Press, 1983.

——. *The Textual Condition.* Princeton: Princeton University Press, 1991.

McNichol, Stella. "A Reply", *Virginia Woolf Miscellany* (Winter 1977 No. 9): 3.

Melville, Herman. *Moby-Dick; or, The Whale.* Berkeley: University of California Press, 1981.

Mendelson, Edward. "The Two Audens and the Claims of History". In *Representing Modernist Texts: Editing as Interpretation.* Ed. Bornstein, 157–70.

Mengham, Rod, ed. "A Note on the Text". In *The Machine Stops and Other Stories* by E. M. Forster. London: André Deutsch, 1997. xiii.

Moore, Madeline, ed. "Virginia Woolf's Orlando: An Edition of the Manuscript". *Twentieth Century Literature* 25.3–4 (1979): 303–55.

Neverow, Vara. "Defying the Dic(k)tators from Freud to Fascism". Unpublished paper. MLA Convention, San Diego, December 1994.

——. "'Tak[ing] our stand openly under the lamps of Picadilly Circus': Footnoting the Influence of Josephine Butler on Three Guineas". In *Virginia Woolf and the Arts: Selected Papers from the Sixth Annual Conference on Virginia Woolf.* Eds Diane F. Gillespie and Leslie K. Hankins. New York: Pace University Press, 1994. 13–24.

Newton, Adam Zachary. *Narrative Ethics.* Cambridge, MA: Harvard University Press, 1995.

Nicolson, Nigel, ed. *Harold Nicolson: Diaries and Letters.* 3 vols. London: Collins, 1966–68.

——. Letter. *Virginia Woolf Miscellany.* 8 (special Summer issue): 1–2.

——. *Long Life: Memoirs.* London: Weidenfeld and Nicolson, 1997.

——. *Portrait of a Marriage.* New York: Atheneum, 1973.

Nunberg, Geoffrey. "The Places of Books in the Age of Electronic Reproduction". *Representations* 42 (Spring 1993): 13–37.

Nussbaum, Martha. *Luck and Ethics in Greek Tragedy and Philosophy.* Cambridge: Cambridge University Press, 1986.

Oates, Joyce Carol. "The Transformation of Vincent Scoville". *Crossing the Border.* New York: Vantage, 1976.

Partridge, Frances. *Memories.* London: Gollanz, 1981.

Pizer, Donald. "Self-Censorship and Textual Editing". In *Textual Criticism and Literary Interpretation*. Ed. Jerome J. McGann. Chicago: University of Chicago Press, 1985. 144–61.

Porter, David. "*Orlando* on Her Mind? An unpublished letter from Virginia woolf to Lady Sackville". *Woolf Studies Annual* 7 (April 2001): 104–14.

Rabaté, Jean-Michel. "Pound, Joyce and Eco: Modernism and the 'Ideal Genetic Reader'". *Romanic Review* 86.3 (1995): 485–500.

Radin, Grace. *The Years: The Evolution of a Novel*. Knoxville: University of Tennessee Press, 1981.

Ray, Kevin. *type/script: notebooks: an examination, An Exhibition from the Special Collections of Washington University, With an essay by Kevin Ray, Head of Special Collections*. St. Louis: Washington University Libraries, 1996.

Reid, Panthea. *Art and Affection: A Life of Virginia Woolf*. New York: Oxford, 1996.

——. "On My Redating: An Answer to Joanne Trautmann Banks". *Virginia Woolf Miscellany* 51 (Spring 1998): 3–4.

Robinson, Peter M. W. "Is There a Text in These Variants?" In *The Literary Text in the Digital Age*. Ed. Finneran, 99–115.

Robinson-Valéry, Judith. "The 'Rough' and The 'Polished.'" *Yale French Studies* 89 (1996): 59–66.

Roe, Sue and Susan Sellars, eds. *The Cambridge Companion to Virginia Woolf*. Cambridge: Cambridge University Press, 2000.

Rogatchevski, Andrei. "Samuel Koteliansky and the Bloomsbury circle (Roger Fry, E. M. Forster, Mr and Mrs John Maynard Keynes and the Woolfs)". *Forum for Modern Language Studies* 36, 4 (Autumn 2000): 368–85.

Rosenbaum, S. P. *Aspects of Bloomsbury: Studies in Modern English Literary and Intellectual History*. Basingstoke: Macmillan – now Palgrave, 1998.

——. *Victorian Bloomsbury: The Early Literary History of the Bloomsbury Group*. New York: St. Martin's Press, 1987.

Rowbottom, Margaret and Charles Susskind. *Electricity and Medicine; History of Their Interaction*. San Francisco: San Francisco Press, 1984.

Rushdie, Salman, ed. *Soldiers Three/In Black and White*. By Rudyard Kipling. Harmondsworth: Penguin Books, 1993.

Said, Edward W., ed. *Kim*. By Rudyard Kipling. Harmondsworth: Penguin Books, 1987.

Scott, Alison M. "'Tantalising Fragments': The Proofs of Virginia Woolf's *Orlando*". *Papers of the Bibliographical Society of America* 88.3 (1994): 279–351.

Shields, E. F. "The American Edition of *Mrs. Dalloway*". *Studies in Bibliography* 27 (1974): 157–75.

Shillingsburg, Peter L. "An Inquiry Into the Social Status of Texts and Modes of Textual Criticism". *Studies in Bibliography* 42 (1989): 55–79.

——. *Resisting Texts: Authority and Submission in Constructions of Meaning*. Ann Arbor: University of Michigan Press, 1997.

——. *Scholarly Editing in the Computer Age: Theory and Practice*. Athens: University of Georgia Press, 1986.

——. "Text as Matter, Concept, and Action". *Studies in Bibiliography* 44 (1991): 31–82.

Shone, Richard. *Bloomsbury Portraits: Vanessa Bell, Duncan Grant, and Their Circle*. Oxford: Phaidon, 1976.

——. Review of *Roger Fry: A Biography*. By Virginia Woolf. Ed. Diane F. Gillespie. *Charleston Magazine* 15 (Spring/Summer 1997): 51–2.

Silver, Brenda. "Textual Criticism as Feminist Practice: Or, Who's Afraid of Virginia Woolf Part II". In *Representing Modernist Texts: Editing as Interpretation*. Ed. George Bornstein. Ann Arbor: University of Michigan Press, 1991. 193–222.

Spalding, Frances. "Editorial". *Charleston Magazine* 14 (Autumn/Winter 1996): 3.

——. *Roger Fry: Art and Life*. London: Paul Elek/Granada, 1980.

Stansky, Peter. Review of *Roger Fry: A Biography . . .* [and] *A Roger Fry Reader*. *Virginia Woolf Miscellany* 48 (Fall 1996): 5–6.

Stape, J. H., ed. Virginia Woolf, *Orlando, A Biography*. Oxford: Blackwell/Shakespeare Head Press, 1998.

Strachey, Ray. *The Cause: A Short History of the Women's Movement in Great Britain*. Bath: G. Bell & Sons, 1928.

Sutherland, Kathryn. *Electronic Text: Investigations in Method and Theory*. Oxford: Clarendon Press, 1997.

Sutton, Denys, ed. *Letters of Roger Fry*. 2 vols. London: Chatto & Windus, 1972.

Tanselle, G. Thomas. "The Editing of the Novel". In *Textual Criticism and Scholarly Editing*. Charlottesville: University Press of Virginia, 1990.

——. "The Editorial Problem of Final Authorial Intention". *Studies in Bibliography* 29 (1976): 167–211, and in *Textual Criticism and Scholarly Editing*. Charlottesville: University Press of Virginia, 1990.

——. "Textual Instability and Editorial Idealism". *Studies in Bibliography* 49 (1996): 1–60.

Thomson, George H. *Notes on Pilgrimage: Dorothy Richardson Annotated*. Greensboro, NC: ELT Press, 1999.

Tribble, Evelyn. *Margins and Marginality: the Printed Page in Early Modern England*. Charlottesville: University of Virginia Press, 1993.

Trombley, Stephen. *"All That Summer She Was Mad": Virginia Woolf and Her Doctors*. London: Junction, 1981.

Werner, Marta L. *Emily Dickinson's Open Folios: Scenes of Reading, Surfaces of Writing*. Ann Arbor: University of Michigan Press, 1995.

Whittier-Ferguson, John. "Virginia Woolf: The Book Unbound". *Framing Pieces: Designs of the Gloss in Joyce, Woolf, and Pound*. New York/Oxford: Oxford University Press, 1996. 75–114.

Whittick, Arnold. *Woman into Citizen*. London: Atheneum with Frederick Muller, 1979.

Woolf, Leonard. "Editorial Note". In *Virginia Woolf, The Death of the Moth and Other Essays*. New York: Harcourt Brace Jovanovich, 1974.

——. Letter to R. & R. Clark, Edinburgh, June 1, 1928. Hogarth Press Files, University of Reading.

——. ed. *A Writer's Diary: Being Extracts from the Diary of Virginia Woolf*. London: The Hogarth Press, 1969.

——. and James Strachey, eds. *Virginia Woolf and Lytton Strachey: Letters*. New York: Harcourt, 1956.

——. Unpublished letters between Leonard Woolf and Donald Brace. Henry W. and Albert A. Berg Collection of English and American Literature, New York Public Library.

Woolf, Virginia. *Between the Acts*. London: The Hogarth Press, 1941.

——. *Collected Essays*. 4 vols. New York: Harcourt, Brace and World, 1967.

——. *The Complete Shorter Fiction of Virginia Woolf*. Ed. Susan Dick. London: The Hogarth Press, 1985; expanded and revised, 1989.

——. "The Cook". Ed. Susan Dick. *Woolf Studies Annual*. New York: Pace University Press, 1977. 3, 122–42.

——. *Flush*. Ed. Elizabeth Steele. Oxford: Blackwell/Shakespeare Head Press, 1999.

——. *"The Hours": The British Museum Manuscript of Mrs. Dalloway* Ed. Helen M. Wussow. New York: Pace University Press, 1997.

——. *Melymbrosia by Virginia Woolf: An Early Version of The Voyage Out*. Edited with introduction by Louise A. DeSalvo. Scholar's edition. New York: The New York Public Library, Astor, Lennox, and Tilden Foundations, 1982.

——. *Moments of Being: Unpublished Autobiographical Writings of Virginia Woolf*. Ed. Jeanne Schulkind. Revised and enlarged edition. London: The Hogarth Press, 1985.

——. *Mrs. Dalloway*. London: The Hogarth Press, 1925.

——. *Mrs. Dalloway*. New York: Harcourt, Brace, 1925.

——. *Mrs. Dalloway*. Ed. Morris Beja. Oxford: Blackwell/Shakespeare Head Press Edition of Virginia Woolf, 1996.

——. *Mrs. Dalloway*. Ed. Claire Tomalin. Oxford: Oxford University Press/Oxford World's Classics, 1992.

——. *Mrs. Dalloway*. Ed. Glenn P. Wright. London: The Hogarth Press, 1990.

——. "Notes for Stories". Appendix A in *To the Lighthouse: The Original Holograph Draft*. Ed. Susan Dick. Toronto: University of Toronto Press, 1982.

——. *Orlando, A Biography*. Ed. J. H. Stape. Oxford: Blackwell/Shakespeare Head Press Edition of Virginia Woolf, 1998.

——. *Orlando, A Biography*. London: The Hogarth Press, 1928.

——. *Orlando, A Biography*. New York: Harcourt, Brace, 1928.

——. "Orlando, A Biography: Author's Corrected Proofs". Frances Hooper Collection, Mortimer Rare Book Room, William Allan Neilson Library, Smith College, Northampton, Massachusetts.

——. *Orlando: The Holograph Draft*. Ed. Stuart Nelson Clarke. London: Stuart Nelson Clarke,1993.

——. *The Pargiters by Virginia Woolf: The Novel-Essay Portion of "The Years"*. Ed. Mitchell A. Leaska. New York: New York Public Library, 1977.

——. *Roger Fry: A Biography*. Ed. Diane F. Gillespie. Oxford: Blackwell/Shakespeare Head Press Edition of Virginia Woolf, 1995.

——. *Three Guineas*. Ed. Naomi Black. Oxford: Blackwell/Shakespeare Head Press Edition of Virginia Woolf, 2001.

——. *Three Guineas*. London: The Hogarth Press, 1938.

——. *To the Lighthouse: The Original Holograph Draft*. Ed. Susan Dick. Toronto: University of Toronto Press, 1982.

——. *To the Lighthouse*. London: The Hogarth Press, 1927.

——. *To the Lighthouse*. New York: Harcourt, Brace, 1927.

——. *To the Lighthouse*. Ed. Susan Dick. Oxford: Blackwell/Shakespeare Head Press Edition of Virginia Woolf, 1992.

——. *Walter Sickert: A Conversation*. London: The Hogarth Press, 1934.

——. *The Waves: The Two Holograph Drafts*. Ed. John W. Graham. Toronto: University of Toronto Press, 1976.

——. *The Waves*. Eds. James M. Haule and Philip H. Smith, Jr. Oxford: Blackwell/Shakespeare Head Press Edition of Virginia Woolf, 1993.

——. Unpublished letters to Winifred Holtby. Winifred Holtby Collection at the Hull Local Studies Library, Humberside Libraries, Hull, England.

——. *Virginia Woolf's "The Hours": The British Museum Manuscript of Mrs. Dalloway.* Transcribed and edited by Helen M. Wussow. New York: Pace University Press, 1997.

——. *Virginia Woolf's "Jacob's Room": The Holograph Draft.* Transcribed and edited by Edward L. Bishop. New York: Pace University Press, 1998.

——. *Virginia Woolf, Orlando: The Original Holograph Draft.* Transcribed and edited by Stuart Nelson Clarke. London: S. N. Clarke, 1993.

——. *Virginia Woolf, Pointz Hall: The Earlier and Later Typescripts of "Between the Acts".* Edited, with introduction, annotations, and afterward by Mitchell A. Leaska. New York: University Publications, 1983.

——. *Virginia Woolf, "To the Lighthouse": The Original Holograph Draft.* Transcribed and edited by Susan Dick. Toronto and Buffalo: University of Toronto Press, 1982.

——. *Virginia Woolf, "The Waves": The Two Holograph Drafts.* Transcribed and edited by J. W. Graham. London: The Hogarth Press, 1976.

——. *Virginia Woolf, Women & Fiction: The Manuscript Versions of "A Room of One's Own".* Transcribed and edited by S. P. Rosenbaum. Oxford: Shakespeare Head Press, 1992.

——. "Women Must Weep". *Atlantic Monthly Magazine* 161:5 and 161:6 (May and June 1938), 585–94, 750–9.

Wright, Glenn P. "The Raverat Proofs of *Mrs. Dalloway*". *Studies in Bibliography* 39 (1986): 241–61.